In the golden...
love reaps a rich bounty...

LOVE'S FIRST BLOOM

They knelt together, his hands on her waist, her hands on his shoulders, and drank deeply of each other. Insatiably. As they kissed, Zach pulled Elizabeth to her feet. She melted against his strength, feeling the warmth of him envelop her. Apple leaves brushed his shoulder, crackled in the darkness, and she stood on tiptoe, leaning into him, while his mouth came down on hers with even more devastating force, and his tongue invaded, caressed, tempted her to respond.

When he dragged his mouth away, he rested his cheek against hers, letting the violet scent of her drug him. They stood there, lips touching each other's skin, hair, afraid to continue the kiss, afraid to let go.

Forbidden. Their desire had been forbidden for too long, and forbidden fruit was sweetest . . . oh, so sweet.

Harvest Song

Karen Lockwood

DIAMOND BOOKS, NEW YORK

This book is a Diamond original edition, and has never been previously published.

HARVEST SONG

A Diamond Book/published by arrangement with the author

PRINTING HISTORY
Diamond edition/January 1993

ISBN: 1-55773-841-6

Diamond Books are published by The Berkley Publishing Group,
200 Madison Avenue, New York, New York 10016.
The name "DIAMOND" and its logo are trademarks belonging to Charter Communications, Inc.

PRINTED IN THE UNITED STATES OF AMERICA

10 9 8 7 6 5 4 3 2 1

For my husband, Frank,
and
my sons,
Barry, Dan, and Mike.
This one could only
be for you—with love.

With special thanks to
Melinda Metz, my editor,
    for her faith in me,
Elda Finnigan, my mother-in-law,
    for sharing all the orchard stories,
    and
Brian Finnigan, big brother-in-law,
    for gently critiquing every
    word about apple growing.

Where the apple reddens
Never pry—
Lest we lose our Edens,
Eve and I.
— ROBERT BROWNING

Harvest Song

Prologue

He stood in indecision, destination unknown, desperate for escape. As each sarcastic word hit home, he flinched.

"You want a real ticket, soldier, then gimme a real city. 'Nowhere Special' ain't listed anywhere in this railroad's timetable!"

Finally the Southern Pacific agent shoved back his visor and slammed shut his ledger as if the matter were ended and Zachary Danvers should move obediently on. After all, plenty of other soldiers, valiant soldiers, stretched serpentine fashion all through the depot, each impatient to catch a train out. The agent drew a watch out of his pocket and glared at it. The unspoken message: *This railroad runs on time, and you, bum, are holding things up.*

"Wait!"

The ship's isolation ward had not run on railroad time, and now Zack clutched the counter, palms slick against the cold marble, voice hoarse. "I need to get out of here."

A veneer of ice came down over the agent's face. His eyes narrowed in polite condescension as he stared down his nose at Zack's disheveled clothes, the dark growth of beard. An insult to the tradition of the railroad it was, dealing with ruffians like this. "Look, soldier, where's home?"

"Chicago, but—"

But that didn't matter anymore. It was a warm April day,

1

and the depot was hotter than a jungle tent. Zack tugged at the collar of his uniform, and sweat broke out on his forehead as yet another group of soldiers entered the steamy depot looking for connections.

"But *what?*"

Behind Zack, the private who'd carried Zack's duffel bag from the pier stepped forward. "Aw, give him a minute to think," he said to the ticket agent, then looked at Zack. "Haven't you got relatives somewhere, Lieutenant?"

Zack did, none of whom he wanted to face. Relatives would question him about the glories of fighting the Philippine insurgents, they would nag and pester him for thrilling stories of valor, and worst of all they would offer advice.

When Zack stared at the counter, the clerk coaxed, "So have you or haven't you?"

"What?"

"Got relatives?"

His brother was somewhere out here in the West. "Idaho." Zack croaked out the name of the city. "Eden Creek."

"Well, now we're narrowing things down. Come on, fella. Most soldiers are faster'n fleshpots at knowing where they're goin'."

The stationmaster walked by, his gray uniform a dead giveaway, and the testy agent changed his tone. All smiles and "Yes, sirs," he rephrased his question. "So . . . Eden Creek or Chicago? Which will it be? *Sir?*"

"Aw, flip a coin, man," a soldier hollered from back of the line. "You must have a cinco piece on you."

Flip a coin? At the suggestion, Zack shivered, grew damp about his shirtsleeves.

"Yeah, swell solution," the agent said, patience ebbing as soon as his boss vanished. Everyone in line set up a din, demanding Zack try his luck, and it appeared once again his fate was going to be decided by the flip of a coin.

He pulled out a handful of change, dug through pennies and

nickels till he unburied the Spanish coin, then stared numbly at its gold imprint. One hundred pesetas. It wasn't his last piece of change, but it had kept him alive, for whatever that was worth, and to anyone who asked, he lied and called it his lucky coin.

Toss it. Helpless, the room blurring, he glanced at the ticket agent, who gave him a wary look.

With a grunt, the ticket agent flung off his visor, patience nearly gone. "Flip that dago coin, soldier. The railroad can't spend all day waiting for you to call it."

His hand shook as Zack balanced the peseta between his forefinger and thumb, while the agent leaned over the counter, smile gone. "Tell you what . . . Heads, I pick your destination. . . ." His voice rose ever so subtly as he ground his words out between his teeth. "Tails, you get outta here and sleep it off!"

With a flick of his thumb Zack sent the coin whirling upward and then watched as it glittered in midair, landed on its edge, and rolled against the marble-sided counter.

Briefly the peseta spun on its edge, poised as uneasily as Spain's newly lost empire, while soldiers craned their necks to look. Even the steely stationmaster leaned over a vacant ticket window to stare.

And then it fell flat, the boyish profile of a king glinting up at them.

"Well, ruffle my feathers," the agent said as he jammed a bunch of green coupons into his ticket stamp. *Bam-bam-bam.* Three times his hand came down on the machine. "I ain't ever sent a passenger on the route to Eden Creek before."

Zack managed a baleful smile for the ticket agent, who shoved the ticket over the counter in exchange for some bills. Turning over the strip of coupons, Zack stared at all the identical stamps, one for each transfer. "Departure: San Francisco, April 20, 1899."

After pushing up his sleeve garters, the agent barked out a sarcastic dismissal. "Lotsa luck, soldier. Now move aside. Next!"

*   *   *

Her mind was made up, her destination and her future
decided, all of it stretching before her at the end of a long
silver ribbon of railroad track. Elizabeth Sheldon slipped the
letter from Joel Emory into her bag, then turned her attention to the details of changing clothes. Outside, Amherst,
Massachusetts, was enduring another blustery spring day,
so she pulled her new worsted suit from her wardrobe. For
warmth. And practicality.

Half an hour later, after stopping to resew a loose hook and
eye at the waistline, she approached the beveled mirror to
examine herself, to make certain everything was absolutely
correct. A double-breasted jacket trimmed with black braid
covered all but the high lace collar of her shirtwaist. And
below that a long skirt flared down from her hips to where
the velvet hem could skim the toes of her high-button shoes,
polished a shiny black.

The rest was incidental, but essential to any well-dressed
lady: a violet-scented hanky tucked up her sleeve, a straw
sailor hat fastened to her hair with a five-inch pearl-tipped
pin, and as always, pesky curls to tuck into place, as if they
didn't know their place was in the demure knot at the nape
of her neck. She wasn't one of Amherst's reigning beauties, but she knew appearance counted, especially for first
impressions.

As she left the house, she slid on black kid gloves, spending
an inordinate amount of time smoothing the leather over her
fingers. Posture erect, she walked with her head held high and
looked neither left nor right.

Ever since Elizabeth had come out of seclusion, the
neighbors invariably peeked from around their curtains at
her, as if since the awful, tragic events of the past winter, she
simply must have grown two heads or three eyes. Worst of
all, though, was hearing her name bandied about in the same
shameful breath as Lizzie Borden's: "Have you heard what
happened to Lizzie now? No, there's more. Wait till you hear
the latest. . . ."

Well, she was about to give them something to really wag their tongues about.

At the railroad depot, she shut the door behind her firmly, and both the ticket agent and the stationmaster looked up at her with the interest usually reserved for a lady of the circus rather than a mayor's daughter.

"Afternoon, Miss Sheldon. Expecting a train?"

"I'm planning a journey."

"To Boston again?"

Shaking her head, she marched to the ticket window. Drawing out Joel's letter, she showed the ticket agent the return address. "You may read for yourself my destination. I should like to know the route and how much money I'll need."

The ticket agent looked puzzled. "Eden Creek?"

"It's in Idaho. My brother's farm is there, and it's mine now."

Eyes widening with surprise, the agent whistled softly, and a faint smile twitched at his mouth. "The Wild West, huh?"

Elizabeth drew her shoulders up straight. "Times have changed out west. I have it on good authority."

Clearing his throat, the agent replaced his smirk with a more sober expression, one befitting his position. "Yes, well, you're talking about a lot of train changes. Going to want first class I expect. A ticket home, too?"

Home? There didn't seem to be much more than a shell left. The framework of an elegant house holding small unhappy memories. Of course, her father had taught her not to burn all her bridges, but he'd ignored his own advice and disillusioned her. From now on, her decisions would be her own. Her life was in her own hands.

Careful to keep the same creases in the paper, she refolded the letter and slid it back into the envelope. Joel Emory's words were still fresh in her mind, committed to memory like a schoolgirl's alphabet:

As I see it, I need a wife and you need someone to help run your late brother's orchard, may he rest in peace for serving his country to the fullest measure. . . . If you're of the education and temperament your brother described, I am sure we can prosper together and in time perhaps form a mutual attachment. The good citizens of Eden Creek are anxious to meet more people of your refinement. Best of all, out here no one asks about a person's past, and neither will I, Miss Sheldon, believe me. Most Sincerely . . .

If Joel Emory had been her brother's best friend, then she could trust his word: "No one asks about a person's past. . . ."

"So . . . Miss Sheldon, are you wanting the cost one way or both ways?" Though the agent waited politely, the gleam in his eye outshone the gaudy brilliant that winked from his stickpin. A gossip of the first order he was.

Elizabeth schooled her voice to keep it even, to convey nothing but her usual clarity of purpose. "One way, please."

1

Idaho, Spring 1899

Just outside of Boise City, on the last leg of the journey to
Eden Creek, the dark stranger appeared without warning at
the head of the car and began staggering like a drunk down
the aisle.

It was Elizabeth Sheldon's worst fear come to life. After
all, at her farewell tea party, hosted by the ladies of the First
Episcopal Church of Amherst, the story had gone around how
females were so scarce in the West that all a woman had to do
was step off the train, a man would grab her, and a preacher
would marry them right there on the platform of the depot.

Of course Elizabeth had pretended not to listen to such
tales, dismissing them as fancy while she fervently prayed
Joel Emory would be more genteel than the men in those
shocking stories. But Joel Emory was nowhere about, and
the stranger was advancing, staggering closer and closer
to the vacant place next to Elizabeth. She shrank back
against the seat and held her breath, praying he'd walk
right by . . . but how could he? She sat in the last row of
the car.

In the few seconds before he teetered over that empty seat
beside her, Elizabeth was assaulted by the stranger's seami-
ness and elegant debauchery. Such a contrast. A stubbly black

beard and wrinkled clothing beneath a black Prince Albert coat—a long coat of uncommon warmth for spring.

"This place is taken," she blurted out to him, panic-stricken. "I . . . I have a companion." Her standard excuse for undesirable-looking travelers had worked all across the country—but not this time. Without a by-your-leave the man sat down and immediately stretched out his legs, leaving her trapped by the window, pulse thumping wildly.

He leaned back and pulled his hat down over his face, as if exhausted from an all-night posse chase. "Wake me in Eden Creek, okay, lady?" He leaned back and within moments slumped sideways, his head lolling closer and closer to Elizabeth, until finally, to her utter mortification, he was asleep on her shoulder!

Well! The West harbored all sorts of misfits, and clearly the journey was not a safe one, not yet, not as long as men like *this* stalked the aisles of trains. Furthermore, the caliber of the passengers was definitely deteriorating. Way back in Omaha, the Union Pacific car had been lit by an elegant Pintsch gas fixture, her seat had been red plush, and her seatmate was a banker's wife. Now, as the Oregon Shortline chugged through the Payette Valley, she sat on stained leather, choked back soot, and fixed her gaze on a kerosene lantern swinging from the ceiling, all the while wondering what quirk of fate had led this . . . this unshaven . . . desperado to sit by *her*. The miles crawled by. Yes, the more she dwelt on it, the clearer it became: He'd ridden all night to escape capture. . . .

"Eden Creek!"

At last.

The conductor, in crisp navy serge, moved down the aisle and, with a wry look at her predicament, reached up to the overhead rack for her valise. Once again the train coughed and gagged, and then spit the stranger's cinder-covered hat right into her lap. With a jerk, he was awake, sitting upright, and reaching for the brim. Ever so briefly he fumbled, and before he caught the thing, his hand grazed her knees.

"Sorry," he murmured, brushing the cinders to the floor, scattering soot on the skirt of her suit. "Appreciate you waking me."

She stood, adjusting her straw sailor. "You can thank the Oregon Shortline for that, sir. I'm not the sort of woman who wakes strange men."

There was a short pause while he blinked and looked her up and down. Black hair, unburdened by hair tonic, fell rakishly over his forehead. His eyes, blue, were fringed by impossibly long black lashes, the only soft feature in a face of long hard planes.

"Let me guess," he said suddenly. "You're the new schoolmarm."

"I've come to farm." Not that it was his business.

With an indulgent smile, he stood up, towering so far above her that when she stared at him her chin pointed straight up. Riveting blue eyes met hers with full-force intensity and sent little tremors down her arms. Disconcerted, she glanced down at her sensible traveling outfit and back up at him, disheveled as a tramp. She was uncertain whether to push her way around him or back up against the window and pray he wouldn't grab her and haul her out to a platform preacher.

In a hiss of steam followed by the squeal of brakes and a whistle shriek, the train slowed and finally came to a stop. And then the answer to her dilemma came miraculously from outside, where a small band began playing a soaring song, a patriotic melody. And even though none of the soldiers was getting off at this stop, they rolled down windows to wave and cheer for the "The Star-spangled Banner."

Pretending to look for Joel, Elizabeth knelt to peer out her own window, and all her wariness over the desperado vanished. She had arrived safely at her destination, after all. Her fears over this unshaven man were nothing more than imagination. He was harmless. Nothing but a weary sojourner like her, listening to the tinny music of a makeshift small-town band.

Emotion stung her eyes. "They're playing for the soldiers . . . how glorious." She glanced over her shoulder and paused, uncertainty creeping back. The stranger's face had gone white, and then he moved so fast that she half expected him to draw a pistol. Elbowing her aside at the window, he stood so close they were thigh to thigh, his warmth radiating through her. With a fist, he swiped at the dust on the inside of the window.

His voice, as he took in the scene, betrayed something raw. "Son of a gun, Ben. . . . I never should have telegraphed."

Elizabeth and he remained shoulder to shoulder, the tension in his body running like a current through her own. His coat had to be hot, yet his face was haggard, pale.

"Who's Ben?"

He stared down at Elizabeth, blinking, as if trying to remember.

"My meddling brother," he mumbled at last. "Look, would you mind stepping off the train and telling them you never saw me?"

"I beg your pardon?" Turning, she realized he was staring at her through narrowed eyes. Oh, Lord of mercy, she'd guessed right. A fugitive, a renegade worried about capture on the very depot platform they'd warned her about back in Amherst. She clapped a hand to her straw hat and fumbled for the only weapon at hand—her hatpin. "You—you're trying to escape the law, aren't you?"

His jaw fell slack; then he recovered. "Lady, there's no time to talk about it."

Heart pounding, she quickly pushed her way around him before she had to stick him with her hatpin. They touched. There was a fierce tension at all the contact points. Arms. Chest. Thigh. All muscular and all male.

At the opposite end of the railcar, the conductor awaited their departure. Without any further warning, the stranger caught her by the arm and pulled her around to face him, his beautiful eyes merciless in their purpose.

"You don't have a choice, lady. I need help, and you're it."

Gulping, she tried to think philosophically. Someday, she supposed bravely, she'd tell her grandchildren how she managed to live through a desperado's attack on the train to Idaho. No pioneer worth her salt lacked some adventure to call up in future years.

Outside, trumpets and clarinets blared away, punctuated by the froglike tones of a tuba. Now the song was "America."

Land where my fathers died!
Land of the Pilgrims' pride!
From every mountainside . . .

The clarinet squeaked, and suddenly the stranger had his arm on hers, firmly, squeezing, guiding her just a step ahead of him. She tried to stop, but he moved in behind her, his body close against hers, male and uncompromising, his deep voice low in her ear, the male scent of him intoxicating.

"Lady, just move up the aisle. Don't talk. Just walk."

With unsteady steps, Elizabeth made her way through the crowded car, a firm male touch propelling her.

Soldiers, crisp in khaki pants and blue shirts, waved flasks of drink.

"Hey, Jack, where ya from?" Over and over they called him Jack, a common name for any private in the army. But of course this desperado didn't respond. He'd have nothing in common with brave soldiers returned from Cuba, from the Philippines, from anywhere.

Ignoring them, they continued down the aisle, his touch burning, moving her on.

Traveling salesmen, hawkers of liniments and syrups, playing poker invited him to play a hand. "Wanna try your luck, buddy?"

Ignoring them as well, they continued on, and Elizabeth was too terrified to cry out for help.

A pair of ready women in garish sateen gowns, the most tawdry spectacle of womanhood she'd ever laid eyes on, invited him to . . . Well, it didn't bear thinking on.

He ignored them, too, and continued moving her down the aisle. Her pulse beat a tattoo in her ears, out of time with the blaring music.

At the front of the car he pulled her around to face him, and she decided if anyone epitomized the wild country she'd come to, it was this man, who exposed everything raw in her.

He pulled back and half smiled at her.

"Now step off the train and pretend they're playing all those pretty songs for you, ma'am."

"Miss! Miss Sheldon." She had to grit her teeth to keep from kicking him in the shins. "And for your information, they don't bring out welcoming bands for mail-order brides, so don't think you'll get away so easily."

His eyebrows went up in surprise; his face set in a bemused expression. "Someone meeting you? The mail-order husband-to-be?"

Self-conscious, she looked away. Hot, sticky, she was painfully aware that her hat had fallen askew and pesky curls clung around her face. He'd totally destroyed her dignity both inside and out. Without warning, he reached over and straightened her hat, tilting his head while he adjusted it just so.

"There's a dear heart," he said. "And don't tell your mail-order husband that Zack Danvers slept on you first. Some men get possessive about those things."

Turning back, *her* jaw fell slack. The last she saw of him he'd darted the opposite way, unhooked the safety chain on the open platform and jumped over the coupling to the next car, where he disappeared.

Resolutely she moved out the door to the platform and allowed the conductor to hand her down, feeling very much like a woman stepping into a vast chasm. The little band struck up an even louder tune, the soaring notes of the new and thrilling "Stars and Stripes Forever." Pressed close to the smelly train, she surveyed the platform, looking around for Joel Emory.

She didn't have to wait long for someone to claim her. Approaching was a bearded man with friendly eyes. Joel? He hadn't mentioned a beard, but maybe he'd grown one since they last exchanged letters.

Instead of returning her smile, though, the stranger virtually ignored her and peered up into the railroad car. "Zack? Zack Danvers, get your butt out here and shake your brother's hand."

Elizabeth's pulse went into double time again. Brother Ben. *And Zack Danvers.* Zack Danvers was the desperado's name, and whatever Mr. Danvers was running from, she hoped he got caught.

The memory of Zack Danver's head on her shoulder, his hands touching her, adjusting her hat in that intimate way, all in the space of ten minutes, had left her humiliated. For that alone he deserved to be locked up away from innocent women.

"Zack?" Ben's voice sounded hollow.

She sighed. As a conscientious citizen, Elizabeth felt compelled to tell the truth.

"Zack Danvers," she said in frosty tones, "escaped through another car . . . something about not liking patriotic music."

Now it was *this* man who raised his eyebrows at her in surprise, all traces of his earlier smile vanished. "Which way did he go?" he said with the grimness of a dime-novel sheriff.

She jerked her hand toward the last car on the train. "Is he in trouble with the law?"

"Trouble? Lady, this ain't the Old West. Zack is my brother, Second Lieutenant Danvers, just home from the war. Did his part in the Philippines, he did."

Soldier? Not that desperado. But then the memory of his clothes under that black Prince Albert coat came back. Khaki pants. Light blue shirt. Wrinkled, but army issue. How could she have been so blind?

As the truth sank in, Elizabeth looked from one band member to the next, ending with a little girl in overalls and bare feet who still tapped out a rhythm on an empty coffee can.

Her heart thudded in her ears, as shock, then white-hot anger took its place. Zack Danvers had duped her. And in the most despicable way possible.

"Hey," the clarinetist said, "where's the soldier? No offense, lady, but we were expecting a soldier, a real soldier from the War with Spain."

Only her grief for her brother tempered her anger. A soldier. Zack Danvers was worse than a desperado. He was a traitor to her brother's memory, and he had no right to turn tail on a welcome ceremony. No soldier did. Turning to hide the sheen of moisture in her eyes, she moved down the platform to claim her trunks and crates while, with a screech of its whistle and a cloud of steam, the train chugged out. Ben Danvers followed her and jammed his hands down into his pockets.

"Son of a gun . . . I mean, he said not to make a fuss, but I thought he was just, well . . ."

"A coward?" she supplied.

"Well, I wouldn't put it quite that strong. . . . What'd you say your name was?"

"Sheldon," she snapped.

Ben rocked back on his heels. "Will's sister, eh?"

"Yes," she said, standing straight and looking him in the eye, "and I'd have given anything if my brother had come home to a welcoming band. Instead he's buried in some ugly grave in . . . in some ugly—"

"Here, now," Ben said gently. "You got a right to feel aggrieved all right. Consider that band, such as it was, a tribute to Will. Fine fellow." Briefly he identified the carpenter, the saloonkeeper, and the blacksmith as the musicians. A motley crew with their scratched and tarnished instruments, nevertheless they bowed and doffed their hats like true gentlemen.

"Your music was wonderful," she said with as much sincerity as she could muster.

Ben shuffled from foot to foot as men will when women get teary-eyed.

"Someone meeting you?" he asked at last.

She cleared her throat. "Joel . . . Joel Emory knows I'm coming." Her voice sounded small, dejected. "I expect he's busy working in the orchard and lost track of time."

Ben Danvers smirked. "Joel, eh? That train whistles like a banshee when it comes around the bend near the orchard. He couldn't miss it. You better come with me. It appears we've both been stood up."

It sounded as if Ben didn't much like Joel. Well, she didn't like Ben's brother either, so that made them even.

The little barefoot girl sidled up, drumstick and coffee can hugged close, like a doll. "Can I ride with you, too, Ben?"

When there was no answer, she began to click her drumstick around the spoke of Ben Danvers's wagon wheel, setting up a racket loud enough to scare away wild horses.

"You git now, Clara." To Elizabeth he explained, "Child ain't got no ma, and now her pa's run off to the mines. Sort of the bad seeds of the town, her and her brother."

"Then your brother's in good company."

"Aw, Zack ain't no bad seed, but something's eating him." In an aside to Elizabeth while handing her up into a rough buckboard, he muttered, "Always was a contrary little brother. Probably got brain fever over in that jungle."

Elizabeth hoped never to lay eyes on the traitor again, and as for Joel Emory, she swallowed back her disappointment and held on to her sailor hat for the ride. Eden Creek, Ben explained, was built near the junction of two waterways. From the snow runoff in the nearby hills came the creek, which flowed into the mighty Payette River. Ben's hotel sat right on the piece of land where creek met river and formed a wide lake of sorts. Her orchard was farther past, beside the creek, whereas his hotel stood near the river. The ride, he said, would take a half hour or so.

The squeak of the wagon wheels was somehow comforting, and for the next few minutes they rode in silence, except for cawing magpies in a clear blue sky. She'd held out hope that perhaps Eden Creek might be a diamond in the rough, but seeing the town stretch out from the railroad depot, she had to gulp in dismay at all the unpainted buildings, the dust, the tumbleweeds. Here and there near the few town houses, long johns and petticoats whipped on clotheslines in the stiff wind.

A big mercantile dominated Main Street, the selection of businesses as sparse as water to a sagebrush; in fact, the attorney-at-law plied his trade in a big white canvas tent, and only one business came in a pair—two saloons faced each other across the street. Here and there people stepped out of stores to wave at Ben as he drove past. They made no secret of gawking at her.

Ben shifted in his seat. "Only fair to tell you, I guess, that the town's divided on whether you'll succeed or not, that being from back east and all. . . . Meaning no disrespect, but they said the same thing to Will. It's the orchard. Now, I ain't a betting man, Miss Sheldon, just opinionated. Fact is, the whole town's taking bets on how any woman'll do."

"Joel Emory will help me."

Ben chuckled at that. "A wedding planned between you two?"

"Maybe," she said. "But I'd like to keep it a secret for a while till we decide for sure."

"Ain't many secrets here. Not for long. Fair warning, miss, some men will use a woman like you."

"Perhaps I want to be used."

She was silent, remembering the last time she'd planned a wedding. Her father's untimely death had been followed in short order by a jilting. "You don't have what a man needs in a wife, Elizabeth," she'd been told. A marriage of convenience, the kind Joel hinted at, was all she could expect in this world.

"I appreciate all your concerns," she told Ben at last, her voice stiff, "but I came here on a one-way ticket. I have just enough money to live on, so the only way I can leave is to bring in my brother's crop."

"Then I admire your courage, miss. Admire it mightily."

At the end of Main Street Ben drove the wagon around a bend, past a little steepled church, and out onto an open country road. There, trudging along, a bedroll slung over one shoulder, a duffel in his hand, walked Elizabeth's former seatmate. The coward. She hated Lieutenant Zack Danvers, but she also couldn't tear her eyes off of him. His long black coat swayed as he walked, and his shoulders were broad, his legs strong.

With a grunt of impatience, Ben Danvers reined in.

"What're you doing hiding your uniform, Zack? Only a man with a fever in his brain would wear a coat like that on a fine spring day."

Silently Zack Danvers walked on, but he moved slowly, as if it took an effort.

Ben tried again. "Looking peaked, Zack. You catch that yellow jack over in the tropics?"

"I don't want to talk about the war or about yellow jack or about the tropics. Not any of it."

Once again Elizabeth swallowed back the emotion in her throat. Quickly she dropped her gaze to her skirt and wondered whether hatpins at twenty paces were considered acceptable retaliation out here.

Ben jumped to her defense. "I expect you to be friendlier than that, Zack. Can't have you scaring away the boarders. Besides that, you could have been buried over there like Miss Elizabeth Sheldon's brother."

Zack Danvers shot her a quick look, half desperate, a little bit apologetic. He tossed his gear in the back of the wagon but kept on walking.

"You don't even know where the hotel is," Ben pointed out.

"How many hotels you got in a town this size?"

"Walk, then," Ben said gruffly. "Might knock some sense into you." With a quick flick of the reins, he drove off, leaving Zack in his dust.

*   *   *

Zack Danvers trudged along the road, his footsteps slowing. The yellow fever had left him feeling as if he could sleep for forty nights. Still, he wasn't about to give Ben the satisfaction of lecturing him with I-told-you-so's. Then, too, the prim Miss Elizabeth Sheldon had pinned a condemning look on him, as if he had no right to be alive.

He walked on toward the big two-story building down by the water and wondered how long he'd last here. It was all he allowed himself to wonder, beyond eating a little humble pie over the fact that he'd ended up here in Idaho. Eden Creek was the sort of town Zack had disdained as too small for his dreams. It was the sort of place where failures went to start over, and Zack had succeeded at everything in life, until he went to war. Oh, this place was good enough to hide out in for a while. Just so no one got any ideas about him staying. That was why he hadn't wanted any welcoming ceremonies, because things like that made a man beholden.

Winded, he dropped his duffel outside the hotel, which Ben had built with his mining savings. Judging by the exterior, Ben must have hit a bonanza up north. For a long time Zack stared up at the Groveland Hotel. Not the Palace by any means, but Ben had spared nothing, not gingerbread cupolas, not a wide veranda. He wouldn't have been surprised if the place came with electricity and running water and back-east furniture in its parlor.

A pretty brown-haired woman stood across the yard at the clothesline, waving. Zack had met his sister-in-law just once, when she and Ben had come to Chicago to see him graduate from the medical college. She was the bubbly, mothering sort who'd be ready for matchmaking before Zack could eat dinner, but he wasn't hungry for food or women. All he wanted was a room of his own and peace and quiet, so he was glad when Ben offered to show him upstairs right away, relieved, too, for a banister to hang on to.

Though he'd guessed right about the elegant parlor, the rooms weren't as fancy as the ones back east. But his room contained the essentials—a mattress, a good one, a washstand, a bureau, and a chair. A kerosene lantern sat on the bureau, and green flowered wallpaper surrounded him. A picture of some Roman goddess wreathed in grape leaves hung from a two-foot wire above his bed.

"Nice," he said in the same tone of voice he'd used when he found his bunk on the ship from Manila. Nice. A bed to collapse in was nice. But the smell of frying chops and browning biscuits wafted up to him, reminding him that Maddie expected him to come down to dinner, and Ben was proudly boasting of his hotel's earnings while fussing with the door hinge. The squeak rattled uncomfortably in Zack's head.

"Unusual little town, Eden Creek," Ben said lazily. "Ladies from the East come here with preposterous schemes about raising apples, crazy miners come with motherless kids, harlots come, but we can't seem to lure a doctor here."

Doctor. The word sent up an immediate alarm. "I'm not staying."

"So what happened to you over in that jungle?"

"Nothing. And for every time you remind me about doctoring, I'll cut my visit by a day."

"Mind if we eat supper before we fight any more?" Ben said grumpily.

Zack stared out the window at the distant view of a young orchard, still naked, but carpeted with wild grass, the same color as his wallpaper. Dizzying, that's what the view was, and turning back, Zack leaned one shoulder against the window, trying to hold on to his strength.

"That Miss Sheldon coming to dinner?"

"You scared her off," Ben said idly. "But it don't much matter. She's going to leave as soon as she gets a taste of farm life." He tossed the room key to Zack, who didn't have the energy to catch it. It clattered onto the floor, which wavered queerly.

Maddie's voice came from the doorway, faint. "For heaven's sake, Zack, why didn't you tell us you were sick?"

Ben drew closer and stared at his brother. "That so?" Ben asked. "I was just joshing about yellow jack."

"Oh, Ben," Maddie said, disgusted, "don't expect a doctor to say any different. Look at him. He's dead on his feet."

"I might skip dinner and sleep a bit," Zack managed to say. He began collapsing in the direction of the floor, but was caught at the last minute in his brother's arms.

2

In his letters to Elizabeth, Joel Emory had not lied about caring for the Sheldon place. He had taken care of it—for the worse. There were signs of habitation everywhere—open soup cans and cracker crumbs in the cupboards, a dirty plate in the sink, and a mug of coffee on the round table in one corner of the kitchen. A splash of amber liquid lay in a puddle on the red-checked cloth. Looking about, she didn't know what to do first—clean, unpack, laugh, or cry. Perhaps it had been a mistake to come here—the rash decision of a woman running from spinsterhood—and wouldn't the biddies of Amherst just love to see where Elizabeth had ended up?

This house, a mere tinderbox, contained but three sparsely furnished rooms, their walls as raw as if the nails were still smarting from the blows of the hammer. She had to give her brother credit for a few amenities, though—real windows, for example. A brass bed in the bedroom and a basin and pitcher bearing Queen Victoria's likeness. A pump over the sink. A cupboard full of mismatched dishes. There were two Windsor stoves—one in the kitchen for cooking and another in the sitting room, a potbellied one for keeping warm.

Overhead in each room a kerosene lantern hung from a nail, and on the kitchen wall a calendar with a voluptuous beauty's corseted figure still languished at April 1898, a

full year ago, when Will's battalion had left for Manila
Bay. Month by month Elizabeth tore off the pages, and then
when she faced December—the month Will had succumbed
to yellow fever, the month her father had died so ignobly, the
month Lawrence had jilted her—she pulled down the entire
calendar and stuffed it into the cold ashes of the stove.

It was a new spring, a new year, a new life, and she would
not fail. *She couldn't.*

She picked up her valise and headed for the bedroom. Idly
she set her hat on the dresser and, gazing out the window,
allowed the overwhelming feelings full sway. She was utterly
daunted, not by the wide blue sky but by what lay beneath it.

Rows and rows of trees stood waiting to bloom, not a one
tall enough to shade the tar-paper roof of the little house.
They were just big enough, according to Ben Danvers, to
yield a first paying crop. But Elizabeth didn't know a thing
about apples.

Thousands of tiny buds were just visible on the trees, with
the promise of blossoms and, later, of apples. As fast as she
saw things, even faster did doubts creep into her mind. What
if the trees never bloomed and all the bees went away and
there were no apples?

Would all the weeds get cut down, all the pesky birds and
bugs get scared off?

How would she ever get the water from that rushing creek
to the miles and miles of ditches that ran parallel to the trees?

And assuming apples did grow, who would pick them all?

Most fearful of all, who would buy them so she could earn
enough money to make it through the next winter?

Elizabeth, Elizabeth, she admonished herself. Joel Emory
would know all that. After all, he was her brother's friend,
a man who'd stood by the orchard even after Will Sheldon
enlisted in the army.

But what if Joel Emory never came to help her?

As if an angel in heaven had heard her, that very instant
someone knocked at the rear of the house, at the door of the
kitchen. Her heart raced almost as fast as she did.

She opened the door a crack and peeked outside. "Joel?" she said, uncertain.

A handsome blond man smiled back at her. "Elizabeth? Elizabeth Sheldon?"

She relaxed. Yes, everything was going to be all right. Joel was here. Ecstatic, she flung open the door and stared in unabashed gratitude.

Her first impression was most favorable. A prayer answered. She had anticipated a sturdy farmer in overalls, had feared an uncouth, boorish, wild man. Just one glance at Joel Emory and her gratitude knew no bounds.

Joel Emory was very different from Zack Danvers's tall and rumpled wildness, was even handsomer than she'd hoped. His straight blond hair was neatly parted in the middle and slicked back. Though not particularly tall, not even very big, he was genteel. That was clear from the neat striped shirt to the crisp wide-brimmed hat, which he held in one hand, and the boots polished as shiny as the skating pond back home.

He smiled uncertainly and ran a hand over his slicked-down hair. His fingernails were immaculate. "Guess I missed your arrival."

She tried not to let her hurt show. No sense being petty. "Ben Danvers gave me a ride in."

He had the good grace to look embarrassed, and the wider his smile, the narrower his squint.

"Look, I'm sorry, Elizabeth, but somehow I thought you were coming tomorrow, and when it dawned on me it was today, I didn't see any point in running up there and making a bad first impression. I hate bad first impressions, don't you?" he went on, his voice distinguished by its slow drawl.

No one could have made a worst first impression than Zachary Danvers. "I don't mind, and neither did Ben. He was meeting his brother."

"Yeah, it's the talk of the horseshoe pit."

"Horseshoes?"

Joel flushed. "Well, I was passing by. Word gets around. Especially about Ben's brother, and them fighting like banty roosters right off the bat."

There was a long pause, and a queer feeling ran through the pit of her stomach. Elizabeth could still see Zack Danvers, that cowardly desperado, trudging along the dirt road. She also remembered the feel of him, the scent of him. . . .

"I've never done this before," Joel said.

"Been late for a train?"

"No, I mean, invited a woman to cross the country for me."

"Neither have I." She'd never have admitted it, but her pride still smarted from Joel's carelessness.

He turned his hat around and around in his hands and looked properly contrite. "I should have been there at the depot, I know."

"It doesn't matter."

"But it does. . . . Look, I'll make up for it. I'll show you around town. Introduce you to people. Refined people."

Joel stretched out one arm to the door frame, in what to her was a slightly insinuating gesture. "I've been taking care of the barn and all, but I never was much good at fixing up a house, not like a woman can." He looked back over his shoulder at the outside yard. "Guess you could use help with your trunks."

It wasn't proper to invite a single man inside the house, but some rules, she suspected, had to be bent out here in the West, and she opened the door wide.

When Joel had brought in the last crate of books, he reached for a coat that had been hanging all this time on a hook and then studied his hands.

"You're very kind," she said. "Judging from Will's letters, he was lucky to have you for a friend."

"Yeah, he was a good man." He rushed on to a new subject. "Now that you're here, I'll move my things to the hotel . . . unless you think it's okay for me to stay in the barn. You want me in the barn?"

She wasn't ready for this. "I think the . . . hotel."

His face fell.

"You know," Joel said at last, slinging the jacket over his shoulder, "this may be a delicate matter, I realize, but I was wondering if you'd thought about my letters, about the arrangements between us."

Her heart clenched. "Joel, I'd like a little time to . . ." What? Unpack? Rest? It all sounded trivial. So she simply put him off.

Everything was happening too fast.

Zack Danvers had touched her and given her a warning: "Don't tell. . . . Some men get possessive about those things."

"Could we discuss this tomorrow?"

"Sure," he said easily. "You had a long train ride. I remember how I felt when I arrived here. I shouldn't have rushed in like an unbroke horse. Tomorrow will be soon enough for everything."

She looked from him back to the orchard, searching for a softer way to wind down the conversation. "There are so many trees. Will you teach me about them?"

He turned back, his face guarded. "Aw, there's nothing to it. Not much to do till the trees blossom and then apples form. A bit of work picking the crop, but mostly you just watch them grow. Don't worry your pretty head about the orchard yet."

His gaze lingered on her a moment.

Even while he spoke, the little barefoot girl from the train depot scampered through the orchard. She was wearing, Elizabeth noted, a pair of overalls and a boy's flannel shirt.

Joel swiveled to follow her gaze. "Those Gustavson kids trespassing again? Don't let those squareheads worry you."

"Squareheads?"

"Yeah. Crazy, dumb Swede of a father went off mining and left those kids here to fend alone. Both play hooky, because the schoolteacher will tie 'em up and send 'em off to an orphanage if she can get her hands on 'em."

"Really?" Maybe Eden Creek wasn't as refined as she'd been led to believe.

"Clara's just a kid. Been known to filch food, but your money's safe. Don't worry, I'll flush her out and send her back to her shack."

"That's a comfort." Actually, the children's plight sounded quite dreadful, but she had too much on her mind now to dwell further on a pair of fatherless urchins.

"Well, till tomorrow, then," he said. Joel flashed a smile and headed off, picking his way along the outside of the orchard, heading in the direction of the Groveland Hotel, its elegant second-story facade just visible at the far end of her property. Which made Zack Danvers one of her nearest neighbors now.

Suddenly she knew what bothered her more than anything else she'd encountered in Eden Creek. That uncouth, cowardly desperado, laughing at her when he'd heard she was a mail-order bride, adding to her humiliation. No, as long as Lieutenant Danvers remained in this town, she was not about to rush into any kind of wedding.

It was always the children Zack dreamed of first. Night after night after night they paraded through his sleep, dragging him back to the tropics. Bedraggled and starving, following the soldiers, they burned with fever. Worst of all were the ones sweating with the yellow jack, begging for water.

"Doc Danvers, Doc Danvers, Doc Danvers," the dream children cried, "I don't want to die. I don't want to die. . . . Doc Danvers, I don't want to die. . . ."

Zack waded into the cluster of dream children, randomly giving out medicine. Here a child, there a child, picking and choosing at random. . . . Then the children ran off and there lay Harry. . . .

Harry . . .

"Zack, I don't want to die. . . . Please, Zack . . ."

"You won't. I promise." And Zack reached for the last of his quinine. "I promise. I promise I'll get some."

"Zack, you won't let me die, will you? You promised. . . .

"You promised. You promised. . . ."

When Zack woke up, he was muttering to himself, the words from the dream still echoing in his mind: "*You promised.*"

The bedclothes were tangled, his body damp with perspiration. All he could do was lie in the darkness, catching his breath.

For a few minutes he remained disoriented, wondering at the darkness and heat, fearing he was still in a medical tent in the Philippines. He jackknifed to a sitting position, then swung his legs over the edge of the bed and sat, head in hands, trying to regain his equilibrium. Desperate. Haunted. Unable to forget. He wanted daylight to come, the dreams to go away. Most of all he wanted the fever out of his body.

When he thought his legs would hold him up, he dragged himself out of bed and over to the window, pulled open the sash to allow the cool night breeze to sweep in over him. The air was laden with the scent of sage and newly turned dirt, sweet in the cold air. He was back in America, in Idaho, he reminded himself, and the war was over.

Zack stared out at the distant moon-dappled orchard. The prim Miss Sheldon stole into his thoughts and, like a mercy, lingered there—her condemnation, as well as her soft shoulder.

He found himself wanting to wrap himself around her softness. Maybe if he had a woman to hold, he would be able to sleep. It surprised him to think of her in that way. But she was the first woman he'd slept that close to in months . . . the only one he'd touched. She had curls like honey. Honey-gold and soft.

He found himself remembering the prim way she'd dressed and talked. . . . It was a pleasant enough diversion, better than flipping his lucky peseta in the dark, and sooner than usual, the memory of his nightmare faded. Then he had to lie awake another hour telling himself that a woman like her was a temptation.

All he really wanted was a few of her apples. Ever since he'd succumbed to yellow fever, he'd had a craving for apples, not ripe ones but green ones. The greener and tarter the better. The kind that were picked in midsummer when they were still half ripe and sour. But Zack knew he'd better control his cravings, because it was only April, and God willing, he wouldn't hang out here that long.

Joel surprised Elizabeth the next day when instead of driving her directly back to the orchard from Main Street, he turned the wagon in at the hotel.

"I thought we'd have dinner," he announced. "Maddie's a pretty good cook, and you need to celebrate settling in."

Dinner. Just the two of them. What a romantic notion—yet, charming as it sounded, Elizabeth knew what was coming. She'd been engaged once before, and she recognized the signs: the slight self-consciousness, the halting awkwardness of Joel's words that preceded the formal proposal of marriage.

Joel reined in outside the Groveland Hotel, and in a moment he was out of the wagon and around to her side, helping her down. She stared up at the place, uncertain if she wanted to go in. "Do we have to eat here?"

With a laugh, he handed her down. "Why not? There aren't many other choices in Eden Creek. Besides, you'll want to meet your neighbors, the Danverses, won't you?" Joel Emory offered her his arm.

Joel had known his share of women, and he could predict how this one was going to react; she was going to play coy and try to delay matters while she looked around to see if there might be a better prospect. Well, she'd look a long time. No one with any degree of refinement lived within fifty miles of this town. Unless you counted Miss Yates, the schoolmarm, of course, and she was female.

Joel had almost settled for Miss Yates, who had only meager savings. But then providentially Will Sheldon had gone to war and died, leaving Joel, his friend, the delicate task of writing to the bereaved sister. Three letters later, here she was. Not a bad investment of his time.

But Joel hadn't hung around Eden Creek all winter and spring writing to her, waiting for her to show up, playing the gallant for nothing. Nobody outhustled Joel Emory when he set his mind on an idea, and darned if he'd slave away all summer over the apples to do it, or lose her and her orchard land to some other fast-talking man.

In the dining room of the hotel he helped her into her chair, the one with the view out the window, the view of the water. Oh, Joel knew what all the ladies liked. No one could ever accuse him of being cloddish.

Maddie came in to greet them, Maddie of the laughing Irish eyes and plump figure. He liked her, liked the way her hips swelled out from her waist, liked the way they swayed when she walked, but today he was careful not to look too close at those hips.

"The house special today is pot roast," Maddie said. "You have your choice of oven-browned potatoes or mashed."

"Mashed." He looked at Elizabeth.

"Oven-browned, please," she said.

"I hope that doesn't mean we're less than suited," Joel joked, and Maddie, laughing, went on to another table. Joel's gaze followed her briefly; then he turned to Elizabeth across the pristine white tablecloth from him. Though he normally took a shine to brunettes, Elizabeth was pretty enough. She was also a petite thing, not strong enough to work that orchard alone. She needed him.

He gave her what he hoped was a look of tender regard, the sort maidens' hearts melted for. "Do you want me to stay and work that orchard?" he asked softly.

Elizabeth paused, wanting to delay what was coming. She looked out the window at the Payette River and caught her breath.

There, walking along the riverbank where sagebrush and wild grass grew knee deep, was none other than Zack Danvers. It was the first time she'd laid eyes on him since yesterday, when Ben had left him trudging along the road.

"Elizabeth?" It was Joel.

"Yes . . ." She turned. "Yes. Forgive me, there are so many new sights to take in at once."

Joel reached for a stalk of celery from the dish in the center of the table and then took a dill pickle, too. Elizabeth was absolutely right, of course. Every woman of her delicate sensibilities needed some time to adapt.

"Bleak view, isn't it?" Joel asked conversationally. "Too much sagebrush and rock. Not enough cottonwoods to shade the boat dock."

"The scenery is . . . unusual."

Zack Danvers was still in her line of view, standing alone on a small dock where half a dozen little rowboats, painted gray to match the hotel, bobbed like corks. He was dressed in a black vest over a white shirt and dark trousers, and he stared out across the water as if lost in thought. He drew out a pocket watch and, after examining it, half turned. With legs spread, the wind whipping his black hair, he stared up at the hotel, almost as if he could sense her watching him.

Quickly she turned away. The big clock out in the hotel lobby bonged the hour, and in the parlor someone plunked out a tune on the piano, a sprightly melody that reminded her of her arrival, of the music at the depot, and worst of all, of Zack Danvers's reaction. Oh, she hated him. If the hotel window weren't separating them, she'd shout out there and tell him off.

Joel, though, was keeping her here, Joel and the plates of pot roast that suddenly arrived. The dish, she noticed idly, had a beautiful border of moss roses, and the potatoes were roasted to perfection. Joel was staring at her, smiling in his lazy, charming way.

She played for time, keeping up a steady stream of questions, all of them as prim as if he'd come to call for tea.

"Where are you from, Joel?" she asked.

He was educated, like her, and she wondered how he'd ended up in the middle of nowhere. Joel shrugged.

"Baltimore, but don't ask me why I left. Like more than one curious man, I boarded a train and ended up here, where I met your brother."

No different than that soldier man.

Zack Danvers strode across Elizabeth's mind with the same bold strides he'd used to come into town, pushing away people. Pushing away from the welcome-home songs. A defiant loner.

"Why do you want to stay here, Joel? In Eden Creek, I mean."

Her unexpected question seemed to jolt him, but he recovered quickly. Again he shrugged. Again the smile deepened the squint lines around his eyes. "I was Will's friend. And I don't like the things the townspeople are saying . . . about Will's sister not being able to make it. It brings out the gentleman in me, I guess. I'd like to help. Besides, don't you know women are scarce, especially fine-bred women like you?"

He was an expert at flattery. "Why, Joel, I'm sure I know nothing about that, but I can't count how many people told me the West doesn't have as many uppity rules about what's proper."

"It's not different, believe me, Elizabeth." His voice was rough. Suddenly he cleared his throat. "I didn't quite get around to saying it formal yesterday, but . . . well, we could marry and set things right."

Elizabeth caught her breath. She couldn't meet Joel's eyes, not yet. Now of all times the parlor piano went quiet. So she turned to stare out the window.

"Did you hear?"

A blush crept up her face. "Yes, we could." She was so alone and so in need of this man. When they'd corresponded, marriage had seemed as far off and remote as the Old West. Now that the reality was closing in, so too were the doubts. She hardly knew this man, and she certainly didn't love him.

But she'd accepted the possibility of a loveless marriage before coming West. Perhaps he could become nearer and dearer to her with time. But love didn't matter. What did matter was making that orchard grow, and for that Elizabeth needed Joel Emory.

"Perhaps at harvest time if we've come to have mutual regard for each other."

"Out here time takes on its own meaning, Elizabeth. Like I said, women are scarce. If I wait, ten other men in this town alone might come courting you and win you over."

Men like Zack Danvers? She shuddered. Never. She managed to tear her gaze away from the window, away from the enigmatic man outside. Let Maddie handle him.

"Zack Danvers," Maddie called as she marched across the yard to the river, "does your brother know you're out here roaming around?"

Zack hadn't been outside more than ten minutes when Maddie came chasing after him. He liked his sister-in-law tremendously, but she had a bad habit of trying to mother people to death. Actually, after sleeping nearly twenty-four hours straight, then bathing and shaving, Zack felt nearly like a new man, well enough to walk along the river and breathe in some fresh Idaho air. Fair-size cottonwoods grew here at the river's edge, their shade a harbor for the hotel rowboats, all well secured against the heavy spring current.

"Zack Danvers, didn't you hear me?" Maddie was upon him, an Irish whirlwind, wiping her hands on her apron and then shaking a finger at him.

"I'm a lot better, Maddie. Don't fuss, now." He backed away a step, but she advanced on him and, before he could stop her, reached up to touch his forehead like some Florence Nightingale.

"You're still pale. Do you have a fever? I'm going to get Ben to help you back to your room, and you can eat there—"

"Don't put yourself out, Maddie."

"I'd be very glad to bring you dinner to your room, and Granny's got potions that might make you feel better."

He had to bite his tongue to hold back the impatience, not at her fussing but at his own vulnerabilities. Zack was used to being in control, making decisions, and he'd had enough of lying around half alive, half dead. Especially did he not want any Granny medicine poured down him.

"Maddie, I'm a doctor. I know better than anyone if I'm well enough to take a walk. I'm okay. Now, don't sic this Granny person on me, you hear?"

Her face registered the rebuff. "I'm sorry. Mothering is a bad habit I'd like to get into."

"I'm okay." His tone was soft, professional.

"But you *will* come in to eat." Hands on hips, Maddie quickly regained her composure. "I made your favorite, and even you've got to admit you could gain some weight back."

Looking down at the loose fit of his trousers and shirt, Zack nodded in agreement. For the first time in weeks he admitted to a good appetite.

Moments later he walked into the hotel dining room and scanned the white-clothed tables.

He saw Miss Elizabeth Sheldon at once, sitting with some strange dandy. Her napkin slid off her lap, and as she bent to retrieve it, she had to turn. As she was rising up, her gaze fell on him. Staring at her straight back, her high-necked dress of lilac, he couldn't help but smile to himself. Oh, but she must have been mortified when he fell asleep on her prim little shoulder.

She remembered him, too. Only a blind man wouldn't have known that. The most delightful shade of pink stained her cheeks as their gazes locked for a moment, and then she turned away. But not before he'd seen the look of fear in her eyes. Fear that he might come too close to her again, as he had on the train.

Well, he was not about to accommodate her. Zack Danvers was suddenly in the mood for a bit of teasing. Oh, yes, he was feeling much better than he had yesterday, and he strode toward the only other table with a window view—the table right next to Miss Elizabeth Sheldon.

The instant she heard him enter the dining room, Elizabeth wanted to crawl under the table. Zack Danvers's boots echoed on the polished wood floor, and she knew before he arrived at the window that he would sit at the table right next to theirs. Indeed, he selected a chair that put his back to the window, pulled it out, and sat down. She could smell the wind in his shirt, that and a hint of bay rum. She conscientiously avoided looking at him, instead smiling up at Maddie who brought Zack Danvers a plate of dinner without asking what he wanted.

"Now, don't bother flipping a coin to decide what you're going to order, Zack," Maddie said with warmth. "I'm choosing today, and it's both mashed and oven-browned potatoes. You put some muscle back on you, now, you hear?"

Joel lowered his voice so that it couldn't carry. "Ben and Maddie, I hear on good authority, were married one week after they met."

"How do you know?" Elizabeth leaned over the pickle dish in order not to be heard.

"Maddie brags about it. That's the way it is here."

Discomfited, Elizabeth stared back at the window and straight into the bemused eyes of Zack Danvers. He was clean-shaven and looked positively civilized. Not handsome so much as compelling. His eyes were the same deep blue she remembered, his dark hair almost as untamable as hers. It was a small thing to have in common.

"Elizabeth?"

She turned back to Joel. "I'm sorry."

"How soon can we?"

Joel's voice demanded her attention as much as Zack Danvers's very presence disturbed her equilibrium. "I . . . I don't know. Please, Joel, can we discuss this later, in private?"

Desperate, she picked up her fork and poked at her potatoes, hoping to steer Joel away from the subject.

But Joel was not to be discouraged by one dark-haired stranger. If anything the competition egged him on. "I know it's not much of a proposal—I've never been fancy with words—but I think Will would like this. A way of keeping the orchard in the hands of two of his favorite people in the whole world."

She glanced sideways to see if Zack Danvers had heard that.

He raised his water goblet in a mock toast.

Blushing furiously, she fixed a steady look on Joel. "Please, Joel, later."

"But we've got to settle this, Elizabeth. I'm offering a fair business proposal, the kind men and women make all the time out west. Don't you see, people will say it's not right for me to work out there from sunup to sundown with a single woman on the place?"

Her mouth dropped open. "Are you saying, Joel Emory, that unless we . . . we marry, you won't keep on helping me?"

"I wouldn't put it that way," he drawled and leaned back in his chair, confident, smiling.

Elizabeth wished Zack Danvers would do another one of his vanishing acts or that the piano would start up again and lend some privacy to this conversation.

Please, Joel. Not now.

But Joel leaned across the table and took her hand in full view of Zack Danvers. "You don't have any choice, you realize. No one else in this town wants you to succeed at that orchard like I do. I think we'd make a fine partnership and show them all."

She didn't have to look to see Zack Danvers's smile.

"Elizabeth?" Joel prompted.

"Yes." The word came out like a desperate note.

"You mean, yes?"

She nodded, blushing furiously, like a schoolgirl.

"You won't be sorry. Soon?"

"We'll discuss it on the way home . . . please?" She might have said yes, but that didn't mean he'd get his way on the wedding date. Harvest time was her choice and no compromising. Oh, she'd never forget the humiliation of this public declaration.

Smiling with satisfaction, Joel came around to assist her up.

She walked out of that hotel with all the dignity she could muster, but every step of the way she felt Zack Danvers's dark blue gaze on her, boring into her.

When it was safe to crawl out from her hiding place under the Groveland Hotel veranda, Clara Gustavson ran through the orchard with the speed for which she was famous. She'd found out two new secrets. Real secrets. Pete wasn't going to believe it.

Her bare feet were used to the cold earth, and so she flew through the trees, her route memorized. In her arm, she carried the still-warm loaf of bread she'd snitched from Maddie's kitchen window. Before heading for the mines up north, Pa had left only a sack of beans and half a sack of flour in the little shack. It got to be monotonous fare.

After running up the road and on into town, she hurried inside their tar-paper shack at the end of Main Street, across the railroad tracks from the depot. The smell of burned beans at once assaulted her.

"Guess what?" she asked Pete.

"Miss Yates quit as schoolteacher?"

"Nothing that good." Clara held out her prize, the loaf of bread.

"You snitched it from Maddie's window ledge?"

"It don't matter. I think she knows it's me, and she leaves food there on purpose."

Clara sat cross-legged on her bare mattress and, twisting the loaf, tore off half for Pete.

"I've got a secret." Her voice was a tease, a dare for Pete to ask for more.

"You've always got a secret." He chewed off a bite of bread. "But never anything about Miss Yates."

"No, this is a good secret. About the missing soldier at the railroad depot. I found him."

Pete kept chewing, but when he looked up, eyes wide, Clara knew she had his attention. Clara's goals in life were to grow up to be the town gossip and to have her pa come back and build them a real house. Which he would.

"He's a doctor."

"Who?"

"The new man, Ben's soldier brother, and he doesn't want anybody to know."

Pete's eyebrows rose in interest. "That ought to be worth a few bribes from Maddie's kitchen."

Clara flopped down on her mattress, arms and legs spread wide. "I know that, Pete. And you know what else? He's having an argument with Ben over whether to stay or not."

"You think he's just here to visit?"

She curled up on her side, head propped up on her elbow. "I couldn't hear it all through the window, but he's from Chicago, and Ben is mad because he won't stay here."

"You sure he's not from that orphanage Miss Yates is always talking about?"

"Naw, they would have mentioned our names."

"What about that fancy lady that got off the train?"

"She's not from the orphanage either. Don't worry, Pete. Miss Yates is the only one we've got to stay clear of."

"What else do you know?"

"Joel's already gone calling on the orchard lady, asking if she needs help. I think he's asked her to marry him. But guess what the best part is?"

Pete stopped chewing, and a worried look crossed his face.

"He told her there's not much work to taking care of the orchard."

Slowly Pete looked up, expression half incredulous, half amused. "She believed him?"

"Why shouldn't she?" Clara hooted. "Not much work! The apples just grow by themselves! Ain't that funny, Pete?"

"You go listening again tomorrow and see what else you can find out. Until I know what she's going to do with the orchard, I'll keep on working down by the creek."

"Pete, what if she catches you? You know what Pa said!"

"Don't worry, I'm not giving away any family secrets. You're the one who'd better be careful or I'll make you eat burned beans for the next week. I'm in charge of you, Clara, and don't forget it."

She sighed with annoyance. "You're always thinking you're so smart because you're fourteen and I'm only eight, but let me tell you, Pete Gustavson, you'd starve on your own cooking without me! So there!"

On that provocative announcement, she rolled over on her straw ticking and wrapped herself in her favorite "blanket," the dark blue Civil War coat that Pa had given her. Pete had a gray one, and aside from the matching hats, they were their most cherished possessions, *and* among their warmest. They were Pa's favorite things, too, out of all his Civil War collection. That alone was enough to convince Clara he'd be back. He might be taking longer than he said, but Pa *would* come back.

He'd promised.

3

The nightmare came back that night, and again, Zack awoke in a sweat. But this time his brother was there, shaking him awake.

"Sorry," Zack mumbled, embarrassed. "Aftereffects of the yellow jack, I guess. I'm okay. Go on back to bed."

"Like hell," Ben muttered. "When are you going to tell me what happened over there?"

"Nothing happened." Nothing noble, nothing heroic, nothing honorable.

Zack pulled on his trousers and shirt and moved to the window, where he watched stars twinkle above the orchard.

"You got a drink?" he asked Ben.

"Water, you mean? Or something stronger?"

A stab of pain shot through Zack. In one excruciating moment the memory of his best friend Harry flashed before his eyes. . . .

"Hey, Harry, I'm thirsty. We got any water in this tent?" Zack had said.

Of course there hadn't been any water, and they'd argued like bear cubs over who was going to go get some. Not because it was dangerous out in the jungle but because it was hot and sticky and a nuisance to have to go find a well. . . .

"Never mind," Zack said to his brother. "I'm not that thirsty."

"How about some fresh air? You know, come with me for a smoke outside? So we won't wake up everyone in the hotel."

Moments later Zack settled down in the darkness beside his brother on the top step of the hotel porch and watched Ben measure out some tobacco for his pipe.

"What do you know about this Joel Emory fellow?" Zack asked at last.

Ben shot him a quick look. "What's to know?"

"How long's he been here?"

Ben contemplated the pouch of tobacco in his hand, then lit the pipe, taking his time drawing on it. He was a thorough man, Ben, the sort of man who measured his words as carefully as he had the tobacco. "He's paid his rent so far."

"And been here all of one night," Zack scoffed.

The sweet aroma of pipe tobacco filled the air. "I didn't know you'd been out and about meeting people."

"Joel Emory ate dinner here in your own hotel today. Proposed marriage to that lady I rode in on the train with."

Ben took a couple more draws on his pipe, then stuck a thumb through his suspender. He stared straight ahead up the lane leading to the town road.

"Women are scarce in a town like this," Ben explained at last. "No woman stays a spinster out here long—except for the schoolteacher. A man's gotta move fast if he wants first pick."

"Or if he wants her land."

"Is that what you think?"

Zack shrugged. "It's none of my business. Just curiosity." Come to think of it, this was the first thing he'd been curious about since leaving Manila. Even now he could imagine Miss Elizabeth Sheldon, all soft and warm in his arms. Probably because he'd fallen asleep on her, he could remember her perfume. Violets or lily of the valley. Something sweet, like her. Someone as cynical as Zack would notice an innocent detail like that. Everything about the lady was as opposite to him as the poles of a magnet.

Ben stretched and leaned back, looking up at the sky with

its myriad stars. "Listen, Zack, a woman like that is better off marrying Joel Emory than an ornery cuss like Orville Gustavson with a pair of motherless kids in on the deal . . . and mark my words, she's going to marry someone." He took a puff on his pipe. "Besides, Zack, I kinda like the idea of a little courting going on in my dining room. It's good for business." He looked up at his brother. "You sound like a country doctor already, knowing more about everybody's business than anyone else in town."

"Maybe I've had a little time on my hands to notice things."

"The town's getting by with Granny Sikes to do our midwifing, but we could use a real doctor."

"I'm not staying. Didn't I make that clear?"

"Too good for small-town medicine?"

"Is there a law that says because I pass through I have to hang up a shingle? I told you, I'm staying anonymous. I don't want anyone to know I'm a doctor."

"Oh, yeah, what if Granny has trouble delivering one of the ranch babies? What if that Gustavson girl falls off a roof?"

A cold fist clenched around Zack's heart. "It won't happen." It couldn't. Ben had helped put him through medical school, so he had a right to expect a favor in return, but not this. Some favors were just too much. "Those urchins, from what I've seen, look pretty tough to me."

"You're stubborn."

"I've called myself worse."

"What are you going to do next?"

"Nothing."

"Well, if you want to do nothing but pound some nails around here that's fine, but eventually you've got to get back to doctoring."

Zack's reasons were locked far away in his soul, and he was not about to pull them out. "I'm done with doctoring."

Ben made a noise as if he meant to argue, but suddenly a light shone over the two brothers, and as one they looked behind them. Maddie stood there on the porch, dark hair hanging loose about her shoulders, a shawl thrown over her nightgown. She held up a lantern, and its light caught the stern expression on her face. Zack had never seen Maddie without a smile.

"Ben, quit badgering your brother and let him go to bed."

"Aw, Maddie, you don't have to fuss over me," Zack insisted.

"Yeah, Maddie," Ben parried, "why don't you come out here on the porch and fuss over me awhile? There's a real pretty moon to look at—a crescent moon."

She hesitated, and Zack could see the longing between husband and wife to sit together in the uncommonly mild April night, with the promise of apple blossoms in the air, maybe wrap their arms around each other and gaze at the stars together while they dreamed about their future.

Zack stood up. When he murmured, "I'll go in," no one objected. He left the door ajar and walked quietly upstairs where he heard the soft voices of Ben and Maddie floating up to him. Zack lay back in bed, hands linked behind his head, unable to sleep. The trouble with Ben was easy to analyze: he still thought the world needed whipping. But whipping the world was simple when you were idealistic and saw your dreams one by one coming true, as Ben did.

His hotel.

His wife.

His children, who would follow, as inevitable as rainbows after rain on a sunny day.

Ben's question cut deep into Zack's gut: What are you going to do next? He had no answers. Did anyone whose dreams had died? It was enough to take life one day at a time and keep his secret between him and Ben and Maddie. By the time anyone else found out he was a doctor, he'd be gone. And meanwhile, if one of those urchins fell off a roof, he'd fondly wring the kid's neck.

The next day, as soon as Ben and Maddie went to church, Zack headed up Main Street to the railroad depot. The sooner he inquired about departing trains the better.

The railroad agent, Otis, was busily transcribing a message from a clicking telegraph. Curious, Zack stepped up to the counter, and immediately the young man turned off the key and held up a hand signaling "Wait a minute" while he kept transcribing furiously. Then he turned back to the key and signed off his code.

"Holy cow," Otis muttered under his breath, still ignoring Zack. "The town's not gonna believe this."

Intrigued, Zack naturally expected some news from either the Philippines or Cuba. "What is it?" The war had been over for months, but *not* the military involvement. The newspapers were still insatiable in their appetite for stories.

"It's the mine—the silver mine up north where that Gustavson fellow's at." Abruptly he stopped.

"Tell me."

Wary, Otis lowered his voice. "This is on the QT."

In a nutshell, the big Bunker Hill mine up north had blown.

"It blew yesterday. Men killed. A lot. Sounds like it was a real doozie, and according to this message, Eden Creek's own Orville Gustavson is there."

Zack caught two words—*Gustavson* and *killed*. "You mean that little girl's father?"

"Yeah, he was close enough to have been in it. Him and a dozen others!" Otis came out from behind his counter and headed for the door.

Otis pushed around Zack. "I gotta get to the church and bang down the door to get the newspaper editor. But no one else hears about this, understand, or I could lose my job."

Acting on pure instinct, Zack grabbed the fellow by his coat sleeve and swung him around. "Wait a minute. You aren't going to send that message out to the newspaper like Paul Revere, are you?"

" 'Course I am." Otis shook Zack's hand away. "This is big news, mister. Biggest since I learned Morse code! Besides, the message is for the paper. Ain't my place to change that."

"Someone ought to tell the Gustavson kid first. Hasn't she

got a brother here somewhere, too?"

Otis paused. "Listen, mister, I told you—I got my job on
the line. These Western Union messages are confidential.
Like I said, this one's for the newspaper."

Something turned in Zack's gut. "His children shouldn't
find out that way."

"Aw, no one cares about those crummy kids." The eager
telegraph agent pushed Zack's hand away. "Out of my way.
Old man Gustavson a goner," he chortled. He was off then,
running down the street in the direction of the newspaper
office, and right behind him followed Zack, railroad time-
tables temporarily forgotten. Western Union law be damned.
Surely someone in this town had the compassion to forewarn
a pair of helpless kids about a tragedy.

After wending her way through the horse-high sagebrush,
Clara Gustavson darted in among the apple trees. The orchard
was her favorite hiding place—at least it had been until this
fancy lady from back east arrived. New people in town had
to be tested before Clara could decide whether to trust them
or not.

Maybe she'd try to snitch some food. That was always a
giveaway as to whether people were friendly or not. If they
said nothing, like Maddie, she knew they were friendly, but if
they hollered and chased her like Miss Yates, then no amount
of nice talk could get Clara to trust them.

The wild grass was still wet and cool with dew, and ahead
of her was a clothesline. Though her mother was a distant
memory, one thing brought the memory back—clotheslines.
On Mondays Clara loved to sneak up to the lines of wash
and sniff the scent of soap and wind. Her mother's dresses
and aprons had smelled that way—not gaudy like the saloon
ladies' clothes but clean. Sometimes she wrapped herself in
a sheet just to envelop herself in the memory. Sunday the
clotheslines were usually not in use, but on this Sabbath the
new lady here had a quilt and some sheets out airing.

As the Sheldon house came into view and beyond it the

barn and fruit cellar, Clara hid behind the quilt and peeked out. Seeing that the coast was clear, she ran for the cellar. A minute later she was prying open the wooden doors that rose at an angle from the cellar. The scent of last year's apples, musky and overripe, assaulted her. She'd snatch a few, and if nothing else came of the search, she and Pete could at least make applesauce.

"Pete," she called. "Are you here? If you're down there, I'm coming in."

She stubbed her toe on a stack of empty apple baskets, and when they crashed to the dirt floor, she froze in place, praying Joel Emory would not hear and come chase her out. Clara worried about Pete getting caught by Joel more than she worried about her sore toe.

Elizabeth Sheldon straightened from making the bed and turned to the window. She was almost certain she'd heard a voice calling, not a deep voice like Joel's but something higher pitched.

"Pete?"

There it was again. It was a childish voice. Quietly she moved outside. She had a strong suspicion about who was trespassing and followed the voice to the doors of the underground cellar that Joel had said was for fruit storage.

Elizabeth knelt and opened one of the doors a crack.

Someone gasped, then let out a childish squeal.

Desperadoes, it seemed, did indeed dwell in Eden Creek, in pint-size form. Shoving the door wide open, she exposed her intruder. A pair of wide blue eyes stared back at her from the fruity dungeon.

"What are you doing here?" the girlish voice asked with bravado.

Elizabeth bit back a smile. "I live here. What are you doing?"

"Looking for my brother."

The little girl scrambled out, brushing past so fast that Elizabeth almost lost her balance. By the time she was able to turn, Clara Gustavson, barely visible in dark overalls, was running through the orchard, and Elizabeth, thoroughly intrigued by her pint-sized intruder, followed.

There was no keeping some things a secret, and Sundays were the best days for gossip. It spread at church, passed from pew to pew as quickly as the hymnbooks could be handed out, and this Sunday two items were of particular interest.

The newspaper editor, Mr. Pierce, had been called out of church by Otis. And Joel Emory had proposed officially in person to the new lady at the orchard, Miss Elizabeth Sheldon. The latter news sorely vexed Eden Creek's schoolteacher, Miss Agnes Yates. After all, Joel had been hanging around her schoolhouse, calling on her, until this—this *eastern* lady arrived.

It was quite a long walk from church to Main Street, and while they walked, Miss Yates let her feelings be known to her closest confidante.

"What's *she* got, Granny, that makes him propose to her the day after she steps off the train?" she muttered crossly.

Granny Sikes, garbed in black cape and frilly hat, looked like everybody's grandmother, and when she spoke, it was clear she was nobody's fool.

"Now, Agnes, Joel was her brother's friend, so it was natural he started corresponding with her, and you have to admit lots of engagements happen through the mail."

Lifting up her skirt, Agnes stepped around a mud puddle. "From men who are desperate, who absolutely can't find a woman within a hundred miles. But when there's a single schoolteacher right in the man's own town, you'd expect he'd look around his backyard a bit before luring some fancy eastern woman out here, as if none of us are good enough for him."

"It could be he wants the orchard, you know. What could you offer?"

Granny could be maddeningly practical. "Joel's above greedy, mercenary motives."

"Well, there're plenty of other men, so you'll find a beau.

You've not yet turned thirty, and you've a good figure about you still, though I wouldn't let the other men see you in such a lather, or they'll all stampede away, especially that handsome sheepman. Men don't like a woman who gets unreasonable."

Agnes had to be careful not to let her anger show, because members of the school board were all about her, waving as they drove off to their ranches or houses.

"Clods, all of them—especially Antonio. I didn't go to normal school to take the first illiterate Basque who came along."

"Choosy, eh?"

"Well, weren't you?"

Granny knotted the bow on her best black cape and set the pace as they headed for nearby Main Street and their habitual after-church walk. "Agnes, I was seventeen when I married the first miner I laid eyes on. He didn't have an education, except what he'd picked up on the streets of Dublin, but he knew more than some educated people I've met, and he tolerated me fussing with herbs."

"Well, a man like that may have suited you, but not me."

"I think you need to come home with me for some Granny brew. Some spring tonic to calm you and end your fretting over the truants, and some camomile tea to heal your heart."

Miss Yates practically stamped her foot in frustration. "Now, don't go patronizing me, Granny, with spring tonics . . . bunch of bark and roots and whiskey put up to look respectable in canning jars. I'm perfectly in control of myself. As far as I'm concerned, Joel can marry whomever he likes. I'm only sorry to see him lowering himself to a marriage of convenience."

As she and Granny rounded the corner onto Main Street, they drew up short at a most unusual sight. There, clustered in front of the newspaper office, were enough people to hold a social on the spot. Others reined in their wagons and jumped down. Dogs barked, and loose children toddled around, while women bowed their heads and wrung their hands in shock.

"Well, I declare . . ." Under her breath Miss Yates muttered, "That message from Otis must have been very important if Mr. Pierce opened up his newspaper office on a Sunday."

Miss Yates drew closer so she could read the news bulletin posted in the office window: "Local resident in area of Bunker Hill explosion. Presumed dead."

"Who is it?" Granny asked.

"Orville Gustavson," someone said.

Miss Yates moved in closer to read more. It was true. She caught her breath and had to bite her lip to keep a smile from showing. "Well, that's a blessing," she whispered to Granny, one hand shielding her words from eavesdroppers. "Orville's been nothing but a nuisance since he arrived here and built that ugly shack. And his children . . . they've done nothing but made me look bad as a teacher. Maybe now someone will do something about those urchins of his and help me pack them off to . . ."

The shadow of a man loomed up behind Granny, and, whirling, Agnes stopped in mid-sentence. A stranger, an uncommonly attractive man, stood staring at her, condemnation in his gaze.

"Begging your pardon, ma'am, but the man is only *presumed* dead. If his children are lucky, he's alive still."

Miss Yates stared at this bold new stranger, and at a glance knew she was face to face with a man of refinement. Not only was he handsome, but his voice was educated, his manner cultured, and even his fingernails clean. His identity intrigued her more than his argument. Why hadn't someone advised her at church that a new man had come to town? Hopefully, an eligible man at that. Why, you'd think all she went for was to drop her contribution in the plate.

"I beg your pardon, sir," she said in her most conciliatory voice. "Of course we'll all hope and pray for Mr. Gustavson's safe delivery from this awful tragedy. But I am the schoolteacher, and believe me, if you knew Orville Gustavson's children, you'd know why an orphanage is the best place for them. A kindness to the poor abandoned little ones, that's what it would be."

The man's expression didn't change one iota. "Do you know where they are now, ma'am?" he asked in a quiet voice.

Miss Yates smiled. Good, someone at last who was willing to help her. "Oh, I'm sure they're hanging around down by the orchard. If they're not at the orchard, then they're playing in the creek. Would you like me to help you search for them, Mister . . . ?"

"Danvers." Then, to her consternation, he tipped his hat and said, "If you'll pardon me, I'll go find them and break the news before they find out from the paper."

Miss Yates's mouth fell open. He was leaving, walking away from her. Quickly she recovered herself. "Well, sir, surely you don't think they can read?" she called out.

Briefly he paused and looked over his shoulder. "Yes, ma'am, I did think they could. You're the schoolteacher. Isn't it your duty to teach them to read?"

"Well!"

Before Miss Yates could gather her wits he was gone, striding off in the direction of the orchard, toward the eastern lady's place.

Enough was enough.

"Who is he?" she whispered to Granny.

"Ben's brother. Arrived in town the same day as Miss Sheldon. An eligible soldier from the war, they say."

"Then why did you let me go on and on? Why didn't you stop me?"

"Agnes, you never shut up long enough to allow a proper introduction, so you may as well calm down. He'll have forgotten all about this by the time of the spring social."

Miss Yates pulled a face. "If he stays that long."

And off she stalked up the street to Granny's for camomile tea and recriminations. There just weren't that many eligible men passing through, especially for a plain-faced woman like her, and she cursed the Gustavson kids and their pa for causing her to embarrass herself in front of one of the most eligible men to arrive in many a season.

Pausing in front of the mercantile, she eyed a bolt of muslin on display, wondering if this man was worth sewing a new dress for. She caught a glimpse of her straight dark hair and automatically smoothed it back. If Agnes had had to choose her best feature she would probably have chosen her small ears. Tiny coral earbobs danced in the reflection, distracting her from taking a really hard look at herself. She'd do, she decided. A man could do worse. Far worse.

Reassured, she hurried on and caught up with Granny.

"Well," she said on a smug note, "at least he can't court that Sheldon woman now that she's engaged to Joel Emory." Now it was Agnes who set the pace, moving briskly up the crowded street.

"I wouldn't talk ill of the Gustavson children in front of him, though, Agnes," Granny advised, huffing and puffing to keep up. "I think he feels sorry for them."

"Don't worry. In all the excitement, my hasty words will be forgotten. Besides, there's no one else in town for him to court, is there?"

Except for a few bees buzzing around the nearest apple tree, impatient for nectar, Elizabeth was alone. Then the wind came up and even the bees were gone. Even though it was the end of April, spring had yet to fully blossom here, and so far only a gossamer hint of pale green leaves, a few early blooms saved the orchard from stark nakedness. There wasn't much to hide a little girl from sight.

"Clara," Elizabeth called again, guessing she was checking on her brother's whereabouts. With no mother or father, her brother would be all the little girl had, and Elizabeth's heart went out to the child. Like an echo, she heard Clara's voice.

"Pe-e-te," Clara cried. "Pete, where are you?"

Thinking quickly, Elizabeth darted in among the trees, hoping to intercept Clara, but before she could, the little girl whooshed by in a blur. Up and down the rows of trees, Clara led her pursuer a merry chase until, winded completely, her heart pounding in her ears, Elizabeth stopped and dropped to her knees, her blouse coming loose from the waistband of her slim skirt. The grass was damp, and while she took in deep breaths, she pushed back the hair that had flown out of its pins.

By the time she caught her breath she could no longer hear Clara's footsteps, but the child couldn't have left the orchard without Elizabeth seeing her. She stood in a patch of dandelions, their bright yellow heads blowing back and forth in the wind.

"Clara," she called to the orchard in general, "you can stay out here all day and scare away the porcupines for me. But I want to thank you by feeding you breakfast."

Slowly Elizabeth began walking along the rows of trees toward her little house. "I'm making hotcakes," she called. "With syrup."

She paused at a tree, but all was silent.

"And oatmeal."

She paused at the next tree. "With brown sugar."

It took, she discovered, exactly twenty paces to span the distance between trees.

"And eggs. Fried."

Twenty more paces brought her to the next tree.

"And bacon for sure."

When she was out of the orchard she strolled up to her porch, where she made a great project of opening the door so that it squeaked on its hinges.

"Breakfast will be ready in a half hour," she said at last and made a point of slamming the door good and loud.

A few minutes later the door squeaked open.

Elizabeth looked up from the stove to see a pair of blue eyes peeking out from beneath the longish blond bangs of a little girl. If it hadn't been so dirt-smudged, the face would have been angelic.

With a hesitant smile, Clara displayed a gap in her front teeth.

"Did you mean it about food?" she asked.

"I always mean what I say." Elizabeth pointed with a wooden spoon to the table she'd set for two.

A half hour later, Clara Gustavson was polishing off the last crisp slabs of bacon and her second bowl of oatmeal with brown sugar.

While sipping coffee, Elizabeth had pried out as much information as the girl would part with, which wasn't a lot. She and Pete, it seemed, lived alone in a shack behind the train depot.

"Temporary, of course. Pa's going to build a fancy house when he strikes it rich."

"Of course."

"Ma died when I was three," Clara said matter-of-factly when asked. "Pa never talks about it much because he says I remind him of her."

"Then your mother must have been very pretty," Elizabeth said.

"I don't know," the girl said. "Anyways, if I did, I'd have to keep it a secret. My pa is away mining, and I promised him I'd always keep our secrets."

"My, that sounds as if you obey your father."

Clara chewed and nodded her head. "Everyone's got a secret, and they're all important. . . . Miss Yates says I have too many."

"Miss Yates?" Elizabeth had not met a Miss Yates.

"The schoolteacher."

Ah, yes.

"Granny Sikes—that's the town midwife—she says Miss Yates had her cap set on Joel, so don't be too surprised if Miss Yates isn't the first one over here with a pie or preserves to welcome you—'less of course it's to spy on Joel. Anyway, Miss Yates never did like me—"

She was interrupted by a knock at the door, and Elizabeth moved to open it. A boy stood there. Pete, so Clara said. He was a taller, skinnier replica of his little sister, right down to the bowl-cut hair. Though he had the same round face as his sister, he lacked her mischievous eyes. Quiet and deliberate—that would best have described Pete.

Pete spoke up then with all the authority a fourteen-year-old could summon. "Pa says we can't take charity, especially from women."

"I'm not offering you charity," Elizabeth put in, adding quickly, "I understand you know something about apple growing."

"Who told you?" Pete asked, flashing a quick look at Clara, who pulled away from Elizabeth.

"Why, Ben did," Elizabeth said easily. "He says you liked to spend time working in the orchard with my brother."

Pete shuffled his worn boots. "Yeah, well, maybe. We've worked at a lot of jobs, me and Pa."

"Good." While they'd been talking, Elizabeth had already thought of a way to help this pair.

"I'm offering you a real job. You can plant the vegetable garden, cut wood for the stove every day, get me some chickens for the coop, feed the horses, and do all the other things that keep the place running. And then when Joel needs help with the orchard, you can do whatever he needs."

"The weeds need to be hoed around the trees," Clara said in a know-it-all voice.

"Quiet, Clara."

Pete and Clara exchanged a quick look, a warning, as if they shared a secret.

"You and your sister can stay here, sleep in the loft, and board with me. I'd rather cook for three than for one anyway, *and* I'll pay you a nickel a day."

Pete's mouth dropped open.

"Well, what do you say? Is it a deal?"

"Let's see the loft," Clara said.

When Pete didn't object, the three of them headed for the barn. Actually, Elizabeth hadn't had time to investigate it yet and was curious about what else she owned.

A lot more than she knew, as it turned out.

"I'm not sure how to get up to the loft," she said.

"Steps are over there," Pete pointed. "Your brother sometimes let me curry his horses," he explained hastily. "He always had lots of hay up in the loft. Me and Clara have got warm coats for blankets."

Elizabeth thought she could round up some extra quilts and pillows. "Well, then, you'll stay?"

"Can we play here?" Clara asked. "And you won't chase us away?"

"There's no time to play, Clara," Pete said. "She's hiring us to work."

Chastised, Clara drew a circle in the dirt with the big toe of her bare foot.

"Did my brother explain any of this to you, Pete?" she asked.

Nodding, he showed her around, and Elizabeth followed, looking at the wagon, the horses in their stalls, the grain bins and finally peering into a room Pete identified as the harness room. The dark room contained not so much harness, though, as equipment for the orchard. For spraying, Pete told her.

"Codling moths get on the leaves and make worms in the apples," Clara said.

Pete gave her a poke in the ribs. "Hush up."

There was a pause, and only a buzzing fly broke the silence. "Anyway, what Clara means is wormy apples don't sell, so your brother filled this room full of chemicals and sprayers for the trees. Spraying's not so complicated, though, as watering. It takes a lot of plowing to open up the ditches—rills, some people call 'em—and then shovel work to get the creek water to flow through them. Your brother was a strong man."

Pete stopped suddenly and stared at his feet, his face beet red. "Sorry. I'm talking too much."

"No, no," Elizabeth rushed to say. "You've saved Joel some explaining, and it's good to know you spent time with Will."

"Yeah, your brother was our friend."

Suddenly a shadow filled the doorway, and as one they turned to see who was joining them now.

In the dim interior of the barn, with dust floating in the air, it was hard to see, and they automatically moved forward, heading for the light. Their uninvited guest was tall and dark and stood with legs spread, hat in his hands.

When she recognized him, Elizabeth caught her breath and put a hand to her heart in shock. She'd never thought to see him again so close up.

It was Zack Danvers, his face somber. After a brief look at the children, his gaze caught and held hers.

Elizabeth sensed from his look something serious. The entire valley seemed to be holding its breath. She couldn't even hear the rush of the creek for the pulsing of the blood in her ears. Should she invite him to sit? On what? A barrel? Before she could decide, he was speaking.

"I've come because of Clara and Pete," he said.

"I see." Again, their gazes met over the top of the little girl's head. Then he walked in, stopping in a patch of light, and met them halfway.

Instinctively, as soon as she could see Zack's face clearly, she knew he'd brought bad news. After all Elizabeth had been through, she'd learned to recognize the signs—the hesitancy, the somber expression, the respectful holding of hat in hand. The only thing she didn't understand was why Zack Danvers, of all people, would be the messenger.

"There's word in town about your pa," he said to the children, and when Clara moved toward him, he knelt beside her. "There's been an accident up in the mines." He hurried on, touching the little girl's shoulder. "But no one knows for sure if your pa's still there or not. It could turn out that he's all right, but you need to know about the accident because the town's full of talk."

Clara flinched as if struck. "What happened?"

Slowly Elizabeth sank down beside Clara, as if to offer extra support. She and Zack Danvers flanked Clara, while Pete stood, quiet.

Zack Danvers told them then about the mine explosion, told both children, who listened in silence as Lieutenant

Danvers couched the awful events at the mining town in words as tactful as any Elizabeth could have dreamed up. Like Clara, she stared at Zack Danvers, at the gentle expression in his eyes, the sheen of perspiration across his lip, the broadness of his shoulders. Though he looked just like the desperado from the train, it was hard to tell by his manner that he was the same man.

He ended with some encouraging words. "Of course, as I said, it's just a first newspaper report, and there'll be more news coming. Let's hope it will be better news."

Pete slumped where he stood, his eyes downcast, and Elizabeth could almost see the shell he pulled over himself.

Then Clara surprised her. With a brave swallow, she looked at Zack Danvers, her face full of trust. "If there were doctors there, could they fix some of the men?"

Zack looked at her, dark eyebrows suddenly lifting. "I expect so."

"And it would take a while to mend the men?"

"Depends how bad they're hurt."

"Then there's still a chance my pa might be hurt and no one knows who he is? He promised he'd come back, you know."

"There's that chance," Zack said.

"Well, I think my pa's still alive," Clara declared.

Zack stood, and so did Elizabeth, their eyes meeting across Clara's head.

The little girl rushed on. "He'll be back. He promised to come back, and he always keeps his promises."

The room was perfectly still. Then Zack said softly, "I like people who keep their promises. Can you be brave for a while till we find out more?" He chucked her chin in a gesture meant to give courage.

Hugging herself, Clara stood there like a forlorn tumbleweed and nodded. "I never learned to pray, but I'm gonna now." She dropped her head to her hands, which formed a steeple. "God, if you're up there somewhere, you're gonna have to overlook all the bread and pies I pinched. I'll explain why later, but you gotta help me now. You gotta make sure my pa's alive, and you gotta do something about Miss Yates because I don't wanta go to no orphanage. Amen and awomen, too."

As Zack turned to leave, Elizabeth closed the space between them. "Lieutenant—"

"Zack." His correction was terse. He'd stopped in his tracks, staring straight ahead, as if he couldn't wait to get outside, away from her.

"Is that all you know?"

"If I knew more, don't you think I'd have told them?" He slanted a look at her, his dark lashes coming down over his eyes.

She gulped. "I hardly know you, so I really don't expect anything of you."

"I guess you don't at that, Miss Sheldon."

"I hope, though, you'll tell me if you learn more. The children will be bunking in my barn. Working for me," she added at his quick look of surprise.

"I'll keep you informed, unless the town does first." He shoved back his unruly hair and placed his hat squarely on his head.

"Zack." She said his first name more easily than she'd expected to, and he responded by turning to face her. Her ears hummed. "Please, could we forget what happened on the train?"

Sighing, he gazed at his boots. "It's probably for you to do the forgetting. For what it's worth, I'm sorry."

She was touched by his somber voice, the quick look he gave her, like a schoolboy apologizing for pushing her out of a tree. "You missed a lovely welcome, but that doesn't matter. All that matters is that we talk once in a while about the children's father."

He swallowed and nodded. "Yes."

Zack Danvers stood there, silent, watching her, a little bit of wonder in his eyes. Their shared gaze lasted the space of a heartbeat before she was the one staring at her shoe tops.

"Thank you for coming." Her voice sounded stiff and far away. As she'd intended, he took her words as a dismissal, and spun on his heel.

She stood there watching him walk out, mystified at this new side to him.

Then Clara sighed. "Oh, Pa . . ."

At once Elizabeth turned, thoughts of Zack Danvers far from her mind. "Come here, Clara." She put her arms around Clara, and the little girl just naturally burrowed against her, desperate for physical contact. A sob broke from her.

"Hush, Clara. I'll be your friend, and as long as you're on my land, no one can take you away. Not even this Miss Yates, whoever she is."

"We're safe when she's in school overseeing the kids with their lunch pails and breaking up fights over red rover, but today's Sunday, and she'll be looking for us."

"Miss Yates won't be able to send you away until we hear for sure about your pa . . . and even then she won't. You're safe with me," and she sent them off then with a list of chores to keep them occupied.

Alone again she wandered out to the orchard, where she stood looking at the hotel off in the distance and thinking about Zack Danvers. A genuine enigma, he'd changed from desperado to guardian angel in days. There was no denying the compassion he'd just shown—to break such news to Clara and Pete and do it so gently.

She was so lost in her thoughts she never even heard the wagon.

"Elizabeth?"

She whirled to see Joel, crisp and smiling.

"You ready for our ride?"

She was startled, especially by Joel's carefree smug expression, and had to force herself to smile.

"What's wrong? Them Gustavson kids aren't prowling around here, vandalizing, are they?"

Her mouth dropped open. "Haven't you heard about their father?"

He shrugged as if the news were about a mongrel found run over on the road. "Aw, they'll get over it."

Her temper threatened to flare. "I've hired Pete to help work the place, at least until we find out about their father. Then you won't be so pressed to do everything for me."

An incredulous look crossed his face, and she hurried on. "I think they're good kids, Joel. They'll live in the loft and take their meals with me. I want to protect them from this Miss Yates. They shouldn't be alone, Joel, not now."

He blinked, opened his mouth as if to object, then seemed to think better of it. "Sure, Elizabeth. You're a good-hearted woman. I like that in you—your generosity. I can handle a pair of kids running around here. Now let's go riding."

"Joel, I don't want to go riding. It's not right. When Zack Danvers broke the news about their father, the children went white. They're in shock."

"Zack Danvers was here?"

She ignored that. "Joel, I want to learn everything there is to know about this orchard. Will you show me?"

His face revealed his impatience. "I've already told you, Elizabeth, there's nothing to learn, not yet. Now let's go riding. I've been looking forward to this all morning."

He used the same petulant tone of voice her father had affected on occasion. Men. Sometimes they needed to get their way to prove they were . . . men.

Sighing, she agreed, but only if Clara and Pete could come along. Standing here wouldn't bring the Gustavson kids' dad back any sooner.

Reluctantly Joel gave in. "And while we're out, we'll set the wedding date."

4

In the next week Joel demonstrated a surprising intolerance
for orchard work and a vast fascination with the sordid details
of the mine explosion as bandied about in talk around the
stove at the mercantile.

"I'm going into town to check on the news from Bunker
Hill," Joel said for the fifth day in a row. "Need anything?"

Elizabeth looked up from the bread she was kneading.
"You got me supplies yesterday, Joel, remember? My cupboards are full. What I need is help watering the trees."

"Don't you want me to find out news for the kids,
Elizabeth? I thought you cared what happened to their pa."

"I do." He always backed her into a corner this
way, every single day. She needed him to stay and
do a full day's work around the orchard, yet all he'd
done so far today was chop fifteen minutes' worth of
wood. And now, like a restless animal, he was ready
for another trip to town. She knew he wouldn't be
back for hours, probably just in time to return to his
hotel room.

"Will you be back in time for the social?" She'd been here
scarcely more than a week, so she told herself not to worry
if she didn't know Joel's habits and likes yet. But a party, it
turned out, was something Joel *did* like.

"I wouldn't miss this social for anything," Joel said, brushing wood splinters off his shirtsleeve. "You and I will be the honored guests." He gave her a sideways look.

"Oh?" This was news. "What about Ben Danvers's brother?" She forced her voice to sound casual. "That band at the railroad depot was quite an honor. I'd expect him to be singled out again tonight." Not that he deserved it. He ought to be pinned to the wall while she threw darts at him . . . but that wasn't fair. Hadn't he been repentant and gentle when talking with the Gustavson children? To be honest, Elizabeth didn't know what to make of him.

"Do you see him around the hotel?" she asked casually.

"Zack Danvers is a very private man. Keeps to himself. I think he'd shoot anybody who tried to pin a medal on him. Why? Does he deserve attention?" Joel leaned against the kitchen door in that negligent way of his.

"Not at all. I only wondered why Ben had made such a fuss the day he arrived."

Joel shrugged. "Tonight is for us, not for war heroes. Haven't you heard, Elizabeth? It's the custom to honor any newly engaged couples at the annual socials."

"How many couples are there?"

"Just us." Joel smiled.

That was worse than ever. Elizabeth covered the bread with a linen cloth and set it aside to rise, then scrubbed flour and dough off the plank counter. She didn't want to be the center of attention; she'd experienced all the celebrity she needed back in Massachusetts. Their reasons might be different, but she and Lieutenant Danvers had one thing in common at least: a desire for privacy.

"What's wrong?" Joel took a step toward her.

"I was hoping to stay on the sidelines and watch out for Clara." In the days since the mine blew, word had trickled down to Eden Creek about casualties and riots and federal troops arresting men. Clara had become more and more optimistic about her pa, but she didn't like to be alone and dogged her brother's every step . . . or Elizabeth's.

"Clara can take care of herself. You know that, Elizabeth. Besides, she's going to have to quit moping about her pa. And you, as the newest betrothed woman, are going to dance your feet off, with me and with every other man there. But mostly with me."

She began icing a cake, her contribution to tonight's potluck supper. "You know, Pete says if it freezes, the bees won't pollinate the trees. I think I ought to stay near the orchard."

"Aw, Elizabeth, don't be a stick," Joel complained. "Do you see me worrying about the trees and the bees? They're buzzing their heads off. If anything's gonna scare 'em it's all this worrying. We're going to announce our wedding date, too . . . and this is the sort of event all the kids go to, even Pete and Clara."

Clara, who'd just come into the kitchen to lick the icing bowl, bounced up and down, the happiest Elizabeth had seen her since she'd heard the news about the mine disaster. Joel was right; of course they'd go to the social. Besides, staying home wouldn't be neighborly, and she needed all the friends she could get. If she was really honest about it, it was Joel who bothered her, not the idea of going to a town social.

She handed the bowl to Clara and moved to the door to watch Joel drive off with her team of horses. Like a naughty whisper, a thought teased her: Joel Emory wasn't worth twenty-five cents a week, never mind a day.

Wiping her hands on her apron, she frowned, surprised at herself. She was being silly, resenting Joel's frequent trips to town. But was she unreasonable? After all, women went to town regularly to trade their eggs and milk, so why shouldn't men have equally frequent reasons to do business in town? Her father had always gone to town in his capacity as mayor of Amherst. True, not every man was a mayor, but every man doubtless had cashboxes to take to the bank. Barbers to cut their hair. Mail to pick up. Newspapers to buy. Parts for equipment to buy. Horses to shoe. Trains to meet.

Trains to forget.

Horseshoe games.

Saloons.

What *was* Joel doing in town? Curiosity was eating at her, but it was also unworthy of her. If he hadn't forgotten to meet her train, she probably wouldn't be reacting this way. Joel deserved her trust, just as she had his trust. His trust that they would marry and share the profits from Will Sheldon's orchard.

She went out onto the kitchen porch and, shielding her eyes, gazed in new appreciation at the farm. The place looked so much better now than it had when she arrived. Better? Why, it fairly sparkled now. The vegetable garden was planted in neat rows, a trio of chickens clucked around inside the coop, the horses had been brushed till they glowed, and Pete had launched a heavy assault on the weeds that choked the trees. He worked so hard for his board. No wonder she questioned Joel's work habits. Pete, bless his heart, would put *any* grown man in a bad light, and the boy deserved a night at the social, not only as a reward but also to take his mind off the worry about his pa.

She moved out among the apple trees, which were now in full lush bloom, a sight guaranteed to soften the meanest heart in this poor world. As the faint scent of blossoms filled the air, she inhaled again and again. Elizabeth loved to look at the orchard, and now she buried her face in a big cluster of sweet blossoms. Joel just grumbled that he'd be glad to see apples growing. How, she wondered, could Joel be blind to this beauty? Walking back to the house, she still felt troubled by that thought.

She supposed it would be good to get away from the orchard and meet people. Besides, she admitted to a curiosity about the infamous Miss Yates. Whether or not Zack Danvers would be there concerned her not the least bit. In any case, she readied her best dress for the big event, taking pains to tack on some fresh lace and ironing the gown twice.

When Joel finally returned to pick up her and the Gustavsons, Elizabeth was fastening a mother-of-pearl brooch to the neckline of her dress. Because they were very nearly late, Elizabeth sent Clara and Pete out with the dessert to wait in the wagon, each with a blanket to ward off the chill.

Elizabeth looked at Joel, dapper in a white shirt and bow tie and slicked-down hair. "What did you do in town today?" she asked casually. He smelled of hair pomade and whiskey.

He smiled. "What did I do? Had a little fun with the boys. Found out the latest on the Bunker Hill mine. If those kids are lucky, their pa might be one of the men who were arrested for rioting. Being thrown in jail is better than dying."

"Well, don't get their hopes up." She sensed him coming up behind her.

Suddenly Joel reached for her and spun her around into his arms. "All we do is talk about those kids. . . . Marry me, Elizabeth. Don't you know how hard it is to be around here all day and not married to you? Why do you think I go to town so often?"

She was speechless with shock at his candid admission.

"There's nothing to stop us. Marry me. I don't want to wait."

But she did. "Not yet, Joel. Not until the end of June."

With a surprisingly strong grip, Joel held her fast. "Elizabeth" was the single word he uttered, and then he leaned down and, cupping her face, kissed her.

If he thought a kiss would persuade her, he was wrong. Actually she was surprised by her reaction. Though his lips teased hers, she did not kiss him back, and after he had broken away, she felt as cold as before. It was up to her to break the silence.

"We'd better go before the children catch their death."

He had the grace to look abashed. "Elizabeth, I'm sorry. I couldn't help it."

"We'll talk later," she said. "After the social." She walked on out ahead of him and fussed over Clara's blanket.

The sky was clear, the air cold for early May, so cold the scent of apple blossoms was now lost.

Joel grabbed the reins and looked straight ahead. "There's nothing to stop us."

"Shh," she said, aware of the children. "At the end of June. I don't care if that's long by western standards. I set my own standards." They would be married at harvest time if she really had her way.

By now her teeth were chattering, as much from the shock of Joel's kiss as from the cold. Perhaps she was infinitely selfish, wanting to bring her crop in before she committed her life to Joel; in a way she was no better than Lawrence, the jilting cad. But what choice did she have?

Zack hadn't planned to dance. As a single man passing through a small town, he was eyed by every single woman and mother there. Consequently, if he had one dance with the schoolmarm, who was rather homely, or a ranch widow who had a passel of kids, everyone would watch him like a hawk to see how fast he proposed marriage. That's how it was when women were scarce. Look at how fast Elizabeth Sheldon had gotten snapped up. He wanted to look at her again, to see if she was as prim as he remembered her, but she wasn't here, and he wished he'd stayed away, too.

His plan had been to stay and mind the hotel, but Maddie, a matchmaker if Zack ever saw one, was having none of that. She insisted he come to this social, declaring she wasn't feeding him supper, so if he wanted to eat, he'd *have* to come. He'd teased her a bit, tossing his lucky coin up into the air as if he needed help making up his mind, but because she'd been so good to him, he wanted to please her and agreed. The minute he saw the jumble of horses and buggies parked along Main Street, however, he had second thoughts. He didn't want to cope with a crowd.

And what a crowd it was, especially since tonight's social was held in the brand-new hall up on the second floor of the mercantile. The room, Maddie explained, was larger than the schoolhouse and had a real hardwood floor. The entire town turned out in force, the talk about evenly divided between the

Bunker Hill mine disaster and the spring crop planting. Zack envied the look of pride some of the men wore. Men who'd built this hall and installed its fine hardwood floor. Men who still took pride in their skills.

Maddie was proud, too. His sister-in-law walked up the stairs and into the hall with a brother on each arm. "Don't even think of leaving early, Zack," she whispered to him. "Ben's going to go off and play his fiddle with the musicians, so I need another Danvers brother as my escort." Despite her reassuring words, the instant she saw some lady friends at the food table she was gone to talk recipes, and Zack made his escape to the rear of the dance floor.

Lanterns flickered on the walls. He shut his eyes, memories of the war closing in on him. He wasn't ready for this, for all the people crowding him like so many wounded bodies. Chattering voices and children's laughter competed with the twang of tuning fiddles. The hum of people could have been the drone of mosquitoes. And the heat up here . . . for a cold night, it was surprising how warm the hall was already. Ever so subtly he edged sideways toward the window and, when he reached it, opened it a few inches, grateful for the fresh air. Still, the dizziness warred inside him, and he knew there was no way he could stand here all night. He inched toward the stairs, intending to go outside and wait by the buggies. Maddie would understand, he told himself. . . .

But then the little Gustavson girl came bounding up the stairs and ran smack into him.

He separated himself from the little girl, pivoted and bumped into yet another person, this one soft in the most intriguing places. He looked up, straight into the eyes of Elizabeth Sheldon. For all of five seconds, their eyes made contact, and inside Zack a match flame touched tinder.

They jumped back, both apologizing at the same time.

"I'm sorry."

"No, I wasn't looking. Did I hurt you?"

She shook her head. Her blush made her even prettier than he'd remembered, and she didn't look at all prim tonight. Her dress, the most feminine thing he'd seen in months, made her stand out like a hothouse flower in a field of wild, scruffy bunch grass. It was pale green, the color of new apple leaves, and the scent of her drifted out to him. Violets. Definitely violets.

Joel took possession of her then. Damn him. Eyes narrowing, Zack couldn't help looking him over, the way he'd not so long ago looked over the enemy. A dandy. From the first time he'd laid eyes on him, Zack hadn't liked Joel. Besides the stiff-collared shirt, Joel sported a bow tie and a fancy straw boater, and he swaggered as if he'd caught the brass ring. A self-important strutter, if Zack ever saw one.

And damned if Zack didn't feel color rise to his face as if he were no more than a strappling twelve-year-old frozen to the spot.

Suddenly it didn't matter if he left the hall or not. He only wanted to find a corner alone somewhere and watch *her*. After sliding along the wall to allow the newcomers to enter the dance hall, Zack watched her surreptitiously. He could stand the crowd, he realized, as long as he kept his eyes on Elizabeth Sheldon. Instantly she was surrounded by a gaggle of town women, the same women who had dropped by the hotel porch in the past couple weeks while in town trading their eggs or cream. Every one of them had peeked into the hotel drawing room to sneak a look at Zack. The only one who'd gone out of her way to avoid him had been Elizabeth Sheldon.

Which, though he hated to admit it, rather intrigued him, wounded his male pride. So he studied this woman who'd lent him her shoulder and concluded he must have been sicker than he thought when he'd arrived not to have noticed her with more appreciation.

The fiddlers struck up a tune, and all around him couples— including Elizabeth and Joel—drifted onto the dance floor. Still Zack watched her, hands jammed into his pockets. Her hair was the color of mountain aspens in autumn, rich honey gold with little wisps blowing about her face. She had green eyes, if he remembered right, and he wished he could see them by lantern light.

Peaches and cream would have envied her complexion, and everything about her spoke of big-city sophistication, except her friendly manner, which drew the other women the way honey drew flies. From the knot of her upswept hair to the toes of her fancy satin slippers, she invited a man's arms, made him ache to hold a woman.

Her tiny figure was like an hourglass, her breasts finely molded by her corset, her skirt clinging stylishly about her hips. The other ladies in their fuller skirts had good reason to cast envious looks her way. When she'd bumped into him, the pearl buttons that ran down her bodice had grazed his shirt, and he had felt the contact right through to his chest.

He looked up to find her watching him over the shoulder of her dance partner, and he felt as if he'd had a relapse of the fever.

They both looked away.

"Come on," someone said at his elbow. "You can't let your brother have all the dances, and I can't allow you to stand here alone all night." Maddie, cheeks flushed with excitement, waited, then finally reached for his hand, and dutifully he led her out onto the dance floor.

Before they began to dance, Maddie whispered in his ear conspiratorially, "You realize you'll have to dance once with Miss Yates or the town will talk. Every new man in town gets to dance once with the schoolteacher."

Agnes Yates doubtless had redeeming qualities; none of them, however, were visible to Zack. Her figure was fine enough, but her features were rather long and horsey, and a vague odor of camphor clung to her. Nothing about her looked soft to hold, and he'd hate to be caught on the stinging end of her yardstick.

"Will I turn into a pumpkin if I don't?"

Maddie laughed and patted him fondly on his cheek. "Dancing doesn't commit you."

"I've never been partial to brown hair, except on my sister-in-law."

His sister-in-law looked up into his face, her own features sympathetic. "Oh, Zack, whatever happened over there in the Philippines couldn't have been that bad. People would be real proud of you if they knew you were a doctor—even your chief competition, our own Granny Sikes."

"I should go on back to the hotel." Before he got roped into dancing with Miss Yates. The midnight supper wasn't worth waiting for . . . and he was being too obvious about watching Elizabeth Sheldon. Some rancher was twirling her right past Zack, and he could scarcely tear his gaze from her.

Quickly, Zack swirled Maddie about, so fast she stumbled.

"Zachary Daan-vers!" Maddie cried. "Where are you going? This is a schottische, not a two-step."

"Sorry. I never learned to do the complicated steps very well."

"You also told me you weren't sick. You're such a liar," she said on a laugh. Pulling out of his arms, Maddie put her hands on her hips and issued an ultimatum. "You have to dance at least once with the bride-to-be."

He assumed she was joking. He'd never heard of such a custom. It was one thing to admire Elizabeth Sheldon from a distance, another to touch her.

Granny Sikes whirled by in the arms of Mr. Gantt, the saloonkeeper. "Call me a charlatan again, you firewater vendor, and I'll cure your bunions good." The laughter had no sooner died down than Granny added, "And don't spit on the floor again, you old goat, you hear?"

Zack caught Maddie's twinkling eye.

"That, I gather, is the venerable Granny Sikes."

Nodding, Maddie said slyly, "She's even more of a stickler than I am for the rules of etiquette. Do you want her after you? She and Miss Yates are friends."

Inwardly he groaned. "Fair warning."

"Either Miss Yates or the bride-to-be. It's expected of you, or else you'll get no midnight supper."

"All right," he promised.

"Before supper," Maddie added.

All day the women had slaved over their favorite recipes, and now across the dance floor the food for the midnight supper was waiting.

Pies. Cakes. Meat. Bread. Vegetables. Home-canned pickles and peaches. Even the table was homemade, long planks propped up by sawhorses, the contraption hidden by white tablecloths, starched and freshly ironed. Every lady had brought her best serving dishes. Why, Maddie had kept Ben waiting while she washed her mother's Dresden bowl for her noodle casserole, then fussed over the cut-glass dish of bread-and-butter pickles. Yes, supper was definitely worth staying for after all, worth dancing for.

Already sleepy children who'd been bedded down in the four corners of the room were waking, crying, "I'm hungry. Quit dancing. . . . I'm hungry."

As he walked toward Miss Yates, who stood next to the table, a movement from under the sawhorses caught his eye. A small hand reached up from under the table and, after groping about, snatched a corn muffin and secreted it down under the tablecloth, which Clara was using for cover.

Clara Gustavson, he guessed, was going to end up six feet tall if she kept eating this way.

He turned to see which man Elizabeth was dancing with now and discovered three different men vying for her hand. He turned back to find Miss Yates watching him, smoothing her dark hair in anticipation of being asked to dance. He'd never hated the ritual of dancing more, but knew there was no backing out.

Already the fiddles were tuning up for the next song. Miss Yates was smiling at him, overeager. His steps dragged.

All of a sudden he stopped. Behind Miss Yates, the tablecloth was moving, and he stared at it, half in disbelief, following a whole line of pies and cakes and pickle dishes moving down the plank board like a slow train. And before he could move to stop the disaster, the engine fell off the cliff with a resounding crash as a potluck supper dish hit the brand-new hardwood floor, splintering and sending meat-balls rolling in every direction. To make matters worse, as Clara tried to crawl out, she toppled over a sawhorse beneath the cloth and, like a domino, the entire table collapsed with Clara beneath it.

Bedlam took over, the dance a near memory as Miss Yates was shoved aside. Women screamed and dashed to protect their best dishes, while men cursed and ran to prevent dam-age to the new floor. Miss Yates, with a schoolteacher's reflexes, hopscotched her way around shattered china plat-ters and pickle dishes, and pushed her way to the end of the table, where the cloth was still sliding toward the floor. The beckoning smile she'd given Zack was replaced by her most formidable teacher's frown as she bent to capture the pint-size culprit.

The tablecloth stopped its progress and little Clara climbed out of all the debris, a half-eaten muffin clutched in her hand. Up came her other hand to balance herself, and down onto the floor crashed yet another bowl, this one of pudding, which dribbled onto someone's once immaculate tablecloth.

A dull red flush spread across Miss Yates's face, and her tiny coral earbobs danced with her emotion. "That was my prize Nesselrole pudding!"

One fiddler had kept sawing away, but now he, too, stopped playing as the entire crowd watched the confron-tation between hungry child and vengeful schoolteacher.

After yanking Clara out from under the table by the straps of her overalls, Miss Yates shook the little girl. "Look what you've done!" As if to punctuate her words, she gave Clara another shake. "Do you know how hard I worked to make that pudding? Do you? You don't deserve to be here, all alone with no one to watch you."

Everyone in the room froze in place except Zack, who re-sumed making his way to Miss Yates and now tapped her on the shoulder. The inclination to ask for a dance was gone now. Long gone. Instead, he said the first thing that popped into his head. "It can't be that bad, can it?" he asked. "Leave the child alone."

Miss Yates whirled, and the instant she saw Zack, her face softened, her voice went down to a concerned murmur. "Now, isn't it obvious the child needs a better home?"

"Only to keep her from getting yelled at, ma'am. And I think if one slight girl can do in a table, maybe someone ought to see to their carpentry."

Elizabeth scarcely heard Zack Danvers's question, scarcely knew how she pushed her way through the crowd and grabbed the little girl. "Let her go," she said. "She's with me. I'm minding her." She didn't care what anyone thought, not even Lieutenant Zack Danvers. Vaguely she sensed his surprise. Most definitely she heard the angry voice of the teacher.

Miss Yates whirled. "You—"

"Yes, me. Clara is under my care. I'm sorry about your pudding, and I know Clara will help clean up the mess."

"You're sorry? What good does that do now? Besides, who gave you the authority to take in orphans? The school board?"

"Myself."

Miss Yates cast an icy look at Elizabeth. "You may be able to do what you want back east in your hometown, Elizabeth Sheldon, but this isn't Amherst and your father's not mayor here, so there's no use acting as if you're better than other folks."

"Calm down now, Agnes." Maddie came up beside Elizabeth.

"I was plenty calm until she, with her citified airs, came along and interfered."

"I'm sorry, then," Elizabeth said, doing her best to turn the other cheek.

"Don't mind her, Elizabeth," Maddie whispered, close up.

When Maddie took Elizabeth's part, Miss Yates lost her temper entirely. "Clara's father is dead, and you're a fool not to tell her so. Dead. Blown to smithereens."

With a little cry, Clara broke loose and took off running across the dance floor, heading for the open window at the back.

"Catch her!" Elizabeth cried, and Zack Danvers, to her surprise, was the first one to run after the little girl. Mouth open, she watched him do battle with elbows and shoulders. Then she gathered her own wits about her and, taking another route, went after Clara herself. But she was immediately tangled in the crowd, caught in an angry debate.

Behind her, Granny Sikes, outspoken as ever, bellowed, "Calm down, Agnes. At least we won't have to eat your pudding now. Don't go on so. Don't put yourself in a bad light."

And then Agnes Yates was crying. "That's not fair. Before she came, you'd never have dared tell me I lack refinement."

"Oh, stop blubbering," Granny hollered. "Just because you always manage to scorch your puddings doesn't mean we don't like you. You're tolerable enough. But compared to Elizabeth Sheldon, all of us could use a little saddle wax."

"That's not true. I'm as much a lady as her."

"Now who's being highfalutin? If you want to show off your good manners, then pitch in and help clean up this mess so we can eat what's left." Granny hollered to the crowd. "All in favor?"

"Aye!" roared the crowd, and the musicians played "Turkey in the Straw" as accompaniment to the rescuing of supper. Mercifully the crowd parted and Elizabeth ran through.

"Clara! Wait!"

Zack heard all the shouting, but gave it scant notice. His attention was focused on one thing. Ben's taunt: "What if that Gustavson girl falls off a roof?" And now the little girl had climbed up on a chair and was shimmying out the window at the back of the hall.

When Zack got to the window, Clara was clinging by her fingertips, but when she saw Zack, she let go. Zack sucked in his breath and leaned out the window, fearing the worst, expecting to find Clara flatter than a weed run over by a wagon wheel.

It was a long drop from the second story of the mercantile to the roof of the lean-to below, but Clara, bless that urchin's heart, rolled down the sloping roof without so much as denting herself. While Zack watched, the little girl got partway up, balanced a few seconds on her haunches, and then with all the ease of a circus acrobat, jumped into a wagon bed full of hay. His heart caught in his craw until her head popped up.

When she scrambled out of the wagon and ran away into the night, he remembered to breathe again. Selfish gratitude that she hadn't hurt herself was his main emotion, for Ben had been right about one thing: Zack might want to quit doctoring, but he'd never be able to walk away and ignore a serious injury.

"Is she all right?" Elizabeth Sheldon took him off guard; he hadn't expected her to follow quite so quickly. Her words fell soft and warm on the back of his neck, and when he turned, she was practically in his arms. Before he could fashion an answer, she moved up close to look out the window for herself, and brushed against him.

Like a pair of awkward kids, they stood there, he with his hands balled at his sides. He dared not touch her. Just standing there feeling the sway of her skirt against his pants legs and inhaling the violet scent of her was heady enough.

"Can you see her?" he asked.

Elizabeth, petite as she was, had to stand on tiptoe, and when she wavered, he moved behind her, unable to help himself. His hand went around her waist to steady her.

A big moon hung over a clear starry sky, and to Elizabeth's relief she could see a little overall-clad figure running down the alley behind the town buildings, apparently none the worse for her jump.

"She's a remarkably agile little girl." Zack's voice sent shivers down her back, and she turned, then paused. "Yes, she's okay. Scared more than anything." Like her, Zack

Danvers stared at the floor, then up again. Their eyes locked.

Someone was extinguishing the wall lanterns at their end of the room, while down at the other end most of the townspeople were sitting on the floor or on chairs enjoying what was left of the food. Only one of the fiddlers was still squeaking out a lively rendition of "Aura Lee." Involuntarily she hugged herself, uncertain how to move away from Lieutenant Danvers. Should she ask if he felt better? Inquire about Clara's father?

Zack pushed down the window, then turned back to her, wondering why his throat had gone dry. With everyone down at the other end of the long room eating supper, the dance floor was deserted here by the window, and the only person to talk to was Elizabeth Sheldon.

He swallowed the lump in his throat. "Back in first grade," he said hesitantly, "I had a teacher who was a lot like Miss Yates. Used to take a strap to the littlest kid in class because he couldn't tie his shoes and she'd trip over his laces."

A light danced in her eyes. "I had one who made us recite the alphabet backwards. She burned everything she baked, too, and the winner of her cake at the cakewalks was too mortified to face the class for a week." A giggle welled up. The laughter of relief. She saw the glint of amusement in his eyes, too. His shoulders shook, and like her he looked down, trying to will the laughter back.

"It's not f-funny." She bit her lip and thought of something that would instead make her mad. Zack Danvers falling asleep on her . . . Zack being scared of a tinny band. . . .

Sobering, she looked up to find him looking at her, dead serious. *It's not funny*.

She was so close to him he could have had her in his arms in a second. The fabric of her skirt swayed temptingly against the tops of his boots while a couple of strands of cornsilk hair curled down around her neck and another curved over her cheek. Her eyes shone in the lantern light. He couldn't see the color, but he remembered well the sight of snapping green eyes glaring at him from a wagon, telling him she hated him. Despite that, after all these months without a woman, he was suddenly starved. As he reached out to touch her waist, his hand shook.

"They tell me it's bad manners if the bride-to-be doesn't dance with all the single men." His voice wasn't too steady either. "Since everything else has been unpredictable tonight, you shouldn't be surprised if I ask you to dance."

She was surprised, though. She hadn't expected this.

"May I?" he said.

Such good manners, she thought. So different from her first impression of the unshaven desperado who'd fallen asleep on her shoulder.

Just moments ago he'd appeared on the verge of asking the schoolmarm to dance. But now it was Elizabeth he was asking.

She nodded her head, telling herself it would be all right. Joel wouldn't mind if she accepted just one more dance. And then all thoughts of Joel slipped away.

Elizabeth was conscious only of the warmth of his hand, the pressure of his arm, the strength of his thigh . . . the memory of his head on her shoulder, the manly scent of him. He was clean-shaven and smelled like bay rum, and she was no longer afraid of him. Yet when he drew her into his arms, she trembled.

Then they were dancing together, the rest of the world blocked out. Very carefully she pressed her hand to his shoulder, way up high. She maintained a respectful distance, staring at the white button on his shirt, at how it moved in and out with each breath he took, which was faster with each whirl.

His hand came up around her waist, and he held her apart a way, the crown of her head resting in the crook of his neck. It was the last dance, and the only dance where no one interrupted. Then the music faded away, but still they danced in each other's arms, staring at each other.

She didn't know what to say, because she didn't dare say what was running through her head.

She wished the dance had lasted longer. Why had they laughed about schoolteachers when they could have been doing this?

"Elizabeth." Joel's voice from across the room might have come from down a long tunnel. "Elizabeth?"

Belatedly she turned slowly as if being awakened from a dream.

"Elizabeth? I fixed you a plate."

Reality slapped her like a blast of arctic air. What was she thinking of? She hated Zack Danvers. Didn't she?

"Are you done dancing?" Joel directed his words at Zack Danvers.

Zack barely heard Joel; the music was still vibrating in his head. Elizabeth slipped out of his embrace then, but he could still smell the lingering violet scent of her clinging to his shirtfront, could still feel the silk of her hair where she'd fit beneath his chin.

Maddie came up, too, and pressed a plate of food on him. "Zack?"

But he just stared at the chicken and salad and pie, and when the first people left, Zack went with them.

"Feels like a frost tonight," someone said.

Miss Yates stood by the door, lips pursed in a pout. "Oh, who cares?" she snapped to Granny, then whispered loud enough for Zack to hear, "He was going to dance with me. *Me.* Until that—that urchin ruined everything."

"Hush up," Granny hissed back. "Didn't I tell you men don't like whining women?" As Zack passed, Granny nodded. "It's going to freeze hard, Mr. Danvers. Pass the word. Maybe a killer freeze."

He tipped his hat to Granny and pulled up the collar of his jacket. Riding back to the hotel alone, Zack gave Granny credit for more than midwifery. It was a cold spring night all right, but the only thing killing about it to Zack was the memory of Elizabeth Sheldon warm in his arms as Joel Emory came up and claimed her.

The lady was forbidden, and he'd best remember that.

5

Elizabeth found Clara up in the loft, burrowed into the hay, snuggled in her pa's Civil War coat. Immediately she took the little girl into her arms. Clara, shivering, smelled of hay and tears. The normally snug loft was uncommonly cold tonight.

"Don't cry, Clara. You're safe with me."

"Miss Y-Yates makes lumpy pudding anyway," Clara sniffled. "Pa hates her cooking, and we can't end up in an orphanage. We can't! Pa promised he'd come for us."

"I'm glad her pudding ended up spilled, then, and I believe you about your pa."

Stroking her hair, Elizabeth reassured Clara, but secretly she cursed Orville Gustavson for his careless notion of fatherhood.

Brightening, Clara swiped at the tears.

"Come on," Elizabeth said at last, "let's go in for cocoa. Inside the house. You can't sleep here until the weather warms up again." Together they made their way down the loft steps and walked through the cold night, their breath coming out in clouds, and in moments Elizabeth coaxed a laugh out of Clara. Soon the kitchen lantern was lit, and as a blaze heated the cookstove, Elizabeth reached for the tin of cocoa.

"Elizabeth?" Pete called from the door, and after wrapping

a heavy coat around Clara she went to invite him in. The boy was so shy and reserved, she'd scarcely seen him all night till the ride home. So it came as a surprise to hear so many words tumble out of him at once.

"I checked the thermometer," he said in an excited voice. "Granny's right. It might freeze tonight, and that could mean the blossoms will die, the bees will quit pollinating, and we'll lose all the apples. We've got to *do* something. We've got to."

Elizabeth hesitated only a moment. "What does Joel say?"

"Nothing."

"Liar," Joel said, and then he was in her way, pushing Pete aside, blocking her from going anywhere. "Come on, Elizabeth, send the kids up to the loft. After unhitching the horses, I deserve a good-night kiss at least, don't I?"

Kissing was the last thing on her mind. "Aren't you worried about the cold, Joel?" Surely if it was anything to be worried about, Joel would know what to do.

Joel scowled, but they all followed Pete out into the orchard and checked the thermometer that was nailed on a scarecrow's stick face in place of a nose.

"See?" Pete pointed. "Thirty-five degrees, and it'll get even colder before morning. If it hits twenty-eight, we'll lose every blossom."

"You're exaggerating, boy." Joel stalked back to where he'd left the wagon and led the team off to the barn.

Torn between Pete's passion and Joel's scorn, Elizabeth stood there, shivering in her dance dress.

Squaring her shoulders, she took Clara's hand and, followed by Joel and Pete, walked back to the kitchen to make the promised cocoa. They'd all think better with something warm in them.

"The whole valley's going to feel this cold," Pete said, and at his direction, Clara ran back out to check the scarecrow thermometer again.

"How do you know so much, kid?" Joel snapped.

Pete flinched, but held his ground. "Me and Pa, we've

worked around at everything. Pa—Pa says nothing gets hurt by a frost more than apples at blossom time."

"Well, who cares if the apples grow or not?" Joel whirled on Elizabeth, and there was whiskey on his breath. "What do you say, Elizabeth? You're not going to spend your life working an orchard like a common field hand anyway. If the crop freezes, we can sell the land and let someone plant something sensible like wheat. Wouldn't that be an easier way to get money?"

For a minute, Elizabeth could only stare, speechless. But this was her brother's dream, this orchard. There was more to it than just money, but maybe that meant nothing to Joel, who was flushed with whiskey. Perhaps the whiskey had loosened his tongue and allowed him to reveal his true feelings.

"*In vino veritas*, is that it, Joel?" Her voice remained level, but she had to fight to control her anger.

He grabbed her by the elbows, his face set. "Fancy words won't help. E-liz-a-beth," he said, enunciating every syllable slowly, "what can we do?"

You're supposed to know that, Joel, a little voice inside her said.

Joel's face flushed an even deeper red. "Shall we sit up all night and stare at the thermometer?"

"I thought you'd know what to do," she said, overwhelmed by her lack of farm knowledge. She felt cold, numb, scared. She wished she could stay near the heat of the stove all night.

The heat of the stove.

She swung away from Joel. "Pete, would it be crazy to light fires in the orchard to warm the trees?"

Pete's eyebrows formed a worried vee. "I dunno. Usually we just open the head gate down by the creek and let the water into the rills, down each row. The water warms the air."

"But wouldn't fires help—just as this fire is warming us here in the kitchen?"

"Aw, Elizabeth," Joel scoffed, "you're thinking like a woman. You'll burn the blossoms up and all the trees with them."

"Maybe . . ." Pete looked at Elizabeth with speculation on his face. "Yeah, it couldn't help but warm the air, just so we build them out away from the trees."

"There are plenty of old pruned branches behind the barn," Elizabeth said.

Clara came running back in.

The scarecrow thermometer said thirty-three.

And a cold cloud fell over Elizabeth. She couldn't lose the blossoms. She just couldn't.

"Let's do it," Elizabeth said. "Will you help me, Pete?"

He nodded.

"Me too," Clara said, her tears forgotten.

Joel stalked to the kitchen door and turned. "Count me out," he said moodily. "I've been dancing half the night, and I'm not staying up till dawn just in case the thermometer dips." With no more explanation than that, he walked out and headed toward the barn.

This was not the way engaged men and women were supposed to treat each other. She ran as far as the porch. "Joel—"

"I'll sleep in the loft in case you need me," he called over his shoulder. "Wake me if it gets down to twenty-eight—or if the orchard goes up in flames. Your brother would have laughed, Elizabeth. Honest to God."

He was gone then, swallowed up in the night, and she couldn't force him to stay, after all. It wasn't his orchard. Yet, to Elizabeth's surprise, tears pricked the backs of her eyes. He was going to leave her alone, her and two kids.

But she was not about to lose this orchard, Joel or no Joel.

While Pete and Clara waited, she marched to the bedroom, dug around in her brother's trunk and came up with some warm clothes—a woolen sweater, overalls, and a jacket.

She kicked off the black satin slippers in which she'd danced, pulled off her ball gown, and changed into her brother's warm clothing. After grabbing a pair of rubber boots for herself, she snatched up a bundle of clothing for the children—mittens and knit caps and wool shirts for Pete to divide up between himself and his little sister.

Moments later they set off toward the orchard. Pete, shovel in hand, trotted away through the starry night. His task was unenviable: to dig open the dammed-up rills and let the creek water flow among the trees. With Clara at her heels, Elizabeth ran out behind the barn, and after untangling branches and breaking them into smaller pieces, they loaded a wheelbarrow and hauled the wood to the orchard.

It was no different from laying out a fire in a fireplace, something she'd done hundreds of times, only this time she needed to light dozens of fires. With the help of some kerosene, the applewood caught fire and burned hot, crackling in the darkness as warmth reached out to the blossoms of the nearest tree. At best, only half the blossoms would be saved, and there were so many trees, so little time.

Way down at the far end of the orchard, Pete was silhouetted in the moonlight, shoveling away dirt to allow water to flow down the rows of trees. It would take him most of the night to open all the rills up to the creek water; it would take Elizabeth and Clara most of the night to lay fires along the width of the orchard. Sharp spikes on the wood had torn through her gloves, and already her hands stung from blisters. But her hands didn't hurt so much as the despair that threatened her. They weren't going to save the blossoms if the temperature dipped in the next hour or so. Only time and hard work could save them.

"We ought to wake up Joel. Should I get him up, do you think?" Clara's voice came out of the darkness, and she patted her mittened hands against her sides.

And beg? "No." Elizabeth's pride had been bruised badly. If she and the Gustavson children could do this alone, why was she even thinking of marrying Joel? But the work was too backbreaking to ponder any future beyond this cold, cold night.

Just then the shadowy figure of a man moved toward her. For a minute, hope soared in her. Had Joel decided to help after all?

She stood frozen to the spot while the man's face came into focus, lit up by firelight.

Zack Danvers stood there in dark pants and a heavy black jacket, his hands jammed deep into the pockets. His breath came out in a frosty cloud that mingled with the smoke of the fire, and the shadow of a dark beard stubbled his face.

He looked straight across at her, his eyes clear, unsmiling. "I thought the place was on fire."

Briefly Elizabeth explained, then said, "I'm sorry we woke you."

He shook his head and half smiled. "I'm of the nocturnal species of man. Sleep by day. Awake by night. You might have noticed on the train . . ."

"Yes." She dipped her face to hide her unbidden smile. Half of her wished she were far away, back at the dance still.

"And you look like Cinderella, home from the ball, turned back to a cinder maid, laying fires in the frost." As he spoke, he turned up the collar on his familiar black coat. He wore no gloves.

"Mister," said Clara, "I hope you've brought us some help."

"Or at least luck," Elizabeth said.

He reached into his pocket and pulled out a shiny gold coin. "Luck's a fickle lady, didn't you know that?" The coin vanished into thin air, and then Zack Danvers reached behind Clara's collar and the coin reappeared, glinting gold in the firelight.

"Hey," she giggled, "how'd you learn to do that?"

"In the Philippines we had a lot of time on our hands," he said, then just as quickly pocketed the coin and rounded on Elizabeth. "Do you need some help with the orchard?" he asked.

"Why?"

"I've been looking for graveyard-shift work, only there isn't much in a town this size."

She had to force herself to stop staring into his eyes. Zack Danvers certainly had a knack for appearing and disappearing at a whim. "Then you're hired . . . but I only pay in cocoa." It didn't matter if she hated him. She'd take all the help she could get.

"Deal."

Side by side, followed by Clara, they walked out behind the barn, where Elizabeth showed him the pile of pruned apple branches.

"Hey, mister," Clara said, "you know how to use an ax?"

Zack winced as Elizabeth grabbed some wood. He was tempted to pull her away so he could tackle the job himself, but decided against touching her.

Soon enough they had worked out a routine. Zack chopped the wood and threw it in the wheelbarrow, the little girl wheeled, and Elizabeth laid the fires and lit them, each one a foot or so away from the outer circumference of a tree. When they had enough wood chopped, Zack worked with her, lighting fires and then adding more wood to keep the other fires going. Periodically Clara, lantern in hand, would run through the orchard to the scarecrow and call out the temperature. Way down at the other end they could see Pete digging, and in the rows nearest the hotel, water began to fill the rills.

When the first one threatened to overflow and flood a fire, Zack crossed the orchard to find a shovel. He expected to see Joel, but instead he found Pete all alone, the gangly boy shoveling with all his might.

"Where's Joel?"

Pete shrugged.

Zack grabbed a shovel from the ground and stalked back to the end of the orchard nearest the house, the end by the fires. By the time he got there, the ditch had overflowed and put out one of the fires, and Elizabeth stood there, cheeks stained red from the cold, eyes brimming. "I need a miracle."

"Sorry, you'll have to settle for me and the shovel." He took deep shovelfuls of mud, dammed off the water, then moved to the next rill and did the same. The water hadn't made it all the way down the third ditch yet, and that fire was safely burning. What a god-awful mess. This was a war with the temperature. What was worse, he knew now that Joel wasn't even here.

He turned back to Elizabeth, who was about to back into a bonfire. "Watch out."

She took a step and walked right out of one rubber boot, then lost her balance and fell right into a muddy rill, ashes and mud floating around her. He reached down and pulled her up.

The impact of her in muddy overalls was no different than when she'd been wearing a dress of green silk.

Intense.

He took her hands in his and peeled off her torn gloves one finger at a time. Then, never taking his eyes off her, he rubbed her hands between his. Her breath came out in clouds and teased his neck.

It was time he got out of here, but he couldn't leave her alone. Clara brought them socks to use as mittens, and like an automaton, he shoveled dirt and mud. His back ached, his fingers were blistered, and smoke stung his eyes, but still he kept working, trying to keep up with Elizabeth Sheldon.

He was a man, for God's sake, and he could barely keep up with petite Miss Elizabeth Sheldon. Nor could he keep his eyes off her. In her brother's hand-me-downs, she looked like an elf prowling about this orchard. He stood up to wipe his brow and studied her, the way she looked by the firelight bent over in those breeches. Quickly, before he could think about it any more, he bent to shoveling again, damming the rills at his end so the water wouldn't flood the place and go to waste.

"It's past four," Clara called from the porch.

"And the scarecrow says it's only thirty degrees." Pete's voice was exultant. "I think we'll be all right."

"You mean," Elizabeth said, standing and pressing a hand to her back, "we did all this work for nothing?"

"We won't know till tomorrow," Pete said. "Then we can test the blossoms."

Pete's knowledge continued to awe Elizabeth.

"Joel was right," Clara said.

"Joel was wrong," Zack said and looked at Elizabeth, who blushed. "He was wrong not to help, but I guess that's none of my business."

His gaze locked on Elizabeth, on her red hands, her frozen smile, the determined look of her, the wisps of cornsilk hair that peeked out of her knit hat. Those crimson cheeks were in need of kissing. He longed to warm her up, but she wasn't his.

"Quit, before you get frostbite yourself. Take the kids inside." He shut up before he started to sound like someone who knew more than he should about medical problems.

She was staring at him in a way that made him feel queer inside.

"You know, you do have a knack for coming and going at the most unexpected times."

There was a slight pause. The stars moved a fraction in the sky. "What you did is worth a lot more than cocoa," she added softly.

She was waiting for an explanation of why a grown man would spend half the night in a frozen orchard with a green-horn lady and two kids, especially when he wasn't a farmer himself. Now he didn't feel queer. He felt positively idiotic, tongue-tied, and was surprised to hear words coming out of his mouth. "I know you think I'm a coward. A man's got a right to perform one noble deed before he moves on, doesn't he?"

He couldn't tell if her face was rosy from the cold or from a blush. She gave him a tremulous smile. "My brother would thank you very much." Her own breath mingled in one frost cloud with his, and they stood there staring at each other, both tongue-tied. Abruptly she turned to look at the sky, where the first streaks of purple dawn promised another clear day. "We'd better move the ladders away from the trees."

"Why?" he asked.

She looked back at him and wrapped her arms about herself. Her muddy overalls clung to her. She looked very small. "B-because they're in the mud."

Didn't this woman ever give up? "But you're not going to climb up in them tonight, are you?"

Pete shrugged. "We'll move them tomorrow. He's right, Elizabeth. It's time to quit."

While Elizabeth and Clara went in to start coffee and cocoa brewing, Zack helped Pete shovel a mud dam across each row of trees to close off the water. Tonight's work was the first physical labor he'd done in weeks, maybe months, and he had to admit that except for the cold it felt good. Yet all the time he shoveled, he had to fight down the urge to drag Joel out of bed by the collar. He was a dandy, too lazy to do a hard day's work, and not deserving of a woman like Elizabeth.

But what was Zack going to do about it?

Nothing, except stay away.

The temperature hovered at a safe, albeit precarious, thirty degrees when Elizabeth finally huddled in blankets on the back porch, Pete and Clara beside her, hands wrapped around mugs of coffee or cocoa.

Elizabeth, who had changed into a plain skirt and one of Will's sweaters, stretched tiredly. They were all going to take a long nap.

"Elizabeth?" It was Clara's sleepy voice. "Will there be apples?"

"I don't know," she said honestly, "but whatever happens, we tried to save that orchard, and we did it together. That's important to remember."

"What if we failed?" Clara nestled up close to her.

"We worked together. . . . I'll never forget this night and how all of you helped."

She looked out over her orchard and knew the intense satisfaction of having struggled to save something she cared deeply about, with a man working at her side, even though the man hadn't been Joel, but Zack Danvers. It was a good feeling. Surprisingly good.

Her thoughts skipped briefly to the memory of Zack Danvers standing in the orchard, warming her hands, his breath a warm white cloud in the black night. She would never forget Zack Danvers's help, and was still disappointed he'd left without a word to her. Strange man. Always ducking out on her, either from trains or from orchards. Sleeping in the daytime, prowling around at night. Touching her, warming her with just his look.

She was disappointed—hurt, even—that Zack had gone on back to the hotel before she could even thank him properly.

What could she do? She slung an arm about Pete in gratitude, and he smiled, proud, just as Joel came walking toward the house, picking his way through mud, pulling on his suspenders as he came.

"Everyone's up early," he observed. "Everything okay?"

She said nothing but stared over at the distant hotel, at the still-darkened windows. Then she turned back to Joel, her fiancé. "We'll know later."

"Then you didn't need me?"

She paused, recalling Zack Danvers and the easy strength with which he'd pulled her up out of the mud, peeled off her gloves, warmed her hands. She had needed a man, and it was Zack Danvers who'd been there for her. The memory of working under the cold stars lighting bonfires with Zack Danvers as her helper lingered. . . .

"No, Joel, you didn't need to trouble yourself. We lit a few fires to keep the trees warm, and nothing burned except a lot of dead wood."

"You stayed up all night, didn't you?"

"And Zack Danvers helped," Clara said.

No, Clara! Elizabeth cried silently. But it was too late.

Joel's eyes narrowed. "How long was he here?"

She stood and busied herself gathering up a few stray apple prunings.

"Long enough to build a few fires. Don't trouble yourself over it."

"You should have come for me. I'd have helped. Will left me in charge."

At that, she stood and faced Joel.

"There's plenty still to do today, Joel. And I'll thank you not to snap at me. Do you know what? I don't believe you know one end of an apple tree from another, Joel. I believe you're just pretending to."

His face set. "I am not. I can prune. I can thin. I can prop up the branches. You want me to grab some sticks and prop branches?" he said in a testy voice. "First there's got to be apples growing and weighting the branches down." He paused for breath. "Give me time to prove myself, Elizabeth." With a rough gesture, he grabbed the wood from her arms.

"I want to make my brother's dream come true," she said, "and if we don't get married until harvesttime, then so be it."

Whirling, she ran off, leaving Joel with his mouth open and arms full of wood.

That afternoon Elizabeth took the wagon to town for the first time, just her and Clara. Clara proudly carried a large envelope addressed to Montgomery Ward and Company in Chicago. As a thank-you for last night's extra effort, Elizabeth had given Clara the catalog to pore over. Clara had taken hours to decide what she wanted to order.

Neither child, Elizabeth found through gentle probing, had ever received a present. She had set the catalog on the table, and Clara had savored it page by page as if it were the first picture book she'd ever seen.

Elizabeth dearly wanted to see the little girl in a dress, but dared not offend the tomboy too much.

Clara had her opinions. "If *you're* giving up skirts and ordering bloomers, then I'm not having anything to do with dresses either." Obstinate, endearing child. Clara, however, did eye the dolls with real envy, admiring a French porcelain model, but in the end she chose a stickpin.

"A stickpin?" Elizabeth had scarcely been able to conceal her surprise.

"For Pa."

Orville Gustavson sounded like a chaw and whiskey man,

not a stickpin man. Still, she was touched by Clara's insistence that the four-leaf clover stickpin would be his good luck charm.

"What did Zack mean about luck being a fickle woman?" She paused. "He meant luck changes its mind."

"Oh." Clara thought that over. "As long as luck's not a real woman. Pa doesn't like women trying to get him to the preacher, he says."

Elizabeth smiled. With the shortage of women, Orville hardly needed to worry. "He'll be safe with a gold-plated four-leaf clover, I believe."

"Good—and for Pete, a pocketknife. There's one at the mercantile he's always liked, but this one's better. . . . How long will our order take to get here?" Clara asked as she sat beside Elizabeth in the wagon.

"Many days. Maybe weeks." Elizabeth took her time driving into town, getting used to the team, enjoying the spring day. Although the sky had clouded over, the air was warmer than it had been yesterday. Best of all, the bees, with their promise of harvest, were busy, pollinating the blossoms. The faint perfume of apple trees filled the air.

"When will I get my present?" Clara asked again, eager. "Will I get it before my pa comes back?"

"That depends on when your pa returns." Oh, what a tragedy it would be if this little girl's father didn't come back, but Elizabeth didn't have the heart to be anything but encouraging, didn't dare tell Clara how many men were missing.

"Will it be by the Fourth of July?"

"Oh, before the Fourth of July."

"That's so long from now. . . . Joel's gonna be surprised at your order."

"I expect so."

Because she lacked any appropriate garment to wear in the orchard, besides her brother's ill-fitting overalls, Elizabeth had dipped further into her savings and ordered a pair of bicycle bloomers. Even outrageous Clara, the "bad seed" of Eden Creek, was impressed with the daring of prim Miss

Sheldon. The bloomers would most assuredly have caused a scandal in proper Massachusetts, but out west they should rate, Clara said, as no more than a surprise. She hoped.

"Miss Yates is going to gossip."

"I don't care."

A train whistle blew.

"I wonder what Zack wants?" Clara said unexpectedly. "Are you going to get him a gift?"

Elizabeth glanced over. "I think he was only being neighborly."

At Clara's puzzled look, Elizabeth added, "Besides, it's not appropriate for a lady to give a gift to a strange man."

"Oh, you mean a thank-you is all he gets."

It did sound meager. "Well, even if we ordered him something, he'll be leaving before the order can arrive." Yet she hoped not. And that thought took her by surprise.

She hoped she'd see him again.

"Joel doesn't get a gift either, does he?"

Clara's question pulled her back to reality. Joel's cavalier behavior last night had hurt and hurt deeply. That led to a more serious thought: Perhaps her haste in accepting Joel's proposal had been a serious mistake.

He'd seemed properly abashed when he'd come back from his inspection of the orchard earlier this morning to find them eating hotcakes, and he had promised to spend the rest of the day cleaning up the orchard from last night. He'd even wished them a good time in town.

After leaving the wagon at the livery and purchasing a bank draft, the two of them headed for the mercantile to mail the catalog order. Then, on Clara's recommendation, they were going to buy some herbal potion from Granny.

"It'll fix your hands, Elizabeth," Clara promised.

Elizabeth was coming to believe Clara knew everything there was to know about Eden Creek. They took their time leaving the mercantile, Clara sucking on a peppermint candy stick and stopping to pet the brown mongrel that sat guard on the front porch. The dog wagged his tail, and Elizabeth bent to rub his ears while people passed on either side of them.

That was when the sound of footsteps slowed, then stopped, and Clara looked up at the owner of a pair of dark brown boots.

"Oh, hello there, mister. You should have stayed a little longer."

Elizabeth had been patting the dog's head. Her hand froze, and the mongrel, hungry for love, moved his head to find her hand and lick it, coaxing.

"Elizabeth would have cooked you breakfast because you helped us last night. We had hotcakes and the stack was *this* high." Clara demonstrated with her hands.

The mongrel had to settle for a perfunctory pat. Ignoring the canine's adoring eyes and thumping tail, Elizabeth stared up.

Zack Danvers was looking down at her. There was nothing adoring about his expression. "I'm sorry I was so hasty in leaving, then," he said.

Her heart thumping against her ribs, Elizabeth stood and extended her hand. Then, self-conscious because it was callused and rough and, on top of all else, covered with dog saliva, she pulled back. "Lieutenant Danvers—"

"Could you call me Zack? I've got an aversion to titles."

Aware that Clara was watching her, Elizabeth found some perfunctory words to say, though there was nothing perfunctory about her pulse rate. "I hope I thanked you." She knew, of course, that she had. The last moments with him in the orchard were photographed in her mind.

He looked ill at ease, as if he wanted nothing more than to run away again.

And then Clara piped up. "How come you're a coward? I thought you were a soldier."

"Clara!" Elizabeth knew a feeling of mortification worse than any in her life.

A frozen mask slipped over his face, and his eyes were averted, shadowed by those long lashes. But his reply to Clara was gentle. "I believe Elizabeth disapproves of me because I ignored that welcoming band."

"Oh, that . . ." As if that explained it all.

"Your . . . your help was more than I deserved." Elizabeth could only stammer out another silly thank-you.

At last he spoke to her, eyes averted. He shrugged. "You saved me from a sleepless night alone."

Heat rushed to her face. She was sure her blush must match the cranberry cape she wore. And of course he turned to look at her then, his expression distant.

"All you did was postpone my leaving town by a day," he went on, "but the world hasn't missed me. . . . I'm glad I could help. Did we slay the dragon of the frost?"

Everything was topsy-turvy. Upside down. Spinning. She was warm and self-conscious; his smile was a mysterious net. "We won't know for a while. We're at nature's mercy." She turned one palm up to emphasize her point, and saw his face change before her. "What's wrong?"

Zack felt the change from the inside out, the inability to hide his reactions from her. The blisters, the scratches on her hand, touched his heart, as did the memory of chafing her hand between his last night. She was practically running that place single-handed. A tiny woman and a pair of urchins whom no one else in town would befriend because people were afraid of old man Gustavson's Enfield rifle.

Before he could think better of it, he once again captured Elizabeth's fingertips in his, tempted to turn doctor.

She slid her hand away and, like a child, hid it in the folds of her skirt. "It'll heal."

"I should have come sooner." Words failed him. He'd seen men gored by Spanish bullets, he'd seen men bleed to death from gunshot wounds, and yet, except for Harry's death, he'd maintained a professional aloofness. It was awful, yes, but it was a part of war. And yet just now, seeing that soft little hand covered with common blisters and a few scratches, he'd felt awash with guilt. The kind of guilt he felt about Harry's death. And more. The guilt of a gentleman who'd failed a lady.

Until that moment he'd thought all his gallantry had been

destroyed, part of last winter's kill.

He wanted to shake her and ask her why she needed the likes of Joel Emory. But the next second he wanted to take her in his arms the way he had at the dance and take care of her.

Jesus. He had to get out of here.

What was she saying?

"We're going up to Granny Sikes's house right now. Maddie says she'll have some kind of potion, so my hands will be healed in no time."

A granny medicine dispenser. Hell! He was tempted to stay and oversee . . . but despite all the superstitions and good-luck charms of Granny's kind of medicine, he didn't figure the old woman could do too much harm to blistered hands. She could probably even hold her own in the Philippines.

While he stood there looking dumbstruck, Elizabeth had knelt down to stroke the dog between its ears, and now Zack knelt opposite her. Somehow, putting a mongrel between them made their conversation more matter-of-fact, less intimate. They both got their hands licked by the adoring mongrel while Clara stood there watching them, sucking on the peppermint stick, relating exactly what Montgomery Ward and Company was going to send her, and informing him that shamrock stickpins were not fickle.

"Well," he said, at length, "I'd best get on to the railroad depot."

But he made no move to stand. Instead, he looked at the woman who knelt opposite him. A loose curl had fallen from its hairpin; it teased the right side of her face. If he could keep her talking a little longer, it might blow against her cheek again.

Elizabeth was looking at the dog instead of at him, and her words were soft. "Thank you . . . again, and . . . and best wishes in your new venture."

He still didn't know where he was going next. He only knew some strong sixth sense told him to go now . . . *now* . . . or he'd never get out of here.

Of course Clara boldly asked the question he couldn't answer. Again. "Where are you going?"

"Points east—whatever place suits my fancy." He answered Clara, but he kept his eyes fixed on Elizabeth, on the curl.

"What're ya going to do there?"

He stood. "You know what, Clara? I'm not sure, but I might end up importing apples from Idaho. How would that be?"

He succeeded in coaxing a smile out of Elizabeth. Then she stood, too, and smoothed the folds of her skirt. The curl blew about her face, and she pushed it away.

For two bits he'd have hung out his shingle right there and stayed. But he couldn't. He wasn't small-town-doctor material. Anyway, she was going to marry Joel.

Besides, he had quit. Quit. Given up watching people die. Packed away his medical bag forever, and dreams of being a beloved doctor were in the past.

For all his resolve, the boardwalk seemed to be holding him there. He felt strangely weighted.

"Well, good-bye," Elizabeth said. She took Clara by the hand and walked up the boardwalk while Clara waved back over her shoulder. "Bye, mister."

"Bye," he called back. Zack lounged against a post and watched until they were out of sight. He decided he'd best not wait one more night. He'd buy a ticket for the first evening train out of here.

6

The wagon had no sooner rumbled into the orchard lane than Clara popped up and rubbed sleep from her eyes. Peppermint candy was tangled in her bangs.

Elizabeth reined in right in front of her barn, but she made no move to get down.

"Aren't you coming in?" Clara had already scrambled down.

"In a minute."

"Are you worried?"

"Some."

"Confused" might be a better word. Was it right to wed Joel? Was he honorable in his reasons for wanting to wed her? Would she lie in her marriage bed consenting to Joel's caresses while she thought about, and yearned for, another man? A man she didn't even like?

She was being silly. Zack Danvers had simply knelt to pet a mongrel and listen to Clara's chatter. That meant nothing.

After Zack Danvers left town—and according to Maddie, he was packing his gear—she'd feel differently. Out of sight, out of mind; that would help immensely.

Still, her doubts were powerful enough that she made a decision: She was going to break her engagement.

Joel wasn't even here to help with the wagon, so she put the horses away herself, then came back out of the barn. It was so quiet in the orchard. A yellow butterfly perched on the barn door, then fluttered off. Down orchard, bees still hummed and the creek flowed, heavy with spring runoff, toward the river. But there was no sound of people. No footsteps. No voices. No whistling. No telltale rustle of apple leaves.

Of course not. She'd given Pete orders to go off and play. And if he didn't know how to play, he was at least to check on his pa's little house. No one would be here but Joel, and with his work habits, he was liable to have slipped off to pitch horseshoes.

"Jo-el!"

When there was no answer, she cupped her hands around her mouth and called again and again.

Clara headed for the scarecrow to check the temperature. "I'll find him. Betcha he's asleep under a tree."

Apart from a few curious bees, the orchard went still again, and Elizabeth plucked a single blossom and tore it open, praying the heart of it would not be black, a sure sign of freezing. She held her breath and looked. The blossom was normal. At least this one was. Lifting her head to the tree, she buried her face in a cluster of blossoms, the sweetness a promise of apples to come, and her heart nearly burst with gratitude.

At first she didn't recognize the sound that echoed through the orchard. But then it came again, a shout as loud as if Clara were shooing away magpies.

Only no birds flew up into the sky. Gradually came awareness. This was not a shout, but a scream. An incongruity in the middle of all those glorious pink blossoms, but there it was again, clearer now.

"Joel! Joel! Joel!"

Lifting up her skirts, Elizabeth hurried down a row of trees, then crisscrossed to another, trying to find Clara in the maze. All of a sudden Clara appeared, running, her bobbed hair flying, little legs pumping as fast as they could go. When she reached Elizabeth, she clutched her skirt and hung on for dear life. There was an urgency in her voice Elizabeth had never heard.

"Come quick" was all she got out before clasping her arms about Elizabeth's waist, her grasp tearing hooks and eyes loose.

"Get Pete! Oh, Pete, please help!"

Nonplussed, Elizabeth tried to calm the little girl. "Pete's gone to check on your place. Remember, Clara? I told him to take the day off. What is it?" With an effort, Elizabeth untangled Clara and held her out at arm's length, looking at her scared white face. "What's Joel done now?"

All Clara could do was point toward the center of the orchard. Following the little girl's gesture, Elizabeth caught her breath. On the ground among the trees, lying beneath a tree as if asleep, lay Joel.

Asleep in the mud beside a fallen ladder.

Her heart skipped a beat. Then she was running, tripping over her skirts, heedless of the mud, and she didn't slow down until she pulled to a stop beside Joel.

"Oh, God." She raised a shaking hand to her mouth and fought back a desire to faint. "Joel . . . oh, Joel!" she cried as she knelt, knowing the scene would remain etched on her memory forever.

Beside him lay a ladder, not a fruit ladder with a wide bottom, but a straight, narrow-bottomed ladder. A branch laden with blossoms, still warm from the sun, was caught between the rungs, and the ladder had left an ugly gash in the tree when it fell. The blossoms, the ladder, and Joel lay together in a tangle.

Joel was crumpled oddly, in a strange heap, and a trickle of blood ran across his forehead and down onto his usually immaculate shirt. Why, the accident couldn't have happened more than minutes ago. A few pale petals blew across his chest, scattering among his shirt buttons.

Clara, moving from behind her, knelt beside her in the mud.

"Is he dead?" Her voice wasn't more than a whisper.

"Of course not." Elizabeth sounded braver than she felt. He couldn't be. "He just fell out of the tree . . . or off the ladder."

The ladders. The mud. Joel didn't know, couldn't have known how dangerous they could be if a man climbed one and came unbalanced. And she'd meant to move them.

She needed to do something, get help, scream, cry, but all she was capable of was shutting her eyes and trembling while she pushed back the recriminations. If she hadn't stopped to talk to Zack Danvers, would she have gotten back here in time to stop the accident?

Joel's chest rose and fell in a shallow breathing pattern.

"He's been knocked unconscious, Clara."

Selfishly, she wanted to yell. She needed help . . . yet she couldn't move.

Clara, the bad seed of the town, the girl who could get away with more mischief than a groundhog in February, laid a trembling hand on her shoulder. "Elizabeth? What shall we do?"

"Clara," she said, fighting dizziness, "how fast can you run to town and get Granny?"

At the depot Zack slid his money across the counter to the railroad agent, at the last minute pulling back the gold peseta. He wasn't ready to part with it yet.

"How much time do I have?" He pulled out his pocket watch from his coat so he could synchronize it with railroad time.

Otis, the overeager youth who'd rushed the tragic news about Bunker Hill to the paper, double-checked his timetable. "Train departs for Boise City in two hours and seventeen minutes," he said brightly. "Eight-ten on the dot."

Zack pulled up the stem and adjusted his time by two minutes, then stuffed the watch back in his pocket. It wasn't even six o'clock yet, and raking a hand through his hair, he paced the railroad depot a few times. Then, with another two hours and six minutes until the train arrived, Zack walked outside, as if watching the track would make the train come faster.

After a couple hours' sleep and a bath, he'd dressed in rough-and-tumble clothes suitable for a long train ride, clothes borrowed from Ben. Maddie had made such a fuss over the Prince Albert coat, mocking and teasing him about how it was just the thing for a country doctor, that just to quiet her, he'd told her to cut the thing off and make it over into a short coat, which she had. Her price: having to listen to another lecture on what a wonderful doctor he was.

"And what do you plan to do for a living in Chicago?" she taunted. "Panhandle? Or become a cemetery sexton? Or starve in a garret while you write your memoirs? I can't think of many other ways you could hide away from the world. Unless you peddle apples on a street corner."

That did it.

By the time he announced his departure, he had an occupation all in order, courtesy of a Western Union inquiry. "I've got a lead on a position," he said. "In fact, I'm not going back to Chicago."

"Why, Zack!" Maddie smiled, pleased, and Ben raised his eyebrows, waiting for the explanation. "Harry's relatives are in Chicago, aren't they?"

"They don't want to see me." Zack's tone brooked no argument.

"Where *are* you going?" Ben asked carefully.

He told them. He'd go to Boise City, which offered connections to all points east, and then he'd head for the coast and sign on as doctor for some immigrant ship. He'd roam the seas, examine the anonymous masses coming to America, treat seasickness and malnutrition. Nothing complicated, nothing that required commitment. He could handle that, he told them with more confidence than he felt.

At the depot the good-byes had been quick. Under no circumstances did he want Ben dragging out the saloonkeeper with his tuba again, or Mr. Atwood with his clarinet. There would be no farewell songs.

Ben had shaken his hand in farewell, and Maddie had kissed him on the cheek. "I hope you meet some beautiful immigrant girl from Italy," Maddie had teased before waving good-bye. "Some beautiful lady who will torture your dreams."

She wasn't so far from the truth. Only her geography was off. The lady was right here in Eden Creek, but he liked holding Elizabeth Sheldon in his arms far too much to linger here and wait for her wedding to another man. . . .

"Zack!" came a voice from far away down the street.

Quickly, not wanting any emotional good-byes, he moved inside the depot, out of sight from everyone except the railroad agent. Industrious Otis was mopping the depot floor, and the scent of ammonia permeated the place. The oaken clock on the wall ticked loudly, its large gold pendulum counting away the seconds till the train came. Each second dragged. All Zack's instincts said to run down the track and find the train before something happened to make him stay.

"Zack!" The voice was familiar.

It was Clara, of course. What other child in town could have found out what he was up to so fast?

"Zack . . . Zack!" Seconds later Clara Gustavson skidded to a stop beside him, panting, her hair flying across her eyes from the exertion of her run, tears running down her face.

Tears? For his departure?

But he'd already said good-bye to her.

"Zack! You've got to come back!"

"It's time for me to go." He held out his train ticket.

She tried to snatch it away, but he was quicker and shoved it in his pocket. "Go snitch some of Maddie's cobbler. It's still on the window ledge cooling."

"No! No! I need you." Frantic, she grabbed his hand and tugged at him. "You've got to come."

Just before she told him the reason for her hysteria, he had a premonition of what was coming. He'd seen children run that way in the Philippines, children of natives struck down by yellow jack or bullets. Frantic, whining little mosquitoes, flitting around him, even in his sleep: "Doctor, Doctor, come quick! It's the yellow death. . . . Doctor, the soldiers have shot my mama. Help me! Help me. Help me. . . ."

He passed a hand over his eyes, thinking he must be having a relapse of the fever. But when he removed it, Clara was still standing there, the terror still on her face.

"Help me." This time she grabbed his coat pocket and clung for dear life. "Zack, you gotta come. I know you're a doctor, and I wasn't going to tell anyone. Honest. It was my best secret, and I was saving it till someday when I could get a licorice stick or some horehound drops out of you. But you can't keep it a secret anymore."

"Why don't you get Granny?" If he argued long enough, maybe Clara would vanish like a windblown thistle.

"Because she's off midwifing a baby. Please, Zack. I don't know why you want to keep the doctor part of you a secret, but you can't anymore. You just can't."

He disagreed. In two hours he'd be out of here.

"It's Joel," Clara finally managed, sweeping the bangs out of her eyes. "He's hurt."

Joel. Having observed Joel in action, Zack imagined a bee sting or a fall in a gopher hole would reduce him to a dead faint. Doubtless Clara, with a child's imagination, was exaggerating.

He warred with himself, flipped the choices back and forth in his mind.

You can't walk away from this. No self-respecting doctor could.

Since when did you care about self-respect?

Well, maybe for a few hours out there in the cold orchard with Elizabeth Sheldon . . .

But no one knows you're a doctor, and you don't have to care what happens to Joel.

Heads . . . Tails . . .

"Zack?"

Fighting his conscience hard, he stared up the tracks, then back at Clara, who stood there gazing up at him with an expression he'd never thought to see directed toward him again—a look of hope and trust.

Stubbornly he turned and stared at those train tracks, as if by ignoring Clara he could push back the dilemma.

But Clara, clever little Clara, had not survived in this town, he knew, without a strong measure of determination. She stood her ground. A quick glance confirmed that her expression was changing, from hope to accusation.

"Joel's hurt, and Elizabeth needs you." All he could hear then was the ticking of his watch in his pocket, and then he realized it was not his watch at all but the sound of his pulse hammering in his ears. *Elizabeth.*

Guilt, white-hot guilt, stole over him . . . and something else—a protective feeling he'd never known before.

"Elizabeth needs you," Clara said again, and those three simple words undid him.

She needs you.

"How bad is Joel hurt?" he asked casually.

"I don't know."

"Well, what did Joel look like?"

"Dead," Clara squeaked. "He was just crumpled up on the ground like he was dead. Elizabeth . . . she's all alone with him."

His defenses crumbled. As he headed for the livery stable to borrow a horse, little Clara couldn't keep up with his stride.

Elizabeth was prepared for Joel to die. She laid her head on his once-immaculate white shirt while saying over and over, "I'm sorry, Joel. I'm so sorry. I'm sorry I hurt you. . . ."

Time had lost all meaning; Clara might have left yesterday. By the time hoofbeats sounded on the lane leading into the orchard, she was beside herself, more frantic than she'd been when her father died. But then she'd been with family and friends. To be left alone on a vast acreage with a dying man was terrifying, so terrifying that she couldn't bear it. Everyone was right; she'd never make it alone here. She ran toward the sound of the rider, stumbled, and fell, crying.

Suddenly someone was pulling her to her feet, and she allowed herself to be held against a solid chest.

A little girl's voice, triumphant with pride, broke through her tears. "I got Zack. I got Zack to come."

Pulling back, she blinked away tears and looked up into the hard blue eyes of Zack Danvers. She was clinging to his shirtfront, to the lapels of his coat, and his arms were around her, supporting her, briefly, and then he reached up and stroked the hair out of her face.

"Elizabeth, what's going on? Where's Joel?"

Mute, she could only blink away tears.

"I'll show you." Clara ran ahead.

Zack put his arm around Elizabeth's waist and guided her to the next row of trees. When she pulled up short and gave a little cry, his hand closed around hers, gave it a squeeze of reassurance, and then he let go and moved toward Joel. Calmly. As if he knew exactly what he was doing.

"Zack's a genuine doctor," Clara crowed. "I found out from Ben, only I kept it a secret."

The afternoon had held too many surprises for Elizabeth. She supposed that Zack was trained as a medic during the war, had probably seen injuries worse than Joel's and knew first aid.

But now, as twilight fell across the orchard, Lieutenant Zack Danvers was kneeling beside Joel, feeling his pulse, lifting one eyelid, then the other, as if examining him. Like a doctor.

Lieutenant Zack Danvers was pressing his ear to Joel's chest, listening. Just like a doctor.

Lieutenant Zack Danvers was calmly opening Joel's mouth, checking to make sure he could swallow.

Again, just like a doctor.

Clara's words punctuated the truth, which was slowly dawning. "But when I told him you needed help, he came." The little girl cast an admiring look at Zack.

By now Pete had returned from town and joined Clara, pulling her back a ways. "Hush up. If he *is* a real doctor, he doesn't want you jabbering while he's trying to fix Joel."

"What happened?" Zack asked over his shoulder, his voice cool and professional. "Did he fall?"

Numb, Elizabeth didn't respond. She was staring at Zack, as if seeing an entirely new person. A doctor! As well as a soldier. Clearly the man had a lot to run away from. She had a hundred questions to ask him, but there wasn't time now. Emotion clogged her throat.

"Were you with him when he went unconscious?" Zack asked. He was running a hand along Joel's legs, feeling for broken bones. "Elizabeth, were you?" His voice was expressionless, all business.

She stared at him, trying to comprehend everything.

Then Zack Danvers stood and in one stride took her by the shoulders and shook her till her buttons rattled against her corset. "Don't turn missish now, Elizabeth Sheldon. Answer me!"

She looked up at him, stunned, hot where he touched her. "He fell . . . but I wasn't with him."

With a ragged sigh, Zack nodded, and knelt back down beside Joel. "We can't be sure about his neck. Pete," he said, turning to the boy, "run and get me some help from the hotel—some props. And blankets to make a stretcher, too."

Coming to her senses at last, Elizabeth knelt down on the other side of Joel.

Zack . . . Lieutenant—now . . . Doctor—Danvers looked across at her.

Numb, she stared back. Black hair falling rakishly about his forehead. Blue eyes . . . unfathomable still. He looked the same; only his title had changed, but she began to understand how he'd been able to deliver the bad news to the Gustavson kids. The only thing she didn't understand was why he'd kept his profession a secret.

"Do you have a pillow we can use?" he asked. "And some clean rags to wrap around his leg? A torn-up sheet'll do."

"I'll get them," Clara volunteered.

"Will he be all right?" Elizabeth asked.

Zack stared down at Joel and sighed wearily. "I don't know."

In short order, Ben and Maddie came running across the orchard from the hotel, stopping at first sight of the accident. At Zack's request, Ben ran to get a buggy and drive to the mercantile for ice.

"If you want," Maddie said, "you can use one of the hotel rooms, Zack."

Elizabeth stood up, suddenly in command of herself again. "No! Put him in the house. He'll stay here with me. It's . . . it's only fitting. We were to be wed—soon."

Zack Danvers turned, his gaze boring into her.

"It was my fault he fell," she said simply, "and so he'll stay at my place."

As Maddie ran up to the house to prepare the bed, Elizabeth crouched at Joel's side again. She picked up a ticket that had fallen from Zack's pocket while he'd knelt over Joel.

In the distance the whistle of the incoming train punctuated the silence of the valley. "Thank you for coming back," she whispered through a tight throat. She held out the rail ticket.

As he pocketed it he gave her a level look, one devoid of tenderness. The man who'd given her comfort just moments ago had vanished just as quickly as the desperado had ducked out of the train.

"I'll catch another train later, when Joel's in better shape."

There was nothing else to say because Clara came running up, arms overloaded with a pillow and a sheet, and Zack went to work, tearing the sheet into strips.

By the time he finished, Pete had arrived back on the scene dragging sticks of all lengths behind him, sticks that would later be used to prop up heavy boughs of apple trees. At once, Zack and Pete knelt together to fashion a crude litter. Then while Pete ran off to summon Granny from the Grissom Ranch, Zack used two of the smoothest sticks to fashion a crude splint for Joel's left leg.

Elizabeth walked over and nudged the fallen ladder with her shoe then stared back at Joel's motionless form. This was her punishment, her penance for coveting a man other than her betrothed. I'm sorry, Joel, she said in her heart. I'll make it up to you, but live. Please live. Zack Danvers was nothing to her. Just an army doctor, it turned out, who'd almost left town without a backward glance. From this moment on, she would ignore him, if it killed her.

With the help of Pete Gustavson and Ben, they got Joel settled in the bed in Elizabeth's house, and then Zack explained the situation more fully.

"I don't know when he'll wake up, but when he does, he'll have a bad headache. Until then we've got to keep him as still as possible."

Maddie was tidying up the room, picking up the excess rags from the floor and delivering a bucket of cold water. As soon as she left for the kitchen, Zack bent over Joel. By morning at the latest, judging by the slow swelling, he'd have to loosen the leg bandage, but the broken bone didn't bother Zack as much as Joel's closed eyes and cold white skin.

"Do you have some more pillows?" he asked Elizabeth. "I want him on his side," he explained. "It's safer in case he aspirates."

There was no answer, and he said it again in laymen's terms. "In case he vomits in his sleep."

For the first time he realized how quiet the room had become since Maddie had shooed Pete and Clara out with her. He glanced over. He and Elizabeth were alone in the room, and her face was nearly as white as Joel's. She sagged against the wall.

A second later he had his arm around her waist and was leading her to a wooden chair.

"Put your head down," he ordered and, to make certain she obeyed, pressed a hand to the nape of her neck. Compared to Joel, she felt like silk. She was just a fragile little thing.

He wrung out a rag in the bucket of cold water and pressed it to the back of her neck. His hand lingered for a moment; then he stepped away and made himself busy with Joel, checking the broken leg for swelling, searching hard for his professional detachment.

"I'm sorry," Elizabeth said at length. "I'm a nuisance." She sat up and reached for the cold cloth and wrung it out in the bucket.

Zack didn't turn. "You don't have to watch over him, you know. I'll stay until he comes to."

"No," she argued in a weak voice, "I can't leave him."

"I've seen grown men fall into a faint for less valid reasons, so don't apologize . . . and don't expect so much of yourself."

He glanced at her over his shoulder. The color had returned to her cheeks, so he was back to one patient instead of two. She was staring at the toes of her high-button shoes, looking utterly miserable, however. The strain was starting to tell. He ran a hand over his forehead and for the first time in over a year prayed for restraint.

The whistle blew as the train left for Boise City, and he allowed himself one consoling thought: There would be other trains.

"Will you stay here . . . until Joel's better?" Her voice was hesitant, shaking.

Nodding, he looked at her terrified face, her slim figure, and wanted to pull her to him and comfort her. But she wasn't his to dream about that way. Besides, he was a doctor, and comfort wasn't dispensed in his arms, but rather in reassuring words.

"Did Pete find Granny?" he asked carefully. Joel's injuries were far too serious to leave him alone. Until Granny got here to act as nurse, Zack would have to remain and watch over him—at least as long as he was unconscious.

Elizabeth nodded. "When the baby's delivered, Granny will come here. Meanwhile I'll help you," she said.

"It might be a long night," he warned.

She turned wary eyes on him. "I don't mind. I won't faint again. I've never fainted in my life."

"They all say that, Elizabeth, every patient who faints." His smile held a hint of warmth.

She looked down at her hands. "Will Joel be all right?"

They all asked impossible questions like that, too.

He shook his head. "Medicine has no absolute answers, Elizabeth."

If he were an honorable man, he'd have sent Elizabeth to the hotel to be cared for by Maddie, but he'd long ago given up on honor. So he did the less than honorable thing and allowed her to stay in the bedroom with him. It would, he told himself, provide her with a measure of comfort, and that was important to the family . . . or in this case, the fiancée.

Elizabeth sat on the opposite side of the bed from him in a rocking chair for a long time, staring at Joel. Then she got up and went to stare out the window at the orchard. It wasn't hard for Zack to read her thoughts.

"You realize Joel won't be doing anything for a long while?" he said quietly.

The trees shimmered silvery under the spring moon. She was so scared and so tired . . . and so glad to have Zack Danvers nearby. She paced once then returned to the rocker.

Behind her, on the chest by the bed, the round-faced clock ticked away in the growing darkness, and nearby a lantern glowed softly in the room, glinting off the brass bed. What was she going to do?

While Zack was sitting there trying not to look at her, she began to talk, to tell him a little of what had happened. In his experience, talking was the best thing people could do.

"In a way this accident was my fault," she said in a wobbly voice. "Joel and I quarreled, you see. After the freeze. That night he didn't . . . Well, Joel's never worked as hard as Pete, and I doubted his industriousness. Even Pete said Joel used the wrong kind of ladder to prop against a tree. But you see he was up there working only because he wanted to please me."

"When is the wedding?" he asked.

She stared down at her hands again, rubbing at a blister on her palm while rocking slowly. "Joel wanted us to be married right away. He said that no one thought anything of short engagements in the West, but I wanted to wait till harvesttime." She leaned her head back against the rocker and wearily pushed a strand of that honey hair out of her eyes. "That's another thing we disagreed on. . . . I'd marry him tomorrow if only he'd live. He'll live, won't he?"

Something down in Zack's gut knotted. How many times was she going to ask? That of all things he couldn't answer.

Zack couldn't meet her eyes. "I'll do my best."

There seemed to be nothing more to say then. They were alone together, one man, one woman, and Joel between them, reminding him that he was a doctor here, not a man.

Silence. Except for the soft ticking of the clock and Joel's soft breathing.

Zack slumped wearily in the chair. He had a feeling this was going to be a long case and damned his luck in not burning all the ladders in town before he bought his train ticket.

Elizabeth straightened in the chair and folded her hands primly, but he could see the dispirited droop to her shoulders, and her hair was falling out of its pins, framing her face with soft blond curls.

Until well after midnight, they sat like that, he watching Joel and trying not to watch her. Her eyes slid shut and then snapped open as she fought exhaustion. Finally she moved her chair closer to the bedside table and propped her chin in her hand. Again her eyes slid shut. . . .

He walked around to the other side of the bed and reached for her, and for the second time this evening he had to catch her from falling into an exhausted heap. This time he picked her up in his arms, intending to lay her down on the parlor sofa.

But she was light, feather light, and just fit in his arms, and suddenly he was tired of playing doctor. She looked too exhausted, too fragile, too lovely, lying next to his heart. And so he sank down in the rocker and held her. In a few minutes, just five more minutes, he'd take her out to the parlor.

At some point he allowed himself to shut his eyes—not to sleep, just to rest for a second. His chin rested against the cornsilk of her hair. . . .

The slamming of the door jolted him awake, and before

he could set Elizabeth down, Granny Sikes came sailing into the room, her gray hair and shapeless black dress haloed by the lantern. A sly smile lit her face as she stared at Zack and Elizabeth, then at the unconscious form of Joel and back again.

Thoroughly awakened, Elizabeth jumped to her feet, her face flushing with bewilderment, still blinking away sleep. She blushed all the harder when she stared at Zack's shoulder. "Why didn't you wake me?" she whispered, backing away from him, pushing a lock of hair away from her face. "Why did you let me sleep on l-like that?"

Zack stood, too, and pushed away the chair. "I owed you a shoulder to sleep on," he said, backing away from her.

Granny stepped between them. "Elizabeth, go boil some water."

"This isn't another birthing, Granny."

"No," Granny replied calmly, "but that baby I just delivered took an uncommonly long time, and I'm hungry. Oatmeal, if I recall, is made in boiling water."

Elizabeth darted a quick glance at Zack, who hadn't moved. "Of course," she said and fled to the kitchen.

Then with her sharp tongue at the ready, Granny turned on Zack and poked a finger in his chest. "Those Gustavson kids tell me you're a doctor, and if that's true, it's about time you owned up to it, because I need a little help." Her sharp-eyed glance cut over to Joel, who lay pale as bleached flour. "And it looks like you need some help, too, Dr. Danvers. But before I start playing nurse, you and me are going to have a talk."

Moving around the bed, Zack rubbed the back of his neck, wondering how he could have done such a foolish thing with Elizabeth. "If it's about your spring tonics, Granny, forget it."

The old woman smiled and shut the door so Elizabeth could not hear their conversation. "It's got to do with that naive little lady in the other room."

7

"You sweet on her?" Granny, hands on ample hips, stood against the shut door and looked Zack in the eye.

Zack met Granny's stare head on. "As I see it, all that matters is that I maintain professional distance." He stood at the foot of the bed and turned his gaze to his unconscious patient.

But Granny was not to be distracted. "That didn't look much like professional distance when I walked in here."

He supposed he deserved that. "Miss Sheldon nearly collapsed with exhaustion, and she's no nurse," he nearly yelled, then softened his voice. "Having her around is like having two patients in one room." Slumping down in the chair, he looked up at Granny, with almost a beseeching expression. "If I watch over Joel's condition, can you do the nursing?"

Granny gave him her best sly smile. "I'll do better'n that. I'll not only nurse Joel, but I'll watch out for Miss Elizabeth Sheldon as well."

Zack passed a weary hand over his forehead. "Yes, I think we've divided the labor fairly. Agreed?"

With a nod, Granny Sikes moved to the bed and assessed the patient for herself. This was not, of course, the first unconscious man she'd seen in her life, but most of the others had come out of gunfights or fistfights or were in the throes of dying. Served Joel right, it did, posing as a farmer to win a woman, for though no one else in town had seen through Joel Emory—especially not Agnes Yates—Granny had long ago decided not to take him at face value.

And as for this other man, Zack Danvers, well . . . nothing surprised her anymore. He wasn't going to sneak out of Eden Creek without Granny knowing why, but there'd be time to pry into his troubles later—after Joel's fate was decided. She went to work.

"Lieutenant, you may have left patients in their muddy clothes in the Philippines, but not here in Eden Creek."

He wasn't up to a lecture on medical hygiene from this huckster of tonics. "Actually, Granny, if the wounded men weren't soaked in mud or blood, we took off their clothes and gave them to the other soldiers."

"The newspapers made it sound like there wasn't a decent nurse within half an ocean."

"Medicine was what we lacked, Granny, not nurses and doctors."

"Humph. That ain't right." She dug some scissors out of her bag and began to cut Joel's shirt off. Zack had cut the trousers off the broken leg with a pocketknife, but the other half of the trousers remained to be dealt with. Granny tackled those too, reducing Joel to near nakedness.

Zack watched, bemused. He'd been too busy to do much about the clothing, and he was impressed now at Granny's fussing over cleanliness.

"My nursing style isn't going to be Florence Nightingale," she said, "but I'm not squeamish and I'm not embarrassed around naked men and bedpans. And I take no time for vanity, so there'll be no shaving. I always liked a man with some facial hair myself, like my departed husband." She moved to the other side of the shirt and continued scissoring.

"I don't take no sass from any man," she warned, pulling away the shirt to leave a bare chest. "On the other hand, I never had a male patient who didn't love being fussed over, and I suspect Joel's going to be a very willing patient."

"I don't care if he's contrary, just so he wakes up."

Granny covered Joel with a sheet and paused from tucking it in to look across at Zack. "You don't bother much with bed-side manner, do you?"

"If we're going to get along, that's as far as we're going to take the subject."

"How come you were leaving town? You hid out here, telling no one you were a doctor, stealing in and out like an outlaw in the night. There's gotta be a reason why you're so secretive about your doctoring skills."

"I got the impression this was your territory medically. I don't want to get in your way."

"Whippersnapper. That's what we used to call men like you in the old days. Of course it's my territory. Always will be. Doesn't mean I wouldn't like a real doctor to give me advice."

Zack smiled, his features softening. "As a matter of fact, I was at the railroad depot when the accident caught up with me. What if I'd gotten on that train? Could you have handled this alone?"

"Of course not," she said. "Guess it's only fair to admit I haven't seen many unconscious men. They don't tend to fall off of plows or hay wagons. I thought Joel knew better than to fall off a ladder and bang up his head."

"Then maybe I should stay around till Joel comes out of it."

They lapsed into silence for a minute, Granny tying on the fresh apron she'd brought.

The door to the bedroom squeaked open an inch.

"I covered him with a sheet, so come in, dear heart," Granny said. "Ain't no use in us all tiptoeing around each other or getting embarrassed. If God didn't blush when he put man together, then there's no reason for a woman to blush either. That's what I always say."

She sighed and cast an appraising eye on Elizabeth, who handed her a bowl of oatmeal slathered with butter and brown sugar and raisins. As dawn cast its first glint of light through the windows, Granny tucked into her food, and Elizabeth stood there smoothing Joel's brow. Zack Danvers, meanwhile, watched Elizabeth's every move, his face impassive. Yes, mused Granny, this was going to be a mighty interesting case. Better than delivering twins on Christmas Eve.

Granny gave orders while she ate. "Now that Joel's settled, we'll organize ourselves. As his nurse, I'll sleep right in here while he's unconscious. Elizabeth can set up a cot in the kitchen—Ben's bringing a couple over from the hotel—and you, Lieutenant or Doctor or whatever, if you feel the need to spend the night, can sit up in a chair or stretch out on that sofa right out there in the living room. What'll it be?"

Zack smiled. As an organizer Granny was unsurpassed—probably one of those women who'd always preferred toy soldiers to dolls. "A chair will be fine."

Time passed, and there was no change in Joel, so Zack wandered out to the kitchen. He was looking for coffee, but he found Elizabeth kneeling on the floor. Wisps of honey-colored cornsilk fell out of their pins again as she struggled over the cot, which was spread out in a tangle of canvas and wooden legs. He'd spent more nights on similar cots than he cared to remember and had thought he never wanted to assemble one again. But as soon as he saw Elizabeth at its mercy he changed his mind. Quietly he moved up behind her and stood there for a few seconds.

"Where'd this come from?" he asked softly.

She jumped and turned, hands to her heart as if she'd lost her breath. "Ben brought it."

"My gallant brother didn't even offer to set it up for you?"

It was the closest thing to a smile he'd seen from her all day. "I don't mind. One of the rowboats came loose, and he had to run, but I'll figure it out." Her voice sounded dubious, and she tucked flyaway hair behind her ear, a self-conscious gesture he'd seen before and which fascinated him. "It can't be that hard to figure out."

He realized he'd moved a step closer and was staring down within touching distance. "They gave out promotions in the army to anyone who could master one of those cots on the first try," he said drily.

"A medal at the very least, I should hope," she said, kneeling and staring at the contraption, as if wondering where to begin.

Well, he did know, and immediately knelt beside her.

With the practiced motions of a soldier, he began to assemble canvas and wood. In silence she watched the expert movements of his hands. Ever since Granny had caught them together this morning, Elizabeth had been stiff with him, barely speaking, never mind meeting his eye.

Kerplunk. He turned the entire contraption over, and the odor of stale baked canvas filled his nostrils.

The aroma of violets drifted up to him, too, disturbing, enticing.

Thump. He banged the legs of one end down on the floor.

He could feel the warmth of her beside him, and it brought back the softness of her in his arms.

Whomp. Wood slammed against wood, and then the cot sat there assembled.

Her bed.

"Where do you want it?"

Without looking at him, she pointed to a corner behind the rocking chair and near the stove.

It was an intimate little corner, and he'd know exactly where to look for her each day when morning came.

"What about you?" she asked.

"Me? I've got a bed at the hotel. Once Joel wakes up, I'll use it. Until then, as I said, I'm nocturnal. Those hard chairs will keep me awake."

There was an uncomfortable silence.

She plumped a pillow and set it down at the far end of the cot so her head would be in the corner. "Would you like to use the cot?" she asked in a stiff voice. "Since you're the doctor, I mean . . . ?"

This conversation about who slept where was getting difficult.

"Elizabeth, I realize how we must have looked to Granny this morning . . ."

"Do you think Joel will find out?"

"Granny hasn't read more into it than what it was—a pair of exhausted people who fell asleep in the same chair. Nothing more."

He knew by the quick blush on her face that he'd embarrassed her. As soon as she finished tucking a quilt under the cot, she looked around. "Well, if everything's in order, I'd better go help Pete with the orchard." Grabbing a straw hat, she fled out the door.

Zack debated for all of five seconds, then against his better judgment went after her. "Elizabeth," he said. "Leave the work to Pete. He's a strong boy." He was genuinely worried about this tiny slip of a woman, but didn't know what to do for her, other than offer to help.

He caught her by her arms at the first tree in a long row and in two more seconds took in the thin muslin dress, the delicate frame beneath it. "Elizabeth, you can't take care of this place alone. Ten women couldn't work this orchard alone."

She averted her face. "Please, leave me. I feel bad enough."

"Look, it wasn't your fault Joel got hurt. Don't be foolish and end up getting hurt yourself."

She tried to duck away from him, but he held her fast, then backed her up against the tree. Bees hummed around them, pollinating, enacting nature's oldest ritual. The fragrance of the apple blossoms was impossibly sweet.

"For heaven's sake, a woman and a pair of kids can't care for all this." HIs hand swept across the expanse of trees. At least twenty rows of twenty to twenty-five trees per row. Four hundred, maybe five hundred trees. Was she crazy? "Hire someone to do the work."

"No one in town will help. They all hope I fail."

"Then fail. Where are you going to find another man to work here?"

Elizabeth stared at him, furious, humiliated, and dizzy by turns. His stubbly beard was back, its black shadow a potent reminder of his masculinity. The image wasn't helped by the disheveled dark hair, the tautly corded muscles in his arms showing where he'd rolled up his sleeves. Most disturbing of all were the steely blue eyes, challenging her.

"You're in my way."

"Lizzie, I'm only trying to make you see sense, so I don't end up with another casualty from the orchard. . . . You got engaged to Joel because you needed help. Now, with him laid up, the work will be even harder."

She hated him, she hated the name Lizzie, she hated the shame of having been found in his arms. And it all welled up at once.

"You're like all the others in town, aren't you?" She choked out the words. "You think I'm an eastern hothouse plant who can't get my hands dirty. You've already tossed your coin and bet on me failing, haven't you?"

He'd struck a raw nerve without meaning to. "Elizabeth, I've tried not to get involved with this town at all. Just hours ago I was at the depot ready to leave. It doesn't matter to me whether you succeed or not. But if you want help—"

"Well, it matters to me." Bright pink spots of anger appeared on her cheeks. "Unlike you, Dr. Danvers, or Lieutenant Danvers, or whoever you are, I am not a quitter, and I'll see this crop through if I have to harvest it myself!" She knew she'd hit her mark, knew she was hurting him, but she couldn't stop the words from pouring out of her heart. "And no, thanks, I don't want any help from *you*. Don't you know how it hurts to see you alive and know my brother is dead?"

He flinched, closed his eyes, and stood there. Tit for tat.

She turned and ran off into the orchard, but he stood there, stung to the core. A quitter, she'd called him, and of course she was right.

"Would it surprise you, Elizabeth Sheldon," he whispered quietly, "to know I agree with every word you said?"

Elizabeth was as angry at herself as anyone. There was no denying how her hasty engagement to Joel must look. It made her look loose. No wonder Zack Danvers had taken advantage and held her in his arms. Well, she'd show him, just as she'd shown the biddies of Amherst. She'd work this orchard. It would be her refuge, her haven . . . but not from Joel.

From having to face Mister-Lieutenant-Doctor Zachary Danvers every day, staring at her, teasing her, tempting her . . . The thought didn't bear finishing. She was going to work this orchard. That was all that mattered.

After all, if a fourteen-year-old boy like Pete could do such work, how hard could it be? The trees needed water, all the bugs had to be chased away, and when the apples were all ripe, she'd need hands to pick them. Period. Simple. Hadn't Joel tried to tell her so?

Never mind that the ditches between the rows were so long . . . or that to start the water running down the rills, little dams had to be shoveled . . . or that she didn't know a codling moth from a mosquito. . . .

She stopped at a tree where the blossoms had faded, and already baby apples, Roman Beauties, each no larger than the nail on her littlest finger, were forming.

She brushed grass off her skirt, picked up a nearby hoe and stabbed at the ditch, attacking the mud and closing up a gopher hole, giving the water a clear path down the entire row, so that every tree would get water. Over and over again, she bent and cut the hoe into the dirt. Hour after hour. Day after day after day.

At the end of a week, Joel was still unconscious, and Elizabeth had not succeeded in completely avoiding Zack Danvers who, with Granny to spell him, watched over Joel and spooned water down his patient's throat to keep him alive. To keep busy, to keep the guilt at bay, Elizabeth helped Pete in the orchard.

Her back ached, the blisters she'd earned out in the cold threatened to break and bleed, perspiration dampened her hairline and three of her delicate summer dresses were mud-stained and torn beyond salvaging. Out of exasperation, she'd burned her confining corset, thrown away yet another torn petticoat. Her "back-East" clothing, she'd quickly learned, was all wrong for orchard life. Still, she worked on, row by row. The orchard went on forever, but it kept her away from the house. Until Joel regained consciousness, there was little point in sitting by the bed, glaring at Zack Danvers.

On the seventh day of backbreaking work, she discovered half a row of baby trees by the next to last row before endless sage desert. Only a few years old, their trunks no thicker than broomsticks, not a one had bloomed; most, in fact, were half dead. They were too young to have borne fruit, but seeing them like this was like an omen of failure.

Her heart sank, and for the first time, her resolve faltered. She sank to the ground by a baby tree and wept.

Clara and Pete found her there. "Elizabeth, look what we found!" Their voices were happy, and in their hands they carried arrowheads they'd dug up from the dirt, a child's treasure. "Look! Arrowheads! From Indians, real . . ." When they saw her face, their excited voices trailed off and they pulled up short.

"What's wrong?" Clara asked. "Did our catalog order get lost?"

"Shush, Clara," Pete said. "That's a dumb thing to think."

"I'm all right." Elizabeth looked up at them, glad for their company. "I guess I'm very tired and very worried about Joel. And then I came on these dead little trees," she said, digging a hanky out of her apron pocket to blow her nose.

Solemnly Pete inspected the seedlings. "Oh, yeah, I forgot, Will bought these two years ago. It never hurt to have some young ones coming along, he said. They don't look too good. I think Joel planted them. He probably never watered them enough."

"They look worse than Joel," Clara said. "Do you want us to pull them?"

Shrugging, Elizabeth said, "Why not?" And for the first time she allowed herself to give in to despair. Maybe they should just pull the whole orchard, because she'd never be able to care for all the trees. Zack Danvers was right. She was wrong and stubborn and proud.

But Pete was more thorough in his inspection. "And even if Joel planted them good, sometimes trees don't transplant. It's tricky getting trees to take to new soil—getting the roots to take, judging the right amount of water, and all."

"Like trying to transplant people, huh?" Elizabeth sighed and stood up. "Once in a while they don't like where they're living, and if they can't move on, they wither up and die."

"You transplanted yourself here in Eden Creek."

"I'm trying."

"What about Zack Danvers?" Clara said. "Did he transplant himself? And Joel?"

Trust Clara to ask the precocious question. Little pitchers had amazingly big ears, especially little pitchers who eavesdropped on all the town secrets.

"I don't believe Dr. Danvers ever intended to set down roots here in Eden Creek. As for Joel, he was trying, but like this little tree, he was losing the battle."

"Well, our pa's got good roots here," Clara said with passion. "That's why I know he'll be back. He's got such strong roots. Not even a mine blast could hurt him."

Elizabeth put her arm around Clara. "I believe you. . . ." And then she had an idea. "Tell you what, Clara. Why don't you and Pete take one of these seedlings?"

"What for?"

"I have too many trees to care for already. Plant it at your pa's place—so when he comes back, he'll have a start on his own orchard. If he likes it, he can get more and he won't need to leave town for the mines anymore."

There was an awkward silence. Pete looked at Clara. Clara looked at Pete.

"But—"

Pete nudged Clara in the ribs. "We'll take it."

"Good." Elizabeth smiled. "You make it grow, and every time you look at it taking root, think of your pa promising to come home. That wouldn't make him mad, would it?"

Pete cleared his throat. "We'll tell him we moved it to our place in memory of Will. He'll like that."

Elizabeth's eyes misted. "Yes, in memory of Will. Won't your pa be proud of you when he sees how hard you've worked with the trees, Pete?"

Before Pete dug the seedling up and dragged it off, he paused and thanked Elizabeth.

Elizabeth brushed the bangs out of Clara's eyes and waved her and Pete away. "Hurry up, now, and get this one in the dirt."

"When we're done, could we swim?" Clara asked.

"No, Clara." It was an emphatic refusal. "You promised never to swim in that creek. It's too close to the river."

"Not even dangling my feet?"

"Not even your big toe."

"You're as strict as Pa," Clara said, smiling.

"Someday I hope to meet him."

"He's got red hair," Clara put in, "and he's the tallest man in town and can spit farther than any man and tell the funniest jokes. Why do you want to meet him?"

"Just curious."

Actually, Elizabeth couldn't wait to meet this man who wouldn't take charity and yet allowed two precious children to waste away alone. The minute that Orville Gustavson came down out of those mountains, he was going to have a welcoming committee of one: Elizabeth Sheldon. And let him aim his Enfield rifle at her.

Pete picked up the root ball while Clara held the delicate branches. At the top of the lane leading from the orchard, Pete and Clara paused with their seedling and, looking back, waved.

Their childish optimism was infectious. Things *had* to work out.

The Gustavson kids, Zack observed the next day from his vantage spot on the porch, had changed in the short time he'd known them. For one thing, they were thriving. For another, there was a spark in their eyes, not of mischief but of having something to live for.

He envied them. Elizabeth was good to those two kids, and he had to hand it to her for taking the bad seeds of Eden Creek and helping them bloom.

Especially changed was Clara who, now that she had no need to forage for food, talked daily about the presents coming from the catalog book. And Pete was working like a man. Zack watched him drive the wagon to town for supplies, just like Joel . . . No, better than Joel. A seedling lay in the wagon bed. Not only was Elizabeth keeping the orchard growing, but it appeared she was expanding already, sending Roman Beauty apple trees into town. He'd been wrong to tell her she couldn't work the place and wished he could find the words to make peace with her. Trying to avoid her was getting hard.

Before he knew it, he was walking toward her, his footsteps crunching in the dirt, and Elizabeth looked up from her hoeing, her expression guarded. They'd scarcely spoken a civil word to each other in a week.

"Is Joel all right?" she asked.

"The same." All Zack knew was that as fast as the apples were ripening, so too was his awareness of her.

"How are you doing?"

"Keeping busy. The blooms are all good. We're going to have apples. Lots of them." This was, she reminded herself, Joel's doctor. This was, her racing pulse said, an attractive man.

"Good."

His gaze took in her prim skirt and blouse, then moved up to her hair. He was bold in his staring, as bold as when he'd fallen asleep on her shoulder.

"Do you need something?" She had to force the prim and proper question, despite the mesmerizing force of his stare. His eyes were as blue as lupine.

"My charm hasn't been very lively since the war. I wanted to apologize for what I said last time we talked. It was poor of me, but I . . . Well, you're an attractive woman."

She looked down at the ground. "Dr. Danvers, I'm engaged."

"I'm telling you what I see, not making an improper advance, Miss Sheldon."

Rebuffed, she kept staring at her feet, at the dust coating her shoes. Of course this man wasn't making an improper advance, or a proper advance. Did she think herself so desirable in men's eyes?

"Let's just say it was my inept way of putting some professional distance between us"—her eyes, he noticed, were flecked with hazel, her mouth fighting back a tremor—"so we wouldn't have the town talking in ways you might not like."

She looked away, then quickly back, her face flushed. The loamy scent of newly hoed earth assaulted her, as did his maleness. His dark hair was blowing across his forehead. Even clean-shaven he had a shadow of a beard, and the effect was magnetizing. "Do you know when I first saw you on the train I thought you might be a gambler or a wanted man? Back East we always hear how men hide out in little towns in the West. Is that what you're doing?"

He laughed to hide his unease. "The war took its toll." Something about Elizabeth invited him to confide in her, but still he held back. He wasn't ready to talk about himself and turned to go.

"I forgive you," she said to his back, and he paused. "My temper wasn't at its best either. But I think it's Joel we should be worrying about more than ourselves."

Something in her voice made him turn back. "I'm trying to remember that."

"Why did you keep it a secret? About being a doctor, I mean?"

She needn't have explained what "it" was. "Granny didn't seem to want competition." That wasn't true, but it took care of a difficult question.

She was looking at a branch with a few miniature apples on it, and she made a fetching picture of another sort as she reached up, bodice stretching against her breasts, wisps of blond hair escaping their pins. Her orchard was in need of a man's attention. Not for the first time, he realized Elizabeth was in need of a man, too.

She turned to look at him, and their gazes locked and held.

"Do you know what I craved coming home?" he asked, suddenly clearing his throat. "Little green apples."

"In about a month you'll have your wish, then," she said.

She let go of the branch and began to stroll down the row. One bite of green apple was all Zack needed. One sour taste to quench his craving. Or maybe he had a newer craving: to be near Elizabeth Sheldon.

Against his better judgment he caught up with Elizabeth, and they fell into step. It was damned hard for him to remember that she was engaged to the patient who lay inside. Her hair blew about her face, pale like prairie wheat . . . or like a summer moon. Her profile, vulnerable and delicate, was attractive; her gaze, when she turned to smile at him, was determined. She drew him like a magnet. And yet the sorrow in him was too deep to share. It was balm enough to be near her—and to draw out her secrets.

"What devils back East are you running from?"

"You mean," she said, "you won't reveal your secrets, but you want to know mine?"

"Call it idle curiosity. What makes an educated woman from back east come west to a barely thriving orchard in a town the size of a postage stamp?"

Elizabeth walked in silence, unnerved by his question, by his insight in asking it, by the concern behind his curiosity. Joel, as far as she could remember, had never asked her why she'd come. He'd proposed without knowing much about her. She could have been another Lizzie Borden from Massachusetts, for all Joel knew or cared . . . but here was Zachary Danvers, asking her to bare her soul.

"You don't have to answer."

His words cut through her defenses. Worse, his voice was soft and deep. It had been so long since she'd had anyone but the children to talk to, and before she knew it, the truth just spilled out.

"Well, you see," she explained, "I suffered a double loss back in Massachusetts. First my father died—he shot himself. . . ." Her voice wobbled, and she pushed back yet another blowing strand of hair, buying time to steady her voice. She hadn't thought she'd ever say that to anyone. She'd even told herself her father died a natural death, but now it was out. "And I was engaged to a young lawyer from my father's firm. Lawrence."

She looked up to gauge Zack's reaction, but his face was impassive. "I took ill after my father's death, and while I was sick . . . while I was recovering, Lawrence sent me a note calling off our engagement. Quite a fall for the mayor's daughter. I was the object of town gossip, my reputation was ruined, and then on top of all else, Will died." She stopped and looked out over the orchard. "After that, there seemed no reason not to accept a mail-order marriage proposal."

He leaned back against a tree and studied a branch closely. "Let me guess. . . . Your first fiancé had political ambitions?"

"Of course." Her voice sounded wistful. "He worshiped my father."

Just as Zack had guessed. Carefully he traced the outline of a leaf as if it were worthy of dissection. "Did it ever occur to you, Elizabeth, that Lawrence might have been using you, that you, as the mayor's daughter, were a prize catch? Wouldn't that be a catch for an aspiring young lawyer?"

"I wouldn't know."

Was Zack the only man besides Joel who wasn't deaf, dumb, and blind? "Well, as a bachelor, I can assure you you're quite a catch."

"I never liked flattery, Doctor . . . Lieutenant . . ."

Their eyes met, locked.

"Try Zack. Try believing that once your father died, you were a liability, not an asset. In short, Lizzie, the cad was using you. You're not the one who was at fault."

"You have a vivid imagination." That was all she'd allow.

She was silent, squirming under his relentless blue gaze, and she couldn't make her breathing slow down. His gaze was on her, watching, watching. . . . Why was he flattering her all of a sudden? She had nothing special to offer a man. Joel had wanted kisses but offered no compliments as a token of his esteem.

"There are some people in town who say Joel is using you too."

It was as if Zack Danvers had read her mind, and the idea unnerved her. "Well, what do they know?" Suddenly wary of this man, she whirled away. He was entirely too good at seeing through her, and she sorely regretted having spilled her heart to him. "They all fawn over my advanced education and then laugh behind my back at my determination to work this orchard!"

"I'm not laughing at you."

"Well, you certainly had an amused look in your eye when you eavesdropped on Joel's proposal."

She felt him come up behind her, temptation in the flesh. He put his hands on her shoulders, ever so gently, and his breath was warm against her neck. "Lizzie . . ."

His voice was laced with longing, the same sort of longing she felt, a longing that cut so deep it hurt, and if he so much as said another word . . . well, it would be so easy to fall into this man's arms. Suddenly it was important to remember that she was engaged. She'd made a promise to another man, however devoid of tender regard her feelings for that other man.

"I'd better go." Without looking at Zack, she slipped away from his touch, then picked up her skirts and ran out of the orchard.

Granny was just coming out the back door of the house, and, catching sight of Elizabeth, she shielded her eyes, waiting.

"Well, Lordy," she declared when Elizabeth reached her, "if you don't look as if you've missed the last train to somewhere mighty important. What's the matter?"

"Nothing." Elizabeth, still catching her breath, brushed at the mud spots on her skirt. To get back here faster, she'd criss-crossed through the orchard, and the entire hem of her skirt was wet where she'd splashed through one of the ditches.

"Well, where's that doctor when we need him?"

"Joel . . . ?"

Granny nodded in pleased satisfaction, as if she were telling Elizabeth the happiest news of her life. "Joel's blinking his eyes, waking up. You can set a new wedding date."

Suddenly Elizabeth couldn't seem to catch her breath at all for the guilt. If people knew she'd been alone with the doctor in the orchard while Joel was regaining consciousness, they'd bubble over like canning jars in a hot bath and seal her reputation. Even out west, if a woman got labeled as a temptress or a Jezebel, she could count on being set on the shelf alone forever.

"Well," Granny said, staring at the mud on Elizabeth's hem, "you didn't go and throw the good doctor in the creek, did you?"

❀

8

As chalk dust settled over the empty desks for the summer, Miss Agnes Yates breathed a sigh of relief. School was out, and at last she was free to waylay Dr. Danvers.

What a fool she'd been to waste her earlier opportunities. Dr. Danvers, refined and eligible, rode by her schoolhouse twice a day—four times a day if you counted the round trips—in order to make house calls on Joel Emory. But with her teaching duties—especially the end-of-year recitation, which Emma Hankins had won by memorizing "The Wreck of the *Hesperus*"—there'd been no time.

Agnes was always a wreck herself when school ended, but this year's ending extravaganza had been a blessing in disguise, starting after the school recital when Emma Hankins's little brother had spilled lemonade in Agnes's open desk drawer. The ensuing cleanup had resulted in a most enlightening conversation.

Mrs. Hankins was a sturdy farmwife who was perpetually suckling an infant. She'd swatted her son and then scooped dissolving chalk out of the drawer. With good-natured spirit, Agnes had helped. After all, Mr. Hankins was the school board member who brought the wood for Agnes's stove.

"This desk needed a good end-of-year cleaning anyway, Mrs. Hankins," Agnes said. "The spill was just an accident—

no different than when Joel Emory fell out of the apple tree."

To Agnes's surprise, Mrs. Hankins pounced on the subject. "If you ask me, the biggest shame is what's going on at that Sheldon orchard. Allowing an unmarried man to bed down at her house right in full sight of good children like mine."

Agnes leaned closer. "Oh, I quite agree," she said quickly. "For all her prim and proper eastern upbringing, Miss Elizabeth Sheldon is creating a real scandal in this community." She knew exactly how to cluck her tongue to sound properly outraged.

"Loose women tend to find a haven in towns like this," Mrs. Hankins noted, frowning. "Why, for all we know, she's a soiled dove come here to roost."

Agnes didn't think so, but saw no point in enlightening Mrs. Hankins. Agnes worried more about herself, one of the few lilacs in a town of tumbleweeds. She deserved to be appreciated.

"It's not fair," she sniffed. "Not fair when women like us try their hardest to bring decency to the West."

Which was exactly what Mrs. Hankins had whispered when she'd departed.

"You know, Agnes, if I were a respectable woman like you, I'd get acquainted with that young doctor who's treating Joel. An educated woman like you couldn't do much better in a town like this."

No indeed. And now a mere day later, with the encouragement of Mrs. Hankins, Agnes was doing just that.

She slammed the schoolhouse door and turned the key in the lock, then marched out to the picket fence, which practically opened right onto the dirt road leading to Elizabeth Sheldon's orchard. The gate that she'd spent an hour prying loose fell conveniently slack, looking as if its hinges were falling off.

Anxiously she looked up the road, watching for a horse and rider, then double-checked the watch pinned to her bodice. Zack Danvers always rode by about nine o'clock on his way to the orchard.

Like clockwork, a cloud of dust appeared on the horizon, and moments later the good doctor reined in, just as she'd hoped. Seeing her "predicament," he dismounted and asked if he could be of assistance.

She was standing there with a hammer trying her best to look helpless. "You're so kind to stop and help. As long as I'm not detaining you?"

Dr. Zachary Danvers leveled an unsmiling gaze on her. "Yes, Miss Yates, you are detaining me, but I feel like being kind today. I don't, however, have a talent for clever conversation." He held out his hand for the hammer.

My, he was no friendlier than he'd been the first time she'd talked with him. A brooding man, given to nightmares, so she'd heard from hotel gossip. However, his assets more than compensated for his liabilities, and by now he'd surely forgotten her gaffe at the newspaper office. . . . While he banged at the hinges of the gate, she stood nearby, watching the play of his muscles through his shirt, admiring his dark hair and fine profile. He was so very attractive. So well educated. So much more appealing in every way than uncouth ranchers like Antonio Mendez, who couldn't even read proper English. Surely Dr. Zachary Danvers would respond to flattery.

"Everyone's proud to know you've come straight from the war. You must have been terribly brave to fight those dreadful Spanish."

"I didn't fight them," he said tersely. "I worked in a medic tent. And the wounded were victims of the Philippine uprising after the Spanish were defeated." Terse and to the point. And impersonal.

"Well, of course, I read all about it in the papers. The town's glad to have a real doctor now."

"I'm not staying."

No, he wasn't one for conversation. She tried again. "Usually I visit my sister in Boise City in the summertime, but I never leave until after the Fourth of July. This summer I might just stay on in Eden Creek." Depending on Dr. Danvers.

"Teaching school?"

She laughed softly. "A bit of tutoring—for the ranchers."

With no effort at all he repaired the hinge. Then he stood and held out the hammer to her. His gaze bored through her, as if he could see right through her ploy. "Keep the hinges oiled, and don't let those nails fall out of the gate so easily." With that, he settled his hat squarely on his head and moved toward his horse. She watched in dismay, disappointed. Surely he wasn't going to leave so soon.

"Do you like huckleberry pie, Doctor?" she asked, rushing after him.

He had already mounted his horse and, without any change in expression, said, "That depends."

"On what?" If he said he preferred apple pie, she'd scream.

"On why you're making it."

"A neighborly gesture, you know. I'm ashamed I haven't been to visit Joel yet and thought I'd take a pie out to the Sheldon place. And since you're often there on house calls, I thought you'd like some, too. Elizabeth Sheldon surely offers you a meal, doesn't she?"

Gathering up his reins, he leveled a clear-eyed gaze on her. "You'd better make Joel's favorite kind of pie. He wants the cheering up more than I do."

With no more encouragement than that, not even a smile, he tipped his hat and rode off down the road. She watched until he was swallowed up in the sagebrush and apple trees. Agnes Yates had never been a practiced flirt, but she knew when she'd been rebuffed, and she didn't like the feeling. She could no longer see Zack Danvers, but she could still taste the dust kicked up by his horse, and between gritted teeth, she made a vow.

"You can brood about that wretched war all you want, Dr. Danvers. It's none of my affair what's eating at your belly, but I'll make you notice me, Doctor, if I have to lace my pie with some of Mr. Gantt's real liquor and shock good Mrs. Hankins to her toes. Just you wait."

Immediately she marched around the school to her little one-room house and brought out one of the many jars of huckleberries she'd put up last summer. With a mighty grip, she unscrewed the lid and sniffed. Huckleberry pie was irresistible to men, more irresistible than apple, and she had the entire summer to ply this most eligible of bachelors with pie. She'd even go so far as to pay social calls at the Sheldon orchard, timed to coincide with the house calls of Dr. Danvers, of course. But on no account was that fancy eastern lady, Elizabeth Sheldon, going to interfere a second time with the quest of Miss Agnes Yates for a worthy husband, no matter how many pies it took.

Elizabeth could measure time in June by Miss Yates's weekly visits and wondered if today the teacher would come bearing another pie. Meanwhile, washing the breakfast dishes provided a rare respite from both the orchard and Joel, and Elizabeth found the simple chore relaxing.

Within twenty-four hours after Joel woke up, Elizabeth had discovered that he was easier to take care of when unconscious. Joel's leg was not mending easily, was complicated by swelling. And Joel, it turned out, knew how to stretch the pain of a mending leg to the utmost. A crybaby.

Consequently, the perfect weather of June had been lost on her, for she'd spent the entire month helping Granny care for Joel and helping Pete care for the little green apples in the orchard. She could recite Joel's demands and those of the orchard in her sleep.

Joel: Read to me.

Trees: Spray me.

Joel: Shut the window.

Trees: Thin me.

Joel: I'm hungry.

And from both of them: I'm thirsty, I'm thirsty, I'm thirsty. Both Joel and the orchard constantly needed water, water, water.

Just when she was ready to scream with frustration or slide off her chair from sheer exhaustion, Joel would moan in pain,

and that would remind her that while he might be playing the
martyr role to the hilt, his pain was real. Then—feeling guilty,
oh, so guilty at her selfishness—she'd gather herself together
and be gracious. But it was hard playing Johnny Appleseed
and Florence Nightingale at the same time. So hard.

She had made a secret decision not to marry Joel, and that
added to the guilt weighing on her. She'd tell him when he
was well enough to get around on crutches, she decided, not
before. Only the meanest person would deliver bad news to a
man who was flat on his back. No, she couldn't tell Joel her
true feelings now, but she would tell him soon. Soon.

After rinsing off the last plate, she handed it to Clara to put
away, then reached for the empty kettle and began to scrub it.
She'd barely finished that task, her hands still pink from the
dishwater, when down the lane came the clop-clop of hooves
from the distance.

Granny poked her head in the kitchen door. "Company's
coming," she said. "Who do you guess will come first today?
Dr. Danvers or Agnes Yates?"

"Neither. I hope it's our catalog order," Clara piped up.

Since the confrontation at the social, Agnes Yates had not
said a word in public about sending the Gustavson children
away to an orphanage. Still, when she came to visit, Clara
made herself scarce.

To Elizabeth's mind, anyone but Miss Yates would be
welcome. Elizabeth grabbed a towel and went to the door,
rubbing her hands dry. Secretly she hoped the visitor would
be Zachary Danvers, for over the past month, she'd come to
regard each of his visits as a short respite in the long days of
hard work.

She and Zack never said much to each other, but morning
or evening, he never left before finding her and informing her,
"Joel is mending fine."

"Thank you for coming. Granny is a good nurse," she'd say
tersely.

But he always got in the last word, and always it was the
same. "Do you need help in the orchard?"

"No, thank you. I told you I don't need any help." In all her years back in Amherst as the pampered daughter of the mayor, Elizabeth had never known such work existed, but she hid her blistered hands, ignored her aching back, fretted in secret over her sunburned skin, and endured. She would not ask for help.

Never again, since that last walk in the orchard, had he shown her the relaxed side of himself. Which was just as well. Though she couldn't explain it, when she and Zack Danvers were alone, temptation walked with them, a temptation she didn't know how to handle. But that didn't mean she couldn't look forward to a brief exchange of pleasantries with him at the house—innocent talk with Granny and Clara looking on. That was enjoyable.

But on the days when Miss Yates came to visit, there was no time for any words. Elizabeth felt cheated out of Zack Danvers's company, and her face burned with the shame of her admission. After all, she was engaged, but Miss Yates and Zack Danvers were both uncommitted and had a right to court.

Still, she hoped that just this once, Zack Danvers might arrive before Miss Yates got here. Then she yanked open the door, putting on an expectant smile. When she saw who it was, her heart sank.

Miss Yates, dark eyes squinting out from under her sun-bonnet, carried the third berry pie in as many weeks— huckleberry once again. Elizabeth smiled and accepted the pie—which, except for a soggy crust, was tolerable. After a brief exchange of greetings, she showed Miss Yates into Joel's room, the same as she did since Miss Yates had begun visiting earlier in June. That was the only blessing to all these visits: Miss Yates, with an empty summer stretching before her, was willing to read to Joel, and that freed Elizabeth and Granny for a while.

Minutes later, as Miss Yates sat in the bedroom, reading from the *Idaho Statesman* the latest accounts from the

Philippines, Joel was blessedly engrossed. The War with Spain had officially ended nearly a year ago, but like many people Joel devoured news about the fighting still going on between Philippine insurgents and soldiers trying to regain order in America's new-won territory.

A while later Elizabeth sat out in the yard with Clara shelling some early peas from the garden. She could hear Agnes Yates through the open window, not reading now, but entertaining Joel with her strong opinions. Miss Yates had a most favorable opinion of herself, her normal school education, and her self-discipline. In fact, Miss Agnes Yates was shameless in her self-congratulation.

"Elizabeth will be sorry when Orville Gustavson blows her fashionable boater off her head for taking his children. But there's no use educating her in the ways of the West. Once a person picks up fancy ideas at some eastern academy, there's no use in someone from a plain normal school talking to her. . . ."

Clara bowed her head and grew very still, but Elizabeth stood, set down the basin of peas, and headed inside.

That was the last straw. Agnes Yates could malign her all she wanted to, but if she was going to start in on the children again, then it was too much. This was her house, for heaven's sake. Who was this woman to come into her own home and insult her and children she'd vowed to protect? Untying her apron, she went in to stand behind Miss Yates, who turned, her eyes narrowing.

"Oh, hello, Elizabeth. We were just talking about you. Joel's dreadfully worried about how you're going to manage. There's so much about the West that's different from what you're used to, you know."

"I'm managing, and the Gustavson children are perfectly safe and comfortable. I don't want them alarmed."

Miss Yates smiled. "Oh, you couldn't alarm those two, especially that girl, if you put dynamite in her overalls. Really, Elizabeth, give me some credit. I'm a teacher and have the best interests of children at heart always."

"Until we hear where Orville Gustavson is, they're staying with me, working for me."

"Working for you? Clara's only eight."

"They enjoy it."

Miss Yates sighed as if with exaggerated patience. "Very well, if you say so, but if you ask me, you've taken on too much. I mean, you do look exhausted, Elizabeth. You've aged five years since the dance."

Before Elizabeth could reply, another set of hoofbeats sounded out in the yard. Chickens scattered, a horse neighed, and Miss Yates, making a great show of having overstayed her welcome, rushed out into the yard to greet the doctor.

"What a wonderful coincidence . . . again," she cooed at Zack. "I've brought a huckleberry pie. Joel's such a baby, saying it's not his favorite, so I hope you'll have some before you leave."

Standing at the window, Elizabeth listened unashamedly till she couldn't stand it anymore. Then she went in to sit beside her fiancé, but she continued to look out the window.

"Elizabeth," Joel said softly without opening his eyes, "you're a patient woman."

She didn't turn, but stiffened in place. "About what?"

"Everything. Me. Miss Yates. The orchard. Honoring your vow to stand by me in sickness and in health, even before the ceremony."

Please, Joel, she prayed silently, don't talk about weddings.

"Did I say something wrong?"

She shook her head and turned back to him. "Don't worry yourself. You're supposed to rest and let that leg mend or it'll swell again."

"I must have the slowest mending leg in history," he said, with a sheepish smile on his baby face. "If we can ever pry the doctor away from Miss Yates, maybe he'll finally give me a pair of crutches. Go get him for me."

She swallowed hard. "Of course, Joel."

But before she could get up, Zack Danvers appeared in the doorway, and Elizabeth jumped to her feet, the chair still rocking behind her. Self-consciously she tucked back a strand of hair and wet her lips. She was certain color flooded her face, giving away her feelings.

But he smiled as if he saw nothing amiss, and instead of moving to examine Joel, he approached her and held out a package wrapped in brown paper and tied with string.

It was her order from Montgomery Ward.

"Someone in town asked me to deliver this to you." His eyes were so blue she could have drowned in them, and her heart went thump at the sight of the man delivering the package.

Clara was right there. "Can I open it, Elizabeth? Can I?"

"In the kitchen, Clara." And she thanked Zack and left the room, Clara on her heels.

As she crossed the threshold, she could hear Zack talking to Granny, sparring about the merits of spring tonics made out of whiskey, and then Joel's voice joined in, demanding crutches so he could get out of bed.

Out in the kitchen, Elizabeth, with trembling hands, helped Clara break the string on the package. Within seconds Clara was tearing away the wrapping paper, while Elizabeth watched, pretending to be happy.

Clara lifted out the pocketknife for Pete, the stickpin for her pa—the shiny gold four-leaf clover. The biggest surprise of all was the doll, which Elizabeth had added to the order, and Clara went squealing around the room with it, hugging it tight.

There was one item remaining, and Elizabeth herself lifted it up, unaware that Miss Yates was standing in the kitchen doorway watching, until she heard her shocked gasp of outrage. "Well, I never!" She whirled away to her horse and buggy. "Wait till the town hears about this!"

A slow grin spread across Elizabeth's face. Her bloomers had arrived.

*   *   *

"Gosh!" Pete exclaimed, looking at Elizabeth the next day. "You look like Annie Oakley."

Not exactly, but close. "We wear these for bicycle riding back east, Pete . . . and they're going to make working in the orchard ten times easier."

"Oh, I think they're great. And so's my pocketknife . . . except Pa won't like it."

"You earned it, Pete, and that's exactly what I'll tell your pa. Let's get to work."

One hour slid into the next, and the sun rose higher and hotter over the sagebrush valley. High up on a ladder, she plucked away excess apples so that where once there had been six or eight, now one or two had room to grow and fatten. She filled in gopher holes. She propped up sagging branches. By now, the eastern dances and tea parties seemed long ago. Blistered hands and aching muscles were all she knew.

Less than a week after her bloomers arrived, on a calm windless day early in July Pete decreed it was time to spray.

In the barn, the pump sat up on the wagon, ready to have lead arsenate poured into it from a huge barrel. They'd have to refill it many times before the horse and wagon made it up and down all the rows and every tree was sprayed. It was a messy, smelly job, this precaution against worms, but as Pete kept repeating, they had no choice, for wormy apples would have to be discarded, cutting her profits. And, though Pete was a hard worker, this job took two pairs of hands.

What made it worse for Elizabeth was the macabre getup she had to wear. Old overalls and an old shirt. Gloves. One scarf over her nose and another over her head and pulled down to her eyebrows. Only her eyes were visible, and still Pete made sure they slathered lots of axle grease on their faces.

With slippery hands, she pulled on rubber boots, and her costume was complete. Elizabeth felt like a cross between a bandit and a minstrel in a town hall. All she lacked was a banjo.

"If I were a codling moth, just seeing us in these getups would scare me off," she told Pete.

"Codling moths are ornery. They don't scare easy," he said, all business as usual.

"Have you seen Clara?" Elizabeth looked around, making sure the coast was clear. Joel and Granny were shut up tight in the house, away from the noxious spray, but Clara had vanished without a word.

"I sent her to town so she wouldn't get in the way of the spraying. She took her doll to show off at Atwood's."

Worried, Elizabeth wished she'd seen the child first. Clara had been begging to go swimming, and today Elizabeth wouldn't be able to check on her.

"She won't go swimming, neither," Pete said, as if reading her mind. "I told her if she did, Pa would whip her when he gets back. And Doc Danvers won't come, neither. I told him to stay away if he sees the spraying going on."

Pete had thought of absolutely everything. Of course, Zack wouldn't come during spraying, but what surprised her was the twinge of disappointment she felt.

"Then let's get started." She wanted this job done so that life could get back to normal. So that Clara could run free. So that Zack Danvers could come.

Elizabeth drove the wagon while Pete stood in back wielding the black rubber hose connected to the pump machine. The task was messy and grueling because they had to work longer and harder than other days to finish, praying no wind would come up to interrupt them. From sunup to sundown, they drove that horse and wagon around while Pete struggled with the hose, spraying a fine mist of lead arsenate on the trees. And still it took them into a second day before they finished. Elizabeth used half a dozen bandannas to protect her mouth and nose.

When they finally finished, she let Pete drive the wagon back to the barn, while she plopped down on the ground and sank back against a tree trunk, exhausted. She turned her hands palm up to inspect them. Dirt caked the axle grease. An aura of chemicals clung to her like the smell of rotten fish. She felt hideous and wanted nothing so much as a bath.

In the distance the swift current of the creek sounded inviting. And disturbing. It'd be one thing if she were to wash off the axle grease and dirt in the water, another if Clara had disobeyed her orders to stay inside and snuck out to go swimming. Ever since the little girl had gotten her doll, she'd been playing more than working, and Elizabeth couldn't begrudge her time to be a child.

At least a dozen times Clara had begged to go swimming, pointing out that the quiet triangle of water created by the stone weir was perfectly safe, but each time Elizabeth had forbidden it.

The sight of that creek—deep and cold and running wild in places—scared Elizabeth at times. It was at once the lifeblood of the orchard and something to be feared almost as much as the river into which it ran.

"Clara," she called down the row.

She received no answer, but she did catch sight of someone darting among the rows of trees.

Her heart skipped a beat. Clara was beginning to make friends in town. If she'd brought any of them to swim in the creek, that would double the reason to worry.

Worried now, Elizabeth rose and hurried toward the creek.

In the distance the water shimmered cold and inviting under the sun. Leaves rustled overhead as she walked, each footstep swallowed up by the damp earth into which her feet sank and by the magpies that flew about, scouting the scarecrow in the middle of the orchard.

She could hear splashing now, a sound at odds with the usual smooth-flowing current, and somewhere in the distance children's voices.

Her rubber boots were ankle deep in mud and slowing her down, and she cursed the slow, mucky steps she was forced to take, her boots working like suction cups. She crossed the row to a drier path and at last saw the ditch that ran parallel to the creek.

Already, the words of a reprimand were forming in her mind: Clara, don't you know it's not safe . . . ?

"Clara—" She pulled up short. "Oh."

She pressed her sticky hands to her suddenly flaming cheeks.

Zachary Danvers was in the water, and he was naked from the waist up. It was the most intimate look she'd ever had at him, and she couldn't tear her eyes away from the sight of bare shoulders gleaming wetly in the sunlight as first one arm and then the other sliced through the water, propelling him along. The sun glistened on his slicked-back hair, black and streaming with water.

Forever after, she would remember the exact moment when he saw her. He stopped swimming and floated on his back, a wicked expression on his face.

She stood rooted to the spot, drowning in embarrassment and an acute awareness of Zack Danvers the man.

Elizabeth knew for the first time the feeling of liquid desire running through her. Eve tempted.

"H. G. Wells must have costumed you," he called out.

She looked down at herself, self-conscious at the ridiculous picture she made. He might as well have caught her in her nightgown.

"Planning to rob a bank?" Paddling easily, he approached the shore.

"We've been spraying," she called back.

He nodded, water trickling down his face.

"Do you want to come in and swim off the mud?"

Backing up a step, Elizabeth shook her head. "I don't swim."

He floated close enough so that she could see his chest beneath the water. "A Massachusetts lady with no mermaid in her?"

In truth, she could think of nothing except the fact that she'd caught him naked.

"You shouldn't be swimming here," she said. "It's only a creek, but Pete says the current can get strong."

What she really wanted to say was unladylike: You shouldn't be swimming naked.

Like Neptune coming out of the sea, he stood, waist deep in the water, shiny droplets sluicing down the mat of fine dark hair on his chest and disappearing in the creek. Her gaze was riveted to that crucial juncture between water and man when he started toward her. She gasped and backed into a tree before she realized he was dressed after all—from the waist down, though his wet trousers clung like a second skin and left little to her imagination.

His shirt dangled from an apple branch. As soon as she located it she squeezed her eyes shut and thrust it at him, ripping a few leaves off with it. She heard them rustle, heard his every breath. How dare he climb out of the water like that? But he did, and he plucked the shirt from her, too, and dripped water on her while he was about it.

When his chuckle rumbled low in her ear, she whirled and bumped into the tree. She stood there, sticky face buried in the rough bark, humiliated beyond belief.

"If I'd known you were coming down this way, I'd have brought a change of clothes," he said easily. Then after a moment, "You can look now."

Obviously his time in the tropics had loosened his inhibitions, if he'd ever had any . . . and now he stirred something within her. The picture of his tanned torso dripping with water was indelibly printed on her mind. She tingled all over.

Embarrassed, she averted her face. "If I were you I wouldn't eat any green apples today."

"Would they poison me?"

Out of the corner of her eye she could see him buttoning his shirt, from the bottom up.

"Because the orchard's just been sprayed." Tempting her, he was. They were crossing over the invisible line between professional distance and something personal.

"Lizzie?"

At that ridiculous nickname, she turned.

"There, you see, I'm not so scary to look on." His shirttails dangled down to his hips, clinging here and there to his damp trousers, and he was fumbling with the button at his throat. Finally he abandoned the effort and pushed his hair back out of his eyes, all the time watching her. "You look like a Lizzie in that getup, you know. It takes away all your primness."

He was running his hand through his hair again and smiling at her. Oh, he knew exactly what he was doing to her. A drop of water wended its way down his jaw and plopped to the ground somewhere near her feet. She looked down at her ridiculous rubber boots, then at his bare feet, strong and finely arched.

She was acutely aware of how awful she looked, how dreadfully oily and awful she must smell . . . and how childish she felt under his knowing gaze.

"Please leave. And don't swim here anymore. You—you're setting a dangerous example for Clara." Her heart was galloping. "Please leave."

In answer, he touched her. It was just a gentle touch, the flick of a wet finger against her grease–smeared cheek.

"Oil and water don't mix, isn't that an old adage?" he said softly.

"I should be at the house. . . ."

Ducking under his arm, she ran along a row of trees to the barn. Mercifully, Pete was gone. She found the basin and harsh soap he'd used to wash, and after filling it at the outdoor pump, she scrubbed her skin until it tingled and turned pink. Then she went into the harness room and changed into an old skirt and blouse.

That evening, when Zachary Danvers finally called on Joel, no one would ever have guessed they'd encountered each other earlier—unless her refusal to greet him seemed suspicious. Elizabeth stood at the stove, stirring a pot of barley soup, determined to ignore him. As she stirred the broth, all she could think of was how Zack had looked wet and half naked. A pin slipped out of her freshly washed hair and she reached up to tuck it in more securely.

She held her breath waiting for Zack to pass through the kitchen and on into the bedroom. But he didn't go to see Joel immediately. Instead, he came up behind her. He never touched her, just stood there a hairbreadth behind her.

"How's Joel?" His breath was warm on the back of her neck.

Her temperature shot up higher than the stove's.

"As usual," she said without turning. "He says it's time he got crutches."

"Even if I get some made for him, you'll still need help with the orchard."

"I'm fine."

"Lizzie—"

"Don't call me that—not here."

"Let me help you."

"No." She shut her eyes and blinked back tears. He was making this all the harder. Didn't he see? She bent over the stove, trembling.

She could feel him behind her, as if trying to choose between moving closer and retreating.

Outside, his horse neighed.

"Elizabeth," Granny called, "is the water in the teakettle still hot?"

As Granny's footsteps sounded in the doorway, Zack Danvers moved away to see Joel. Elizabeth never moved, except for the in-and-out motion of her breathing, but there was nothing she could do about that.

An hour or so later Zack left the house. Elizabeth immediately wiped her hands on her apron and fled to Joel's bedside.

She knelt at his side. "Joel," she said with a touch of urgency.

He opened his eyes and looked at her.

She covered his hand with her own. He felt cold.

When he said nothing, she rushed on. "I've changed my mind about staying away from the Fourth of July celebration in town tomorrow."

He put on a frown, but she remained undeterred. This man's broken leg was not going to weaken her. "Joel, my imagination's running away from me. I've been cooped up here too long. I can't stay here another day."

Joel's frown faded to a satisfied look. "I knew you'd hate it in this small town. You want to go back East?"

She pulled back, shocked. Of course not. For a minute she'd thought he sounded hopeful. Didn't Joel want her to stay here in Eden Creek?

"No, Joel, I only want to get away from the orchard for one day. Granny's offered to stay here. I'm going into town tomorrow, Joel."

"Why?"

"It's a patriotic day, Joel."

"Zachary Danvers doesn't want to be honored."

"This has nothing to do with him. Oh, Joel, you'll be on crutches soon. I need to meet the other women from town. I need to."

He sulked. "Go ahead." His tone of voice told her he would hold a grudge. "Spend the day in town. They'll all be jealous of you, and you'll have a rotten time. I'll miss you, but go if you must. Do whatever you want."

She stood, unmoved by his obvious attempts to make her feel guilty. "What I want is to spend July Fourth in town."

She stood up and walked into the kitchen.

Men. She didn't need any of them. Not Joel. Especially not Zachary Danvers. Yes, a holiday in town would calm down her imagination. For good.

9

The next day Elizabeth stood solemnly watching from the kitchen door as Zack Danvers fitted a pair of crutches to Joel. Her fiancé had managed to slick down his hair and don a dressing gown, but he looked at the crutches as if they might bite.

Zack frowned. "I thought you were anxious for crutches."

"They don't look much more stable than one of those tree props," Joel said, his voice whiny.

"Well, what'd you expect? To take Elizabeth out dancing right away? . . . Sure, Mr. Atwood's made more coffins than crutches, but count your blessings. Be glad it's crutches he made for you and not—"

"Yeah, yeah," Joel said. "Granny tells me every hour how lucky I am to be alive. I shouldn't expect anything more than homemade crutches in a town like this."

Elizabeth moved to Joel and put a quieting hand on his arm. Immediately Zack turned away, studying the length of the crutches. They were a touch long, so Zack borrowed a saw from Pete and, with Elizabeth watching, sawed off some length right there in the bedroom. He turned back, saw Elizabeth, and paused, his face darkening, as if he were annoyed with her. A second later he was coaxing Joel away from her.

"Now come on. Let's try them."

With an easy strength, Zack pulled Joel to his feet and supported him with his own weight while he tucked the crutches under Joel's arms. "Steady as she goes."

At first Joel wavered, but Zack's arm was there, and Joel, looking like a wobbly newborn colt, dragged his splinted leg while he took his first hesitant step, then moved the crutches, swung his hips forward to take another step, and promptly declared himself dizzy. A second later he collapsed on the bed, banging his head against the brass frame.

"It'll take some practice," Zack said, standing over him. "Don't wander too far."

Joel grimaced in pain and rubbed his head. His splinted leg stuck out off the edge of the bed. "Thanks, Doc. Now take Elizabeth to town for me, will you?"

Nobody moved.

After a pause, Zack turned toward the door where Elizabeth stood wishing she could vanish. After giving in to her fervent plea last night, Joel had turned gallant today and asked Zack Danvers, as a favor, to escort Elizabeth into town. Ever since, Elizabeth had been having second thoughts about Independence Day. The idea had been to get *away* from Zack, not end up alone with him again.

"Are you ready?" Zack's voice was uncommonly soft, a touch unsteady, yet when she looked up, his expression was hard, and she couldn't tell what he thought of the idea.

"I'm not sure." She fled ahead to the kitchen, where she stood at the counter pump, confused.

Granny was right on her heels. "Nothing's wrong, is there?"

She managed to shake her head and made a great show of pumping water to wash her hands. "I don't think I should leave Joel. He's too unsteady on the crutches . . . and he'll be bored."

"Pshaw! No one's ever been bored here on July the Fourth," Granny Sikes declared as she followed her in and carefully set a cake into a cardboard box. "Not even Joel."

Despite Granny's encouraging words, Elizabeth couldn't seem to stop her hands from shaking. She grabbed a towel to dry them as she quickly reviewed all the reasons she shouldn't go anywhere with Zack Danvers.

"Zack has his own horse," she said.

"He can tie it to your wagon," Granny pointed out.

"He doesn't want to take me to town."

Granny cast a suspicious gaze on Elizabeth. "Something wrong with the doctor?"

"No, nothing," she said too hastily, adding in a more relaxed tone, "nothing at all. It's just that I'm probably inconveniencing him."

"Humph," said Granny. "Don't know what else he's got to do now that he's seen Joel."

He might want to go swimming, Elizabeth thought. The image of Zack Danvers swimming in the creek, water glistening off his strong bare shoulders, taunted her. Zack must have been laughing at her, seeing her in that ridiculous clothing yesterday. "If I'd known he was bringing crutches for Joel today, I'd never have said I wanted to go."

"I'll make sure Joel doesn't slip and fall," Granny said. "I'm going to watch him practice."

Footsteps approached the kitchen, and then Zack Danvers was once again looking at her. "Ready now?" he asked softly.

"She's as ready as an apple crop come fall." Granny looked from one to the other and then opened the door. "Now get on, Elizabeth, and for one day don't worry about this place. The apples don't know it's a holiday, and you can bet they'll keep on growing without you watching them." And with that, Granny pressed the cake box into Elizabeth's hands. "This is turning staler than a fence post in January. Take it away."

Zack smiled good-naturedly and moved toward the door. "Don't do any doctoring I wouldn't."

Granny grinned. "I've got remedies your medical books never dreamed of."

"If it's a jar of twigs and leaves steeping in whiskey, keep it hidden away from Joel."

"Get." She waved a broom at them. "You never mind my tonic."

Pete and Clara stood in the doorway, staring wide-eyed at the shelf of canning jars, which as far as anyone could tell, contained nothing more potent than peaches, then ran for the wagon.

And so they went to town, side by side, Zack and Elizabeth in front, Pete and Clara in the back of the plain old buckboard, rambling past the apple trees and bunchgrass and sagebrush. Overhead a clear blue sky promised a hot day.

The box containing the lemon iced cake was covered with a linen dishtowel and sat on the seat between Elizabeth and Zack. Nothing else separated them. Once, Elizabeth hazarded a glance at Zack, enough to admire his high collar and bow tie. A gold watch chain dangled from the pocket of his vest, and his sleeves were rolled up to reveal his muscled forearms. His denim pants fit his legs snugly and were tucked into western boots. His hat brim was worn low over his forehead. She could see the shadow of his beard, dark and masculine, and there was a fine sheen of perspiration on his forehead.

She fanned herself because already her dress clung to her. Only her good taffeta dress had seemed special enough for the occasion; however, it was hotter than she'd been prepared for. She tried to look at the scenery, but Zack's hands moved on the reins, spurring the horses on, and her gaze was drawn to them. They were sensitive hands, slim-fingered and gentle, and she'd spent hours watching how his hands moved over Joel's leg. She still remembered those hands on her waist, holding her tightly, sending sparks up and down her body, while guiding her through a dance.

What was she thinking of? She was prim and plain, not the sort of woman a man like Zack would desire. Her first fiancé had as much as said so. . . .

A moment later they went over a rut, and the box containing the cake jumped. Both of them reached for it at the same time, he with his right hand, she with her left. Their hands touched, and they both pulled away as if burned.

The cake box was wobbling on the buckboard seat, rattling softly. Elizabeth took the cake box onto her lap and looked straight ahead, praying the wind would not blow off her straw hat or the dust coat her dress.

"It's going to be a lovely day," she said.

"Yes."

"I'm surprised how the sagebrush grows."

"That it does."

It was an agony, that last half mile to town.

"Where do you want to be let out?" he asked, slanting a glance at her.

She looked up, startled by the haunted look in his eyes. "Anywhere on Main Street," she said, her throat tight, her voice quiet. "It's a small town." Too small. However was she going to avoid this man all day?

"Your brother's making a speech," she said stiffly.

His voice reflected some pain she could only guess at. "No disrespect to Ben—or to your brother, Elizabeth—but I'm not much interested in all the patriotic stuff today."

Somehow she was not surprised. If a man would run away from a patriotic band, he'd run away from speeches, too. On the contrary, Elizabeth was most interested in Ben's speech. It had taken her two evenings bent beside the lamp at the kitchen table, but polishing Ben's speech had been a welcome change from all the physical labor. She was proud of her efforts and anxious to hear Ben's address.

"Where'd you say you want to get out?" Zack said as the town came into view.

Words came so much harder with this man. "Anywhere you want to park the wagon would be fine," she said at last.

He reined in right in front of the mercantile, the Gustavsons jumped out, and while Elizabeth handed the cake to Clara, Zack came around to hand her down, his grip tight and sure. When she was out, he held her hand a second longer than was necessary. "I'll park at the livery—"

"I can find the wagon myself, so don't trouble yourself about driving me back."

She looked him square in the face, steeling herself against his blue eyes, his tousled black hair, the taut expression on his lean face, but her knees weren't as strong as she'd thought. Why didn't Joel, her fiancé, make her feel this way?

After tipping his hat, he was gone, and she watched him till the crowd swallowed up him and the wagon. That, she told herself, was the last time she'd have to deal with Zack Danvers today. And good riddance. She turned to survey the celebration.

Across the street the mercantile was decked out in red, white, and blue bunting, and on the boardwalk the familiar tuba and trumpet and clarinet players were rehearsing, still as out of tune as when they'd welcomed her at the railroad depot. She was actually jostled in place. Why, she'd never dreamed that when all the people in the valley came to town there'd be this many.

Mrs. Hankins rushed up and took the cake from Clara, and it was passed hand over hand to some anonymous person in charge of food for the picnic. The Gustavson children ran off, and Elizabeth was still watching Clara's little overall-clad figure when Maddie, pretty in brown silk that just matched the soft brown of her snapping eyes, bustled up.

"I've heard about your bloomers," Maddie whispered in her ear. "What does Joel think?"

"He hasn't seen them, but Pete thinks I could pass for Annie Oakley."

They laughed like two old friends. Oh, but it was a grand day, and as she looked around, Elizabeth decided that the Fourth of July was the Fourth of July, no matter whether it was in the staid East or in the wild and woolly West. True, the speakers' platform here was made of raw timber, the listeners stood in dirt instead of on lawns of mowed grass, the ladies wore homespun dresses and had sun-darkened skin. As the clarinet squeaked its way through "The Star-spangled Banner," contentment washed over her.

The band was the signal for the start of a parade of returning volunteers from the Philippines, old veterans from the Civil War, children waving American flags from a wagon decorated in red, white, and blue, and last of all the town's only three bicycles. On either side of Main Street bystanders cheered wildly.

Ben and the mayor of Eden Creek both stepped up to the makeshift platform. A stiff wind came up, blowing dust down the street. The women held on to their hats, and men's ties blew wildly, and then a quartet of men stepped up on the platform and led the crowd in reciting the Pledge of Allegiance. As soon as they finished, Ben stood, hat in hand, and began talking about the great lessons of 1776 remaining alive for the children of today.

When the speech ended, there was more applause, and Maddie leaned over. "See? It was a wonderful speech, wasn't it?"

"It was an insult, that's what!"

Both Maddie and Elizabeth whirled to find Miss Yates behind them. The schoolteacher, in starched blouse and dark skirt, looked as prim as a new-sawed two-by-four. In her wake trailed a rancher whom Maddie had identified in a hurried whisper as Antonio Mendez, a sheepman who was taking English lessons from Miss Yates.

"What happened to *my* speech?" Miss Yates demanded of Maddie.

Elizabeth's heart dropped to her stomach. Miss Yates's speech? Her knees quivered like those of a schoolgirl who'd forgotten her times tables, and she waited for a ruler to lash her knuckles. She'd had no idea . . . Maddie hadn't said Miss Yates had had a hand in Ben's speech.

"It didn't sound at all like what I wrote for Ben."

"There's no need to carry on so," Maddie said. "Your speeches are good, but your style could use a bit of smoothing."

"Eastern polish? Finishing school polish?" Miss Yates turned on Elizabeth. Her voice was withering, her straw hat shaking. "You . . . you did that, didn't you?"

There were some women it wasn't worth reasoning with. Smoothing the road was the only way to get along with them, and Elizabeth was determined to get along. "I'm sorry you didn't like what I did."

"Ever since you came here you've tried to show me up. It wasn't enough to get yourself engaged to Joel. Now you've got to show me up in matters of education."

With a swirl of petticoats, she stuck her nose up in the air and headed off, handsome Antonio trailing her, using broken English to offer up words of consolation.

Elizabeth stood there, shoulders slumping, until Maddie said softly, "Miss Yates considers herself the town's reigning authority, the fountain of wisdom, the arbiter of all things cultural. That's why she thinks Antonio isn't good enough for her."

"She hates me for taking Joel, doesn't she?"

Maddie hesitated, then said carefully, "She had her hopes pinned on Joel—she likes his big-city polish—but don't worry, I heard through the grapevine that now she's set her sights on my brother-in-law."

"Zack?"

Elizabeth's heart skipped a beat at the thought of any woman with Zack Danvers. She came close to telling Maddie about her decision to call off her engagement to Joel. Then word could get back to Zack and to Miss Yates . . . but no, she decided that wouldn't be fair without telling Joel himself first. And then the moment for any confiding was lost.

The men's quartet was singing "Flow Gently, Sweet Afton." Looking across the sea of serious faces and military uniforms, she found him, his expression unreadable. Just briefly she caught his eye, then turned away, embarrassed at her own wanton thoughts. Whatever would he think?

Zack stood at the back of the boardwalk, torn between riding off to the hills for the day and staying to stare at Elizabeth Sheldon. When she turned away in the crowd, an anchor was pulled, and once again he was adrift. He felt surprisingly numb.

The red, white, and blue seemed less vivid than he remembered, the music less rousing. The uniforms still managed to bother him, though. The crisp khaki freshness, the men marching proudly with their medals. It was all he could do to keep his hands balled into fists and not lash out at some innocent soldier, lash at the smug pride they dredged up for the Fourth.

You're alive and Harry's dead! How can you march in a parade and celebrate your heroes? How can you, when Harry's . . . dead? He jammed his hand down into his pocket and closed it around the only coin remaining there, his lucky peseta.

Another nightmare had awakened him last night, and he'd spent the hours till dawn flipping that coin in the air. Heads, he'd please Maddie and attend the Fourth of the July party. Tails, he'd ignore it all and go for a long ride across the tall sagebrush. It was natural, then, to tune out the speechmaking and one by one listen instead to the memories.

Harry died. Too many men died.

But it wasn't your fault.

The medical supplies weren't there.

But it wasn't your fault.

You got thirsty.

But it wasn't your fault.

You were not God. Men were flesh and blood. They got thirsty, ached, envied, cheated. . . . No, he was not God.

His throat constricted.

Desperately Zack searched the crowd for Elizabeth and ran a hand over his perspiring face. There she was, her honey-blond hair barely visible in the crowd, and then just as quickly he lost sight of her.

The mayor was droning on and on about the lessons of war for the young people. . . .

Zack turned away from the parade and staggered up the narrow alley between the mercantile and the newspaper

office, heat pulsating through his head like a fever coming
and going. He braced an arm against the side of the raw
board building, afraid he might be physically ill. Then, after
gulping in air, he turned and leaned back against the board
siding.

As soon as he felt better he made his way to the boardwalk
with quick strides, intending to make his escape, and that
was when he saw Lizzie again. The panic subsided, at
least momentarily. As the speeches and songs dragged on,
he found a way to watch her surreptitiously. She was remarkably easy on the eyes, prettier than the view from his room,
and despite his better intentions, he decided to stay awhile.

Her dress was the color of a mountain bluebird. All the way
into town he'd wanted to tell her how pretty she looked, but
hadn't found the right words. How did you say something so
personal to a woman who was engaged to another man?

It was Joel's fault he was here, Joel's fault for demanding
escort service for his fiancé. When Joel had asked him to drive
Elizabeth into town, it had never occurred to him to beg off.
Never mind that the night before he'd debated attending the
celebrations at all, had even flipped a coin to decide. He'd
called heads, but the coin had come up tails.

Tails. Tails, and he told himself he could skip the celebrations. But then this morning Joel had, out of the blue, mentioned Elizabeth and all of a sudden Zack wanted to go into
town.

Oh, he invented all manner of excuses to explain his sudden change of heart: He needed to fix that squeaky wheel on
Ben's wagon. He wanted to hear Ben's speech. He wanted
to avoid a lecture from Maddie. It was a practical decision,
having nothing to do with Elizabeth's need for an escort.

Lizzie. The petite figure. The soft blue dress. The honey-
colored curls. By turns prim, petulant, passionate in her
hatred of him, determined . . . vulnerable. He couldn't get
her out of his mind. If he was smart, he'd go back to the
hotel, shut himself in his room, and forget her. After all, Joel
was on crutches now. It was only a matter of time before she

wed the dandy. It was time to visit the railroad depot again, time to think about leaving Eden Creek for good.

Without warning, someone clapped an arm about him. "Hey, Lieutenant Danvers, how come you're not wearing your uniform today?"

It was Johnny Morgan, a rancher's son, recently returned from Manila. "You came home on the *Grant,* didn't you? I know you docked at San Francisco same time as I did. Where's your uniform? You on furlough?"

Zack shrugged. Damn fresh-faced kid had too many questions.

"I was mustered out and left the uniform in my duffel."

"Aw, don't pack it away already. You should dress up for the picnic. Impresses the single ladies, you know," he said with a wink, "and the competition's keen. It's a great day for the veterans, Lieutenant Danvers."

"No!"

Johnny blinked and shrank back as if he'd been shot at point-blank range.

Try again, Zack. "No, thanks, Johnny," he managed to choke out, hunkering down against the building.

"Hey, Doc Danvers, I'm sorry. I know the war wasn't a bed of roses. . . . Maybe you'll stay for the races, huh?"

"Yeah, maybe." When all the patriotic displays ended and the sport began, no one was more relieved than Zack. He managed a nod, and satisfied, Johnny Morgan left, calling out to a pretty girl who passed by and running to catch up to her.

Someone grabbed Zack and without waiting for a refusal told him he was needed to act as a referee in the footraces.

Hesitation came first, then a shrug of the shoulders, and moments later he moved with the crowd down the street to the finish line. The wind had died down, and he was hot. He longed to take a swim, that was what, and the thought reminded him of Elizabeth Sheldon standing on the bank of the creek dressed in overalls and rubber boots, her face smeared with amber axle grease, looking as if she'd caught

Adam without his fig leaf. For the first time that day he smiled.

He looked around in the crowd for her again and found her standing with Maddie way down by the starting line for the girls' races. She was bent over whispering encouraging words to the only little girl who was not outfitted in a starched white dress.

Clara, in overalls and bare feet, stood out from the other girls like a thistle in a daisy patch, but she didn't seem to care. Like a practiced runner she knelt low, awaiting the signal. Maddie dropped a handkerchief, and they all flew forward, Clara moving as fast as if a Spanish Mauser were at her back. Even Zack was impressed. Seconds later Clara was first over the line, a girl with a big white bow in her hair a close second. Immediately the two girls collided, and Zack moved to untangle them.

"I won! I won!" Clara shouted, tugging at his watch chain so hard she nearly ripped his vest pocket off.

Emma Hankins, who was still bragging about winning the recital at school, pulled a long face. "It's not fair! You shouldn't have run in your bare feet. None of the other girls did."

"Oh, yeah? Ask the umpire."

"Who's the umpire?" sniffed Emma.

Johnny Morgan walked up. "Call it, Zack. You're the ump."

Flinching, Zack suddenly was the cynosure of all eyes, the very thing he'd dreaded. He considered flipping the coin in his pocket. In fact, he drew it out, and tossed it in the air, then changed his mind and caught it. This clearly called for a ruling, not a coin toss.

He looked at the two little girls, Clara in her bare feet and Emma Hankins in black high-top shoes. He looked at their feet, first one then the other. He hadn't come to Eden Creek to play God and judge, and the irony of this task was not lost on him.

"There's nothing in the rules," he said at last, "about whether shoes count or not. Clara Gustavson can't be disqualified for running barefoot."

Clara jumped up and down for joy.

Emma Hankins was yanked away into the comforting embrace of her plump mother's dress. "Well," huffed Mrs. Hankins, "if we'd known that, Emma could have stripped off her shoes and stockings and come in first."

"Clara would be glad to have Emma's shoes if Emma cares to give them up," Maddie said from the background, and the crowd laughed.

Even before the laughter died out, Johnny Morgan called for the crowd to move to the field across from the mercantile—one of the few vacant lots on Main Street for the three-legged races.

"Single folks will compete first." Not a surprising request, since Johnny Morgan, so handsome in his uniform, had a pretty girl in tow.

When the crowd had reached the vacant lot, Maddie pushed Elizabeth into the circle of participants. "Come on, Elizabeth, this is no fun unless some new people try it. Antonio, you team up with Miss Yates," she suggested, ignoring Miss Yates's longing look at Zack Danvers.

Miss Yates shook off the sheepman and stalked off, declaring in a most dignified voice that she could put her time to better use helping with the food.

Before Elizabeth could retreat, Ben had taken her arm and drawn her over to where Zack stood. "Zack can stand in for Joel, can't you, Zack?"

Elizabeth looked at Zack, and she gulped. It wasn't a question of whether Zack could stand in for Joel. It was a question of whether he should. Just the suggestion had made Elizabeth's pulse speed up. Her heart was pounding, her face felt as hot as the stovepipe, and she was sure everyone must be laughing inside at her predicament. Prim Miss Sheldon having to race with that brooding Lieutenant Danvers. What a spectacle that would be! She was so aghast at the idea she couldn't move.

And then Zack looked at her, his eyes dark blue, like a midnight sky.

Please say no. . . .

But he didn't. On the other hand, he didn't say yes, either.

"Get over here, Zack," Ben said with a smile. "You owe us something for your board. Something fun."

Where was the strict and sanctimonious Miss Yates when Elizabeth needed her?

Maddie joined in the chorus of approval. "Zack, you're the perfect choice. If Elizabeth falls and breaks her leg, we know you can heal her."

He started walking toward her, and she backed right into Maddie. "I'm not sure . . ."

"Nonsense, this event is only for unmarried people, so you have to, Elizabeth, you simply have to. Just think of Zack Danvers as a substitute for Joel."

Zack Danvers, with his dark brooding face, was anything but a substitute.

He was simply overwhelming, and suddenly she wished she hadn't come today.

The next thing she knew he stood shoulder to shoulder with her, staring down at her from so great a height. There was a smile in his eyes, a wicked smile she didn't think he'd learned in medical school. It was the sort of smile some men were born with.

"Gotcha," Ben said, laughing. He swung a rope before her eyes, then bent and knotted it around Zack's ankle.

He hesitated before touching Elizabeth's ankle, and Maddie stepped in. "I'll take it from here." She knelt before Elizabeth.

How could you do this, Maddie?

As if Maddie had read her mind, she said, "Come on, Elizabeth, be a good sport about this. Joel will feel bad if you don't have fun, you know. Now, give me your ankle." Kneeling, she reached for Elizabeth's black high-top, the right one, and with her hand, exerted enough pressure so that Elizabeth had to move her foot next to Zack's. Her black shoe was dwarfed next to his big brown western boot.

The rope went around her ankle, in a moment resourceful Maddie had secured a knot, and Elizabeth was shackled to Zack Danvers. Why, she barely had time to untie her little straw sailor hat and hand it to Maddie.

She wobbled, almost lost her balance, and Zack reached around to the back of her waist and steadied her. His thigh touched hers, burning right through her dress.

She wobbled again, and everyone tittered.

"Hey, Doc," Harry called, "what d'ya think of *that* leg splint? A little more fun than the one you put on the lady's fiancé, huh?"

Oh, they were all going to have their sport with this.

"There's a trick to this, I believe," he said gently, his voice neutral. Then his voice, deep and dark, was close to her ear.

Zack's hand went around her waist again, sending little shivers down her. "Don't let them make you nervous or we'll fall," he whispered against her hair.

She froze.

But he kept talking, his breath warm where it taunted her hair. "Balance on your outside foot, and move the other one when I move."

"I can't." Suddenly she was giggling, embarrassed as a schoolgirl.

"It's like hopping. Try it," he said, ignoring her lack of composure.

All she could feel was the insistent pressure of his thigh against her, strong, ever so masculine.

She felt the gentle pressure of his arm about her waist, warm, perfectly fit. She was drawn, as if her body had a will of its own, close against him and simply melted against him. It was no different from dancing when she had responded to his lead.

Don't think, just move in rhythm with him.

One, two, three . . . hop on the outside foot. His own outer foot matched hers in distance, and when they landed, his arm gripped her waist to steady her.

One, two, three . . . hop on the inside foot. Their feet moved at the same time. Her skirt grazed his pant leg.

She got to the starting line without falling.

There were five other couples at the start line, drawn in the dirt with a stick. The finish was the outer wall of the barbershop, about three wagon lengths across the vacant lot.

Someone counted: One, two, three, go!

Beside her, Antonio Mendez and the blacksmith's oldest daughter fell in a heap of arms and legs. But Elizabeth managed to jump with her inner leg and then, as if on some unspoken signal, hop with her outer leg at the same time as Zack. They moved as one. They were leading.

"Win this one for Joel," Clara called out above the laughing crowd, and that was when Elizabeth lost her rhythm.

She felt it happening as if time had slowed down, in a fall that she could watch happening. One of them—was it her?—hopped on the middle foot while the other one stood still. Their knees bumped against each other. Instinctively she clutched at Zack's shirt. Something ripped. She went dizzy. The world spun around.

The wild grass and the sky tilted crazily while Zack tugged her toward him. She pulled against him and screamed like a silly schoolgirl. Oh, God. No. This couldn't be happening, not in front of everyone in town.

But it did.

They fell in a tangled heap into the scraggly sage, Elizabeth on the bottom, and for the first time she was in Dr. Zachary Danvers's arms, molded against his contours.

Zack.

No, not Zack. *Joel.* She had to remember. She was Joel's.

But it was Zack's warmth pressing against her, sending fire through her body. It was as if she'd never seen before, never felt, never existed until this moment lying beneath him, smelling his musky skin, touching his warmth, hearing the vibration of his muffled curse, and shamelessly she wanted to go on lying like that.

But then, with sure movements, he rolled away from her and pulled her to a sitting position.

Without once looking at her, Zack calmly reached down and untied the rope. His hand fumbled with the knot a couple of times, and finally flung the cord aside. Ever so gently he reached for her and pulled her to her feet, silent, his expression giving nothing away.

She stepped back, smoothing her wrinkled skirt, and stood, blushing, staring at the toes of her shoes. Somewhere deep inside her a clock had been wound. It didn't just tick; it sang. It shouted. It sent vibrations right down to her toes. She'd never felt this way, not in a million dreams, and not even the cheering crowd could still the sensations.

She turned to see Johnny and a pretty ranch girl touch the wall of the barbershop, then collapse against it, laughing. The winners.

Zack was also watching the winners. His shirt was grass-stained, his black hair ruffled.

In her mind she was still lying in the sweet summer grass tangled in his arms.

And still engaged to Joel, his patient.

She was so far off that she never noticed when Zack came up behind her. "We lost," he said softly, so close behind her that his breath ruffled the hair at the nape of her neck.

She nodded and swallowed hard; then they were separated in the crowd.

For the rest of that day Elizabeth kept occupied. She attended a picnic in the cottonwood grove by the hotel riverfront, but she couldn't remember what she ate. She listened to singing at the hall, but the songs were not as memorable as the beating of her heart. And at the end of the day she heard the firecrackers set off by the boys of the town, though their explosions paled compared to those she'd heard earlier when she and Zack collided.

She dared not put a word to what she felt.

She did dare, though, to leave town as soon as politeness would allow.

And later, alone in her makeshift cot in the house, with her fiancé asleep in another room, she lay awake long into the night.

10

On the fifth of July, Zack didn't wake up until dawn. For the first time in a long spring of nightmares, he had slept without interruption.

He lay there, trying not to remember the soft curves of Elizabeth Sheldon, but soon discovered waking dreams could be as agonizing as any of his nightmares.

Abruptly he threw back the covers and got up. The hotel slumbered late, uncommonly so for a weekday. He figured that everyone else, exhausted from the night of excitement, was still asleep, and for an hour he had only the crackling cookstove to keep him company. In less than half that time he'd brewed himself a pot of coffee.

He was sipping the second mugful when Maddie, with her familiar smile and soft brown eyes, joined him. Without warning, she set his black satchel on the table. A gift from his mother when he graduated from Northwestern Medical College, that bag contained everything he wanted to forget.

"I found this in your bag and thought you might like to have it."

"What were you doing in my duffel?"

"Moving it. Seeing if your uniform could use an airing. You don't want to get it moth-eaten." While she talked she heated up the frypan for eggs.

"Did you enjoy yourself yesterday?" she asked while tying on an apron.

Enjoy himself? He didn't know what that meant anymore. Was he supposed to have enjoyed holding Elizabeth Sheldon in his arms in full view of the entire town? It had taken all his willpower to act nonchalant, all his strength to fight off the immediate reaction of his body, which had been to meld with hers. Enjoy himself? Hardly.

And looking at his black bag nearly undid two months' worth of healing. Nothing in it would help anyone. Not his scalpel, not his amputation saw, not his forceps. Cholera, the grippe, the ague, diphtheria, measles, tuberculosis, gunshot wounds—that was what a country doctor had to look forward to. And that didn't count dealing with spittoons and slop pails and assistants who were more likely to faint than hold the lantern steady. Death gave no quarter.

"Granny does all right here," he said, voice gruff. "I tease her a lot, but some of those folk remedies aren't bad."

"I thought you might have some real medicines."

Real medicine. She probably meant the little pieces of paper folded up around crushed powders and crystals, little vials of tinctures: laudanum, ipecac, paregoric, belladonna, quinine, morphine. They were all there in his satchel. But from what he'd seen last year in the Philippines, he knew that the results from the contents of his bag were less reliable than tossing a coin.

He pulled the peseta out of his pocket and, after tossing it up for Maddie's benefit, caught it. "Tails . . . the patient will live . . . or shall we try for heads? It doesn't much matter, you know."

Maddie put a sisterly arm on his shoulder. "Zack, you're too hard on yourself. If you're not going to tell us what happened, at least quit berating yourself. Grief takes time. You can't carry all the sorrow from the war on your shoulders."

No, only one death. Harry's death. Zack's little black bag had been useless there.

She gave him a sideways look, then took a deep breath. "A

couple of people from town—Mrs. Atwood and Mr. Gantt— have been asking if you'd examine them."

"No!"

"You can't turn them away now. They know you're a doctor, Zack."

And when he met her gaze, she said again, "They know."

"Maddie, don't ask it." Shoving back his chair, he stood, like a man caught. Expression hurt, his sister-in-law bit her lip and turned away to the stove. Immediately he was sorry. In a conciliatory voice, he said, "Maddie, I can't spend the rest of my life sitting beside patients waiting for them to die."

"Life has to go on, Zack. Most people are not dying. They just want you to treat simple problems like aches and bunions and . . . you know."

He knew only too well. "When I'm ready for it."

"Shall I tell them you'll think about it?"

With a harsh exhalation, he nodded. "All right." Maybe he needed something to occupy his mind, after all.

Maddie's shoulders rose and fell in a sigh, and she changed the subject. "Has Joel paid you for setting his leg and for all those house calls?"

"I don't need the two bucks. It was on the house."

So he simply bent his head over his coffee mug. He drew his timepiece out of his pocket. Only five minutes had passed since the last time he'd looked.

"Where are you in a hurry to this morning?" Maddie asked.

Were all females so nosy, even the friendly ones? Zack poured himself more coffee and walked casually to the kitchen door.

"Same as always."

Maddie held a bowl against her hip and whipped eggs. "You looked pretty funny in that three-legged race yesterday."

"I felt funny," he growled. This of all topics he wanted to avoid.

"Well, you've got to admit you and Elizabeth didn't break any bones in the fun."

That was a leading question if he ever heard one, and Zack knew exactly how to steer away from it.

"Any professional dignity was probably lost in the fall."

"Oh, I don't know about that," Maddie mused. "Joel would say you were the perfect gentleman."

Darn her matchmaking instincts. He'd rather have heard what a coward he was; he'd rather have fended off another plea for him to stay and be the doctor in Eden Creek. Anything but this.

"I don't know that being a gentleman has anything to do with losing the race." He got up to pour himself another cup of coffee and put a hand under the bowl before the eggs could slide from Maddie to the floor.

"Zack," Maddie began, then paused. She set the bowl on the counter and wiped her hands on her apron. "Zack?"

"What is it?"

"Well, this is none of my business . . ."

"You're right." The subject of medicine was closed.

"Please, Zack, just once, take off all that tough bluff you're wearing and talk to me."

He stared at the stovepipe as if it contained patience.

"I won't repeat a thing we say to Ben. I promise."

Zack remained silent, his back turned to Maddie in defiance, but she rushed on nevertheless.

"I mean, it's rather bold of me to speculate, but I like Elizabeth tremendously, and yesterday I finally got to know her better. . . . She's out there on that orchard all alone so much of the time that you're probably the one who sees the most of her."

Maddie paused.

Zack felt the dull thud of his pulse, and his throat was as dry as a summer desert.

"Do you think Joel and Elizabeth are suited?"

Turning, Zack looked Maddie in the eye. "Does that matter?"

She shrugged. "Why shouldn't it?"

In three strides Zack stood at the back door, which looked

out on the wide spot in the river. A hotel guest was rowing around in one of the little boats. Ducks were following.

For a few seconds the only sound was the hiss of eggs being poured into the pan. When the sizzling died down, Maddie said, "To a woman it matters a lot. I worry that she's done so much of the work around that orchard that she'll decide she doesn't need Joel."

"Maybe that's for her and Joel to decide."

"What do you think of Joel?" Maddie asked.

What Zack thought of Joel personally was not repeatable to a lady's ears. "He's a willing patient."

"No, I mean as a man. When he's well enough to work, what do you expect he'll be like?"

"I don't know. By then, I'll probably move on."

He could feel Maddie's gaze on his back, challenging him. *Are you certain, Zack Danvers?*

Reaching into his pocket, he wrapped his fingers around the peseta. It was till there. Chance. Luck. Fate. Whichever way it fell, did it really matter?

"You don't have to move on. People here like you, and I happen to think you like *them*."

Zack wasn't sure whether that was a hint or just an idle comment. He had to turn to read the expression on Maddie's face. What he saw was a challenge.

You like Elizabeth, Zack, and you know it, she seemed to say.

She's forbidden, he wanted to reply.

"I wouldn't worry, Maddie," Zack said with as nonchalant a shrug as he could manage. "If Joel doesn't marry Elizabeth, there'll be another man. Aren't there ample single men around here?"

"Orville Gustavson, for example?" Maddie's voice held an ironic note.

"He's too wild."

"You've never met him."

"I feel as if I know him already."

"Then our liveryman, Bill Brown."

Zack whipped around. Brown was an oaf. "You mean he's single?"

"Very, and so's the clerk at the depot. Otis."

"A boy." With a boy's impetuousness.

"Elizabeth's not that old. Now, the sheepman, Antonio Mendez, is a solid man, but he's not right for her."

A slow hammering began somewhere inside his head. Zack leaned against the frame of the back door. It was open and the sound of birds squawking covered Maddie's voice. Clara must be scaring magpies from the orchard.

"Actually none of them are right for her." Maddie stood there waiting for a reply.

"No." His monosyllabic answer came from far away.

Of course not. No one in this town was good enough for the prim Elizabeth Sheldon from Massachusetts. Not even Zack.

"She'd be better off with Joel," Maddie said on a sigh.

A shaft of pain shot through Zack.

Maddie was busy stirring scrambled eggs, folding them over and over and salting them.

"I just think she's too good, too nice, for a marriage of convenience. I mean, she doesn't love Joel, does she?"

She looked at Zack as if he should know, and he slowly lowered his mug. It was suddenly hard to swallow. "I haven't asked."

Maddie held a plate of steaming eggs in front of his nose and lured him to the table, to the seat right by the window. "Well, I guess it's none of my business. Eat up. You said you were anxious to get over there."

He had. He still was. But he didn't feel like eating breakfast.

On the way to the orchard, he rode as slowly as possible.

If he had his way, there'd be no Joel Emory there. No Granny, with her talk of spring tonics.

He turned into the lane leading past rows and rows of green apples waiting to mature. The screen door of the little house slammed, and he expected to be accosted by a barefoot Clara, who had beamed all yesterday after learning her name would be in the paper for winning first place in the footrace. "I even beat you and Elizabeth," Clara had taunted smartly.

And so she had. He and Elizabeth had ended up in a heap, tangled in each other's legs and arms. He'd never taken a woman in his arms in quite so warm and unexpected a way.

"What have you got to smile about this morning, Dr. Danvers?"

Granny's voice startled him, and he looked up to see her standing there shaking out a checkered tablecloth.

"That's the happiest I've seen you look since you found out about the tonic I poured into Joel's coffee. It's a good restorative. I've used it to treat a dozen ailments . . . but you think you're smarter than an old lady." With a flick of her wrists, Granny sent the tablecloth cracking through the air, and then it landed in a limp heap in her arms.

Zack moved up onto the porch and held open the door to the kitchen for her. "Don't flatter yourself, Granny. Could be I'm going to see Joel walks proper on those crutches and then leave on the next train. I don't care if you want to pour a dozen spring tonics down him. Keep him sober, though."

Granny pursed her mouth into a wrinkled prune. "Could be you'll decide to stay, too." She preceded him into the house, chattering all the way to the kitchen table.

"Something tells me this town isn't big enough for you and me, Granny," he said with a grin.

She was spreading the tablecloth, running her gnarled hands over the wrinkles, smoothing them out. "I can make room for you in this town if I have to. I never claimed to be an expert at setting bones, but I can do it."

While she talked, Zack tried to politely stare around her, through the kitchen toward the parlor and bedroom. He wanted to know the whereabouts of Elizabeth. And judging by the gleam in her eye, Granny knew it.

The old woman moved to the stove where a pot of some strange-smelling liquid brewed. If that was lunch, Zack would go hungry. Usually he liked Granny's cooking, but not if a magic potion was included among the ingredients.

"Joel's staring at those crutches you brought him as if they were pricklier than summer sage."

He didn't move.

"But if it's Elizabeth you want to talk to first, she's not here. . . . Clara tells me you and she got hog-tied into the town's annual three-legged race."

"You might say they roped us into it," he deadpanned.

"Clara says you fell."

"Clara's quite a chatterbox, isn't she?"

"Not around Joel, she's not. Elizabeth and I see that she eats, but the child's without a father even. She's got a need to confide in someone. Follows Elizabeth around like a puppy."

"So Clara's working the orchard today?" Subtlety didn't matter anymore. What mattered was finding Elizabeth and knowing if his pulse would run normal. He needed to confirm his suspicion that his reaction to Elizabeth yesterday had been only imagination.

Granny smiled and, after crumbling a few more fragrant leaves into the pot, stirred her concoction. It smelled like a combination of anise and sage. "Clara's been invited to the Hankins ranch to play dolls and try on hand-me-down dresses. That was Elizabeth's doing. She told Clara it'd be nice for her to wear a dress when her pa comes home . . . *if* he comes home, that is."

"And is Elizabeth at the Hankins ranch, too?" Granny knew how to drag this out longer than a first baby.

Bobbing her head toward the far side of the orchard, the edge farthest from town, she said, "She's out in that orchard. She wouldn't wait for Pete. Won't wait for nobody. If you ask me, she needs some man to talk sense into her about climbing all these trees."

It was tantamount to giving him the job. Granny might be thickheaded when it came to defending her spring tonic, but in other matters she was remarkably clearheaded.

Too clearheaded.

"Tell Joel to practice up," Zack said. "When he can walk

by himself, I'll turn him loose to help Elizabeth out in the orchard." He was already walking before he'd finished talking.

All he wanted was to see her, no matter what excuse it took, and he wanted to see her alone before some busybody like Miss Yates arrived bearing pies and flirtatious smiles.

Behind him he heard a soft chuckle and the slam of the screen door.

Still in her nightgown, hair streaming down her back, Miss Agnes Yates yanked open her dresser drawer and pulled out her writing box. She pushed aside the stack of metal pie dishes on her tiny table and, ignoring the clatter, sat down and assembled her writing materials—paper, quill, ink bottle, blotter—then lined them up with precision.

Oh, but she was in a fine mettle. For ages, she'd been calling on Joel Emory and plying Zachary Danvers with homemade pies. Now she was out of canned huckleberries. Worse, she was out of patience, and it was all Elizabeth Sheldon's fault.

How dare that eastern bluestocking be so forward as to arrange a truce between Clara and Emma Hankins? To allow the bad seed of Eden Creek to play with the fine children of a member of the school board? Didn't Elizabeth know her place at all? It was too much, especially the way she threw herself at Zack Danvers yesterday in that race. A truly shocking spectacle of abandon. Agnes had fought back tears of frustration until she reached the picnic, where the women had brought up the idea of forming a Ladies' Literary Society.

Agnes had jumped at the chance to be president, to be in charge. It was going to be her crowning achievement. Think of the meetings, the intelligent discussions of books and ideas, the beautification of the city. Agnes's dream was to have a park named after her, of course . . . but that would take time, and she had another matter to take care of first—a matter named Elizabeth Sheldon.

Why weren't those silly apple trees and Joel enough to keep Elizabeth away from the other ladies, away from Zack Danvers? But no, she thought bitterly, Elizabeth was one of those rare creatures—a remarkable woman who could juggle everything.

Well, Agnes Yates had a way to divert all that remarkable energy. Division was her favorite subject both in and out of school. So Agnes's plan to divide and thus conquer was neat, absolutely without untidy loose ends like remainders. After dipping her pen in her ink, she shook off the excess drops, addressed an envelope to an orphanage in Boise City, and wrote a brief letter.

Kind Sir:
   As a Christian and a schoolteacher, it pains me to perform such a sad task, but on behalf of the newly formed Ladies' Literary Society of Eden Creek, I feel it incumbent upon me to seek help for a pair of recently orphaned children who have no home in their hour of greatest need . . .

"Granny, where's Doc?" Joel, sounding restless, was sitting on the edge of the bed.

When Granny appeared in the doorway, she stared at him. "What's your rush? You know he won't give you any more laudanum. . . . You haven't been up on crutches today," she noted.

"It's hard to walk on crutches," Joel whined. "Doc Danvers says to take it easy still." He eyed Granny. "How long's he been out there with Elizabeth? They've been getting awfully social lately."

"Never you mind. Maybe he's helping her a bit, too. She's been out toiling in that orchard while you lie here."

"I can't help being laid up, Granny," he said in a peeved voice. "And making me feel guilty doesn't help me. . . . Everything's hard."

"Taking care of the orchard's hard, but Elizabeth's never complained."

In all Granny's years here, no patient had done more to plant new lines on her face or new gray hairs on her head. She'd told him that a dozen times, and that was what her expression said now.

"Doc was here," Joel said. "I heard you talking, and I want to see him. Now, what's taking him and Elizabeth so long?"

"Joel Emory, you bide your time. I've got a new tonic brewing. Sage and bark and a nip of whiskey. Better than any laudanum. Unless you'd rather try honey and vinegar. That cures all."

Joel flopped his head against the pillow and shut his eyes, as if tired. "Bring me some, and then I want the doc."

"Good, then you just lie there and wait for him," Granny called back over her shoulder. "Unless you want to walk some more, and in that case get those crutches out and use 'em."

Moments later, she brought him some of her whiskey-laden "tonic." He gulped it down and sent her off for more. As soon as she left, Joel's eyes snapped open. He could use those crutches all right. There was nothing better to do, but why show off to Granny when he could surprise the good doctor?

Zack heard Elizabeth before he saw her. Granny was right; there ought to be laws against women working this hard. Walking between the last two rows of trees, careful not to fall into the rill, he couldn't see a thing, but soon enough a rustle up in the leaves gave her away.

The wooden ladder stood propped against one of the largest trees on the orchard not far from the scarecrow. Elizabeth was standing on a branch up so high he could barely see her. She was, if one could judge from the number of little green apples cascading to the ground, thinning, reducing the number of apples per branch. Without any warning, an apple hit him hard on the shoulder. A second one battered into him and bounced off to the ground.

"Ouch!" Little green apples had the impact of Mauser bullets if propelled hard enough.

With a baleful glance, he watched it roll to a stop.

The rustling, meanwhile, stopped.

"Who's there?" It was Elizabeth's voice, soft, sounding slightly lonely.

"For God's sake, Lizzie, didn't Joel tell you that people could get killed falling out of trees?"

There was a pause. "Zack?"

"Lizzie?"

"I hate that name." The tone was censorious.

"Come down. This is Joel's job."

No answer.

"Lizzie, I want to see you."

What happened next was so fast that it was all a blur. She started to back down, her bare feet probing for the ladder. She missed the top rung and, before he could move, kicked the thing over. He tried to catch it, but missed, and it landed with a thud in the mud and weeds.

Then she gave a little scream, the leaves rustled, a branch went Cra-a-a-ck and snapped off to fall at his feet. Crouching to dodge it, he remained in place, arms poised to catch her.

A second later she emerged, hanging from a branch, her ankles and feet dangling about a rifle's length off the ground. While she hung there, swaying, he ascertained that life or death was not in the balance and then admired the view from his angle. She was wearing bloomers that clung to her hips in ways skirts never dared. He'd seen a lot of women back east in bloomers, but none of those bloomers had revealed quite so much. So the prim miss was loosening up.

"Don't just stand there, Zack," she squealed, breathless. Her voice was pitched an octave higher than usual.

He was in an advantageous position. While she clung, he circled, deciding if he could possibly help her down without taking her in his arms. Fortunately, body contact seemed the only option.

"I'm here," he said calmly. "All you've got to do is drop."

"While you flip a coin, trying to decide if you'll c-catch me or not?" She said the words between gritted teeth.

"Do I detect a once independent woman now begging for help?"

"Yes, I take back everything I ever said about growing apples alone." With each syllable, the pitch of her voice rose a notch till she was fairly squealing. "Help—me—down—from—here, Zack. I'm slipping! The ladder! Get it!"

"That doesn't sound very efficient."

She closed her eyes and made a sound of exasperation, like a true damsel in distress.

"I owe you this for sleeping on you on the train," he said.

And when his hands closed about her waist, she kicked him in the stomach.

Oomph.

Stung, he let go and circled her from a distance.

"Why'd you kick me?"

"You scared me."

"Well, that was a mean kick, Lizzie. If I were you, I wouldn't kick the only rescuer you've got, especially a man with a shady past."

"Horse manure, Zack. I don't care about your past, only my future."

If prim Lizzie was resorting to unladylike language, clearly enough was enough. Besides, the lady could get physical when provoked. He moved closer and positioned himself to catch her. "All right, I've got you." Reaching up again, he once more encircled her waist with his hands. "Let go."

The instant his hands made contact with her waist, the tension shifted from her to him. Suddenly falling into his arms, she very nearly slid through his hands, but he tightened his grip and slowed her progress, savoring every inch of body contact as she slid down his torso. Her legs against his chest. Her pelvis against his chin. Her breasts against his nose. Her breasts against his chest. Soft woman against taut male. Lizzie . . . Lizzie was a delightful armful, and he prolonged the slide down, in the name of caution. Male caution, as much as caution against broken bones.

Too soon her feet touched something solid—his boot tops,

as a matter of fact. Her toes made little indentations in the leather as she simultaneously threatened the seams of his shirt with her grip. Then she threw her arms around his neck and clung for dear life. He kept his hands at her waist, waiting for her to catch her balance. She pressed tighter.

"Oh, Zack, I was so afraid!"

"I've got you." He made a movement to let her loose, but she clung all the tighter.

"So afraid."

Moments later neither of them had made a move to step away. They were chest to chest, and he could feel the frightened beating of her heart right through her blouse. He could also feel the soft contours of her uncorseted breasts.

"Foolish Lizzie," he murmured and for the first time allowed himself to touch the curls at the nape of her neck.

"I couldn't help it," she murmured. "You scared me."

All he had to do was lift her up by the waist and set her on her feet, but he didn't do so. "Are you all right?" he asked softly.

She nodded, her hair brushing against his cheek like silk against sandpaper.

"It was all your fault, you know," she whispered. "Sneaking up on me like a thief in the night."

"Is that all the reward I get?"

She was clinging so delightfully that he forgot what he was about and leaned down to give her a kiss. It was meant as a teasing kiss, nothing more than mistletoe in July, big brotherly affection. His reward for rescuing her. Her penalty for falling out of the tree. The kind of kiss Joel would not have objected to. Repayment for that kick.

His lips touched hers, and parted as her arms tightened around him. Any second she'd push him away.

Only she didn't. And at some point he realized she was kissing him back, tentatively and naively, but ever so sweetly. He thought he'd stopped breathing as they stood there, bodies barely touching, arms wrapped about each other, kissing.

As her lips parted, gently opening to his boldness, he forgot about Joel and what a nuisance he was. Lizzie was everything. She was every bit as soft as he remembered, and he drew her closer as if he were breathing in life. His senses flared to life, just as she, with a gasp, pulled away.

Before he knew what he was about, he'd grabbed her by the hands. Her fingers closed around his, warm and callused. It was the calluses that tore at his control. He wrapped his arms around her again, burying his face in her hair.

"Zack?" she said in a small voice. "Let go."

He hadn't been this right in a long time, hadn't known he'd ever be this right. Elizabeth was a tonic in herself, better than anything Granny claimed could stir the blood. In fact, if he could package whatever quality Lizzie possessed, he could peddle it around the world and make a fortune.

He also felt immense guilt. This time he did push her away and looked into her slightly dazed face, her mouth still open to his kiss.

"You're an engaged woman, Elizabeth Sheldon."

"Well, don't you think I know that?"

"You're engaged to Joel."

"Don't you think I know that too?" She shoved her hair back from her face, her eyes flashing. "Why'd you kiss me?"

"Maybe I need to think that over."

"No, you don't think about a kiss after it's over. Can't I even trust you to pull me out of a tree?"

"You deserved it."

"That's no answer."

No, it wasn't. The answer, he decided, was somewhere in the vein pulsing in his throat, the same heavy longing he'd felt since yesterday when they fell in a tangled heap, but he couldn't explain it.

"Lizzie, you can't go falling all over a man and expect him to have no reaction."

"I hate you." She said it softly, without passion.

"I know." He closed the gap between them and took her in his arms. "Don't talk," he murmured into the spun silk of her hair. With her heart thudding so close to his, he couldn't concentrate. He forgot about yesterday and tomorrow.

She wrenched herself away. "Zack . . . please. We can't do this." Her mouth was swollen still, her cheeks flaming with her fury, eyes confused.

"You kissed me, too, Lizzie." Though he tried to sound mocking, his voice came out with a bit of a shake in it.

She turned, as if to hide her flaming cheeks.

"Why did you kiss me, Lizzie?" He turned the tables on her. "I'm Joel's doctor, for heaven's sake. I've done my best to keep a respectful distance. I didn't ask you to dangle out of that tree."

"I don't want to talk about it." And she was kneeling down, retrieving a battered pair of black rubber boots from beside the fallen ladder. Unaware of the picture she made, she bent over to slip her bare feet into the boots and then straightened up.

"We shouldn't have kissed," she said as if that ended the discussion. "It was a mistake."

"Did you think I was Joel?"

"No." Startled, she looked up, her eyes wide and green. "No, I forgot myself. . . . You must think me wanton."

He looked at her, flushed and confused. "I think a lot of things about you, Lizzie, but wanton is not one of them." Good God, men and women didn't just fall into each other's arms and kiss for no good reason. He felt dizzy.

"You won't tell Joel? He'd never understand how it happened."

Zack smiled. Joel wasn't the only one who wouldn't understand. "Dear Lizzie, believe me, no sensible man tells another man he's just kissed that man's intended."

She sighed. "Well, that's a relief. I was so worried you'd say something. It was simply a mistake. We both forgot ourselves."

"No, it was my fault."

"You're being a gentleman and taking the blame, but we both forgot ourselves."

"If you say so." She'd fallen out of a tree like a piece of ripe fruit, the ultimate temptation. Could any man blame him for taking her into his arms?

He'd kissed her, and the earth had shaken, and he couldn't ignore it, especially because he suspected she felt the same way.

"Lizzie, could we talk alone, later?"

"No. We should forget it. And you should call me Elizabeth."

Already she was running up the row between the apple trees, her slim hips swaying, her hair streaming down her neck, her feet ridiculously big, like a duck's in those black rubber boots. She stumbled once, and then continued on through thickening mud.

After one second lost in dumbstruck silence, Zack strode after her, calling her name. He darted around a tree into the next row, and then the next, looking for a rill without mud. When he reached drier ground, he was able to overtake her and pass by her. Calmly he walked from his row to the row up which she ran and, arms folded across his chest, blocked her way.

The instant she saw him she veered, as if to dart into another row . . . and walked right out of the rubber boots she was wearing. She was two steps into the mud, the boots standing encased in mud behind her before she stopped, barefoot. Her expression verged on tears.

"Lizzie, stop. We *can* talk about it. You don't just forget things like that." Determined, Zack walked to her where she stood entrenched in mud. He retrieved the rubber boots and dangled them in front of her like bait for a scared rabbit.

She grabbed for the boots, but he pulled them out of reach.

She looked up at him from under her lashes, her expression scared. "Why do you want to talk about us kissing?"

He advanced on her. "Don't you think we should?"

"No. You can't follow every inclination that comes along. That's why we kissed. It was an inclination, an impulse, and it was wrong. There, now, we've talked. I have to go."

With a tug, she wrenched a boot away from him and balanced on one foot, like a stork in the mud, while she put it on.

She didn't see anyone else in the whole world . . . which was why the deep male voice caught him off guard.

"What's going on out here?"

Only one man in the world would have cared. *Joel.*

Startled, Elizabeth planted both feet on the ground, one booted, the other bare. Behind her, Zack froze in place, her other rubber boot still in his hands.

Joel had made his way out of the house on crutches and stood on the porch, blond hair blowing in the breeze, baby face taut with unasked questions.

Without smiling he looked from Elizabeth to Zack then back again. "What's been going on out there?"

11

Elizabeth's breath caught in her throat.

"Joel . . . you—you're walking! Outside."

His handsome face creased in a smile. "Wasn't that the idea—that eventually I'd walk outside again? Or did you expect me to stay conveniently out of the way?"

"No . . . no, of course not." Joel had so many complications—swelling for one, that Elizabeth thought he'd never get on his feet. "It's just been so long since I've seen you up and about."

"Did you expect me to look the other way while you toyed with your reputation?"

"What's wrong with my reputation?" She looked down at her feet, one bare, the other in a rubber boot, and glanced helplessly over at Zack.

Joel could draw any number of conclusions from the sight of Elizabeth running out of the orchard barefoot, hair flying loose, one boot on, one boot carried by Zack Danvers. She reached over and took the mate from Zack, then, bending down, slipped it on.

"Did you touch her?" Joel lifted the base of one crutch off the ground and jabbed Zack in the stomach with it. "Did you?"

"Of course he touched me," Elizabeth replied calmly, all

the time wondering if she looked as guilty as she felt. "History almost repeated itself with a ladder."

"What does that mean?"

"Zack rescued me from a—a tree." She couldn't help stammering.

Joel turned to Zack. "Well, then, now that she's safely got her feet back on the ground, are you here to pay a house call?" There was no mistaking the sarcasm in his tone as Joel looked from one to the other, his face still taut with anger.

"Why don't we go in and check your splint?" Zack managed with a cool voice to restore professional dignity to his presence.

"Maybe if I stayed in my splint, I wouldn't be in your way when you want to meet in the orchard." Joel's face darkened angrily, and he wavered.

Zack reached out a supporting arm. "Maybe if you were out of your splint, you could be of more help to Elizabeth."

"How could I help? By fending off your advances?" Joel moved the crutches forward and swung down the two wooden steps to the ground to face Zack at eye level. "At what?"

"Joel!" Elizabeth cried, then took a deep breath. "It's not what you think," she said more calmly, then stepped forward and, in what was meant to be a reassuring gesture, touched Joel's arm. "Please, Joel, I know how you feel."

"Do you?"

"Yes." When she'd explained to Zack about her jilting, he'd been understanding. When she'd told Joel, he'd merely shrugged.

"You can't know how it feels to have someone you trust deceive you." Joel's voice held bitterness as he pulled away from her and hobbled closer to Zack.

"You're wrong, Joel," she said. "And you're looking pale. Don't you think now you ought to go in, so Zack can examine you?"

"Zack!" he sneered. "Is that what you call him out in the middle of the orchard?"

She stayed silent, staring at the ground. *Please, Joel.*

"Is that why Dr. Danvers has kept me off my feet so long? So he'd have an excuse to come see *you*?" He turned on Zack, whose face turned dark at the slur on his judgment.

"I did what was best for you, nothing else."

"I've heard you're a yellow-bellied coward who ran from the war, so how do you know what's best? You could have sent me back to the hotel long ago, couldn't you?"

Like a pair of wary jackals, the two men circled each other, stalking, stalking. "The stairs there would have been too hard on you," Zack said

"You black-hearted liar!" Again Joel hobbled close enough to jab one crutch into Zack's chest. "As long as you kept me here, under Elizabeth's roof, you got to make daily house calls, only it wasn't my leg you were as interested in—"

"That's a lie!"

"It's not!"

The screen door slammed. Out of the corner of her eye, Elizabeth saw Granny raise a bucket, and suddenly both men were dowsed in water, their heads and shirts soaking wet.

Then Granny came marching down the steps. She looked at Zack, who was shaking water out of his hair. "Hot weather we've been having, but what can you expect for July?" She set down the bucket and wiped her hands on her apron. "Now then, are you releasing him as a patient, Dr. Danvers?"

"It's a few days sooner than I'd thought, but if he wants, he can return to the hotel." He looked at Joel. "Just go easy on the stairs."

"Suits me fine." Water running down his arms and legs, Joel swung his crutches and headed for the house.

"Suits me too," Granny declared, lifting her skirts out of the mud. "I've got more patients needing me than just Joel. It's time I returned home." She turned on Joel. "I'll help you pack. You put on a dry shirt before you appear at Maddie's hotel." At the door she turned back to Zack and Elizabeth. "Nice crop of apples, Elizabeth. Will Sheldon would have been proud of you. Keep those Gustavson kids working hard now." Her sharp eyes went to Zack. "And you, Doctor, I'll be calling on you if I need help, unless of course you're fixin' to leave town soon."

It wasn't a question. At least Granny didn't wait around for any answers. She disappeared inside the house, slamming the screen door behind her.

After the briefest exchange of glances, Elizabeth went to hitch up the wagon for Joel, and Zack rode back ahead of him to the hotel. Granny packed up and left, too, leaving Elizabeth back where she'd started—alone, except for the company of the Gustavson children. She stoked up the fire in the stove and dug out the largest kettle, then picked through a bucket of fresh-picked elderberries that Clara had brought her. She spent the afternoon making jam. Very tart jam. And she never once thought about Zack kissing her.

It didn't bother her, of course, being alone. The orchard was coming along fine, thanks to Pete. It was only proper that Joel leave, especially since she planned to break her engagement with him, but not now, not in the heat of accusations. And her decision had nothing to do with Zack kissing her, either. She'd been planning it since before Joel's accident, after all. And having seen his pain and anger, she didn't have the heart to hurt him yet. But at the first appropriate moment, she needed to tell Joel—gently—that she was breaking off the engagement. Just not now, or he would think it was somehow connected to this afternoon's episode in the orchard.

Joel was no sooner established in the hotel, splint replaced with a tight leg wrapping, than he realized the error of his anger. He'd promptly retrieved his horse from the livery and begun to call on Elizabeth, with ribbons and sweets, every other evening. That didn't count the days he rode over in the buckboard to oversee Pete's work on the orchard. Meanwhile, only Pete knew how little Joel did around the orchard, and the kid would never talk. Elizabeth was sympathetic and never once did she accuse him of not pulling his load. If he so much as mentioned that his leg was paining him, she mothered him.

But at the same time, she'd grown rather distant since he'd had that fight with Zack Danvers. That made Joel nervous about losing her, so he played the perfect gentleman and pressed her to marry him without any further delay.

Naturally, the sooner she married him the sooner he'd own her orchard. He'd sell it, of course, to the highest bidder. That lucrative creek-front land would be his ticket out of here.

This particular Saturday evening he managed to get Elizabeth alone in the sitting room for all of five minutes before Pete and Clara, like self-appointed chaperons, knocked on the door and walked right in. He wanted to order them out, but that might have alienated Pete, and he needed Pete's hard work.

So he thought of another way to get rid of them. Pulling out of his coat pocket a news article he'd torn out of the paper, he cleared his throat and held it up. "I brought something to read after Elizabeth is done reading Mark Twain."

At once he had her interest, as he'd hoped. She set down her book after marking her place with a velvet ribbon.

"Read it to us," she insisted.

"It might not be suitable for the children."

"Oh, Joel, they've read every story about the Philippine fighting and never had a nightmare. Heavens, you don't think a reputable newspaper would print anything that could hurt the sensibilities of Pete and Clara? After all the articles about the mine explosion?"

"You're sure they're tough enough?" Clara was tougher than molasses in a snowstorm, but it was worth asking for effect.

"I'd like to hear it before Granny gets here," Elizabeth said.

"Granny?" Joel sensed some conspiracy against him being alone with his own fiancée. "Doesn't she know we're an engaged couple?"

"I asked her to stop by and help herself to some of the jam I made. Don't look at me so. I know Miss Yates is rather jealous of me, you see, Granny told me I'd be wise to have a chaperon."

Joel's face split in a crooked smile. "I'm flattered. You're worried Agnes Yates might accuse you of brazen behavior if Granny's not here as a chaperon?"

Elizabeth shrugged. Why didn't she just get it over with and tell Joel she would not marry him? Not next week. Not next month. Not next year. Then Miss Yates could work her wiles on him.

She knew why. Because she'd been jilted back in Amherst, jilted right after her father's death, and she knew how wretched a thing it was to do to a person, what a humiliating thing. Especially now that she realized Lawrence probably only wanted to marry her for her father's political connections. Devastating.

"You're too much a lady for me to take liberties, Elizabeth."

"Fiddle, you're a sweet talker." This came from Granny, who stood in the kitchen doorway.

"Granny!" Clara ran to hug her, and after greetings all around, Elizabeth turned back to Joel.

"Read the article, please."

He leaned back against the horsehair sofa and began to read the clipping from the *Idaho Statesman* as Pete and Clara sat on the floor listening with rapt attention: " 'Chicago: An Illinois native was acquitted by a jury last Wednesday of the shooting death of his fiancée. John Burns shot to death his fiancée last winter after she told him she wished to break off their engagement. The jury ruled with the defense that an engagement is a legally binding agreement and that the man was within his rights in expressing his indignation. Mr. Burns will be released pending the judge's final review of the case. . . . ' "

While Joel read, a cold silence stole over the room. Elizabeth just sat there, hands clasped, feet close together, head bowed. Not even Pete and Clara said a word, their dominoes still, the old maid cards scattered, and a game of Country Auction languishing on the floor, the board bare, playing pieces in disarray.

"The man who did that ought to have his mouth washed out with soap. Where'd you get that? One of those sensationalist eastern papers?" Granny said her piece and then returned to the kitchen to stack jam jars in a basket.

"Still bullying me, eh, Granny?" Joel had wanted to make more of the article, use it as a warning to Elizabeth, but the best he could hope for was that she'd listened.

"I only read it because it's so preposterous. Can you imagine a man behaving like that?" He directed his gaze at Elizabeth. "Can you?"

Elizabeth's stomach contracted in fear. It was a threat. Joel was warning her. She didn't know if he still suspected her of any untoward behavior with Zack or not, but this was a warning. No, a threat.

"Elizabeth, didn't you tell me a man jilted you once?"

She nodded.

"Did you want to shoot him, Elizabeth?" he asked smoothly, then moved to take her hand as if in comfort. "Didn't you want to kill him for how he hurt you?"

"No, Joel." His touch felt as cold as a floor on a January morning, and nothing in his words melted her. She jumped up. "No."

"Will you go on reading *Huckleberry Finn* now?" Clara said uncertainly. "Or can we make fudge?"

Elizabeth had promised Joel a proper evening the way people used to court. He said he missed the ways of the East. If Joel read anything like that in front of the children again, she'd lace his fudge with castor oil.

They made fudge and returned to the parlor. After picking up her volume of *Huckleberry Finn*, Elizabeth turned the pages and for the rest of the evening read aloud. Joel stayed on, rocking by the Windsor stove, and listened until the Gustavson children fell asleep. His parting kiss did nothing

to warm the chill that had fallen over Elizabeth, and she slept
fitfully.

It was midmorning when Granny returned to the orchard
with Maddie in tow, both of them demanding Elizabeth climb
down from her ladder.

"Never mind propping any more branches. Pete can do it.
And don't even think of opening the ditches and watering the
rows. We've come on behalf of the Ladies' Literary Society.
We want you to join. There'll be no talk at all of apples
now." Granny stood there, hands on hips, black cape and
black bonnet shaking with excitement. "Our first meeting is
scheduled."

The women sat in the shade of one of the largest trees, skirts
tucked under them, fanning themselves with their straw hats,
and spelled out their plan. When Maddie had explained the
where and when, Elizabeth looked from her to Granny.

"You've chosen Miss Yates as president?" she said carefully. Miss Yates felt threatened by her, and she didn't want
to worsen things.

"We've also got Florence and Geneva and Helen . . .
and . . . and even the saloonkeeper's wife."

"Her name is Gretchen," Granny put in.

"I know that," Maddie said on a blush, as if she found
socializing with the saloonkeeper's wife embarrassing.

Elizabeth was more worried about the schoolhouse than
the saloon.

"If Miss Yates is president, perhaps I'd better not even
come to meetings."

"Nonsense. She may want to sass and be in charge, but
you're the person who can bring us culture. Why, you've got
books and eastern ideas. *Real* eastern ideas."

"Miss Yates doesn't care for my ideas."

"Now, now, there's room for all kinds of ideas. Agnes may
be good at teaching the ABC's and teaching English to the
likes of Antonio Mendez, but we've been yearning for something far more edifying, far more sophisticated."

How would Miss Yates behave if Elizabeth showed up? Would she be angry? Resentful? Rude?

Maddie pressed the issue. "Elizabeth, you wouldn't use Miss Yates as an excuse not to join, would you? I know we look a bit rough around the edges here. But just because we dress in calico and homespun and have work-roughened hands doesn't mean we don't yearn to discuss the news of the day. No one's had much time for news and culture up till now, to tell the truth, but the town's built up nicely. We've got everything—a livery, a barbershop, a mercantile, a hotel, a bank, a blacksmith, a carpenter who also makes coffins, and maybe even a doctor."

"Dr. Danvers is leaving town."

"Then we'll find another doctor. Besides, the literary society is for women, Elizabeth. If nothing else will persuade you, then do it for us. We want you to get away from this orchard more often."

Maddie added softly, "We'll even organize a memorial statue to the war dead. Your brother will be remembered with more than just the orchard, Elizabeth. Oh, do say yes."

Elizabeth grew pensive. A memorial for Will. How could she say no to that?

She stared at her little house, where lately she'd spent so much time with Joel, and then at her orchard, where she spent so many of her days in backbreaking labor. She hadn't realized till July fourth how confined she was, how limited her horizons had become. And actually the apples were growing nicely. The orchard was under control, at least until harvest. Moreover, she was leery of Joel's threats and guilty still over her thoughts of Zack.

So far, in the week since he'd kissed her, in the week since Joel had started hobbling about, Zack had found her in the orchard several times, either near the creek or near the hotel property. Their conversations had been quiet, fraught with shyness on her part. If that shyness succeeded in hiding her longing for the man, all to the good. After all, now that Joel was mobile again, it was only a matter of time before Zachary

Danvers—bitter, cyncial, and dashing Zack—bought a new train ticket and moved on.

"Elizabeth?" It was Maddie.

She needed to put both men out of her mind for a while, and the sooner Zack Danvers left town the better she'd sleep.

She wanted to be an independent woman. The dream she'd come after was coming to fruition. Beneath the summer sun, her rows and rows of trees flourished as hundreds and hundreds of apples swelled.

Somehow that was scant comfort.

"Do come to the meeting," Maddie pleaded.

"I'll think about it," Elizabeth said.

But thinking about the literary club didn't help her sleep. That night when the clock said two in the morning, she got up and tiptoed over to the window and looked out at the moon playing on the creek and casting shadows out of the orchard. She chose the window that had a view of the tall hotel. But it wasn't Joel, her fiancé, whom she missed. It was Zack. Whenever she got up during a sleepless night, it was always Zack who haunted her.

Zachary Danvers stood at the window of his hotel room, looking out at the moonlit orchard, aching with a longing he couldn't shake, a longing worse than the fevers of the tropics. He'd have given anything to be asleep and having another nightmare. What he felt now was a waking nightmare of what Joel might do to Elizabeth . . . if Joel married her.

The little three-room house stood beyond the expanse of ripening trees, and in his mind's eye he saw Elizabeth and Joel together. They were betrothed. Never mind that theirs would be a marriage of convenience. If they wed, Joel would enjoy rights Zack envied. The right to lay his hand on the nape of her neck and entwine one finger around the honey-colored curl that lay there like a stray wildflower. The right to blow out the lamp and lie beside her. The right to wake up next to her.

His mind couldn't take the picture any further. His throat felt thick with the longing to touch her.

He didn't want to be a doctor here and have to help Granny deliver Elizabeth's babies—babies conceived by Joel. He didn't want to spend his future avoiding her, watching her grow old before her time because she'd married a lazy lout like Joel, knowing she valued all the things that Joel would never understand—like courage and honor and the memory of a dead soldier brother. He slammed a fist into the door, so hard the impact stung and the slam knocked his black bag off the corner of the bed.

Somewhere in that bag was a scalpel, and after fumbling for it, he tensed his arm and aimed it at the wall, like a dart at a board.

Just then a knock shook the door. "Zack?"

Slowly the tension drained out of his arm, and he dropped the scalpel on the bed, his gaze following it. For the first time since Harry died, he'd allowed himself the luxury of anger.

"Zack?" Ben cracked open the door.

"Yeah." Zack turned. "Sorry, I didn't mean to be so noisy."

"Something wrong?"

"I got mad and slugged the door. Sorry. I'll repair it."

"Sorry? A little anger's better than the moping you've been doing. . . . Do you want to talk?"

"No."

Ben paused, as if deciding whether to push the point, then nodded. "You get a good night's sleep, now, you hear? You'll need it for the Ladies' Literary." At Zack's puzzled look, Ben said only, "Don't say I didn't warn you."

Agnes Yates positioned herself at the schoolhouse gate and waited. Now that Joel was no longer laid up at the Sheldon house, she found it harder to invent ways to bump into Dr. Danvers, but sooner or later he would head up this road. Way out past the Sheldon orchard there was a ranch where Dr. Zachary Danvers was treating a woman for swollen ankles and a child for tonsillitis. He was in demand, just like Granny, and he never said no.

This time she had the perfect excuse to talk with him.

Never mind that the other women intended to make the Literary an exclusively female club. The others, except for Elizabeth, were all married and could afford the luxury of social evenings without men. To Miss Yates, who had lived through her twenty-seventh birthday last week, a social event without a man was a total waste of time.

When the doctor finally came along the road, Agnes managed to position herself nonchalantly at the gate, a few wild asters in her hand, as if he'd just caught her in the act of picking them.

"Why, hello," she said, feigning surprise and enduring the cloud of dust that enveloped her best skirt. With her free hand shading her eyes, she remained as close to the road as possible, so that if good manners didn't make him stop, the possibility of running her over would.

To her immense satisfaction, he reined in and, after briefly frowning at her, tipped his hat and dismounted.

But there was a tired, preoccupied look about him, and so she didn't waste any time getting to the point. "Good morning, Zack. I was going to seek you out at the hotel and ask a favor, but didn't want to appear too forward."

"What is it, Agnes?" he asked, his voice impatient. "What favor?"

She cleared her throat and straightened her shoulders with purpose. "Will you think me brazen if I ask you to attend the opening meeting of the Ladies' Literary? And please don't say no. I'm the president, and I do so want to surprise the other ladies."

She tried to bat her eyelashes the way Elizabeth Sheldon did, but her eyelids wouldn't cooperate.

"Do you have something in your eye?" Zack asked, coming closer, touching her shoulder.

"No . . . I mean, yes. A speck of dust, I think. I'm fine."

For a moment she stared wide-eyed, mesmerized by his touch. This was what she was starved for, an educated man. If it hadn't been for Elizabeth Sheldon, Agnes would have had both Zack and Joel courting *her,* fighting over *her.*

"Will you come and join the ladies?"

Zack paused. "What other ladies?"

Miss Yates ticked off half the wives in town. "There's Elizabeth Sheldon," she added, as if an afterthought, "but why would she bother coming to anything remotely cultural in this town? She's far too good to be bothered with us. Besides, she'll be busy with Joel."

For a long moment Zack, who'd known a fair share of women and how they cast out lures, studied Agnes Yates, her straight dark hair and her horsey face. What was she up to? Certainly not flirting, and even if Miss Yates had been good at it, which she wasn't, he wasn't biting.

"No, thanks."

Miss Yates's face fell. "But it's a political debate about the wisdom of digging a canal across Panama. How can we possibly do a credible job without a man who's actually been in the tropics?"

Briefly he shut his eyes.

"Dr. Danvers, Dr. Danvers, it is my mama. My papa. They are sick. They need you. Don't you have any medicine?"

"I don't know anything about Panama, Miss Yates."

"We can debate rural medicine if you prefer," she said smartly. "The topic doesn't matter, you see. It's the challenge of the debate. How about this—'Resolved: Children should be seen and not heard'? Any topic will do."

"No, Agnes."

Another voice echoed again out of the distance: "Ag-nes!"

Zack had been about to tell her he'd be packed and gone before the Literary got its shoes buttoned and its hat on. A few medical favors here and there in Eden Creek and then . . .

"Ag-nes . . ."

When Zack looked, there on the horizon appeared Antonio Mendez, cantering along on a dapple gray horse. In a moment he was there, gathering up a sheaf of papers, and leaping off the wheezing animal as if he'd come to Miss Yates's rescue.

"What are you doing here now, Antonio?" she asked with little enthusiasm.

"You forget me? You said you'd help me read all my accounts, Agnes."

"But you should have made an appointment for my time," she snapped.

So, mused Zack, pausing before getting on his horse, Miss Yates had a secret admirer. Antonio seemed like an up and coming sheepman, a man who'd prosper, and he was handsome to boot. Miss Yates could do worse.

But her annoyed expression told another story. "How many times have I told you, Antonio, not to come uninvited? How many lessons will it take to get that through your head? Must I teach you manners in addition to English?"

"Ah, but the Mercantile owner asked that I bring you a letter—from the orphanage." He held it up and pointed to the word in the return address, as if proud he could read it.

The orphanage! If Miss Yates had been a man, Zack would have connected with her chin. He settled his hat on his head and took a step toward her. "I thought we agreed to stop all this orphanage talk until we heard if Orville Gustavson had survived the mine explosion. It's the decent thing to do."

"Well, even if he did survive, he's probably in prison up there with all the other rioters. He's no fit father, Zack. Surely you see that."

"Leave those children with Elizabeth."

"Now, Zack, it's merely an exchange of letters. A possibility, should the worst news come." Her face brightened. "Join us at the Literary and we'll discuss *that* topic."

He had a feeling this first meeting of the Ladies' Literary of Eden Creek was going to be memorable. "I'll be there."

Clara rubbed her nose and then pulled up a fallen overall strap. She was perched up on the rocky ridge overlooking the Sheldon orchard and the creek. Nearby, Pete was inspecting the new growth of leaves on the seedling Elizabeth had given them.

"Is it taking root, Pete?"

Happy at his nod, she tilted the bucket, which she'd dragged all the way up the incline to the ridge, then jumped back while the water puddled around the base of the tree.

"Don't pour it so fast. It'll wash all the dirt away." Pete spoke with big-brother sternness as he continued to inspect the pencil-thin branches and their new leaves.

"Then you water it. You're the one who knows all about trees." She fell onto her stomach and propped her chin on her hands to better admire the view over the Sheldon orchard.

"What're you looking at?" Pete asked.

"Nothing. . . . Is it true, Pete, about the orphanage?"

"If I heard it told around the stove at the mercantile, it's true, especially if Antonio said it. He may not be good with English, and he's no good with chaw either, but he don't lie. A letter came to Miss Yates, and Antonio hand carried it to her. Don't worry, though. Elizabeth will help us . . . and Zack will, too."

"Then how come when I saw them in town yesterday they passed each other without saying a word?" Clara had found that especially baffling, since she'd seen them kissing in the orchard a week ago. It was her best secret, one too good to even tell Pete.

Pete didn't look up. "People change. Could be Zack's changed his mind about being Elizabeth's friend."

"Will Pa change his mind then about coming back?"

"Naw, that's different."

Clara pondered that. She had no idea why it was different. Being eight years old was very confusing, especially when you had secrets to keep.

12

On a Saturday evening at the end of July, the Ladies' Literary Society of Eden Creek gathered for its first meeting. After much debate over location, it was decided to use the schoolhouse, which Miss Yates opened early to freshen the air and sweep away spiders and chalk dust.

Up until an hour before, Elizabeth had second thoughts about attending. Without her there, Miss Yates could have no further reason to resent her. Besides, she rationalized, the orchard needed watering, and a few of the larger trees required propping. Her place was here with the orchard, with Pete, with her brother's dream. Will's dream . . .

Alone, she walked around the orchard, ending where the irrigation dam flowed parallel with the creek. A canvas dam allowed her to force the water to flow in whichever direction it was needed, but that dam was high and needed a man's strength to move it, and it needed to be moved—soon—or the ditch would overflow and flood the orchard. Why did some dreams take so much work? And why did one need men?

She'd have to find Pete.

She sought him in the barn where, earlier in the day, he and Clara had been forking hay down to the animals. No childish voices greeted her. Instead she heard someone moving about in the harness room and, curious, walked to the entrance.

Her eyes weren't accustomed to the dim light yet, and she could barely see. "Pete?"

"No, Elizabeth, it's me, your future husband." The voice held a taunt.

"Joel," she breathed, startled. She'd no idea he was on the property. Yet, ever since the jealous argument with Zack, he'd done all sorts of small tasks in an attempt to win back her favor, but usually he announced his arrival.

"How'd you get here?"

"I rode from the hotel, as always."

He was standing on his own power, ripping off the month of July from his calendar. As her eyes grew accustomed to the square of light from the small window, Elizabeth could make out a drawing of a voluptuous beauty with upswept hair and nothing on but a camisole and corset, the same sort of calendar she'd removed from inside the house the day she'd arrived.

"What are you doing here, Joel?"

He looked at her then, the expression in his face a mixture of guilt, wariness, desire. His gaze roamed over Elizabeth, lingering on her bloomers, and then moved back up her face.

It was a hot day and Elizabeth's shirtwaist clung to her. After a moment he put on a smile and, gathering up his crutches, hobbled out to the wagon, Elizabeth following him. He leaned close to her. "I was hoping you'd come out of the house. . . . I can't wait till harvest to marry you, Elizabeth. Do you know how hard it is waiting for you?"

Her heart beat more quickly, and she shook her head and looked over his shoulder for signs of Pete. "How hard?" Her voice was expressionless. Joel had no idea she was about to send him packing.

"This hard," he said and, with remarkable ease for a man on crutches, reached for her, pulled her to him, and kissed her.

She remained rigid beneath his kiss, her lips unyielding, her body stiff.

He pulled back, his hands still on her waist. "You don't

act as if you enjoy being kissed."

Half turning, she pushed his hands away. "Please, Joel, the children might come in."

"Then come back inside the harness room." He dropped his crutches, grabbed her arm, and despite his limp, pulled her into the harness room. The instant he slammed the door, he turned to her. "We're engaged, Elizabeth. People expect us to do a little spooning."

She backed along the wall to the door. "Joel, I didn't come for this."

Smiling, he tilted up her chin. "You aren't going to be one of those wives with rules about when and how to kiss, are you?"

He reached for her again, but she dodged to one side. "I won't be your wife at all unless you show you can help around here. You forget this was a business arrangement."

He looked momentarily stunned.

She couldn't believe she'd said the words. After Lawrence's calculated rejection of her, this was hard. Hardest of all was the flash of pain she saw in Joel's eyes before he put on an expression of bravado.

"I've been hurt, Elizabeth. If you're mad because I haven't helped enough, I understand, but I'm trying to do better." With one hand, he gestured to the harness he'd been repairing.

"That's not a lot, Joel. The entire orchard needs work, but you've let Pete do it all—right from the start."

"He's a strong boy."

"That's not the point. If Pete can do it all, why do I need you? Did I ever need you? Who was taking care of this place before I got here? You or Pete?"

The color faded from Joel's face, and where a moment before he'd been leaning against the wall, now he stood up without benefit of crutches.

"My, my, you sound like a scolding wife already."

The moment of confrontation had come. She couldn't put off telling him.

"Joel, this is my orchard."

"I hear Zack Danvers has been making house calls since I moved out."

"He's stopped by. Just to talk."

"You mean, hundreds of nice fat apples still couldn't keep the doctor away?"

She flung open the door. If Zack's name was going to dominate the conversation, she wouldn't continue. "That's not worthy of you, Joel."

He limped after her, out into the open barn. "Elizabeth, wait—"

"No."

"Don't be upset. We'll talk later. I can limp down to the head ditch and try to move the canvas dam, or I'll get Pete to help. It'll get done, Elizabeth." Oh, but he was trying to soften her up by playing the martyr. Oh, why did this have to be so hard?

In an instant he was hobbling after her without his crutches, his voice echoing off the roof of the barn. "I can help Pete watch over things while you go to that shindig at the schoolhouse. You're invited, aren't you?"

She stopped, back to him. "I've been invited." Now that Joel mentioned it, she decided she would definitely go after all.

He made a scoffing sound. "Those old biddies need something more to do with their time than sit around and talk about building a canal through Panama. They ought to leave the talking to the menfolk. But go ahead. You worked hard while I was laid up."

She kept walking out into the sun and on toward the house to change.

"Just remember, Elizabeth, we have an agreement. You promised."

"We'll talk about it later, Joel."

And with no more explanation than that, she went to change, her hands shaking from anger. Tomorrow, she would end the engagement officially, and she dreaded it. Yes, an evening at the Literary would calm her.

She quickly changed into her pale green dress, the one she'd worn to the spring social, when she danced with Zack Danvers. She placed her hands on either side of her waist, just where his had been, remembering that dance. Then, abruptly, she called herself foolish, clapped on her straw hat, and jammed a hatpin through it. When she emerged, Joel was waiting beside the wagon, horses hitched to it. On his face was a decidedly meek look. She'd never seen him so humble.

"I'm sorry, Elizabeth," he said, voice contrite. "I'll drive you to the schoolhouse."

Climbing up onto the seat of the wagon and picking up the reins, she promised only, "We'll talk later," and drove off by herself.

Miss Yates scowled when Elizabeth arrived, and Elizabeth wanted to hide in a corner and blend in with the woodwork. She was tired of confrontations with Agnes Yates.

Inside the little white schoolhouse the air was hot despite all the open windows. On Miss Yates's desk sat a pitcher full of wilting wildflowers—red paintbrush and white asters with giant yellow throats. Though dressed in her usual severe schoolmarm skirt and blouse, Miss Yates had turned uncharacteristically romantic in the decorations.

A train whistle blew in the distance, and Elizabeth thought immediately of Zachary Danvers, the blue of his eyes, the black of his eyelashes, the warmth of his head on her shoulder.

Zack Danvers—and her wanton thoughts shamed her. He was a traitor to her brother's memory, for heaven's sake. The best thing she could do was occupy her mind, mingle with some other ladies, and give her foolish imagination a rest.

Zack Danvers listened to the faraway whistle of the train and wished he were on it. If he'd been smart, he'd have bought his ticket. Anything to get out of this Ladies' Literary thing. He'd considered skipping the meeting entirely and dealing with the orphanage issue in private, but then Maddie found out he'd been invited and cajoled him into driving her there in the wagon.

"As long as you have to drive me, Zack, you might as well come in and talk—a bit."

He scowled.

"And even if you don't want to talk, maybe the dessert will be good. You could still use a few more pounds, you know."

Maddie, he realized, needed someone to baby real bad. Until Ben gave her a six-pound one, though, he guessed he was it.

And now here he was, at the little white schoolhouse, feeling like all sorts of a fool for giving in.

Women.

Agnes Yates met him at the door of the schoolhouse. She was standing there looking prim and innocent, her dark hair pulled back in a severe knot. He shook her hand, and then moved toward the piano, away from all the women who'd crowded into the desks.

And that was when he nearly tripped over Elizabeth Sheldon, hiding in the corner.

His heart slammed into his ribs, and he took a ragged breath. He hadn't thought she'd be here in Agnes Yates's domain.

Elizabeth looked his way, and at once her face paled, as if she was every bit as surprised to see him here.

I thought you weren't coming, her eyes said.

"My, my, Elizabeth," said Miss Yates, uneasy black eyes glancing at Zack. "It's so nice of you to take time away from your orchard to join us. I didn't think you'd find our humble meeting of interest."

"I had a change of heart," Elizabeth said, her voice distracted. Zack's hair was windblown, his expression somber, almost pale. Heart-stoppingly so. And he was dressed up, his gold watch chain dangling out of his vest pocket. She'd never seen him in a tie.

Immediately she whirled away to sit in the front of the room, leaving Miss Yates and Zack together to talk while she sat on a bench and looked down at the plank desktops. No groove for the pencils and no inkwells, but plenty of inkstains and carved initials, one of which she traced over and over with her finger. Pure, raw jealousy bowed Elizabeth's head. Why had he come? Why?

Someone lit the kerosene lamp that hung from the ceiling, and the cloying smell mixed with the hot summer air. Dizzying. Homely. Intimate.

Miss Yates, as president, moved to the blackboard on which was printed, "Welcome to the first meeting of the Ladies' Literary Society of Eden Creek." Tonight, she announced, the society would hold its first public debate.

Florence Atwood, wife of Eden Creek's carpenter, stood to speak some words about the importance of exchanging ideas. "You know, I buried two children in the Great Plains just getting out here in a covered wagon some years ago. I never thought I'd see civilization again, but now the ladies of Eden Creek have a chance to change that situation forever . . ."

Zack didn't concentrate on the words so much as he enjoyed the view of Elizabeth. A honey-colored curl had escaped from its pins and dangled down her neck, tempting him to move into the desk behind her and tease it. She looked more petite than ever, and her head was bowed as if her mind were far away.

Elizabeth barely heard what Florence was saying. She wanted to get up and leave. If Miss Yates had gotten Zachary Danvers to come here—even if he was a guest speaker— then Miss Yates and Zack must be getting friendly; they must have talked in town. Of course he had the right to talk to other women. He'd talked with Miss Yates for a long time before the meeting began. He'd stood tall, hands thrust into his pockets, laughing at some witticism of Miss Yates, who utterly monopolized him. Every woman here had gazed at him in rapt attention. Miss Yates, simpering and fawning, was no different. Oh, how was she going to look him in the face when he got up there to speak?

And yet she did, as surely as if he were the opposite pole of a magnet.

When Agnes Yates cleared her throat to announce the topic of debate, Elizabeth, like the other ladies, sat up straighter.

As Miss Yates spoke, there was a sound of surprise, from Zack.

"What?"

Miss Yates repeated herself. "Resolved: The War with Spain was advantageous for America."

"No." The single syllable was torn from Zack's soul. He half stood. "No."

"Oh, yes." Miss Yates smiled. "It's perfect. You said any topic would be agreeable."

"I thought the topic was to be the orphanage."

Miss Yates waved a hand in dismissal. "Oh, that. I decided the ladies are here to get away from discussions of children. We want something edifying, something men discuss."

As Zack sat again, Miss Yates herself took the affirmative argument and spoke for five minutes on the glories of America's newly acquired empire. The self-satisfied smile never left her face.

Zack sat there, to one side of the blackboard, looking stunned, even after Miss Yates finished and sat down by the stove.

It was a sticky summer night, and Elizabeth was growing hotter and hotter waiting to hear his voice. He would of course speak with candor about the dangers of yellow fever, about mosquitoes and medical practice in tropical countries, about how many men had died from gunshots and how many from disease, and then he would talk about Admiral Dewey and perhaps drop in a mention of the Rough Riders and Roosevelt. And doubtless he'd end by announcing his imminent departure from Eden Creek.

Briefly she felt his gaze on her and glanced up to see him looking at her. At once he turned in the other direction, as if he hadn't recognized her. A muscle jumped in his jaw.

Carefully, Elizabeth looked at Miss Yates, who sat smiling like the cat who ate the canary. "Lieutenant, it's your turn."

Slowly Zack stood. "There's nothing to tell," Zack said bleakly. "You've read it all in the papers."

"But what's your personal opinion?" Miss Yates pushed, ever the teacher.

"My personal opinion?" He was very white, very pale, and fumbled for words.

When he put his hand in his pocket, Elizabeth was sure she saw it tremble. Even more sure when he pulled out a gold coin.

"What is that?" Miss Yates asked.

"One hundred pesetas. That's all a life is worth in war." His words were cool and dispassionate, devoid of emotion, directed at the center of the room.

"Go on," Miss Yates urged. The other ladies leaned forward expectantly, except for Elizabeth, who sat perfectly still.

His hand came down so hard on the front desk that Elizabeth jumped. Then she sat still, trying not to breathe while she stared at his hand, at the dark hair that spread from his wristbone and disappeared up into the pristine whiteness of his starched cuff. She let her gaze slide up his torso to the haunted sadness of his face.

His Adam's apple worked. Elizabeth was close enough to touch his hand, if only she knew what nerve had been bared.

Maddie stood. "Zack . . . would you care for a drink of lemonade before you continue?"

He looked disoriented, as if he couldn't find the source of the voice. Miss Yates had surprised him with the topic; that much was clear.

"Zack, are you all right?" It was Maddie again.

"But tell us more, Lieutenant," Miss Yates urged.

"Zack?" Maddie's voice held concern.

"Lieutenant, tell us."

A hush fell over the room. "I can't." He was white around the mouth, jaw set, eyes hard, dark blue in the lamplight.

Miss Yates's words were sharp. "Are you going back on your word, Lieutenant?"

Suddenly he stalked toward the door and every woman there turned to watch. There was a chalk mark on the back of his coat where he'd leaned against the blackboard. Elizabeth stared at her lap.

"Lieutenant Danvers," Miss Yates called out, "you can't just walk out on us."

He could and he did, slamming the schoolhouse door behind him.

"How dare he?" Florence Atwood said, outraged.

"Now, now," Miss Yates said. "I predicted certain men wouldn't be willing to discuss serious subjects with women." Her tone was snide.

Maddie stood up. "You had no business asking him to discuss the war."

Miss Yates looked as if she'd swallowed a prune, and several other ladies had their lips pursed. "Why? Aren't women smart enough to understand war?"

"That's not what I mean. Of all the subjects you could have chosen, that one was . . . well, thoughtless."

"And haven't men been thoughtless toward women, leaving us out of their smoking rooms and after-dinner talk?"

"Agnes, you don't understand!" Maddie's voice shook with rage.

"Yes, I do. I understand it will take time to get men to come around to take a ladies' literary club seriously, but never fear, ladies, we'll get it going."

One by one they began standing up and talking, debating informally, not the war, but whether men and women were capable of discussing serious subjects together.

All Elizabeth could do was stare straight ahead, the picture of Zack emblazoned on her mind. Zack, white-faced and numb.

Suddenly she had to find him. Picking up her purse and hat, she slid sideways out of her bench, stepping on ladies' toes all along the way. "Excuse me . . . excuse me . . . pardon me."

She couldn't get out fast enough. She had to hurry, before he left.

At the aisle, she almost collided with Maddie, who raised her eyebrows meaningfully.

"Let me find him," Elizabeth said, and Maddie nodded.

Once out in the aisle, Elizabeth made her way to the back door. Miss Yates stood near a wall decorated with paper chains left over from May Day and was cutting a coconut cake.

"Can't you stay long enough for dessert, Elizabeth? Or do you also think serious subjects are best discussed with men in private?"

Behind in the crowd, Maddie was loudly giving all the reasons why the war with Spain had been so wretched.

Elizabeth couldn't get outside fast enough and leaned against the door, scanning the tangle of buggies and horses.

He was standing, back to her, about to get in the wagon.

"Zack, what's wrong?"

He froze at the sound of Elizabeth's voice. Lizzie. "What are you doing out here?" he asked, his voice harsh.

Before he could move, she hurried up to him and grabbed the wagon reins. "I'm glad you walked out. That was a dreadfully stuffy topic, wasn't it?"

She was so close Zack could smell the violet scent of her.

"Will wouldn't want me to hate you," she said softly.

He swallowed hard. If she left now, dropped the subject, he could handle it. From the schoolhouse drifted the muted sounds of ladies' voices. Nearby a cricket chirped.

She looked up at him, her eyes shining, heart aching for the wretched look on his face.

"I'm sorry about Miss Yates and the others. They didn't warn you about that topic, did they?"

He was silent, eyes shut, and she couldn't stand seeing him hurt any more than she could have stood it if Miss Yates and her Ladies' Literary had gone after Clara and Pete. Zack stood facing her, his expression impassive. "That's really why you left, isn't it?" she asked.

There weren't any words in her that seemed appropriate, especially since she had no idea what hurt or where or why. So she did what seemed most natural. She wrapped her arms around his waist and held him, her cheek against his heart, her heart aching for him, wishing she knew why. "Oh, Zack, I'm so sorry."

He tensed for a second, startled no doubt at the way she'd thrown herself at him, but he made no move to push her away. Her hair was soft and warm against his face, and carefully, ever so carefully, his arms came up to hold her as he leaned against the wagon wheel.

"I'll never get over being sad about my brother's death, but that doesn't mean I have to hate you for it." Her words were very soft. "I don't care if you don't want to talk about it."

Stars filled the sky that night, like a million souls daring him to tell his secret. The story had to come out, and leaning back against that wagon wheel, he stared at the stars and told. How much he said out loud and how much he simply remembered he would never know. All he remembered clearly was Elizabeth holding him as if she'd never let go.

"Harry was my best friend . . ." he began.

"Go on, Zack."

"But it was my idea to sign up for the war. Harry and I shared everything, from medical school to space in the ship. Remember the *Maine*? That was when we signed on. No one said anything about yellow fever or bullets; people just talked about patriotism. We were in a medic tent in a jungle when the shooting broke out. We had no water, no medicine. . . . Can you imagine every one of those apple trees a sick man and the only water a tiny creek through a jungle infested with Spaniards carrying guns?"

"No." She shook her head against his chest.

"Harry got shot going for water." He stopped, wondering if he could go on.

"Lizzie, don't make me say any more."

"You don't have to tell me any more." But she didn't move out of his arms.

"Lizzie, I need to tell someone, or I'll die from the guilt of it. It was carnage. Soldiers, who only two days before had drilled in tropical white uniforms, lay sweaty and blood-splattered. The Spanish knew no mercy, and when there were gaps between the gunshots, mosquitoes filled in the silence, droning and droning and droning. . . .

"The bees in your orchard reminded me of mosquitoes at first. I had to keep looking to make sure they were bees—you know, pollinating, not stinging and passing the fever from one man to another. Bullets . . . bullets flew over our heads, and we lived on our bellies as much as on our feet. Cowardice became relative, you see, because a dead doctor couldn't wield a scalpel."

"No, of course not." Her voice was soft with encouragement.

"I was on my belly when Harry went for the water. We took turns, you see, and he was gone so long that last time . . . but the bullets were raining down, and all I could think of was stupid things like whether it would rain and whether I could get from the tent to the grove of coconut trees . . . you know, to look for Harry . . . and find the water, because everyone in the tent was thirsty. Always thirsty. In Manila, where we trained, there were mangoes and coconuts for sale on the streets, but out in the jungles there wasn't even a drop of water to drink, never mind clean out bullet wounds. Do you believe that?"

"Yes." Whispered.

"I fell asleep then, and when I woke up, someone had brought Harry back to the tent. . . . The sky was dark with gun smoke, and I was on a cot, listening to singing. 'The Girl I Left Behind Me.' You know that maudlin song?"

She nodded against his shirtfront. Of course she knew the song, and now she hated it. She swallowed the lump in her throat. "That's enough. You don't have to—"

"Yes, I do have to talk, but you don't have to listen." His words were harsh, but his voice was warm against her hair. When she didn't move, he continued haltingly.

"Harry never batted an eye at danger. Would do anything for a friend, and all he could talk about was how he'd never found the water. . . . He was dying because he went to get the water.

"That's all." Stark.

"No water . . .

"No more quinine . . .

"And after he died, I helped put him in the mass grave."

Nearby, the cricket chirped away, the only sound in the world. Tears welled up in her eyes. For her brother. For Zack. Across the school yard, Miss Yates called out to departing members of the literary society.

Elizabeth tried to think of something to say, but the knot in her throat prevented words from getting out, and then Zack set her away from him and looked at the ground. "It was the coin toss," he said as if to himself, then looked up at Elizabeth, wove his fingers through her hair, framed her face with his hands. He looked into her eyes, his expression bleak. "We flipped the coin to see who'd have to get water. I won . . . and Harry went." The words were torn out.

She might have managed a syllable or two, but any words she spoke were swallowed up in the darkness. And then he turned as if to go, and she came up behind him, caught him by the arm. "Zack, it was bad luck," she murmured against his back. "Don't you see that?"

He took his time replying, and when he did, his voice was quiet. "Such a trusting thing you are, Lizzie. Don't you know you can't trust people, especially when they're gambling?"

"That doesn't mean you haven't got a right to win. Zack, we all do what we have to. *All* of us."

"I haven't told you all of the story yet. That was the easy part."

She waited, silent, so quiet she could hear the darkness pulse around them. Their need to touch each other was palpable, but neither moved, and then his voice came, bleak.

"I was too sick to care, so I made sure Harry went to get the water. Death was all around me, but I didn't think it would happen to my best friend." He stopped, voice breaking. "I cheated."

Something in her shattered. Elizabeth bowed her head and waited, at length saying only, "I see."

No, she didn't really. Every time she thought she knew this man, he surprised her, either for good or for bad . . . but then, she had known that this was the sort of place people came to when they wanted to hide from the past. People like her, even.

"Well," she said in a small voice, her forehead bent close to his back. "Do you think any of us are here because we're perfect? I'm not. Why . . . why, I've even been known to get mad and yell and stomp and say 'I hate you' and accept proposals through the mail because I—"

"I'm leaving town, Lizzie." Suddenly very focused, he rounded on her.

"When?"

"As soon as I can."

He laid his palm against her face and grazed her cheek with his thumb. "No man's good enough for you, Lizzie, I want you to know that. You deserve a lot of happiness."

With another man. "Thanks. You, too."

"Aw, don't waste happiness on me. I'll settle for honest luck."

As soon as he drove off, she headed for the schoolhouse, and she did not allow herself to look back.

13

Ben jammed his pipe into his mouth as he bent to help Joel Emory untie one of the rowboats from the hotel dock. Boating on the Payette River was a dangerous sport, except for one wide spot in the river. Almost a lake it was, and it was for the river view that Ben had built his hotel there. But whenever guests asked to take out a rowboat, he cautioned them and casually gauged their skill with a boat.

"Planning to do some courting?"

Joel squinted up. "How'd you know?"

"You're the only man in the entire county that I know of's got a claim on a lady's hand. Elizabeth's a fine woman. A lot of men would want her."

"I plan to keep her for myself."

"Yeah, well, just watch out where you're rowing. There's eddies here and there; don't let them fool you. You understand, don't you, that Eden Creek flows into the Payette River about a mile upstream? And if you don't pay attention to your oars when you go downstream, next thing you know you'll be in white water dodging boulders."

"I've rowed back east."

"Yeah, in lily ponds. It's different out west, Joel, so mind me now. Stay right here in front of the hotel where the water's wide and calm."

"Don't worry. I'm taking my lady out, not going fishing." It had been a long time since he'd taken a rowboat out in the lake in his hometown park, but what the heck, when you'd rowed one boat, you'd rowed them all.

Row back to make the boat go forward. Row front to go in reverse. Anyone smart enough to drive a wagon could work oars.

Ben was chuckling. "The day a man pays more attention to a fish than to a pretty lady like Elizabeth Sheldon is the day I close the doors on this hotel."

Joel, who honestly liked Ben, chuckled in appreciation. The man was honest and straightforward, not moody and devious like that brother of his. Most important, Ben was happily married, and so no distraction to single ladies like Elizabeth.

Ben ambled off up the embankment, rocks crunching under his feet, and soon was helping Maddie restring the clothesline. Satisfied that he'd be left alone, Joel stepped into his boat to test how much it would wobble. Dangling his hand in the water, he tested the temperature and, stung by the icy cold, quickly pulled his hand out. No wonder Ben provided rowboats. Swimming was clearly out of the question, except by the robust. Anyway, swimming didn't suit Joel's purposes today.

After adjusting the cuffs of his shirt and straightening his bow tie, he plopped a straw boater on his head and waited for Elizabeth, who'd agreed to meet him at the boat dock at two o'clock. He fidgeted, hating the bow tie, but to put Elizabeth off her guard, he'd dressed like a gentleman. For a moment he allowed himself a second thought about his plan, but there was no turning back now.

Elizabeth Sheldon was his train ticket out of here. Of course, Joel was going to sell the orchard, but to do that he had to marry the woman who owned it. That didn't mean, however, that he would wait until harvest to make her his. Ever since he'd caught her in the orchard with Zachary Danvers, he'd felt her slipping away from him, growing more remote. Well, let her try to run away from his kisses once he got her out in the middle of the river.

Like an angel from heaven, she appeared from among the ripening apple trees and approached him, all dressed up in a pale green summer dress, floating toward him, smiling, trusting, vulnerable.

When she reached the hotel dock, he climbed out of the boat and, with all the gallantry at his command, handed her in, directing her to sit opposite him. Moments later he was rowing them out into the deepest part of the water.

"It's beautiful, Joel," she said, staring at her orchard a ways upstream. "I can't believe we've brought it this far." Turning back, she said, "You've worked so hard since . . . since . . . well, you know, lately. Both you and Pete."

He pulled the oars a couple of times. "Pete's a smart boy. I've learned as much from him as he has from me. Will liked him, too."

She played with the ribbons on her hat. "Joel, about the words we had in the barn . . . perhaps we should talk."

Darn right, and a reminder about her brother might make her feel guilty enough to apologize. Since that splint came off his leg, he'd worked hard, harder than he ever cared to work again. Propping apple boughs and digging in the mud to siphon water to trees was not his idea of how to court a woman. And no woman, not even the Princess of Wales, was worth spraying for. But he'd hidden his distaste and tried to match Pete's work habits.

"I hardly know where to begin," she said.

"Aw, Elizabeth, let's go back to the beginning."

They were over at the far side of the water, away from the strong currents, and he pulled in the oars. Now the little boat could float on its own for a while, and he could devote himself to romancing Elizabeth.

"What do you mean you want to marry me?" Agnes Yates rose to her feet and looked down with incredulity at Antonio Mendez. "I hardly know you."

Antonio, handsome in western garb, shrugged. "In the old country, men and women do not need to know each other to wed. We only need assurances of good character. We can become acquainted after marriage."

Agnes Yates was horrified. Antonio was handsome, yes, but he was nothing to her but a smiling face and broken English and clothes that smelled of sheep manure.

They had crossed the water in a boat from the hotel and were seated in the midst of sagebrush. Early mule-ears blossomed nearby in a glint of yellow.

Rarely did Agnes stammer or lose her composure, but she came close now. "You—you said this was a picnic, to thank me for teaching you better English. You never said you were going to propose marriage!"

His dark eyes smiled. "Do you know, Agnes, your eyes sparkle like . . . like a million midnight stars over Seville?"

Agnes stood and whirled away, utterly dumbstruck and slightly dizzy. Antonio remained seated on the brightly patterned blanket. She didn't care if it was from his home in Spain. She didn't like the spicy Basque food he'd packed for lunch, and she especially disliked the wine.

Though Agnes didn't usually indulge, today she had sampled the wine, and that was why she couldn't think straight. She'd taken only a few sips from a tin mug, but it wasn't her custom to drink wine in broad daylight. Even while she stood, the sagebrush wavered in front of her eyes, and the river . . . well, it roared by fiercely, much more fiercely than tame Eden Creek.

Antonio came up behind her and had the audacity to put his hands on her shoulders. "Dearest Agnes. It is the fire in you that makes me choose you, don't you know that?"

Whirling, Agnes stared at him, aghast. There was no denying his handsomeness. Tall, dark, and even-featured with tanned skin and flashing white teeth. But never in her wildest dreams could she see herself married to a foreigner, and an uneducated one at that. Worst of all, a Basque sheepman.

"I can't marry you," she said with no preamble whatsoever.

"Why not?" he asked, calmly sitting down on the blanket and smiling up at her. "Tell me what is wrong. I shall change for you."

"You're not educated, that's what's wrong. Do you think a schoolteacher would marry a man who can't even spell?"

He leaned back on the blanket and laughed. "But, Agnes, I am going to be much rich," he said. "Soon."

"Very rich? You?"

"Yes, that is what I said. You would rather have a poor man who can spell than a rich man who can't?"

"I want an educated man."

"But explain, please, what is the difference? I am a graduate of a university in Spain. It is English I lack, not university."

"I don't believe you."

Instead of looking discouraged at this blunt rejection, Antonio merely smiled.

Her stomach fluttered.

His smile always put her at a disadvantage, and she hated it. Was this the sort of man her mother had scraped her knuckles bare for? Put her daughter through normal school for?

"There are only two kind of men in this world, Agnes," her mother had said. "Educated men and brutes. I'd rather you never wed than ended up as chattel to some beast who only wants you as a brood mare."

Why, Agnes had chosen the Eden Creek school deliberately because of the acute shortage of eligible women in Idaho. Within a year she should have been spoken for. Men, educated men, should have fought over her.

Only they hadn't . . .

"Agnes," Antonio said, "you want to think about my proposal? I wait. I am with the sheep for two summers and I wait and wait for family to come before I take a wife, but now this summer my brother takes the sheep up for the hills—"

"*To* the hills."

"To the hills, and down in the valley I start to build my house—"

"No, Antonio, don't you hear me? I can't marry you."

He stood there smiling, as if amused at her modesty. Oh, this was getting her nowhere. "I need to be alone," she said.

"But of course," he said. "I wait while you think."

She was beside herself with frustration. "You may leave, Antonio. I'll get home by myself."

"I have the boat, Agnes," he reminded her. "You cannot swim across the creek."

"Oh!" The man could be infuriatingly logical. "All right, I shall take a walk. A long walk. I shall think, and then we shall go back."

"But of course. You think all you want. I will wait."

Agnes Yates couldn't flee through the sagebrush and mule-ears fast enough. It wasn't fair. It just wasn't fair that she had to deal with marriage proposals from illiterate sheepmen when . . . when . . . Her gaze fell on the view across the river at the hotel, and she came to an abrupt halt as the object of her anger came into focus. Elizabeth Sheldon, for once not working in the orchard, was on the hotel boat dock being handed into a little rowboat—by none other than Joel Emory.

"Elizabeth Sheldon, this is all your fault," she muttered.

Elizabeth had taken Joel and was going to condemn Miss Yates to a lifetime of blackboards and schoolroom stoves to stoke, a lifetime of dense ranch children who came to school only when there were no crops to work. It wasn't fair. She sat down on a rock by the sage and put her chin in her hands.

After she had sat there sulking for a while, she blinked away her tears of rage and focused on the opposite shore. Across the rushing water, a figure moved from the hotel steps toward the grove of cottonwoods near the shore, then stopped.

Zack! Like her, he was watching the rowboats.

Miss Yates's heart did a flip-flop, and then hot, raw jealousy stole over her. Agnes had been certain that Zack Danvers was interested in her—until the subject of war came up at the meeting. Perhaps if she'd chosen another topic . . . Infuriating man. And as for Elizabeth, chasing him outside the schoolhouse like a brazen strumpet when she already had Joel. It was too much.

Sitting very still so there was no chance Zack could see her spying on him, Agnes shaded her eyes and followed the direction of his gaze. The rowboat. The boat with Elizabeth and Joel. And then Clara ran up and distracted Zack. That child. And Elizabeth. Agnes hated them both.

Her jealousy seethed up and bubbled over into hot angry tears. Why wasn't one man enough for that eastern snob? Agnes hoped perversely that the boat would tip over and that Elizabeth would drown.

"Wait, Zack," Clara called as she crawled out of her hiding spot under the hotel porch. "Why are you carrying your gear?"

"I'm leaving." He stopped on his way to the lane.

"Weren't you going to say good-bye?"

The best-laid plans . . . how many times had this child ruined them?

"You'll be okay, Clara. I've seen the list of casualties from the mine, and your pa's name isn't on it. I don't know where he is, but he's not on the list, so you can rest easy on that account."

Clara stood in a wide stance, hands on hips. "You think that means anything to Miss Yates? If that orphanage sends someone here before Pa comes back, Pete and I'll have to hide, just like Billy the Kid."

"Clara the Kid, huh?" Zack smiled. He'd grown fond of the little girl and gave her a reassuring pat on the head. "Elizabeth won't let anything happen to you and Pete."

"You aren't going to leave without saying good-bye to her?"

Zack groaned inside. "I said good-bye."

"Uh-uh. You didn't even look at her when you passed her in town. Elizabeth says it's okay for a gentleman to kiss a lady's hand if he's saying good-bye. Did you know Antonio kissed Miss Yates's hand one day? Right on the schoolhouse steps."

He had truly underestimated the child's ability to be everywhere. "A gentleman doesn't overdo things like that. And a young lady doesn't run around telling such things about other ladies."

"I'm not a young lady. I don't ever want to be a young lady and wear corsets and petticoats. I just want my pa to come back. You going to say good-bye to Pete?"

"Do you think he wants me to?"

" 'Course I do. You have to see our tree before you leave, too. The one Elizabeth gave us. It's up on the bluff, up in a secret place." Turning, she pointed, and when Zack looked he saw, not the ridge, but the water and a rowboat tied up across the river, where a couple had gone to picnic. Another boat, the one he'd been watching, now floated near the rapids.

"What's Elizabeth doing out there?" he asked.

Clara shrugged. "I think Joel's going to ask her to pick a wedding date. I heard him telling Pete in the barn that there won't be much work after he marries Elizabeth. Aren't you going to stay for the wedding?"

Zack stared, thunderstruck, at Clara. "She's going to marry Joel?" After all that had happened? In the back of his mind, the engagement hadn't been real; it was just words, like in a book. But what did he expect? To confess his sins to her, then ride off into the sunset and leave her to run the place alone?

Clara, who sometimes struck him as wise beyond her years, gave him an unaccountably sly look. "Well, where've you been all this time, Doc Danvers? That's why she came here is 'cause of Joel's letters. I thought you knew that. All the time you was out there mending Joel's leg, he was her fiancé. If you don't believe me, wait awhile till they come in off the water and you can ask her yourself."

"That won't be necessary. It's only that . . ." She couldn't marry Joel. He'd been certain she would call off the match. She *had* to. Because if Zack was any judge of character, Joel was not trustworthy and not worthy of her. Period.

There was a long silence, during which he thought Clara had run off. Then her voice floated up to him as if from a long distance.

"Zack, if you wind your watch again, you might break it."

He stuck the watch back into his vest pocket, unaware of how many times he'd fumbled with it. "Thank you, Clara."

"You're welcome. I'd stay if I were you. Wait till it cools off before you leave."

Absently he nodded and set down his gear. "You're right, Clara. I just might wait—at least long enough to wish Elizabeth well."

When he turned back to the river, the boat had drifted out of sight. He moved closer to the grove of cottonwoods at the shore.

The hot August sun beat down on Elizabeth without mercy, and the sagebrush bordering the river offered no shade. A flock of magpies flew up from the hotel lane, as if they'd been scared away—perhaps by children. Clara had run past the hotel moments before. A string of ducks paddled downstream with the rowboat, darting in and out of the wild grass that grew close to the bank.

"It's a near perfect day, isn't it?" she said, while removing her hat. Stray curls fell about her face, and she pushed them back, then trailed her hand in the water. This was such an idyllic excursion, yet she couldn't help wondering what it would be like to have Zack Danvers across from her. All she had to do was recall the feeling of his arms about her and her body went limp and warm.

"What are you thinking about?" Joel asked casually.

She kept her eyes shut.

"Just feeling the breeze on my face. It's a sin to be away from the orchard. I feel as if I'm playing hooky."

"You look pretty," Joel said softly. "As tempting as Eve outside *her* orchard."

Elizabeth's eyes snapped open. Slowly she turned from the distant view of the orchard to stare directly at him, and her face paled while her hands gripped the edge of the seat. This, she remembered, was not gentle Eden Creek she was on. It was the Payette River and beyond this wide spot of calm lay rapids. The man who rowed the boat was not Zack Danvers, either, but Joel Emory, a man with motives all his own.

She didn't like the look on Joel's face. It wasn't vulnerable like the way Zack looked at her, but something else. His smile was not tender, but . . . calculating.

She sat facing the bow, so she could clearly see where they were going, and it wasn't in a circle, which is what the rowboats were meant for—to row about the wide spot in the Payette River. They were passing sagebrush-strewn land, far from the hotel, and she'd rather have dangled her feet in the quieter waters of Eden Creek than rowed around in the unpredictable river.

"Joel, I know you can't see which way we're going, but don't you want to go the other way?" He was letting them drift, and the longer they drifted the farther they moved from the hotel. There were boulders and rapids just beyond the wide place in the river, and opposite the hotel a rough shore awaited with another rowboat tied up.

"Joel, let's go back."

"Elizabeth, I know what I'm doing."

Nervous, she pulled in her hand and hung on to the seat.

Joel squinted against the bright sun and focused his gaze on Elizabeth, studying her as if he could see right through her summer dress. The lawn fabric clung to her camisole, and she wished now she'd worn a less flimsy dress.

"Joel, lots of men come west and decide that a life of hardship isn't for them." She fought for the right words, the kind words. The sooner she said her piece, the sooner she'd get off this water. But she'd have to be gentle. Joel was weak and hated the orchardist's life, but she would not use that as a weapon to hurt him, only as a way to explain why she couldn't marry him.

"We don't suit." And never would.

Casually he reached for the oars and rowed the boat away from the shore, away from the bow of the other boat.

Except for the soft swish of the oars in the water and the breeze blowing around her, pressing the fabric of her skirt against her legs, all was silent.

"You can't break our engagement." Joel's words were as matter-of-fact as if he'd told her she couldn't harvest the fruit of a tree yet.

She blinked once at the starkness of his statement, then swallowed hard and took her time drying her hand on an old rag in the boat. While she did so, she said without looking up, "Joel, I never said that—"

"But you're going to."

"Let me explain something that happened to me; then you'll know why I've tried hard to keep from hurting you."

"What's to understand about breaking a promise?"

"I know it hurts."

"So you are going to jilt me?" His hands tightened about the oars, whitening his knuckles.

"Joel, I came out here to start over."

"And I was part of the bargain?" Joel's voice sounded bitter. Again he pulled in the oars.

"I wouldn't phrase it so crassly." She bit her lip in frustration and wiped a hand across her brow. "I don't want to make any mistakes." She looked out ahead of the boat, nervous again about the direction they were drifting.

Staring at her, he squinted. "You aren't holding out hope that doctor will marry you, are you, Elizabeth?"

She felt the blood drain from her face and turned back to look at him.

"Because if so," he said, "you're going to be disappointed. He's leaving, and no other man in this town is going to be foolish enough to pledge his troth to a crazy woman who raises apples. I'm the best you'll find, Elizabeth."

She couldn't put it off any longer. She'd have to tell him and be blunt about it.

"I'm sorry . . . I can't marry you." And she never would. Her words were more blunt than she'd wanted, but the water was distracting her. She glanced nervously at Joel to see if he'd heard her.

Joel had the good grace to look abashed, but just for a few seconds.

Letting go of an oar, he reached for her hand and held it. "Come here, closer." It was as if he hadn't heard a word she'd said.

The boat floated with the current. "Joel," she said nervously, pulling her hand away, "we'll crash into the bank."

"Naw, we'll just float with the current. Nothing wrong with drifting for a while." And he smoothed down his slick blond hair, loosened his tie and collar, intimate gestures both of them. With no warning he leaned over to kiss her.

"Don't, Joel. This isn't a private place to kiss." Or a safe one.

"Who wants to kiss? Is that all Zachary Danvers has done—kiss you? You've got a lot to learn, Elizabeth."

When he reached for her, it was with the strength of a man, a man not about to let go. "You want to learn about love, Elizabeth?"

Her stomach went hollow, tense, and she slapped him. But slapping him only succeeded in rocking the boat.

With dawning comprehension of what Joel intended for her out here alone in the boat came the realization that she could not run away. She was trapped in a rocking boat, surrounded by icy water.

Joel slid off the seat onto his knees. Then he seized her waist and pulled her off the seat so that she was on her back, in a puddle of water. He grabbed her hair and pushed her back against the seat so hard that the impact nearly knocked the wind out of her. And then he ripped open the hooks and eyes at the waistband of her skirt and pushed the skirt down over her hips.

"Joel, don't do this!" she pleaded, her heart pounding in her ears, like the rushing water all around her.

"You're mine. You promised." He pressed his weight onto her, while the boat wavered.

"Joel, stop!" she gasped. "Stop, and I'll never tell." Her heart was beating so fast she could barely think rationally.

His hand slid up her bodice. She knew fear then, not of the water, but of this man, a weak man who was determined to have his way.

"No-o!"

She kicked out at him, and with a vicious grip on her ankles, he held her legs down, then reached for her arms. With one hand she tried to scratch his face, but he twisted her other arm back over her head. All of a sudden, the boat fishtailed as its bow was sucked into an eddy.

Oblivious of the danger, Joel leaned over her, his breath hot on her face. "Don't scream, Elizabeth. We're only going to have our little private wedding night here in the boat. I'll try to treat you gently, but you have to lie still. Women are supposed to be docile in the bedchamber. Quiet and submissive. Didn't Lawrence or Zack teach you that? Too bad they were so slow. Now you'll be mine." And he sprawled across her in the boat, pressing himself down on her and kissing her brutally, his body heavy across hers. She turned her head from side to side, but he kept capturing her lips, and the boat rocked violently as she pushed at him.

I'd rather die than give in, she thought. I'd rather die . . . rather die. . . .

She went dizzy from the motion of the boat, and then once more his cold wet lips found hers while he reduced her skirt to a torn, soggy heap of cloth at her ankles. She had two choices, it seemed: rape or drowning.

She screamed, and her thoughts went fuzzy; the world became a place of terrifying sensations and movements. Reality was reduced to fragments, parts of a whole.

A leg pinioning her.

Water sloshing over her bodice.

Bile rising in her throat.

Whiskers scraping her face.

Hands that wouldn't let go.

She was aware of the desperate scrape of her fingernails against his skin . . . and then the taste of blood.

Time shattered like a comet running out of energy, cascading downward. Then the world tipped upside down and water washed over her, filled her mouth, cut off her scream, reduced her life to a nightmare in which words begged for release but couldn't cut through the black icy ceiling that imprisoned her.

Please God, let me breathe. Mama . . . Mama . . . Mama!

Numbing water closed over her head, and the world went black and cold. She couldn't tell up from down until all of a sudden her hand touched bottom. Desperate, with all her strength, she pushed off and floated up . . . up . . . up, and just before her lungs burst, she broke the surface, gasped, and grabbed a chunk of wood. A sliver pierced her hand. Then there was nothing, not even breath or hope.

She heard a scream, her own, and then as she choked and gasped, cold water once again closed over her head and sucked her down into its dark depths.

14

Lizzie.

At her first scream, Zack was running down to the river, and just before he dived in, he saw the boat tip over. As he swam out to where Elizabeth had disappeared, the cold numbed him to the bone, but he didn't slow his pace.

The last he saw of the boat, Joel was clinging to it and the current was quickly pulling it toward the rapids. A yard away from Zack, Elizabeth bobbed to the surface, limp as a rag doll, disappeared, then lifted a frantic hand from the water and grabbed at Zack and missed.

An oar floated by and he flung it away, then dived under the water and felt for her slight figure. He came up, gasping for breath and empty-handed. Then, after shaking water out of his eyes, he dived again and got lucky.

Honestly lucky.

Elizabeth's hair had come unpinned and streamed out behind her in the water. Although he couldn't see her, he swam right into her glorious honey-gold hair, reached for a lock, and hand over hand, pulled her closer to him until he had her molded against him.

With only seconds left before he lost his breath, he twisted her hair into a coil, like a lifeline and, after pushing off from

231

the bottom of the river, floated upward, pulling her with him. Up and up and up till together they broke the surface, and he gulped in greedy lungfuls of air.

Beside him, she coughed, choked, gasped for air—desperate little noises that were wonderful to his ears. Sounds of life and pain. She cried, and he could see the tug of hair against scalp, but he held on for dear life, wanting to hug her to pieces, but not daring yet.

For she wasn't safe yet; nor was he. The current reached for both of them, pulled, dragged, sucked with a mighty force of its own. Hanging on to Lizzie for dear life, Zack strained with each stroke, sliced the water again and again, but went nowhere. With one monumental effort, he raised his hand like a hammer and cracked the water open. Again and again and again. With Lizzie in tow, he fought to escape the grasping arms of the Payette River until finally, having stroked as far as he could, he nearly collapsed, spent. He knelt as dark water eddied around his waist, and he gathered Lizzie to him, pulled her up against his shoulder, cradled her to his heart, her hair streaming across his face.

Instinctively she wrapped her legs around his waist, clung to his chest, her arms locked about his neck, choking him, coughing out water on his neck. And then he held on to her for dear life. It was the best thing a woman had ever done to him: spit water on him.

Twice before he reached shore, Elizabeth rolled partway over and grabbed for his shirt, both times threatening to drag them under. Mercifully she fell slack, and he carried her the rest of the way, collapsing at the shore.

He woke up to feel at least three pairs of hands gripping him and pulling him out onto the hard shore. His head and shoulders rested among grass and rocks, while from the waist down water still lapped at him, freezing his legs. Rolling over, he choked and spewed water.

Small sensations returned.

The sun on his face.

The grass tickling his shoulder.

The blue sky staring down at him.

And prim Elizabeth, dear, dear Lizzie, entwined about his legs, wearing only her pantaloons.

Then voices. Granny's voice was louder than the others.

"Well, looks like we caught ourselves a doctor at last. Somebody untangle them before decent folks get ideas."

Absurdly, Zack hoped there weren't any "decent folks" for miles around, and then blankets came down around them. Blankets to end the shivering, as in the yellow fever wards, and then at last reality intruded. He remembered where he was. And, worse, who.

Some things would never change.

When Agnes screamed on the opposite shore, Antonio came running to see what was happening.

"Terrible. Terrible," he murmured when he saw the overturned rowboat.

"It's Joel." Agnes was frozen in place, terrified of crossing back over the river. "Joel's in the water."

"Hurry, then," Antonio said and, to her amazement, grabbed her arm as if . . . as if he owned her. Why, he didn't even stop to collect his blanket and picnic basket. He pulled her along like one of his straggling sheep, and his quick wits surprised her.

While Antonio jumped in and positioned the oars, Agnes untied the boat, and in moments they were rowing across the creek, Antonio's arms straining through his wet clothes. Frantic, Agnes looked downriver in the direction she'd last seen Joel. His head was bobbing about the overturned boat, and then suddenly he went under and disappeared.

"*She* probably pushed him in. I hate her."

"Hate is a strong emotion, little one," Antonio said, breathing hard, rowing with all his might. "If you can hate, you can learn to love. Even the black sheep are good for something."

Did Antonio have to choose this particular moment for a homily? She didn't want to talk. She wanted him to get her across the river in one piece. Agnes did not speak while they crossed the creek, but instead clung to either side of the little rowboat as if it were not to be trusted, and watched Antonio row like a Roman slave. Perversely she hoped if anyone had to drown, it would be Elizabeth Sheldon.

The instant Antonio handed her onto shore at the hotel boat dock, she picked up her skirts and ran up the shore to where Clara Gustavson was jumping up and down screaming amid a gathering crowd of onlookers. Shielding her eyes, Agnes peered out at the two wringing wet people who lay at water's edge, and her heart sank.

"You're a brave man, Zack," Maddie said softly and tucked the blanket up under his chin as if he were a small boy in need of humoring.

Groaning, he opened his eyes and saw all manner of faces peering down at him. The one with the pursed lips had to be Granny. The one with the soft brown eyes was Maddie. The one with the white face and scared expression was . . . was Miss Yates.

"Bravery has its price," Granny said sagely. "And I'm going to get my heart's desire and do some doctoring on both of you."

Granny, mused Zack, opening one eye to peer at her, was in her glory now, but for once, Zack was not about to argue medicine with her. The way he looked at it, he was halfway dead anyway, so any fool tonics Granny poured down him would either leave him half dead or finish him off. He shut his eyes.

Zack's ears were plugged with water, his movements slow from the cold, but he could still hear the faint voices from the shore. Women. Men. Children. People pleaded with him from every direction, from the shore, and from the water. From his memory and from his longing. He had to do something. *Dr. Danvers, help us. Please help . . . help.*

He wanted only one. "Where's Lizzie?"

There was a long pause. "Elizabeth's right beside you."

He could feel her shaking beside him, and he crawled the two feet to Elizabeth, summoning all his strength to reach her, to pull himself up and push on her back until water gushed from her mouth.

"Breathe, Lizzie," he commanded. "Breathe, breathe."

She choked, a strangled sound, and then gasped in air, and all he could do was straddle her with one leg while with his hands he pushed up and down on her chest, up and down, willing her to keep breathing. When she quit choking and her lungs moved up and down on their own, he collapsed on top of her and rolled to one side, holding her from behind, spoon fashion.

"Joel . . ."

"Help's coming, Lizzie. Don't talk . . . don't talk—" He choked on the last word and buried his face in her wet hair. Rocks scraped his knuckles, his legs were freezing, but he was content to die here as long as he could feel her heartbeat beneath his fingers.

She'd called for Joel. What did she want with him? Anger welled up inside Zack. Though he couldn't stop to articulate the feelings, he knew a brief rush of emotion, hot and painful.

"What the devil were you thinking of, going out in a boat with that city slicker? What? Are you crazy, Lizzie? What? What? What?" Coughing, he doubled over.

"Joel . . ." she whimpered.

The name cut him to the quick. Half dead, she still thought of Joel.

"Where's Joel?" Ben asked.

Zack rolled away from Elizabeth. "I hope to hell he's dead."

"Dead?" It was Miss Yates's voice.

"He's gone," someone said in a hushed tone. "We'll send people out to search, but . . ."

"If he dies, it was no accident!" Agnes said.

"Hush up!"

"Maybe that's what Zack wanted. Didn't you hear what he said? He hopes Joel's dead!"

"Hush your mouth!" bellowed Granny. "Hush, I say, or I'll take your ruler to you, Agnes Yates."

Miss Yates sniffed. "Well, I know perfectly well what I saw. Did anyone besides me see the boat tip over? I'm a witness."

Zack was instantly awake and by now clear-eyed enough to make out the smug expression on Agnes Yates's face. When no one answered, she continued in a know-it-all voice.

"I am the only eyewitness," she bragged. "If I say I saw all three of them together at the boat, who's to doubt my word?"

"Go on up to the hotel and get some water boiling." Granny was giving orders. "Damn impertinence." She turned to Pete and Clara, who peeked out from behind a cottonwood. "You two. Go help."

"Well," huffed Miss Yates, "it's what Elizabeth Sheldon deserved, acting like Eve, tempting all the men for miles around with her apples and—"

Whatever Miss Yates had been going to add was to forever remain a mystery.

"Now is not the time for such words," a man said.

"Antonio—"

"Did you not teach me there is a time and place for everything?"

"I know what I saw—"

Mercifully, Antonio dragged Miss Yates away by the elbow, and her accusations were silenced.

If Elizabeth had heard the diatribe she said nothing, and Zack groped for her beneath the blanket they shared.

He touched her hand. She was limp and her skin was icy cold, but he found her wrist and, with his thumb, felt for himself the reassuring beat of her pulse. He had just enough strength to rub his thumb across her inner wrist, warming that one square inch of her.

There was comfort enough for him in having held her, pushed the hair from her eyes, absorbed her trembling, seen her salty tears. He felt her pain and took it for his own, a loan repaid.

"Joel . . ."

His thumb stopped caressing her in mid-stroke.

Again a stab of unreasoning jealousy shot through him. She and Joel were engaged. An engaged couple going for an intimate ride in a rowboat. An honest accident.

Lizzie was shivering badly now. "J-J-Joel?"

"Shh," Granny said, and then someone picked her up with orders to carry her to the hotel.

Zack caught a glimpse of her in someone's arms, hair streaming down her back, pantaloons torn and clinging to her legs.

Waving off any offers of assistance, Zack jackknifed up to a sitting position and sat there, dizzy and weak, watching as Ben emerged from the creek, shaking his head, defeat written on his strong face. Ben dropped a single oar near Zack. Far down the creek bank, Zack spotted the second oar, the only sign left of the accident.

Zack drew up one knee and slumped against it.

"You okay?" Ben asked, reaching down to pull Zack up.

"I didn't like Joel," Zack said, then coughed and raked a hand through his wet hair.

Ben stood there waiting while he gathered his voice again. "I didn't like him . . . but—"

"I know," Ben said.

Zack was determined to say the words, if he had to choke them out. "But I'd never . . . never want this." Zack was a healer, for heaven's sake. "I was mad . . . because he almost drowned Lizzie, but I didn't mean what I said."

"I know what you meant, Zack." Ben hauled him up and slung an arm around him.

But Miss Yates's accusations rang in Zack's ears. If he had one shred of idealism left, it was the hope that somewhere he could find a place to belong. But here he was staring into the face of grief again, as if it owned him, as if it were laughing at him. *You may be a doctor, but all you do is bring death and dying.* Like a curse death followed him wherever he went.

*   *   *

The town turned the wicker and bric-a-brac parlor of the Groveland Hotel into a makeshift recovery room. The women had removed Elizabeth's wet clothing and now she lay on the horsehair sofa wearing one of Maddie's robes as well as a cream-colored quilt over her shoulders, Indian style. Despite the hot day, she still shivered from the shock and so Clara's Civil War coat was tucked around her hands like a muff, and a hot-water bottle warmed her feet.

Zack, who had gone up to his own room to change into dry clothes, just stood in the doorway a second looking at her. He'd never seen her hair—that lovely spun-gold hair—hanging loose before. Nor had he ever seen her face so drained of color. Granny was pressing her to drink some concoction that smelled suspiciously like a spring tonic.

Elizabeth looked up at him with red-rimmed eyes, and he slumped down in a nearby chair. He'd saved her life, but he'd failed to save Joel, her fiancé.

"Zack?" Elizabeth's voice was stronger. "Are you all right?"

Nodding, he looked up and guessed at her next question before she asked it, waved aside the cup of tonic Granny was pressing on him, and went to kneel at Elizabeth's side.

"Have they found Joel?" Her whispered words were barely controlled.

Granny cleared her throat, a warning signal if Zack ever heard one.

"Not yet," he said carefully.

Her eyes filled with tears, and he wanted to take her in his arms, but Granny was watching them. Granny and Maddie and Ben and half a dozen other townspeople. The next best thing he could do was usurp Granny's authority and examine Elizabeth. As if she'd read his mind, Maddie handed him his medical bag.

When Granny had herded everyone out of the room, Zack pushed back the quilt and the silk robe and with his stethoscope pressed against her bare skin, under her breast, listened to her heart, then her lungs. When he was done, he pulled the quilt around her again.

"You're lucky," he said.

"No, I'm not," she said, as one tear spilled down her cheek. "Joel's dead, I know he is, and it's all my fault."

And then he couldn't just walk away from her, not without some comfort, a listening ear.

"Lizzie," he murmured, not caring if she liked the nickname or not, "what happened out there?"

Elizabeth shook her head. She remembered everything up until the moment the boat tipped over, but Joel's attack on her was not the sort of thing a lady spoke of. "The boat tipped over." That's all she said. "The boat tipped over."

If anyone understood her inability to talk about the horrific experience, it was Zack. Moving to her, he knew he didn't have much professional detachment left, and he didn't much care. He cupped her face in his hands, with his thumbs tracing away the tears.

"I've got to go back to the water," she sobbed. "I've got to find him."

"No." The room was silent, heavy with summer air, with the steamy scent of herbs brewing, and the taste of tears.

"People will think it's my fault," she said so softly he could barely hear. "I made him angry when I broke our engagement."

"Elizabeth Sheldon, what a far-fetched thing to say! Miss Yates saw what happened. She'll tell it straight."

Granny reappeared in the doorway, and as one they turned to her. "This may come as a shock at a bad time but I wouldn't count on that little schoolteacher to be any help. She left one fine mess in the kitchen while she was supposed to be helping Maddie fix tea, and she'll make a mess of Elizabeth's life, too, if you ask me."

"What do you mean?"

Zack sensed the entire hotel eavesdropping, and Granny lowered her voice. "Agnes Yates is as jealous as a polecat what's got its eyes on a mountain lion's dinner. And don't ask me to do no explaining. Figure it out yourself, Doc Danvers."

When Miss Agnes Yates returned from a ride up into the hills beyond the valley of Eden Creek, she had two bucketfuls of fresh-picked huckleberries dangling from her saddle and a crucial decision about her future settled.

After much soul-searching, she had decided to stand by her impulsive statement. There *had* been three people in the river—*after* the boat capsized—so she hadn't told an outright lie. It also wasn't quite the truth, but as schoolteacher she had her reputation to uphold. She had a right to embellish her story, she told herself. The schoolteacher and arbiter of ethics couldn't suddenly change her story. Moreover, if the town found out her statement had more spite than truth in it she might lose her position.

Inside the house she tipped the contents of the buckets out onto the table. She picked through the berries, sorting out the leaves and twigs. The berries, the first of the season, were dark blue and plump, and by the time she'd scooped half of them into a pot and washed them at the pump, her fingers were blue as well.

She stoked up the fire in her cookstove and when it was blazing hotter than the August sun outside, she tied on an apron and added sugar to the berries. Then she went to work on the pastry. She was going to make fresh huckleberry pie for her expected company.

She wasn't sure who would come calling, but someone would. She could count on that. Any time now the townspeople would descend on her, asking her to repeat exactly what she saw. It was important that she have her tale memorized, so that she wouldn't get it mixed up. A fresh huckleberry pie could sweeten the entire ordeal, and soon the scent of cooking huckleberries began to drift from the stove, filling every familiar nook and cranny of her house.

It was a bittersweet scent. In fact, everything about life in Eden Creek had been bittersweet since Miss Elizabeth Sheldon arrived. Pretty, educated, and able to do anything.

She could have at least failed with her crop, but even the apples were growing, though Agnes held out a hope that they would all be wormy. Which was a mean thought, but Agnes had a right to feel mean.

For three years now she'd lived in this room alone.

Alone.

In a town where men outnumbered women three to one, at least. She had a roof over her head, and she wanted for nothing. When anything around the school needed to be repaired or the woodpile grew low or the roof leaked, always one of the men from the school board came—Ben Danvers or one of the mercantile boys or a rancher. But no one on the school board was single. Except for socials and dances, where men ignored her, Agnes had no chance to meet other men, except those she tutored—like Antonio.

Antonio. How could fate send her a man so handsome and yet so unschooled?

It wasn't fair.

By the time she'd rolled out pie dough and baked three pies, she'd convinced herself that all was fair in love and war. And by the time the knock came on her door, Agnes had three pies cooling. When she opened the door, her heart thumped, but she didn't betray her uneasiness.

She smiled. "Hello, Elizabeth," and invited her in. The time had come to make life fair.

Miss Yates paused, looking at her pies. "Shall we take refreshment first? You must be feeling weak still."

"No, thank you," Elizabeth said, looking remarkably fit, which dashed Agnes's hopes that Elizabeth might take a chill and come down with pneumonia.

Elizabeth stood just inside the doorway, as if reluctant to come closer. "Agnes," she said, "it appears you're the only witness to the tragedy."

Agnes lowered her head and traced a huckleberry spill on her table. "It appears I am."

So Agnes was going to play coy. Elizabeth took a deep breath. What she saw and felt and remembered about Joel's attack was unspeakable. To avoid speaking about it she had to press the truth out of Agnes about that boat accident. She pressed on. "You said something untrue, and the entire town is at odds, wondering what to believe. Zack Danvers's reputation is threatened. You wouldn't do that deliberately, I know, so I wish you'd rethink what you saw."

"Do I have to talk about it now? Perhaps after the memorial service? I'm feeling distraught myself. Such an awful thing to witness."

"Agnes, what *did* you see?"

This was the moment Agnes had been waiting for. "It all happened very fast, and I was so scared." Agnes kept her gaze fastened on the table, traced a scar in the wood with her finger.

"Well . . ." she began, "it was so shocking . . . I feel as if I'm tattling, telling tales out of school . . ." Her voice quavered. "It wasn't so much what happened to the boat as what happened inside the boat. It was dreadful the way Zack Danvers pushed at poor Joel when his back was turned. Didn't you see?"

Agnes was lying. Lying! But the only way Elizabeth could dispute her lies was talk about Joel's attack and . . . she realized she couldn't face another besmirched reputation. Just couldn't. Not even to save Zack's reputation.

"Zack wasn't in the boat with us, Agnes."

"Well, of course not, but Ben has several rowboats. I suppose Zack rowed another one out, and then jumped out and swam to your boat."

Elizabeth bowed her head and pressed her lips together in shame. "That's not what happened, Agnes." But she couldn't bring herself to tell what really did. To tell Agnes Yates about the shameful assault by Joel Emory would put Elizabeth in the worst light. Only a loose woman would invite such behavior.

Agnes remained standing, her face set, coral earbobs dangling. "Well, what do the details matter? All I really know is that Zack saved you while Joel foundered right nearby. It was all so convenient."

And then she was silent, staring at her hands, waiting for Elizabeth's reaction.

"Agnes," Elizabeth said, "are you saying Zack Danvers or I planned this? If so, that's not true."

Agnes met Elizabeth's gaze head on. "I suppose you're going to tell the entire town that Joel—decent, hardworking, gentlemanly Joel—assaulted you, and like a knight to the rescue, Zack Danvers swam all the way out into those currents just to save you. Really, Elizabeth, how gullible do you think the townspeople are?"

"Agnes, you're wrong."

"If you have a different version of the truth, then tell it."

"I can't." She bowed her head, shame blinding her, her throat tight, guilt overwhelming her. "You're wrong, Agnes," she managed to whisper. She was the coward. For not telling the truth and clearing Zack's name. For caring more about her own name than about him. But her name was all she had. It was why she'd come west. Her name and an orchard full of apples were all she had left in this world. "You're wrong," she choked out again. "Wrong."

After a pause, Miss Agnes Yates advanced on her, mouth pursed, as if Elizabeth had been caught passing notes in class. "No, you're wrong. Wrong in coming here. You were wrong to befriend those urchins." There were so many wrongs Agnes couldn't get them all out. Elizabeth was wrong to spend so much time with Zack Danvers when she already had a fiancé. Wrong to accept Joel's proposal. Wrong to attract the interest of two men and leave Agnes none.

Calmly and with stiff back, Miss Yates opened the door the same way she did when sending a child out of school to stand on the porch wearing a dunce cap. They said quick good-byes, stiff words, and outside again Elizabeth welcomed the fresh air, a relief from the camphor smell of Miss Yates's house.

"Zack Danvers deserves better from you, Agnes," Elizabeth said, then walked out past the big wild sunflowers that grew up around the school property.

"I'm sorry I can't help him . . . or you," Agnes said to her back, "but as Eden Creek's schoolteacher, I have my reputation to uphold, and as I'm sure you know, Elizabeth, reputation is all a body's got in this life, isn't it?"

15

Eden Creek quickly took sides on what had happened in that little rowboat. Some, like Mrs. Hankins and the ranch wives and the Kelseys of the mercantile and the Pierces of the newspaper and Mr. Brown of the livery stable, believed Miss Yates's story of a lovers' triangle in which Zack and Elizabeth had conspired against Joel. Others, like Mr. Gantt and all his saloon customers and Mr. Atwood who'd made Joel's crutches, believed it was an accident made more tragic by a woman scorned.

Caught in the middle was Granny Sikes who, when asked to take sides, pursed her lips and muttered, "I'm getting entirely too old to have my heart torn apart. Until I have proof with my own two eyes, I won't say what I think"—a statement that angered Miss Yates no end.

They all agreed on one thing, however: Joel was gone, vanished as surely as if he'd never been here. But when or where his body would wash up was anybody's guess. With the tragedy heavy in their hearts and gossip loose on their tongues, the people of Eden Creek came together a few days later for a church service in Joel's memory, the congregation divided on either side of the aisle according to the way their minds were leaning.

On the left in the front pew sat Miss Yates, weeping into a camphor-scented hanky all the way through the service. On the right in the front pew sat the Danverses—Ben and Maddie, and even Zack, who slipped in late and avoided looking at Elizabeth. She sat right behind him, clutching a violet-scented hanky, the Gustavsons flanking her. Pete wore a shirt and pants borrowed from Will Sheldon's trunk; Clara tugged at the collar of a made-over dress and hid her borrowed shoes under the pew.

The congregation was about evenly divided. Granny, not knowing where to sit, finally volunteered to sit by the minister and read the Twenty-Third Psalm.

Elizabeth tried to avoid looking at Zack for fear people would find that reason to confirm their suspicions. Too much temptation in the orchard, indeed. Head bowed, Elizabeth stared at her hands and when Clara reached over to slip her hand into hers, she swallowed back tears.

"I don't mind Miss Yates hating me," Clara had said earlier. "Cause I've done things that deserve it, like writing my letters backwards and playing hooky and sticking grasshoppers in her desk. But you haven't stolen anybody's cobblers or eavesdropped on any secrets. I guess Miss Yates is just plain mean, right to her crooked little pinky."

Or jealous. Elizabeth squeezed the little girl's hand and drew comfort from it while a soft summer breeze wafted through the open windows of the church. For a moment she allowed her gaze to rest on Zack Danvers as the breeze ruffled his dark hair. He sat directly in front of her, after all, and it was no crime to stare at a man's back in church, was it? Or to give thanks that he'd been brave enough to rescue her from drowning?

Across the aisle someone whispered, and when she turned her gaze to the altar, the whispering stopped. She was being watched. She and Zack. Cynical Zack. After his agonizing confession to her, this of all things he didn't need. As for her, this was a hundred times worse than any pain she'd known back in Massachusetts. A thousand times.

How could so many people believe she was so wicked? How could Miss Yates be so mean, so hateful? But then she remembered the day she'd arrived in town. Ben Danvers had warned her then that the town was divided on whether she'd succeed or fail. Maybe there were those who wanted her to fail—in any way possible.

The service closed with songs—"A Mighty Fortress is our God," followed by "Amazing Grace"—and then it was over. At once she slipped outside without a word to anyone, especially Zack, and with Pete driving the wagon, she and the Gustavsons made their way back to the orchard.

In the afternoon she thought she'd die of loneliness. The clock in the bedroom ticked away while she tried to compose a letter to Joel's family in Baltimore. All Joel had wanted was to get back to them. She didn't fault him for his objective, but his means . . . She could still feel the touch of his hands, could still see the suggestive leer on his face, and could reexperience his desperate assault, the panic.

Memories of the icy water, the echo of her desperate pleas, Zack breathing life back into her were like balm. But why did Agnes Yates have to lie? If it was jealousy, there was no dealing with it. All Elizabeth could deal with was the day at hand, and a letter to Joel's family. No matter what Joel's actions, his family deserved a decent letter.

"Dear Mr. and Mrs. Emory," she wrote. "It is my sad duty to pass on the news of a boat accident involving your son. He fell into the river and is missing still. As his betrothed who has worked with him on an orchard here in Idaho all summer, my opinion of him is that he was a fine, hardworking man of integrity . . ." She scratched out the last part. For some reason she couldn't, just couldn't bear to write of Joel in the past tense. "He is a fine, hardworking man, and we hope yet that he might be found. . . ."

What were the odds of Joel surviving that current? It didn't bear thinking of.

The screen door squeaked open.

"Elizabeth?"

Clara, in the familiar overalls, wore a lace mantilla that Elizabeth had made her from an old curtain, and she had tucked the cuffs of her pants into an old pair of high-button shoes. Her balance was wobbly, her femininity taking uncertain steps.

"Do you want to come out and see the apples? They're starting to turn color."

"I know, dear." Earlier she'd seen for herself the first traces of pink on their skin, faint, as if they'd blushed to see all the goings-on beneath them.

Suddenly she wanted to be out there among the trees and, with Clara, walked out into her orchard. *Her* trees. Although she was weighted down by anguish, they were heavy with the promise of harvest. She'd brought them this far, with help from Clara and Pete, and she found comfort in walking the rows, looking, touching, knowing she'd made her brother's dream come true.

"Pete's propping up a few more branches. There's lots and lots of apples, so you can feel glad about something."

Clara's attempts to console her were sweet.

"Are you still sad about Joel?"

"Of course."

"Will you never marry now? Pete says you'll pine for Joel forever."

"Sadness is no more than a passing seedling, Clara. Spring and harvests return to our lives over and over."

"You won't leave?"

"I won't leave you till your pa comes home, Clara. You know that. I promised. What makes you even doubt it?"

"Because it's almost harvest. And I don't know what you'll do after, because . . . well, people are talking."

"What did you do when they talked about you?"

"I let 'em talk. Nobody can say lies about my pa or take me away from here . . . not till he comes home."

"So I'll guess I'll have to let them talk about me, too, especially Miss Yates. She won't take you away from your pa, and she won't hurt me either, unless I let her."

"Pa would like you . . . I think."

"You've got me curious about this pa of yours and what he's been up to."

"Oh, he just loses track of time. I know the town doesn't think he's a good pa, but that's just because he's big like a grouchy bear and because he lets me and Pete do what we want. That's Pa."

Clara stopped at a particularly lush tree and stared at the apples, full-size now, lacking only the colorful red stripes that more hot days and cool nights would bring. "What makes apples turn red?" she asked suddenly.

"What do you think?"

"I think," she said, "that they must get sunburned."

Pete came up behind them and headed for another tree. "You're silly, Clara. You might as well say they've got blood in 'em."

"Shut up, Pete. Pa didn't teach you everything."

"You be quiet."

"Shush, you're upsetting Elizabeth."

"It's all right, Pete," she said when she saw the abashed look on his face. "I appreciate the propping."

In a way Pete was right. Elizabeth had, after all, poured her heart and courage, if not her blood, into these trees, receiving only blisters and aching muscles in return. But she had another answer for Clara's question.

"I think," she said softly with a wink at Pete, "that God probably took a piece of a rainbow from the sky and told the color red to drift onto the apples."

"Sort of like painting them."

"Yes, sort of."

Pete mumbled something about "girls," then lifted a heavy branch and pushed under it a prop at least twice the height of a broomstick.

Then he turned and looked at Elizabeth, a more matter-of-fact question on his lips. "Do you think there'll be a harvest, Elizabeth?"

They all three knew what he meant. Since the accident, since the awful scandal, the town was so divided about what it believed that no one wanted to help with the apple harvest. And even Pete had said it was going to take lots and lots of people to pick these apples.

"I don't know," she said, heartsick to think all these lush red apples might rot on the trees for want of hands to pick them.

"We can harvest a few rows ourselves . . ." Pete's voice trailed off.

"But," Clara said, "Miss Yates told all the literary ladies that if they come help you, she'll quit as president."

"You've got a big mouth for a sister who says she can keep secrets." Pete propped up yet another heavy apple bough, then scowled at his little sister.

Elizabeth left abruptly followed by Clara.

A long time later, composed and under control, she sat in her rocker, listening to the train whistle and wondering if Zack, despite all that had happened, might say good-bye before he left town.

Or would he leave the same way he arrived—sneaking out through a back door?

Staring out his window at the hotel, Zack looked over the entire Sheldon orchard. True, it was a distant view, but that was for the best. For the last few days, by unspoken agreement, he'd never gone near Lizzie. Now he was tempted.

No, Zack, don't risk any more. His own brother had as much as said so.

That wasn't why he stayed away from Elizabeth, though.

It was so she wouldn't risk any more for him.

After all, she was here to stay. He could leave . . . maybe . . . if only they'd find Joel and know for certain his fate . . . if only Miss Yates would take back her lies.

A hundred times he'd kicked himself for not having seen what Miss Yates was up to with her berry pies. If he'd flirted back more, if he'd danced with her . . . Over and over he recalled the summer, trying to understand why a woman would tell such a lie. . . .

Was she jealous of Elizabeth? He'd never understand women, but then, he guessed Lizzie had good reason not to understand him, not to trust him. He wanted to change that, to let Elizabeth know she could count on his strength. He laughed bitterly at the irony of it. If anyone saw him holding her in comfort, it would lend all the more credence to Miss Yates's accusations.

When he laughed, a shadow moved outside, below his window.

Clara was at the windowsill, no doubt reaching up for one of Maddie's fresh-baked cookies, and he called down to her to wait until he could walk down there. Mercifully, the child obeyed.

"How's Elizabeth?" he asked when he had joined Clara at the window. "And don't tell me it's a secret."

"How come you want to know? You're not going to make her sad, are you?"

"No." Blunt and to the point. Did every female since Eve have to talk at cross purposes?

Damn it, child. Talk.

He reached for the cookie she'd stolen, but Clara was a much more practiced thief and hid it in her overall bib. "Then you'd never do anything to hurt her, would you?"

"No."

"Not even hurt Joel?"

"What do you think?"

"I think Joel was jealous because Elizabeth liked you better."

Out of the mouths of babes.

"Elizabeth's crying. Are you going to be her beau again?"

He gritted his teeth and spoke with as much patience as possible. "I never was her beau, Clara, but maybe later, after a decent interval, I can be her friend again."

"What does 'decent interval' mean?"

"Go ask Maddie. And let me know what she says, will you?" His feet were moving, taking him toward the orchard.

"Where are you going?"

"To ask Elizabeth if a decent interval has passed."

At sunset he came to her door.

At first she just stared through the screen at him.

"Lizzie," he said softly, "can I talk to you?"

She stood still, looking at him and took her time deciding what to do. He never moved.

Finally she moved toward him and opened the door. The house smelled of cooked apples and cinnamon, and she wore a plain white apron. "I've been canning some early applesauce. I'll send some jars back with you to Maddie."

He had not come for applesauce. "Lizzie, this is ridiculous—avoiding each other, not talking, all because of town gossip."

"I've decided the same thing." But she didn't invite him in. Instead she folded her arms and looked out at the orchard. "Maybe, though, it would be best if we walked outside."

Outside it was just turning dark. The trees had lost color, but their outlines were clearly visible. He watched Elizabeth come down the porch steps.

Her profile was delicate, and she had never looked more vulnerable. Wisps of curls fell down her neck. He jammed his hands in his pockets so he wouldn't reach for her, at least not immediately.

"Will you walk with me?" she asked softly, still avoiding looking at him.

His heart turned over. In that moment he'd have walked to hell and back for her, and he fell into step beside her.

They walked a few moments in silence, and then she stopped and looked up at the sky. "The first star is out, and Venus." The air was heavy with the scent of loamy earth and wildflowers. A lone cricket was chirping.

"I don't know why she hates me, Zack." They both knew she meant Miss Yates.

"Why did the boat overturn? Tell me. You know you can tell me."

She was silent, counting the stars.

Constellations of stars flew by while he waited for her to speak. The moon ebbed and waned. The sun burned out, along with the sun inside his soul.

Finally, Elizabeth spoke. "When I was a child I'd lie in the grass after dark on summer nights and locate the Big Dipper up in the sky."

He touched his thumb to her cheek, just the touch of a moonbeam. He wasn't expecting big things like smiles, but he wished she'd talk to him, look at him, cry. Anything but silence.

"Can't you tell me?"

"No."

He sucked in his breath. "That son of a bitch."

She bent her head, and a tear rolled down her face.

He reached for her then and pulled her to him. "Lizzie, Lizzie—"

"That's a stupid name." She was in his arms, but stiff, not embracing him back.

"Zack, I can't see you again. I feel so guilty."

His hand came up to burrow in her hair. "Lizzie, if anyone's guilty I am."

"But you were a hero. You saved me."

"I told you . . . I'm no hero."

"Well, do you think I'm a heroine? If I told the town what Joel tried to do, I'd be a loose woman and the town would invent all sorts of awful things about you and I . . ."

He laid a finger over her mouth. "Shh. I don't have a good name to worry over."

"Zack." His name came out like a whimper, and she pulled away and sat down under a tree, her knees drawn up, like a child, her skirt tucked under her.

He strode over to where she sat and knelt beside her. "I'm not a hero," he repeated, "so there's no need to protect my honor and good name and all that rot."

"Oh, Zack."

"If you want the real unvarnished truth, I let every puppy owned as a boy die."

"Zack, don't—"

"And since I've come to the hotel, every fern of Maddie's has withered and died."

Now she smiled. "You're exaggerating. You probably poured formaldehyde on them."

"You're lucky I didn't do it in your orchard."

"Zack, you're being too hard on yourself."

"Am I? I kill things instead of healing them. Do you know how that feels?" Before she could answer, he told her. "You don't, of course. Everything you touch turns to life. Blossoms or thrives. Orchards. Urchins. Is there anything in this town you've tried and failed at?"

Tears splashed down her cheeks, and she turned her face from the moonlight. You, she thought to herself, face averted so he wouldn't see the tears. Only you.

He turned her to face him then, and in the moonlight his own face reflected the same bitterness and cynicism he'd worn when she met him. "I let your fiancé drown. I wish I could feel guilty about it, but I don't feel any more regret than if a rather nasty rat had drowned. I guess that makes me heartless. The only really noble thing I've done lately is keep you at arm's length."

"Stop it," she said. "You're right. You're heartless, and don't know why."

"Sorry, Lizzie," he said softly, "but I'm trying to talk myself out of kissing you."

"Why?" His touch was so gentle and yet so mesmerizing. She felt as if she might melt and run into the universe, become one with the stars.

She bowed her head, uncertain. This was wrong. She picked up an apple and twisted the stem, tried to change the subject. "There's an old saying about the apple stem. Do you know it? If the stem comes right out, you'll be unlucky in love. If you can twist it forever . . ."

The tension leapt between them, palpable. A breeze was coming up off the creek and ruffling his hair. A lone leaf floated down and landed on his shoulder, and she brushed it away.

He was warm and virile, and there was a half smile on her face. His voice made her tremble in ways she never had.

"Somehow I suspect, Lizzie Sheldon, that you're trying to tempt me."

Tossing it down, she looked up. "Oh, it's just a silly saying. It doesn't matter."

With his hand he tipped up her chin and looked into her eyes. If she was going to protest, now was the time, but she sat there frozen, watching this scene play out as if it had been ordained on the stars millions of years ago, and was just now sparking her desire.

"Kiss me, Lizzie." His voice was hoarse.

"Why?"

"In an act of defiance against all the gossiping biddies of Eden Creek. How's that for a reason?"

He bent close to her then. His lips touched hers as gently as when he'd pulled her out of the tree . . . and just as then, something ignited between them, a fire that had been in the universe forever, only waiting for the right two people to collide like this.

They knelt together, his hands on her waist, her hands on his shoulders, and drank deeply of each other. Insatiably. As they kissed, he pulled her to her feet, never once losing contact with her lips. She melted against his strength, feeling the warmth of him envelop her. Apple leaves brushed his shoulder, crackled in the darkness, and she stood on tiptoe, leaning into him, while his mouth came down on hers with even more devastating force, and his tongue invaded, caressed, tempted her to respond.

Oh, Zack, she cried silently. This was wrong, but it was so sweet. The taste of him, the feel of him, the scent of him, so masculine and scratchy and sweet all mixed into one man's kiss.

For one second she pulled away to catch her breath. She was drowning, but he pulled her back hard against him, and she had no doubt of his desire, or hers. When he dragged his mouth away, he rested his cheek against hers, letting the violet scent of her drug him. Spent, they stood there, lips touching each other's skin, hair, afraid to continue the kiss, afraid to let go.

Forbidden. Their desire had been forbidden for too long, and forbidden fruit was sweetest . . . oh, so sweet.

He touched the corner of her mouth, trailed his finger across her lips, still swollen from his own passion.

"What do you think about us, Lizzie?" he whispered.

"I don't know. I've never kissed a man like that."

"Not Joel?"

"Never." What was he getting at? "Is it wrong?"

"Not if it's what you want, Lizzie."

"I'm afraid, Zack."

"Of what the town will think? Now who's the coward?"

She hung her head and didn't think beyond the touch of his hand stroking the nape of her neck.

"I don't know what to think anymore, Zack."

"If we kiss, what are we guilty of? The town's already condemned us as guilty."

"Not everyone."

"Then they're blind, deaf, and dumb. If I could turn back time and pull Joel out of the creek, I would, you know, so you wouldn't be sad about all this. That doesn't mean I liked the guy, though."

No, she didn't think Zack and Joel could ever have liked each other. And right now it wasn't Joel she was thinking of.

"Will you kiss me again? I want to see if I feel the same."

"No."

"Why?"

"Because I know it'll feel the same. It'll be just as soft, and you'll taste like violets, and I'm only human, Lizzie. Let me stop while I'm still noble."

She looked embarrassed. "I'm sorry."

He didn't have to remind himself she was a virgin. For weeks he'd thought about the possibility of Joel marrying her, tortured himself with the possibility. He couldn't stop thinking about it. "A second kiss would be worse, because it would make me want you more."

They stood so close he could feel her breath, warm against his shirt, and if he blew softly he could tease a curl at her ear. He couldn't resist.

"Zack, stop." She arched against him, and he caught her in his arms. They were closer than a kiss ought to have allowed. For a few minutes he held her, nuzzling her, trying to ignore his darker urges, trying to content himself with just the pulsing of her heartbeat.

"Lizzie, go home now," he said quietly. He tried to push her out of his embrace, but she was immovable. She threw her arms around his neck and clung to him.

For a minute he vacillated. He knew he should ignore this, push her away, and take control. But his body didn't obey. He was embracing her, kissing her deeply, ever more deeply.

When they broke away, winded, he ran a shaky hand through his hair.

"I said go home, Lizzie."

"I am home," she reminded him in a small voice.

"Then go inside. Hurry up." His voice was hoarse.

"You're not leaving yet?" She tried not to choke on the words, tried to keep the question casual.

"You mean leaving this orchard?"

"No, I mean leaving town."

He shook his head, wondering what he'd have to do to stay away from her.

As for him, he had no reputation left to save. They could carve him up in the most scandalous papers of New York City and serve him for Sunday breakfast and it wouldn't much matter. But he didn't want her reputation to be ruined along with his.

"I told you once before—you deserve better than this," he said and strode off. Ignoring the tears that ran down her face was harder than watching Harry die.

Damn prim Lizzie Sheldon had no business coming out on that train to a town like this or, for that matter, consorting with men like him in dark places.

16

"It is much trouble, fierce trouble, you make for people when you do not tell the truth." Antonio stood in the schoolroom in front of Miss Yates's desk, his hands splayed on it, his eyes passionate.

Agnes Yates looked at this new Antonio, the man whose billing accounts and letters she translated into English.

He had hardly been able to speak English when he first came to her carrying a sheaf of accounts for sheep he'd sold.

Would she be so kind, since she was the schoolteacher, as to help him read the English words? "Dear Antonio, Enclosed find an order for ten sheep."

The teacher in Miss Yates—no, the little girl who'd always been first in her class, the teacher to whom everyone in town came for counsel—had not been able to resist. She liked being superior to everyone, and Antonio needed much help with his English. She hadn't looked beyond that, had assumed he was not worthy of a second glance.

Except for his accented English, he was just another boorish rancher, the sort who'd pull his children out of school to plant and harvest crops, the sort who walked around with mud on his boots and sheep on his mind.

259

But now, she realized, he spoke English much more flu
ently. Her lessons had sunk in well. Too well. A graduate o
a Spanish university, he claimed to have come to America
to herd sheep only to earn money for his own ranch. Hi
children, he vowed, would all be raised in luxury, and hi
family in Spain would follow him out. Yes. Agnes recalle
helping him write a letter in English to his mother, describ
ing this land of plenty. At the time, Agnes had thought he
was boasting. Now she realized there'd been much truth i
what he said.

Now for the first time she saw him not as a crude
sheepman but as an attractive and prosperous businessman
Not as a student but as a man. Not as a stupid, weak ma
who was beneath her aspirations but as a very wise man
wise enough and strong enough to take her, the teacher
to task.

She wasn't certain if she should be frightened o
intrigued. Why had it taken her so long to notice how
handsome he was, especially when he was angry? Thos
dark eyes sparkled, and he towered over her. Moreover, h
cared, cared that she'd lied.

"How do you know I'm not telling the truth?" she asked
gazing up at him.

"Because, my little teacher, I know Joel Emory, I know
Zack Danvers, and I know you. Your words may be fine
English, but they do not fit the people I know. I may no
speak as good as you, but I know in my heart that wha
you have said is wrong."

Her hair was slipping out of a pin, and she didn't push
it back. She could imagine Antonio kissing her, tearing al
the pins out of her hair, the fiery passion of his word
transferring to his lips.

Shocked by her own thoughts, she stood and backed into
the blackboard. An eraser fell to the floor, sending up
cloud of chalk dust. She picked up a piece of chalk and
crumbled it into little bits. She was in her own schoolroom
and yet she didn't feel entirely in control. She had to pul

herself together, regain control of him, as with her class.
"Antonio, I insist that you sit down or I'll—"

"Or you'll what? Rap my knuckles with your ruler? Put
me, Antonio, graduate of one of Spain's finest universities,
in the corner of your little schoolhouse? Who do you think
I am?"

"A sheepman?"

"The second son of one of the richest Basque ranchers
in Spain. Do you think I come here because I am stupid?
No, it is because I am wise enough to know that here in
America I can start my own sheep ranch and become rich
enough to send for my other brothers, the younger brothers
who have no land."

"Y-you never told me that before."

"I could not speak good enough English before, Agnes,
but I have you to thank for that. For teaching me English
and . . . the difference between truth and lies."

He advanced around the desk toward her, and her heart
pounded. Was he going to kiss her?

But she was justified in what she'd said. "Why don't you
say all this to Elizabeth and that . . . that doctor? They're the
ones who plotted to push Joel out of the boat, not me."

"No, Agnes. Your lies cannot hurt two more people."

"Antonio, you make it sound so awful. All right, maybe
I didn't exactly *see* them push him. But I saw Joel floating
in the current, and . . . and—"

"The truth." Antonio reached out and pulled some of the
pins from her hair.

"I wanted revenge," she whispered.

"Revenge," he taunted, "is not a woman's game, and as
Granny Sikes says, it is unbecoming to you."

"Granny says that?"

"I am not the only one who is disappointed in you."

"But you don't understand what they did to me."

"I understand about revenge better than you—how do
you say?—give me credit about."

"Give you credit for."

"Revenge to a Basque man is as natural as breathing. We revenge the wrongs done to our family. For example, if you were my wife and Zachary Danvers had hurt you, I would track him to the ends of the earth and kill him."

Agnes flinched, then opened her eyes, seeing Antonio in a new way. No man had ever spoken of fighting for her virtue before. Just the suggestion startled her, and still he talked.

"But you, Agnes, you have no ties to Zachary Danvers and therefore no right to any revenge, even if he did hurt you. What did he do? Not court you?"

Agnes felt herself blush.

"He is not the man for you, Agnes."

"He's not?" She gathered her wits. "I mean, of course he's not." Antonio was the man for her. That was what he'd tried to tell her on their picnic.

She pressed a hanky to her neck to cool the strange warmness she felt. However did Antonio get so wise, so fierce? How did he turn teacher on her?

"Agnes, you have a duty and honor to tell the truth."

"Why? Because I'm the schoolteacher?"

"And because I expect women to behave honorably."

"But I'll be humiliated."

"From humiliation can come honor. Agnes, you must go to town and seek out Zack and Elizabeth and take back your lies. Say they were spoken in haste. That you regret them. I shall be glad, and you shall be a model to all your other students as well."

"I can't."

"But you will."

"I can't."

"Why not?"

"I . . . I . . ." She could not think of a good reason.

She was facing spinsterhood and had no right to be choosy. Besides, hadn't Antonio said he was educated in Spain? There weren't likely to be that many more men of quality come along.

"Yes," she heard herself say from far away. "Yes, all right. And then what?"

Antonio came towards her, passion in his dark eyes. For a moment she thought he was going to kiss her, but all he did was cup her chin in his hand.

"And then I have something to ask you."

No, Antonio did not seem like second choice at all, and gratefully she accepted his implied bargain: an apology to Elizabeth and Zack in exchange for a proposal.

It took all of one day to pass the word and round up the residents of the valley in the schoolhouse for a special meeting, not just of the ladies but of the men, too, ranchers and townsmen both—everyone except Elizabeth Sheldon and Zack Danvers.

With Antonio looking on from the back door of the schoolhouse, Agnes rose from her desk and cleared her throat.

"Good evening, ladies and gentlemen," she began. "Since it's almost time for school to open again, I've gathered you together to share some thoughts on the coming year. . . ."

At least a hundred pair of eyes stared back, curious.

When she was done apologizing, the room was as silent as if she'd pulled her ruler out of the drawer and stalked around the room.

"Are there any questions?" She looked around the room, smiling. "We'll have a Christmas pageant this year—"

"You going to penalize the younguns what miss school for harvest?" Mr. Hankins asked.

Harvest. She hated the word.

Antonio was staring at her, eyebrows raised.

"Ah, no, of course not. Harvest break is good for the children. I look forward to harvest."

"Are there no more questions?" she said.

It was over. Slowly, without talking, the people of Eden Creek filed out.

Antonio lingered. "You said a well speech."

"I made a *good* speech."

"Is that not what I said?"

Dear Antonio. She saw clearly now that he was twice the man Joel was. How could she have been so blind as to very nearly throw him away for want of English grammar?

"You said when I had confessed you had a question to ask me," she prompted and moved closer, close enough so that he could kiss her if he so desired. On their picnic he'd proposed, and she'd said no. This time she wouldn't waste any time in modest protestations.

There was a long pause.

"Antonio? What did you want to ask me?"

"This, little teacher: Someday I shall ask a woman to marry me. When I do, I want your word of honor that you will not tell her I once asked you to marry me. This bad judgment on my part must remain a secret."

"What are you saying?" The room began to spin.

"That I cannot have it said I once proposed to you. It would harm my chance to marry a woman of honor. Do I have your word?"

He didn't want her. Antonio, an immigrant sheepherder to whom she had taught English, who had once proposed marriage to her, was rejecting Miss Agnes Yates, graduate of a fine American normal school. He was rejecting her, Agnes Yates.

"I wish you find happiness," he said softly.

"Hope." She could barely summon her voice to correct his grammar.

"What?"

"I hope you find happiness."

"Thank you for teaching me," he said and, turning on his heel, walked out of her life.

She stood there alone dusting the black potbellied stove and listening to the crickets begin to chirp. School would start soon; harvest was in the air. Nothing had changed.

Nothing at all.

*   *   *

Harvesttime was near, the season of plenty. On a perfect September day Elizabeth Sheldon and Pete Gustavson walked along the rows of the orchard, and Pete picked a sampling of apples. Clara tagged along, picking up the apples that had fallen to the ground and been bruised, collecting them for Mr. Gantt's cider press.

"Another cold night or so and they'll need to be harvested," Pete said after biting into one.

"Yes." She stood there, holding a branch, her face buried in the warm leaves.

It was a bittersweet moment. Ever since apple blossom time . . . No, earlier. Ever since her arrival she'd dreamed of harvesting this crop, of seeing her brother's dream come true.

But she had not exchanged words with the townspeople since Miss Yates confessed at the schoolhouse. Maddie spoke with Elizabeth, and so of course did Zack Danvers, who had repeated his offer to help. He had discovered the little apple tree up on the ridge, the one the children had planted in memory of her brother, and he sat up there for long stretches, alone.

"The town is ashamed that they believed Miss Yates," Pete said. "They'll be sorry when they see you take your apple crop to the railroad depot."

"*If* we harvest it."

"You have to let Zack help us, Elizabeth," Pete said. "We've only got about two weeks to get the apples off the trees. The sooner the better."

"I know." This was no time for pride. Trees stretched for ten acres, at least half of them fully mature and heavy with fruit. Pete estimated that five hundred trees would need picking, and every tree contained enough apples to fill several bushel baskets. Why, Will Sheldon didn't even have enough containers in the barn. They'd have to get Mr. Atwood to nail some big bins together. It was almost more daunting than irrigation had been.

"Zack's waiting to talk to you," Clara said.

"I know."

"Are you going to go see him?"

"Hush up, Clara," Pete said. "Put the cider apples in the wagon, and you and I'll take them into Mr. Gantt."

"Why?"

"I'm gonna ask if anyone in Gantt's Saloon wants some cider in exchange for helping us harvest."

"How many do we need?"

"More than Gantt has customers, but two or three are better than no one."

"You wanna come, Elizabeth?" Clara asked.

" 'Course she doesn't." Pete glared at his little sister. "Come on."

"If you've got some secret plan that I don't know about, Pete, it's not working. You want me out of here so I won't tell anyone that Elizabeth and Zack met and talked, huh? She can talk to Zack Danvers all she wants, and who cares what Miss Yates thinks? That's what Granny says and Maddie, too."

While Pete stood there with his mouth open, Clara handed him the gunnysack full of cider apples and took off, calling over her shoulder, "Race you to the barn."

As soon as they left, Elizabeth looked up at the ridge. Zack stood there, the way she'd seen him on one of her first days in town, legs straddling the earth, white shirt whipping in the valley breeze, the baby apple tree waving bravely beside him.

"Lizzie!" His voice floated down to her. "Will you come up here? Or shall I come down there?"

Frozen to the spot, she could only look. Forbidden fruit, that's what Zack had been, and she couldn't get used to the notion that they could freely meet. Joel was gone from her life. Miss Yates had confessed to a lie. Elizabeth could now actually talk to Zack in broad daylight with no one having cause to gossip.

If they wanted to, they could climb up on top of the church steeple together.

She wanted to, but Zack Danvers wanted to leave. That made every moment precious, and that was *her* secret.

In moments she climbed the path to the ridge and took his hand so he could help her up the last steep stretch.

"Will you leave soon?" she asked at once, as if needing to know whether to hoard the moments or stretch them out.

Zack took her by the arm and walked beside her up on the ridge among the sage. They stopped to admire together the seedling that Pete and Clara had nourished. Then they looked out over the valley, at Eden Creek slicing through it before joining the Payette River, at the patchwork of ranches and farms, and finally at her orchard, just below where they stood.

The apples were blushing red, ready to be harvested.

"You're going to need help picking the crop," Zack said.

"Pete and I can do it."

"I'll be there."

"You don't have to . . . if you don't want to. If you need to leave . . ."

"Lizzie, I don't have to do anything. What I want to do, I think, is kiss you again."

Her face went so white he was afraid she'd run away. "Why?"

Because he'd kissed her once and found himself longing for more. Because he was a romantic at heart, who wanted to know if he'd been mistaken the first time he'd kissed her. He wanted to know so he wouldn't spend the rest of his life wondering. Why indeed? "I don't know. Do I have to answer that before I kiss you?"

"Yes . . . I mean, no." She backed away. "We can't. It was a kiss that started all this." She dropped to her knees by a patch of sunflowers and broke one off. "Maybe I'd better leave."

In a heartbeat he closed the distance and knelt facing her, his hands gently cupping her elbows. He stared deep into her eyes. "Joel's gone now."

"And I've got to work Will's orchard all alone."

Will Sheldon, the hero of Eden Creek. Doubtless Will Sheldon and Harry Crebbs were up in heroes' heaven tossing a coin to see whether Zack Danvers deserved a fair hearing at the pearly gates. If they knew what they were about, they'd use a rigged coin.

Zack dropped down into a cross-legged position and pulled her down beside him. They sat amid stray sunflowers and looked out at the orchard.

"I've sent a telegram to Harry's father. I think it's time I went back to Chicago, told him the honest truth, and asked his forgiveness. But I won't leave until I see this harvest of yours."

She was silent a moment. Still, he had to ask her something.

"Did you ever wonder, Lizzie, what you'd be doing if you'd never come here?"

Restless, she lay back and stretched out flat on the cool earth. "All the time. I know what I'd be doing, and I'm glad I came. I'm staying," she said through a swollen throat. Why, if she had to fall in love, did it have to be this man, of all people, a man who'd never stay in Eden Creek? She watched him as he stretched out beside her, propped up on his elbows, legs long.

"You're not glad you came here, are you?" she asked.

"I came here on a coin toss in San Francisco," he admitted, staring straight ahead. "I haven't been glad of anything in a long time, Lizzie."

Turning away, she plucked off another sunflower and buried her face in it briefly, then teased the crook of his elbow with it. If the townspeople were going to buzz with suspicion still, maybe she ought to give them good cause. "I'm glad of lots of things," she said softly. "I'm glad you saved me from the water. You were a hero, Zack Danvers, and you ought to be proud of it. Don't you know that?"

"It's not as simple as arithmetic, Lizzie. Courage doesn't subtract the cowardice. Heroic acts are all relative."

"I know what I'm talking about, Zack Danvers, whether you want to believe it or not. Any sensible woman would rather have a real live caring man with a good heart and feet of clay than a hero, whatever that is. What is a hero? Do you think Will cares? Or Harry?"

"Yes."

"They don't!" Discarding the flower, she sat up again and looked him in the eye. "A dead hero can't turn the earth, can't hitch a wagon, can't comfort a couple of lost kids. And a dead heroine can't cook a man's meal or darn his socks. I didn't come out here because I'm some sort of heroine. I came here because I had no more heroes to choose from, and I did what I had to. All any of us can do in life, Zack, is what we have to, to survive. Granny knows that."

Silence. But he sat up straighter and leaned over her.

Gently he took her by the shoulders and turned her around, smiled down at her, then wrapped her in his arms.

"Dear Lizzie," he murmured against her hair, "you've been awfully busy being brave."

"I've been too busy surviving and living to care if I'm brave or not. And so should you."

She pulled away, embarrassed at her outburst. Who was she to tell Dr. Zachary Danvers how to live? And what did it matter to him what she thought? His heart belonged in Chicago, with other people, didn't it?

Turning over her hand, he kissed the palm. A slow ache began in her chest, and when she looked up, he was watching her, his eyes serious.

For too long she'd yearned to wrap herself in Zack's arms again. He was too close, and so it was natural to lean her forehead against his chest, to listen to the pounding of his heart. If she failed with her harvest, she could accept it. What she couldn't bear failing at was love, and though she'd never tell him, she was sure this was love.

As for Zack, he didn't move for a minute, but sat there, staring at her, and then his hands moved up to her face, her hair. Whatever his thoughts, she didn't dare intrude.

A ladybug jumped from her shoulder onto the hem of her petticoat, and immediately bending, he chased it, his hand slapping her skirt.

It jumped out from between his fingers, back onto her shirtwaist, this time to her ribs, right under her heart. With a swoop of his hand he captured it.

"Zack!" Her pulse raced.

The ladybug jumped out, and she made a dive for it at the same time he did. They collided, and she fell backwards into the sage, taking him with her. Zack and the ladybug.

She swallowed hard, aware only of his weight pressing against her. "Zack, I think you're squashing it."

"Naw, it's right here." His hand, pressing down with each breath she took, cupped the ladybug against her ribs, right below her breast.

"Let it go." Please, Zack.

He removed his hand, the ladybug flew away, and then he levered himself up, an arm on either side of her. He was staring down at her intently, purpose in his gaze. The scent of warm sage rose up all around them.

She shut her eyes to escape those impossible blue eyes, and then his lips came down on hers, slanting, hot and dry, thirsty. She tilted her head back to reach into him, her mouth open to his warmth, his passion. Without warning, he tore his mouth away and moved aside, leaving her dizzy, still longing, trying to find her breath.

When she sat up she hugged herself against the strange yearning in her belly. Zack was sitting apart from her, face averted, unsmiling. He got up and brushed the bits of sage off himself and then her. And after stopping only long enough to pick another floppy sunflower, Elizabeth ran back down to the orchard.

The next day the sun shone bright on the apples, perfect picking weather—neither too hot nor too cold, this mid-September day. Elizabeth welcomed harvest for the distraction.

The horses were hitched to a wooden slip, which Clara rode like a sled, balancing a big stack of bushel baskets. Out in the orchard, Pete and Clara set the baskets beneath the trees, and pulled the straps of canvas picking sacks over their heads.

There was an art to picking, so Pete explained. One didn't just willy-nilly pull off apples. Elizabeth learned she'd have to twist and lift gently enough to protect the spur on the tree, the source of next year's buds. On the other hand, she couldn't work too slowly or they'd never get the trees all picked. Elizabeth gave a wry smile, matched by Pete. "I guess that doesn't matter in this case." There was no way a young woman and a fourteen-year-old boy could harvest the entire orchard. No way, even with Zack's help, that three of them could bring in the crop.

"But we'll try." With a final determined smile, Elizabeth climbed a ladder and began. With a deft twist of the wrist, she lifted an apple, and it dropped off, leaving its stem behind. Not so good. She tried again, plucking one apple, stem and all, and carefully dropping it into the bag. Then she plucked another . . . and another. Care counted in every way, so the apples didn't get bruised in the sacks.

The sack was fashioned with an open bottom that had been folded up to hold the apples in while picking. When the sack was full, Elizabeth climbed down and, holding her hoard of fruit over a soft wooden basket, unfastened the bottom of it. Gravity took over, and apples rolled out, dropping into the basket with a soft clatter. Then she folded up the bottom of the empty sack and headed back to the tree, moved the ladder to a new position, and continued picking.

All of them knew how daunting their task was. It was slow, tedious work, and Elizabeth was no match for Pete, who could pick twice as fast. Clara picked the lower branches and kept busy counting baskets and moving empty baskets nearer the trees. Then, too, every so often Pete had to stop picking to load baskets brimming with red apples onto the slip, which the horses then hauled up to the barn area. There Pete and Clara transferred the crop to the waiting wagon for a later trip to the rail depot in town.

After a while Elizabeth looked to see how much progress they'd made. Half a dozen trees. Not even a row. At this rate, they'd accomplish only one row a day. Not fast enough by any means to get all the apples picked before they fell off the trees or got blown down by the wind.

She despaired. To come this close and fail was wrenching.

"When's Zack coming?" Clara piped up from the base of the tree. "He didn't change his mind, did he?"

Bereft, Elizabeth didn't answer. It didn't matter. But when he came a half hour later, her heart surprised her and soared.

"The little kid with tonsillitis," was all he said.

Secretly she couldn't resist a smile. Oh, Zack. He was giving. Fighting it, but giving. "Do you want a lesson in how to pick apples?" she said, pleased, radiating happiness the instant he appeared. She guided his hand to a nearby apple, touched his wrist. "Just a flick." His pulse was strong, his hand warm. She looked up to find him watching her. "Look, Zack, at the apple, at how easy it is to pluck." Her mouth went dry then. "I need to get a drink," she muttered and moved away.

But later, out of the corner of her eye, Elizabeth watched him from her tree, her senses flaring to life, a flutter in her stomach, a sudden shake to her hand. An apple dropped to the ground. A perfect red apple fell a dozen feet, to land, bruised. Annoyed at herself, she stared down the ladder at the ground far below.

From the next tree over came Pete's voice. "Is it going all right, Elizabeth?"

"Yes . . . yes, fine." And she went back to picking, not looking at Zack. Anyway, there was no time to talk or even think, and so the only sounds for a long time were the rustle of branches, the gentle thunk of apples spilling into baskets, and the excited beating of her heart.

Then at noon the squeak of wagon wheels broke the silence. Elizabeth climbed down, expecting to see Maddie and Ben who'd accepted her invitation to come and pick some apples for themselves. Wiping the sleeve of her blouse across her forehead, she pushed aside a branch and squinted up the road. Maddie had been kind all along, never more so than yesterday when she'd offered to come over and pick apples as soon as she could leave the hotel.

"Take all you want, Maddie. Serve them up in the hotel. Better than letting the apples rot on the trees because I can't get help to harvest them—except Zack."

"Then I don't think this town deserves anything from you, Elizabeth, especially not free apples," Maddie'd said. Her voice was soft, but her eyes were angry.

Elizabeth had been downcast. "I guess the town is going to win the bet after all, that I'd never succeed as an orchardist. A crop unpicked is not success. I'm going to fail." She'd been too humiliated, of course, to face the town and ask for help, even after she learned of Miss Yates's confession.

Maddie had looked off into the distance, as if thinking. When asked whether she was coming for her apples or not, Maddie had given merely a cryptic, "That depends."

Now here she was, with Ben Danvers, and they were not alone. Why, it looked as if they had brought every guest in their hotel. But the hotel had been only half full, and Ben didn't own more than one wagon. And now wagon after wagon rolled into the orchard, each filled front and back with familiar faces.

Mr. Atwood, Florence Atwood, the Gantts, the railroad agent, the members of the Ladies' Literary Society of Eden Creek.

Why, it was all of the townspeople . . .

Still more wagons rolled in.

The ranchers had come from far and wide in the valley.

Antonio came.

Everyone she knew came.

Slowly it sank in: The town had arrived to help her harvest her apples. Not just Zack. Not just Maddie and Ben, but all of Eden Creek, except Miss Yates, was arriving here at her orchard.

And then Maddie leapt to the ground and said the strangest thing. "We wanted to offer to help all along, you see, but people said they were too ashamed to come by."

"Ashamed of what?"

"Of believing Miss Yates . . . of even listening to her." Her eyes were soft and kind.

Elizabeth stared, dumbfounded.

"Well, are you going to show us how to pick?"

"How many apples do you want?"

"You silly goose," Maddie said. "We're not taking any till you've got enough for a paying crop. We'll take what drops on the ground later."

Her gaze went to Zack, who was standing next to her, helping her open a full sack of apples. Several times, like now, she'd caught him looking at her, but she refused to meet his eyes. Let him see her as she was, dirt on her hands, her hair clinging damply to her neck and forehead, her smile vanished into bone weariness.

They worked together, the entire town, for more days than she cared to count. They couldn't work consistently from sunup to sundown, only when the temperature was just right, and that made the work take longer. Still, she was awake from dawn to dusk, stalking the orchard, watching the temperature rise to ideal picking conditions. She counted trees still to be picked, made room in the apple cellar, rode into town to send telegrams to the Boise City and Omaha apple buyers. She saw to every detail. Everything except talking to Zack Danvers.

Eden Creek's citizens laughed and sang at that harvest, and when the trees were nearly plucked clean, they planned a celebration.

"You're going to break a lot of people's pockets, Elizabeth," Ben said. "Fact is, a few people who bet against you are here helping." He chuckled to himself at the irony of that.

She thought back at once to his words the day she'd arrived in town: "Fair warning. A lot of people are betting you'll fail."

"And you, Ben? Did you bet against me?"

He was silent. "What makes you think I'm a betting man?"

"Your brother's a betting man. I thought it might run in the family."

She turned then and allowed herself to look at Zack, who was standing at the foot of a ladder, framed by the wide sky and the lush trees. His back was to her, and he didn't see her. It hurt deep inside to look at him, at his strong, tall form, at his dark hair, at the sensitive hands, hurt to remember how she had felt in his arms. . . .

"My brother's a foolish man, Elizabeth Sheldon," Ben said, and her attention snapped back to the conversation at hand. "I'd never bet against a Sheldon. Had too much respect for Will. He was a hero."

"There are many ways to be a hero," she said in a pensive voice. "I rather think my brother would like most to be remembered for this orchard."

Ben climbed down off his ladder and paused a moment with his sack of apples. "Funny how everyone's saying the same thing."

"What do you mean?"

"Well, Granny was saying the same thing to Zack just a while ago—that the difference between heroes and cowards is how they live the rest of their lives."

"Granny is a wise woman." Very wise.

Ben nodded and pushed back his hat. "And you, Miss Sheldon, are a very successful woman. I hope you've had Otis wire ahead for a railcar for all these apples."

She should have beamed because she was going to succeed at making her brother's dream come true. Yet she hadn't the heart to join in the singing. Zack, too, she noticed, worked in silence.

Around noon on the following day they finished up, and Clara announced that Mr. Gantt had a surprise for them in town. It took a caravan of wagons to load the baskets of apples onto the platform of the railroad depot; they hauled the rest down into the fruit cellar.

By late afternoon they were all celebrating, most on the cool porch of Mr. Gantt's saloon with fresh-pressed cider. It was on the house, and for a while Elizabeth allowed herself to feel content.

Just when it didn't seem the day could hold any more surprises for Elizabeth, yet another wagon creaked down the Main Street of Eden Creek, the driver singing an old Civil War song, "When Johnny Comes Marching Home Again." He wore a red beard, and on his head was perched a dark blue Civil War hat. Immediately the hue and cry went out throughout the saloon from those on the porch. Men came out of the saloon and off the porch and stood, mouths agape in disbelief. Women, including Elizabeth, gasped in surprise, and children squealed, calling excitedly for Pete and Clara. When the newcomer spotted the revelers, he reined in right there on Main Street and hollered, "Well, am I in time for the harvest? Is there a tree left for me to pick?"

Elizabeth didn't have to ask who this was. The blue Civil War hat told enough. The stranger swept off his dusty hat to reveal hair that matched his beard, wild, unkempt, but very red.

Pete and Clara's father had come home, and though he still sat in his wagon, he was already guzzling fresh cider, passing another mug to a woman who sat beside him. In the back of his wagon, shovels and pickaxes stuck out from under a canvas flap.

"Orville Gustavson!" Mr. Gantt roared and handed up a tin cup of cider, the second. "I always said you'd be back. No mine could blow up a cuss as mean as you, and no jail could hold you!" He laughed heartily, and Orville Gustavson joined in, then looked around the crowd. "Where's my younguns?"

"Come quick, come quick, Clara," Pete called from across the street. "Pa's home!"

Clara was running down the street then, feet flying faster than when she'd won the race, and she flew up into her father's embrace. "Pa!" she cried. "Oh, Pa, I knew you'd come!"

17

Elizabeth hung back in the shade of the saloon porch, watching the reunion as Clara went running up to the wagon, overalls stained from bruised apples, bare feet dusty, bobbing up and down, dancing with excitement. Like his children, Orville Gustavson wore overalls, only about ten sizes bigger.

He took yet another mug of cider—his third—and swilled it long and deep, then smacked his lips in pleasure and wiped his mouth. Next thing Clara knew, she was lifted up and lost in her daddy's bear hug, giggling, shrieking with laughter one minute, wide-eyed and serious the next minute as she told her pa she'd known he'd return.

With shining eyes, Clara turned around, looking for someone to share her excitement with, her gaze stopping on Elizabeth before she looked back at her father. "I told everyone you'd come. I told them you promised."

"Heck, Clara, did they make a big worry over that mine fuss? You'd 'ave thought a Spaniard invaded Bunker Hill the way it blew. I lost my temper and got in the middle of the riots, so they locked me up for a while, but everyone knows you can't hold a Gustavson down, don't they?"

"I tried to tell 'em, Pa. I tried to, but they wouldn't believe me, not all of 'em, not Miss Yates."

Orville frowned. "Here, now, you weren't supposed to let the town ladies fuss over you."

Pete and Clara exchanged quick glances and then, as one, shook their heads. " 'Course not." Clara was quick to change the subject. "We even had a real job, working for the new lady in town. Elizabeth."

"Who's Elizabeth?" Orville Gustavson asked, squinting around, searching for a newcomer.

Clara's stubby finger immediately singled out Elizabeth. "Will Sheldon's sister. We helped her work the orchard."

Elizabeth grew warm under everyone's scrutiny, but now she saw smiling faces instead of suspicious ones.

"That little lady brought in the harvest?" Orville boomed the question so loud that the nearest people fell back, allowing Elizabeth to make her way closer to Orville's side of the wagon.

"We all helped Elizabeth." Clara beamed, running to her. "Pa's proud of us." Suddenly her face fell, as the ramifications of her father's return sank in. "I guess now Pa's back, Pete and I'll have to go home and live with him. You don't mind if we move out of the loft, do you?"

Elizabeth shook her head. "Of course not." After a whispered discussion, she told Clara to go on back to their pa's place while she gathered up the Civil War coats and other possessions that had gotten transferred to her loft.

"And I need Pa's present."

His present? Of course. The four-leaf clover stickpin from Montgomery Ward and Company had arrived long ago. The night of the near freeze. The night when Zack's hand had felt warm on her face, when his breath had mingled with hers in the icy air. Quickly, before more unbidden memories returned, Elizabeth made arrangements with Clara.

"I'll bring it into town next trip. Don't worry. The best gift you can give your pa is to become a family again." She looked at the quiet woman next to Orville. "Maybe he brought you a mother."

"Naw, not Pa. He ain't the marrying kind. I wish he was though . . ."

Elizabeth let the subject drop, for strangely, Orville was staring at Elizabeth as if she'd grown wings. "Well, whatever the case, they're waiting for you," Elizabeth said.

Even after Clara climbed back into her father's wagon, Orville Gustavson stared at Elizabeth, almost as if he knew her. "I been looking to meet you. Now that I know you took such good care of Clara, I'm indebted."

She moved closer. "Your children have been a big help to me on my orchard."

As was his way, Pete mumbled his thanks and shuffled his feet, biting back a smile of pride at the compliment.

Orville turned back to Elizabeth. "You and me need to reminisce about Will and the orchard later, miss."

Elizabeth started to reply, then decided not to. Besides, someone new had joined the crowd.

From out between the newspaper and the mercantile stepped Miss Yates, her prim dress and ruffly hat in stark contrast to the scruffy costumes of the people who'd been helping with the apple harvest. It was the first time anyone had seen her around town since her public confession at the school. The school year had begun quietly.

Miss Yates came up behind Clara first, the expression in her dark eyes contemptuous, her mouth as straight and hard as a ruler. She never said a word of greeting to anyone in Eden Creek, but directed her attention to Orville, her words loud enough for everyone to hear.

"Afternoon, Mr. Gustavson. Your children played hooky for most of the spring, and without any parent here, I looked out for them."

"That's not true," Clara said. "It was Elizabeth who—"

"It's not polite to interrupt, Clara." Miss Yates looked at the sweet-faced woman beside Orville. "Could be your pa gave a ride to the orphanage lady himself. There've been cases, you know, where it's in the best interest of the family if the parent gives up—"

"No!"

"Could be he's been gone so long he doesn't want to be a pa anymore and is going to ship you off to an orphanage himself."

Suddenly Orville Gustavson pulled out his Enfield rifle and, squinting, drew a bead on Agnes Yates.

Immediately the crowd parted and gave a wide berth to Orville and Eden Creek's schoolmarm, who stood there as cool as celery in ice water.

"Miss Yates, you aggravated me before I left here, but I thought my children would be safe from you. Now I see I miscalculated." He turned to his daughter. "This schoolteacher been annoying you like this all summer, Clara?"

Orville Gustavson was a big bear of a man indeed, and Elizabeth did not envy Miss Yates, who now was staring down the barrel of his gun.

Elizabeth looked from Orville Gustavson to the quiet woman who accompanied Clara's pa, and Clara, too, darted a nervous glance at the dark-haired woman who sat by her father.

Clara replied, her voice a bit shakier than before. "Miss Yates has been trying to send us off to an orphanage."

Steadying his aim, Orville said to Miss Yates, "That so?"

"The children had no parents," she said.

"Well, now it seems we've got a whole mess of misunderstandings happened while I was gone." After setting down the rifle, he draped an arm about the woman in calico who sat beside him. "Hellfire and brimstone, this here's no orphanage lady. Clara, Pete . . . meet your new mama, Sarah. She was widowed in the Bunker Hill, and she married me three weeks later."

After a surprised buzz went through the crowd, the women pressed close to shake the new Mrs. Gustavson's hand, while the men moved around to shake Orville's.

Caught in the crunch, Pete blushed and once again shuffled his feet, but Clara climbed right up in the wagon and perched between the bearded man and his shy wife, who promptly opened a satchel and pulled out a rag doll—handmade—for Clara.

There was a long pause, as if the entire town held its breath. "Somehow," Orville Gustavson drawled, "I get the feeling the summer here's been as exciting as anything that happened up Bunker Hill way, so if anyone'd care to divulge the details, I'd be mighty happy to have another glass of that cider. Sarah's been anxious to meet the younguns and buy 'em a sweet at the mercantile. Isn't that right, Sarah?"

A warm glow stole over Elizabeth as she looked at Clara with her father, her new mother, and a brand-new doll. This was the perfect ending to harvest. Absolutely all she could wish for.

Almost.

As Pete climbed into the wagon bed, and Clara wedged in between her father and her new stepmother, Elizabeth continued to stare at them, still basking in the glow of the happy reunion. Suddenly aware of someone's eyes on her, she looked up to see Zack Danvers watching not the reunion of the Gustavsons but her. His face was shadowed, his smile enigmatic.

She broke away from his look, turned her back on him. It hurt too much to contrast the Gustavson reunion with her solitude. A family like that was something she'd never have, and staring at Zack Danvers didn't make things easier. Fighting her way through elbows and mugs of apple cider, she found her wagon and headed home.

Her orchard, when she arrived there, was absolutely silent—a strange feeling after the harvest. She didn't know if she could bear it.

What would she do all winter? Next spring? The next ten summers? And every harvest for the rest of her life?

With a sigh, she headed for the loft to gather up the Gustavsons' belongings. She knew why Clara liked staying in the loft so much. It was a refuge, smelling of sweet hay and the warmth of summer. The Gustavsons had made it homey, with catalog pictures nailed to the walls, arrowheads and old maid cards and Civil War coats and Mark Twain books scattered around.

The air was dusty and sweet, and tired as she was from days of hard work, she was tempted to curl up in the hay and stay awhile, but the Gustavsons needed their things, and so she bundled them up and headed down the stairs. In the dim stairway of the barn it was hard for her to see, especially with her arms filled with coats and childish possessions, so when the figure filled the doorway, she stopped, squinting.

"Zack?" But it couldn't be. This was someone shorter, less rangy in build. Carefully, she moved on down the remaining stairs.

"Have you forgotten me so fast, Elizabeth?" came the lazy drawl.

Joel!

Elizabeth's head went light. Joel. Alive and standing there blocking her way back down from the barn. She dropped everything she'd been holding on to the barn floor and stared open-mouthed. He wore a rumpled shirt and dusty denim pants, but his hair was slicked down with pomade. His smile was as ingratiating as ever.

"Hello, Elizabeth. Aren't you going to rush over and greet me? Ask how I managed to survive and who hauled me out of the water? And how I got back here finally?"

"You came back with Orville Gustavson, didn't you?" she guessed.

She supposed she ought to have a hundred questions to ask her own fiancé, like where had Orville Gustavson found him and why and when. But she was in no rush to ask them. After all this time, Elizabeth had begun to forget, but now the memories closed in on her, destroying totally the earlier festive mood. "Where did he find you?"

"Old man Gustavson picked me up last night on the road and offered me a ride back to town, so I took it. Saved some shoe leather, but I told him I'd just as soon be let off near the orchard instead of going all the way into town, if it was all the same with him. I told him how I'd been late to meet my fiancé's train, and this time I didn't want to be late to her house."

Her heart hammered in her ears. "Orville never mentioned you."

"I slept with a mining drill in the wagon bed most of the way. Besides, there's nothing uncommon in giving me a ride. It's not as if I'm a stranger to him. I bet he just didn't think to mention that he had a passenger. Won't remember me till he's belted a few." He took a step toward her, and automatically Elizabeth took one back. "Clara's pretty excited to see her pa, I bet?"

Did he really care? White-faced, Elizabeth could barely still her quaking knees. She was more shocked than afraid. Joel was too pathetic to inspire more than pity. "We got the harvest in." Without his help, she wanted to add.

"So I see." Then he shrugged in his familiar way. "Harvest be damned. Can't you spare a word of welcome? Won't you tell me you're glad I'm alive? That you've been pining for me?"

"Of course I'm glad you're alive. But I'm not going to marry you. That's in the past. . . . Joel, I think you'd better leave."

"Such a single-minded lady." He stepped around Clara's belongings. "I could have married anybody, Elizabeth. I could afford to be choosy."

Elizabeth backed toward the loft steps. "Well, now you can choose anyone else you want. Only not me."

"So self-righteous for a lady with a less than perfect past. If it hadn't been for me, you wouldn't have had the guts to come out here, Elizabeth, and you know it."

"Maybe not, but that doesn't mean I can't change my mind about marrying you."

"Putting a harvest of wormy rotten apples ahead of a chance to be courted—that was a mistake, Elizabeth. You should be overjoyed to see me. We can still work out a marriage to suit us both. Maybe there won't be mutual attachment, but—"

"No." She jerked away, ready to run, but with a quick reflex he caught her by the arm, pushed her back against the wall, and there in the manure-scented barn, caught her face in his grasp and bent to kiss her.

"So Joel passed himself off as a man who knew how to climb a ladder and get up a tree?" Orville Gustavson, having left his new wife with his children, had returned to town and now sat on the wide porch of Gantt's Saloon, listening to Zack. "Well, I'll be hog-tied. Didn't think he could walk in rubber boots, never mind thin a tree. If he'd sold the place, I'd have killed him. Seems a man can't leave town for a few weeks without the world turning upside down."

"Joel didn't fool everyone," Zack muttered under his breath. "Especially not Elizabeth. It's her place."

"Half."

"Half?" Zack was too stunned to do more than echo Orville. "No one in town said a thing about Will owning only half of the orchard."

"No one in town knew." Orville stuck out his hand. "I think it's time I introduced myself, Doctor. I'm Will Sheldon's silent partner. He ran the orchard, taught Pete a lot, and I went up to the mines looking for markets for the apples. Left Pete here to care for things. But we let Joel think he was manager, beings he was of age and all. Big mistake, I see now." Orville pushed his hat back. "I told the younguns to keep it quiet. I like my privacy."

"Clara has a knack for keeping secrets," Zack said, still stunned by Orville Gustavson's revelation.

A silence fell over the listening crowd too, many of whom, Zack knew, had written Orville Gustavson off as a no-account.

"How'd you know about Joel and Elizabeth?" Zack asked. He didn't care if Jack Frost owned the orchard.

"How'd I know what?"

"The part about Joel knowing Elizabeth. How'd you *know?*"

"I found Joel about ten miles out of town a while ago and gave him a ride, that's how."

Slowly Zack rose and towered over Orville.

"Now what'd I say?"

"Joel's alive?"

"Joel? Yeah . . . Wasn't he supposed to be?"

The crowd remained silent, and Zack's heart nearly stopped beating. "Where is he?" Even as he asked, somehow he knew what the answer would be.

"I dropped him off by the orchard, looking fit as a new-tuned fiddle."

Orville was still talking as Zack pushed his way through the crowd, a slow ache in the vicinity of his heart, worse than if the Spaniards had jabbed a rifle to his back.

Then jealousy, irrational and white-hot, seared him. He rode to the orchard like the wind. When he got there he made a quick search of Elizabeth's house, then strode to the barn. In one instant he forgave himself for everything he'd done in war, because now he realized he was capable of even worse.

When Zack burst into the barn, Joel retreated to a corner of the barn.

"I'm not going to touch Elizabeth."

"Get out," Zack said, voice hoarse.

"You're not going to fight me, are you?"

"Naw, that'd be too easy."

Joel looked around uneasily at the taut faces. Elizabeth, pale and white. Zack, fists clenching, breath ragged. No one else was in the loft, except a lazy fly buzzing about the hay. Elizabeth stood between the two men like a shield, her face white, terrified.

All Joel managed was a shrug. Then he said, "I came out west to see if I'd like it. I don't. I've got a right to go back where I came from."

"Yeah, but not on the purse strings of women, you lily-livered—"

"Who do you think you are, talking to me that way? You always were sweet on her, weren't you?" He jerked Elizabeth against him, but she tugged away so fast he lost his balance, fell into the heap of Gustavson possessions, and landed face first amid the Civil War coats and old maid cards. Immediately he doubled over, howling in pain and clutching his left hand with his right.

Edging closer, Elizabeth saw what had made Joel howl. Smiling, she reached down and pulled from his hand the weapon he'd fallen on—Clara's gift for her daddy, a sparkling gold stickpin with a four-leaf clover on it, for luck.

Before Joel was done howling, Zack lunged for him, and the two of them hit the straw. The thought of strangling Joel crossed Zack's mind, but he discarded it. "You big baby." He rammed a slew of punches to his gut.

Elizabeth was down on her knees, tugging at his collar. "Zack. Zack, please. He can't hurt me anymore. Let him go. Please. You'll break something."

Zack, his hair slick with perspiration, sat back on his heels, and slowly, as Elizabeth placed a calming hand on his arm, allowed his fists to uncurl. Fierce heat of anger burned away, flared, and then was replaced by tenderness at this woman's touch. Warming him. Cooling him. She was right. Joel was not worth wasting his doctoring skills on. Already he knew what he'd do with him.

"You're going on a train ride." He spoke between gritted teeth. Grabbing a rope from the horse stall, he tied Joel up like a trussed hen and dragged him to the wagon. "Maybe," he said as he heaved and pulled and pushed, "maybe, we can get up a collection to send you as far as Omaha. I know it's not home, but it's civilized, and maybe you can find a job at a soda fountain or squiring ladies around mud puddles—something where you won't have to get your hands blistered." With a final shove, he wedged Joel between the empty apple baskets in the wagon bed. "Miss Yates witnessed the boat excursion, so don't expect any sympathy."

And he got none. Just a bumpy ride into town behind a team of fast horses.

"You running me out of town like some one-man vigilante?" Joel said as the wagon left the orchard.

"Why don't you worry about it for a while?"

And then Joel's world went black.

When he came to, he was lying in the bed of the wagon, which was rumbling down Main Street. His head hurt, and the inside of his mouth tasted like blood. He sat up, only to see Zack Danvers in the driver's seat.

Zack reined in so fast that Joel fell back and bumped his head again. Immediately at least two dozen people were staring wide-eyed at the captive.

"Holy cow!" someone said. And that pretty well summed up everyone's reaction at learning Joel had survived the icy rapids of the Payette River. It was the closest thing to respect he heard.

Zack looked around at the cluster of townspeople and ranchers. "What d'ya think we should do with him?" he said.

"Well," huffed Mr. Hankins, "we can't have him around here assaulting our innocent women."

"Exactly my thoughts," Mr. Atwood chimed in.

Mr. Gantt pulled a face. "And I wasted an hour of my life praying over that rotten apple."

"What gives you the right to run me out of town?" Joel whined.

"You'd rather we lynched ya?" Gantt shot back.

The men's eyes met, held, and it was Joel who looked away first.

Zack decided to give him a dignified send-off and untie him for his last moments in Eden Creek.

"What'd you think you'd gain by coming back?" Zack snarled.

Without another word Joel rubbed his sore hand. "I only came back for my things."

Maddie pushed her way into the circle. "Don't worry about your things, Joel. I've got them all packed at the hotel, and I've sent Ben back to get them. Forget about the rent."

Joel hung his head.

"So how do we get rid of him?" someone asked.

"We could take a collection," Maddie said, tongue in cheek.

Orville pulled his timepiece out of his pocket. "If we get enough donations, we may be able to stick his ass on the evening train."

Word got around town fast, mainly because Clara had sneaked between two buildings and hidden behind the lilac bush while Zack was telling the crowd about his plan.

She looked innocent enough, but Zack knew whose idea it must have been to borrow a milk pitcher to take up a collection in.

Orville Gustavson tossed in a coin. "I ought to charge you for the ride in, but after what I've heard it'll be worth it to have you leave."

Ben donated a whole half dollar.

Maddie raided her Mason jar of pennies.

Then with a crowd following, Zack drove the wagon up Main Street to the depot. Joel sat beside him like a condemned man being shipped off to Australia. All the way up Main Street, tradesmen and customers came out to see what all the excitement was about.

From the mercantile . . .

From the carpenter shop . . .

From the barbershop . . .

And from ranches.

Those who kept track of gossip came out to watch, as did those who were new in town, including the Olsens, just arrived from Kansas and in town buying supplies. The woman's belly was fat with child; she and her husband eyed Zack with awe.

Oh, but the townsmen had their fun. "Hey, Zack," someone said. "It's a little early in the season for hunting varmints, ain't it?"

"A collection to run a rat out of town?" said someone else. "That's worth half my poker winnings."

At the railroad depot, Zack dumped the pitcherful of money he'd collected under the metal bars of the agent's booth.

Otis clicked off his telegraph key and looked up, pencil poised. "Where to?"

"How far will that money take one man?"

"How much you got?"

"We haven't counted it yet."

While everyone waited, Otis separated the coins into piles by denominations. Silver dollars. Quarters. Nickels. Pennies.

At last Otis pushed back his visor and wiped his forehead with a handkerchief. He cast a nervous look at Joel, as if he were a train robber. "You in a hurry?" he asked Zack.

"Next train's soon enough."

The agent rubbed his chin and then, scratching his head, consulted a timetable. "Eight-ten for Boise hooks up with a train for Pocatello, and that hooks up with a train for Denver and Omaha."

"How much?"

"You're a dollar short."

For a minute Zack considered buying a ticket for one city short of Omaha. Then he reached in his pocket, and his fingers closed about his lucky peseta.

He pulled it out and tossed it up, then caught it and paused. He'd had that coin a lot of months, hung on to it through thick and thin.

Suddenly he tossed it onto the counter.

The railroad agent stared at it. "Gold?"

"Yeah, one hundred pesetas. Comes straight from a dead Spaniard's pocket."

Young Otis's eyes grew wide.

"So have I got enough now?"

"Anywhere you want."

"One way to Omaha is good enough."

He waited along with half the town till the eight-ten pulled in and then personally escorted Joel onto it. "I won't say hope to see you again."

"I've wanted all along to leave this godforsaken place," Joel grunted.

And Zack would wait, by damn. Wait to see Joel off.

At the last minute a woman stalked into the depot. Miss Yates, back straight, face set, said not a word to anyone, but the pair of satchels she carried made it was clear she hadn't just come to wave Joel off. Indeed, with crisp efficiency she purchased a ticket to Boise City. Then, brushing aside Mr. Atwood, who made a move to help her with her luggage, she proudly picked it up herself and headed for the waiting train, leaving a trail of camphor scent in her wake.

"There goes our schoolteacher," Mr. Atwood said, looking around at the dispassionate faces. "Isn't anyone going to stop her?"

Clearly Granny and Maddie weren't, for they went up to say a polite good-bye to Miss Yates, then immediately returned to a bench in the depot and, sitting beneath the big clock, put their heads together as if in conspiracy.

"Well?" Mr. Atwood had six children, all school age.

Orville Gustavson crunched into a red apple and chewed with appreciation. "You know, my Sarah's in possession of a normal school certificate, and from now on, I have a feeling Clara and Pete are going to like school just fine. Smart as whips they are, and the teacher's dumb who don't know that. Yes, sirree, plain dumb."

The train whistled, and Mr. Gantt turned to Mr. Atwood.

"Ya think Miss Yates is still sweet on Joel?"

"If she is, Joel ain't that desperate to care."

"Still," said Mr. Pierce, ever the curious newsman, "I wonder if Joel will manage to stay single until he gets to Omaha."

Bets were quickly exchanged. Then hoots of laughter filled the depot as slowly the train pulled away from the depot with Joel and Miss Yates in separate passenger cars. The first big apple crop from the Sheldon orchard was piled up in a specially ordered refrigerated car, the first one ever to take perishable produce out of Eden Creek.

Now there was nothing for Zack to do but move on, take up that offer to doctor the immigrants . . . or go back to Chicago. But now that Joel was out of the way and the harvest taken care of, he didn't want to leave without Lizzie. That would have been like leaving his heart behind.

"Hey, Zack, you want to pitch some horseshoes?" Mr. Atwood asked.

"No, thanks." Maybe it was Maddie who had put it in his head, but he had a much more important matter on his mind.

"You aren't going to leave, are you?" Maddie had asked.

"What is this? Not so long ago, you and Ben applauded the idea."

"Then go, but don't leave Elizabeth here alone."

"You said marriageable women were scarce. She'll find someone."

"Not after all that's happened to her reputation. She *has* to marry someone, Zack, or be fair game for every horny galoot in the valley."

Zack hadn't thought of that, and was taken aback. Lizzie fighting off less than honorable advances. The idea of any man touching her the way Joel did in that rowboat made his blood boil.

"You know I'm right," Maddie said, smiling slyly.

Dammit, Maddie was exaggerating. "Lizzie doesn't want to be taken away."

"From what? Gossip? People say they saw you kissing her up on the ridge above the orchard, Zack."

Clara. And now he did want to wring the child's neck.

"You've made Elizabeth a loose woman, Zack. Now make her an honest woman. Isn't it time you did the courageous thing?"

Courage, hell.

A pile of empty apple baskets led him like pebbles to Lizzie. She was down in her apple cellar, deep under the earth. Bins of apples hid her from view. He tripped over one and swore.

"Who's there?" It was Elizabeth's voice, muffled, from behind some bins of apples.

Zack held up a lantern. "Lizzie?"

She stepped out from behind a bin of apples into the pool of lantern light, and his senses devoured her. The entire world came down to this slip of a woman who smelled like violets and cinnamon. Sweet scents.

"Will you marry me?" he asked without preamble.

Elizabeth stood there, stunned. "Marry you?" She sounded as if it were a foreign word, yet Granny had prepared her for the question.

She'd gotten Elizabeth alone after Joel was railroaded out of town. "Gossip isn't easy to endure in a town like this," she'd said.

Remembering the gossip Elizabeth had left behind in Amherst, she almost laughed, but it wasn't funny. "Gossip isn't easy to live with, no matter what size the town."

"Be that as it may, the situation would be eased if you'd marry Zack," Granny said.

"He won't ask. He wants to leave."

"Nothing wrong with a man wanting to roam a bit, but who says he's got to do it alone?"

Elizabeth stared at Granny, words failing her.

"Be practical, Elizabeth. You saw your brother's dream to the end. Think carefully about your own dreams."

Now her very own dream—Zack—was standing before her, only a lantern separating them. "Lizzie?"

"This isn't a time to tease," she said, reacting to his use of her nickname.

"When you're afraid of being rejected, teasing makes great armor, sort of a civilian version of a foxhole." Like a gauntlet he tossed the possibility in her face. "Unless you're determined to stay here in the orchard with"—he gulped over the name—"Orville Gustavson."

"I might be. Half of this orchard is mine. Why?"

"Because I want you with me."

It was so quiet all he could hear was his heart beating. The atmosphere was charged with raw emotions. "I don't know how to make it sound romantic, Lizzie."

"I didn't come west looking for romance, Zack Danvers."

There was a long pause.

"Will you come to Chicago with me?" he asked at last. "It may be forever. It may be just for a visit. I can't tell you which, so please don't ask."

He didn't use any sweet words, so she gave none in return. Anyway, they would only have tangled over her tongue and need to be pruned and thinned of all the emotion.

"It might work fine," she said. "When shall we get married?"

"Could we kiss first, Lizzie?"

When he set down the lantern on the floor of the cellar, she started toward him. The door blew shut, and out went the lantern, leaving them in pitch blackness. But by then he'd already found her, and he'd pulled her against him gently because he was afraid he'd squeeze her to death. Shutting his eyes, he picked her up in his arms and swung her around in the dark until, dizzy, he began to kiss her. As she kissed him back, he slowed and set her down, unable to think, unable to do anything but pull her closer against him and feel her mouth open to him.

The heavy cellar doors suddenly creaked open.

"Is anyone down there?" It was Clara.

"This is one of her hiding places," Elizabeth whispered.

"Pete?" Clara called. "Pa's looking for you. Pete? Pete?"

"What is it, Clara?" Zack asked without encouragement. He pulled Elizabeth's head into the crook of his neck and smoothed a wisp of her hair away from his throat.

"Zack?"

Reluctantly Zack gave a reply. "Pete's in the barn."

"Then I'll find him later. Guess what?"

"What?" Zack said.

"A letter came from the orphanage to Miss Yates, and they don't want us. They're all full up, so even if Pa hadn't come back, Miss Yates wouldn't have got us. Don't you wish you could see Miss Yates's face?"

"My imagination will serve me fine, Clara."

She moved in closer. "What are you doing down there?"

"Stacking barrels for the winter. What else?"

"But it's dark."

Elizabeth couldn't stifle a giggle and linked her arms about Zack's neck. "Stop teasing her, Zack."

Clara gasped. "Ahhh, Elizabeth's there, too! I know what you're doing. Kissing in the dark!"

"I don't suppose you can keep it a secret?"

"For how long?"

Just long enough for me to finish kissing Lizzie, he thought. He whispered in Elizabeth's ear: "She'll tell, you know. The whole town'll know before we can climb out of here. Now you're thoroughly ruined."

He sounded quite pleased with himself, and a stab of regret shot through her, regret for the lack of romantic words in Zack's proposal.

Swallowing back a lump in her throat, she forced a normalcy to her voice and said matter-of-factly, "Then I'd best ask her to be a flower girl. Light the lantern, Zack. I have a wedding to look forward to, you know, and I don't intend to let you rush a moment of the preparations."

Maybe not, but that didn't mean he couldn't rush the day.

18

One week later, on a golden October day, Elizabeth stood in Maddie and Ben's bedroom while the town milliner and seamstress, Mrs. Moss, took a few last stitches in the hem of her skirt. In less than an hour she would be married in the Groveland Hotel parlor, at a window that looked out over the waters of the Payette River. Oh, how fast this wedding had come together. She felt indeed as if she'd been whirled off the train and into Zack's arms.

In fact, she was breathless from all the wedding preparations, and couldn't help but remember the way she'd dragged her feet whenever Joel had mentioned marriage. Maybe at harvesttime, she'd said over and over, thinking that seemed forever away. But now harvest was upon the valley of Eden Creek, and irony of ironies, she was indeed getting married—not to Joel but to Zack Danvers, the man she'd tried to push out of her heart for so long. Temptation had fooled her. Her feelings for him had been real, and, selfish as it sounded, she thanked Joel for breaking his leg, for bringing Zack into her life. And now, soon, the longing and the temptation would all be over and she would belong to Zack completely.

Of course the secrecy wasn't over, for although she'd accepted his proposal, she'd never told him why she'd said yes. Contrary to what he thought, he didn't have to marry her to salvage her reputation. She'd given up worrying about reputations. She was marrying Zack Danvers for a reason he would never have suspected.

Because she loved him.

She was standing in front of a cheval glass while Mrs. Moss, a quiet sort, sewed away. When the door to the bedroom squeaked open, though, Elizabeth looked up to see Clara in a ruffly white dress with big bow pinned to the back of her straight hair. She had always known Clara would be pretty as a picture in a dress. All the little girl lacked was her familiar gap-toothed smile; Clara was uncommonly solemn.

"Mr. Pierce wants to know what you're wearing. You know, so he can write it up in the newspaper, in a so-shall story, he said."

" 'Social' is the word," Elizabeth replied, "and what I wear is a secret." As Clara's expression brightened at the idea of a secret, Elizabeth added, "Mr. Pierce can wait and see me when Zack does."

Actually, Elizabeth was pleased with her wedding dress. It wasn't new, but it was her favorite, and Mrs. Moss and Granny had come up with just the right touches.

To begin with, the dress was dark blue silk trimmed with velvet. Velvet and black jet beads decorated the cuffs and collar. Her hair, piled up on her head, was adorned with a sprig of dried roses and on a rocking chair waited her bouquet of flowers—the last of the red roses from Granny's garden, the wild summer kind, mixed with one stem of precious apple leaves, and a few late asters.

Granny had tied the bouquet together with blue ribbon, and streamers hung down from the flowers. Again, dark blue. The color of Zack's eyes. What a foolish and sentimental notion, yet it pleased her, and suddenly yearning to be alone with him, she was impatient for all the formalities to be over.

But Zack was not here. Not yet. And no one seemed to know where he was. Elizabeth swallowed back the lump in her throat, afraid he was going to duck out on this wedding the same way he'd ducked out of the railcar the day she met him.

"Is Zack here yet?" she asked a trifle too casually.

"Nope, but you look pretty," Clara said. "Just like a fairy princess."

From downstairs came the tinkling sounds of the piano. Mrs. Gantt, the saloonkeeper's wife, played a slightly out-of-tune version of the "Moonlight Sonata" on the parlor piano.

Suddenly Clara hugged Elizabeth around the knees and crushed the silk panels of Elizabeth's gown. "Why do you have to go away? Why can't Zack be a doctor here? I want you to stay."

"I know you do, dear, but Zack made a promise to go somewhere else. You understand about promises, don't you? Remember when your pa promised to come back to you, and how much it meant that he kept that promise?" *And Zack had promised to marry her.*

Straightening, Clara nodded and, sniffling, yanked the big white bow out of her hair and flung it on the bed.

To distract herself, Elizabeth reached for a brush and, to soothe Clara, brushed her bobbed hair, paying special attention to the bangs. Finally she replaced the bow, pinning it double.

"What a lot of work Sarah went to to dress you up. You've got a lovely new stepmother, you know."

"She's nice," Clara admitted on a trembling note.

"You're more grown up now, after waiting all that time for your pa to keep his promise and come back. And I made a promise to myself, too, to look after my brother's orchard, and I kept it. Now it's Zack's turn to keep a promise, a promise to visit someone who lost a son in the war. And when I promise to be his wife, that means I'll go with him."

Looking up out of red-rimmed eyes, Clara sniffled. "Quit? Leave? Elizabeth, you said you'd never do that!"

"Not quit, just postpone . . . Oh, Clara," she said, giving the child a hug. It wasn't fair when life made you choose. "I'll be back to visit. After all, your daddy's here now to care for my half of the orchard, so in a way I'm still here."

"That won't be the same."

No, it wouldn't. Which reminded Elizabeth of a piece of business she needed to take care of before she left. She needed to discuss the orchard with Orville Gustavson, work out some business arrangement for her half of it.

The door opened, and Maddie entered. "Elizabeth," Maddie said now, taking Clara by the hand and allowing Mrs. Moss a last chance to straighten the hem of Elizabeth's skirt, "have you something borrowed?"

She stood, her mind back where it belonged for the next few hours—on Zack and her wedding. "Your garter," she said.

"And something old?"

"My grandmother's mother-of-pearl brooch. My dress is something blue, and as for something new . . . a bridegroom." She hoped.

She was ready. And still Zack wasn't here.

Finally a knock came on the door.

Pete, looking handsome in a coltish way, was all dressed up to give the bride away. Simultaneously the piano launched into "Greensleeves," the song Elizabeth had chosen for the procession downstairs.

"But we can't start without Zack." A lump swelled in her throat, and she stared out the window, trying to ignore the silence behind her. The song swelled and fell empty about the hotel. Mrs. Gantt played a few more bars of the sonata, all out of tune, and then some tavern songs.

At the seventh playing of the sonata, he came hurrying in, breathless. A cheer went up from the assembled guests, and Elizabeth turned to hide her relief.

Granny found out the story. "It was that baby way out on the Zimmer ranch. New folks in town. Didn't even know me. Just came asking for the doctor, and he delivered it breech . . ." Granny grew momentarily vague, then brightened. "Well, I'm glad the lady timed the birth for today and not tomorrow, when Zack won't be here."

Elizabeth only felt relief that Zack was here, down the hall splashing water, changing into his wedding suit.

Less than half an hour later, smiling, she tucked her arm in Pete's and headed downstairs to the tune of "Greensleeves," Clara leading the way with a basket of rose petals.

As they proceeded into the parlor, the guests smiled, but Elizabeth scarcely saw them. There, waiting by the window, handsome in his three-piece suit, stiff wing collar set off by a four-in-hand of silk, stood Zack, black hair wet, jaw so freshly shaved she could see a tiny razor scrape. Their gazes caught and held, and then he smiled at her in a way that made her knees go weak.

But at the same time the lump in her throat swelled. He had come back. He would never know how much he'd scared her. Tears blurred her eyes, and to her utter chagrin she walked down the makeshift aisle to Zack with tears running down her face. As the piano music stopped, sniffles from the assembled guests filled the silence.

With a tender gaze, Zack reached for her, drew her close to his side, gave her a reassuring squeeze, and whispered to her, "Don't let Ben see those tears."

For Zack, of course, had no idea they were tears of relief; he thought they were tears of regret. Ben, after all, had given his brother a stern talk before the ceremony, so loud several people had overheard and repeated it. Even now the admonition echoed in the air: "I've got one thing to say to you, Zack. You're aware, aren't you, that you're breaking everyone's heart, taking Elizabeth away from us? Unless you've got a better prescription, I think you'd better plan on bringing her back for a visit. Agreed?"

Zack would have agreed to anything at that moment in his life. Lizzie was so beautiful, so tiny, so vulnerable, that he'd have promised anything to keep her, for nobody else could heal him. He had to fight the sudden moisture in his eyes. He didn't deserve her, but he damn well intended to keep her, and if she was crying because she was sad at leaving, he'd make it up to her a hundred times over. He would make her the toast of

Chicago. She'd forget this place, just as he thought he would. Gently he reached for his bride's handkerchief, which she clutched in a knot, and with an embroidered corner, blotted away her tears, the scent of violets floating up to him.

While the minister read the brief service, Zack held her hand. Then he slipped on a gold band, one of two the mercantile kept under glass with the pocketknives and watches. There hadn't been a lot to choose from, and naturally the ring was not her size; it slipped a bit, but they'd get that fixed in Chicago as well.

He said the vows in a daze. *For better or for worse.*

She had shared in a simple way his worst moments.

Now she was beside him for the best.

"You may kiss the bride," the minister said.

Zack bent to kiss her, tasted the salt of her tears on her lips, and lingered over the kiss till a few of the female guests sighed and old man Gantt went on a coughing jag. Let them gawk. He held her, burying his face in her honey silk hair, silently promising she'd have no regrets. Ever. He lived with enough regret for both of them.

"Don't cry, Lizzie," he whispered against her hair. "I'll make life perfect for you. All of it." And then he pulled away.

His reward was a tremulous smile, and her eyes were so green he almost got lost in them. He wanted her alone, but the women of the town had planned a reception, nothing simple, but a festive affair with a sit-down potluck dinner and a wedding cake. Maddie had outdone herself, and Zack bided his time, watching Elizabeth enjoy a bride's attention. He felt like a shy kid again, wanting to dip a girl's pigtail in an inkwell. The thought of having her alone later left him weak, tongue-tied, heavy with longing, his desire held at bay. The night ahead was constantly on his mind, and for him the celebration dragged. But he put up with it all—the toast from a bottle of champagne, the throwing of the bouquet, every man in town claiming a kiss from the bride.

And finally Zack was helping her up into a smart buggy loaned by Ben and tied with old shoes and apple prunings. But still they weren't alone. Pete rode ahead as escort. "I've got a wedding surprise for you," he said.

"A gift?" Elizabeth said.

"Sort of."

As they waved good-bye to the guests, her ring nearly slipped off, and he caught her to him, folding his larger hand over her tiny one. After a last wave to the crowd, Zack took the reins and followed Pete. Mystified, he drove past the lane leading to the Sheldon orchard—Sheldon-Gustavson orchard, he amended—and on up to the ridge overlooking Eden Creek.

At once Elizabeth gasped in delight. Pete was already standing proudly by the little tree Elizabeth had given him earlier that summer. A half dozen fragile branches blossomed pale pink.

Blossoms in October.

"It's got a lot of seasons to grow yet, and you can't expect any fruit this year." Pete's face shone with pride. "It bloomed for your wedding, though; that's what Clara says. I think that's sort of girl talk, but I wanted you to see. We did it. It took root."

Elizabeth got out of the buggy and went to sniff the tiny blossoms. "It's a miracle," she whispered, and it was. A tree had bloomed out of season—it was a pure God-given miracle.

"The town wants to make a park here. Sheldon Park, in memory of your brother. A wedding gift from the Ladies' Literary," Pete relayed the message shyly. "Maddie said to tell you when we got here."

Elizabeth shot a quick glance at Zack for his reaction, and then she relaxed. He was smiling at her. "A fitting tribute," he said. "I wish I'd known the man who was your big brother, Lizzie."

Relief rushed through her, and she planted a quick kiss on Zack's cheek, lingered to rub her own cheek against his stubbly one, the pit of her stomach aching at this tangible sign of his maleness. Blushing, she turned to Pete who was once again staring at his shoes. "Thank you, Pete," Elizabeth said. Wordless, she turned to Zack.

"I wouldn't have missed seeing this for anything," he said simply, then shook the boy's hand in farewell. Elizabeth climbed back into the buggy, he turned it around, and at last, at long last, he had Elizabeth to himself. She sat close to him, but not too close. Still a touch prim . . . or else not in love with her bridegroom. He intended to stare straight ahead. Her bouquet was gone, and now it was the scent of violets that clung to her, stole up, and surrounded him, threatening again to steal his control. Despite his better intentions, he turned to her and did what he'd longed to do all summer—he dropped a kiss on her cheek and at the same time pushed back a lock of hair from her face. A simple gesture, but one fraught with sensation.

"Happy?"

She glanced up at him, as if uncertain how to answer. It was a foolish question. Every bride was happy, wasn't she? And he gave a rueful smile and turned his attention back to the road. They were going to spend their wedding night at her little house. One night before they left town. The desire he'd tried to hold at bay surged through him, too strong, too soon, and he sat up, straightened his back, and refused to look at her, concentrating instead on the reins and the loud humming in his ears. It had been so long since he'd wanted a woman that the need he felt now overwhelmed him. But it wasn't just a male need. He wanted her tenderness in return. He wanted to make the lovemaking good for her so that down through the years she might come to feel something for him.

She stood waiting for him while he put the horses away. When he returned, he saw written on her face uncertainty. He swept her up into his arms. Her arms in turn came around his neck, and he carried her across the threshold and into the kitchen, where he set her down.

They lingered in each other's arms, stood as still as if an invisible circle bound them. Secretly he reveled in the feel of her hands against his back, the softness of her breasts crushed against his coat front. The entire room smelled of cinnamon and coffee and, amazingly, her violet scent.

"We're here," she said, a wistful look on her face. "Our first night together and our last night in Eden Creek." Her breath, warm against his shirt, sent a tremor through him.

"Someone forgot to come ahead and light the stove," he said with utter practicality. "Do you want to wait here a few minutes?"

Crushed by his prosaic remark, Elizabeth listened to his heart beating against her cheek, to each inhalation and exhalation that moved his shirt against her. This was enough. She had come west expecting to marry for practical reasons. This was enough. To expect romance was frivolous. She stepped back from the circle of his arms, and immediately he shed his jacket and slung it over a chair, a proprietary gesture that touched her.

Enough.

But, she told herself, as she took off her cape, that was like saying a tree in bloom was enough, when it was really only the beginning of a long sweet journey to harvest. And so, too, with her wedding night. Determined to make the best of it, she moved to the pump to fill a pitcher with water.

They performed their chores in silence. After all the conversations they'd shared, suddenly she was tongue-tied. What did people say on their wedding night when there were no words of love to speak? What was she expected to do?

He lit a lamp, then stoked the fire in the stove up high, and stood watching it. She reached for the pan of apple cobbler.

"Would you like some—"

"No." His hand over hers stopped her. Strong. Gentle. Possessive. What was he thinking? Did he dread the coming night, loving her without his heart in it?

Zack wanted nothing more than to make Lizzie his, now, this instant. Weddings had been designed for women, and wedding nights as well, he knew. Lizzie's wedding night would be for her and her alone, but he prayed for the restraint to please her, not use her. He'd been half alive for too long.

With an easy gesture, he leaned over and kissed her ever so gently, lingering over her lips and then, unable to help himself, trailing kisses on her cheek, her earlobe, her throat. At each touch of his lips to her skin, she gave a little gasp, each one threatening his control. Abruptly he pulled away.

"Don't be scared, Lizzie. I'm not going to rush you." He wanted her as he'd never wanted a woman. Even now, his need was tangible, begging for release. He ached physically, from his heart to his loins, and there was no disguising his raw need when he held her. She hesitated a moment, then leaned into him, molding herself against him, allowing him a momentary reprieve as she pressed her softness against him, promising eventual fulfillment. He kissed her hair, running his hands down to her waistline, to the sweet curve of her hips in that silk dress. He forced himself to stop there. They were fully clothed and still in the kitchen, for crissake.

If he wasn't careful, he'd ruin it for her. And for himself. He turned to tend the stove, and she stood beside him, waiting.

"Lizzie," he said to the stove, "I've never been married before. I mean, I've never been with a woman who's . . ." He hesitated over the explicit word.

She tilted her head, smiling at him as he tried to explain so intimate a subject.

His fingers raked his hair. He'd never talked about love-making with women in the past, but they weren't Lizzie.

Swallowing hard, he tossed one last stick of kindling into the stove and clanked down the iron lid. The humble chore helped him gather his wits. He half turned to her and then looked down at his soot-covered hands.

She dabbed at the soot on one palm. "Now isn't that just like a man?" she teased softly as she reached for a towel. "Getting your hands mucked up the minute the wedding's over." Gently she rubbed his hands with the towel, up and down his fingers, across his palms, taking her time with the crease that was his life line. . . .

He pulled his hands away.

"Zack, I'm sorry," she said softly.

"Sorry for what?" Alarm shot through him. She was going to call it off. Say she was sorry. She couldn't go through with the wedding night after all; she would have the marriage annulled.

"I'm sorry I cried at our wedding," she said. "I didn't disappoint you, did I?"

Was that all? Shaking his head, he loosened his tie and undid the top button of his shirt. Then he began to roll up his sleeves, his eyes on her all the while.

She ran a nervous tongue around her lips, once slowly, and he stopped in mid-roll, one sleeve up, the other half down.

"What's wrong?" he asked.

She was watching in fascination as the dark hair on his chest and arms was exposed. With his finger, he traced the moist line around her lips. She pressed her hand to his and kissed his palm.

He snatched his hand away.

"Was that wrong?" she asked.

"No." Exquisite. Provocative.

"I've thought of you as forbidden for so long, Zack, I'm afraid to touch you."

"I understand. You don't know how many times I looked at you, envying Joel, reminding myself that you were not mine . . . and hating Joel for having you, even while I was supposed to be healing him."

"And now I'm yours, and you can show me everything."

"I don't know everything, Lizzie." At the moment he'd forgotten everything. He had no idea what romantic words a man should say on his wedding night. He couldn't risk declaring his love and having her laugh at his foolishness. If that made him a coward, then he wasn't surprised. It was enough, he guessed, to have this woman for himself. Her reasons for wanting him didn't matter. She was his, and that was enough. He knew only one thing: He'd never thought to have this kind of happiness.

She laid a hand on his arm. "Don't avoid me, Zack."

"You're impossible to avoid, Lizzie."

"Tell me to slow down. Tell me what you want. Tell me . . ."

Tell me you love me, Zack pleaded silently. No, Zack, don't expect the moon. She's more than you deserve. Don't get greedy. Besides, he guessed words of affection were rightly expected from the man first, and he was a coward. . . .

He pulled back and looked at her gravely. The lamp that swung from the kitchen ceiling threw the most delightful shadows on her face, shadows that moved when she did. For a delightful few minutes, he chased the shadows around her face with his kisses, over her eyes, her cheeks, her throat, until she moaned and pressed herself against him.

Abruptly he let go, turned away from her in an attempt to regain his composure and to hide the dark passion on his face. Maybe she didn't want what he did. To keep from grabbing her to him, he hooked his thumbs in the pockets of his vest. The struggle for control came hard.

Slow down, Zack, he told himself, take it easy. Give her time. Give yourself time.

"I'm not certain I'll do this wedding night right," she said, lingering so close behind him that he could feel her breath, warm on his shirt.

He turned and reached for her hand. "How can we know before we've tried?" And finally, as a slow warmth filled the little house, he led her to the bedroom.

At the threshold, she stopped, eyes wide, staring at the brass bed where Joel had spent so many hours holding them apart.

Zack stood at the foot of it, shucking off his vest, his black hair falling over his forehead, his movements stiff.

Never had Elizabeth known more doubt. Entering this bedroom with Zack was more frightening than embarking on a journey across uncharted land.

"I hope you won't think I'm going to be prim. Joel said that I was."

"Lizzie Danvers, it is not my intention to spend my one and only wedding night discussing other men."

Lizzie Danvers. Elizabeth Danvers. Mrs. Danvers. She tried out her new name in all its forms, unable to choose a favorite.

Stiffly she walked around the bed and lit the lamp. A circle of light lit up the ceiling and fell over the bed. She'd put on a brand-new wedding quilt from Maddie's own cedar chest, dark blue in the wedding ring pattern.

They stood as they had when they'd tended Joel, one on either side of the bed. This wasn't going to do at all. It was as if Joel were between them still, with Zack the doctor on one side and Elizabeth the frightened fiancée on the other.

"We're not discussing Joel anymore ever," he said, as if reading her mind. "I don't expect either of us to forget what happened, but we'll not have it between us. Come here now."

But he moved, too, as if he couldn't wait to touch her, and met her at the foot of the bed, where he began unpinning her hair, dispensing first with the dried roses and then letting the honey gold locks tumble down, something he'd longed to do since he'd first laid eyes on her. Her hair shone like gold in the lamplight, and desire washed over him, dangerous and explosive. In the darkest moment of his fever, he'd never felt quite this kind of weakness.

"Perhaps we married in haste," she murmured.

His heart clenched. "Then we shall repent in leisure." No regrets, Lizzie. Not now. He touched the shoulder of her gown, the sleeve.

When she heard the tremor in his voice, her eyes grew wide with comprehension. "I can't take this dress off without help." Heat rushed to her cheeks, so he turned her so that her back was to him. Honey-blond hair hung halfway down her back. He wanted to wrap his arms about her waist and pull her back against him, wanted to bury himself in her right now. But at least two dozen hooks and eyes stood in his way. That and her innocence, her trust.

Hooks and eyes, he decided, after undoing half a dozen, had been invented by a mountain hermit with nothing but time on his hands and no idea of wedding-night fever. Or perhaps he'd taken perverse pleasure in making them too small for a man's fumbling fingers. Gowns, for that matter, like weddings, were all designed to try a man's patience.

"How the devil did you get out of your dresses without—"

"Without a husband to help me?"

"Just how?"

"Clara helped. Whoever was handy."

"From now on, I'll be handy."

His gruff words made her smile.

"All summer I watched you touch Joel."

"You took unfair advantage of the rocking chair once."

"I'm only human, Lizzie." He kept on jerking open hooks and eyes, peeling back satin to reveal more and more of the white lace beneath while she stood impossibly still. It took all of his professional experience to maintain some semblance of control, because as he opened each hook and eye, he grew impatient. He longed to rip the dress from her, bury himself in her breasts, slake his desire.

When his hands touched her waist, she half turned. "Let me do the rest." Backing away, she shed her bodice and stood there in white lacy corset and camisole. More obstacles, he realized.

With a hand to her chin, he kissed her lightly on the lips. "You're beautiful, Lizzie. I can't help staring at you. Do you mind?"

A quick headshake. His melting blue eyes were nothing to mind.

But as she slipped off the skirt, he turned away to the window, one arm stretched out against the frame. He could stare dispassionately at his patients disrobing, but not at her.

He wanted to hurry . . .

He needed to be gentle. . . .

"I'm ready."

Turning back, he caught his breath. She sat on the edge of the bed in her undergarments, a froth of white lace, and carefully, slowly, he moved toward her. He decided he could get used to years of lingering yearning before lovemaking. Bending over, he dispensed with the petticoats—three layers of them. One by one he pulled them off until she stood before him in pantalets and camisole.

"Do you know what happens next?" he said.

"I put on my nightgown."

Tense with desire, he shook his head. "Not tonight."

He peeled back the quilt and before her wondering eyes stripped off the rest of his clothes until he stood before her, easy in his nakedness.

He waited while her gaze went up and down him, then quickly up again. Her breathing came faster.

Gently he pulled her to him, sat on the bed, and took her onto his lap. "You're beautiful, Lizzie. Don't be afraid."

"I'm not afraid, except of disappointing you, making you regret you married me. . . . I don't know what to do." Her voice trembled with her confession.

"Then I'll show you."

He helped her remove her camisole, then the corset, and with a few more movements she was naked in his arms. The sight of her creamy skin and feminine curves took his breath away, but he drew her back onto the bed to lie side by side with her.

"Don't be scared."

"Zack Danvers, stop saying that. I'm not scared, not with you. Why are you shaking?"

"I'm cold," he lied and pulled the quilt up over them.

"You know," she said softly, her head in the crook of his arm, her hand splayed across his chest, "I'm not completely naive. In the East we girls weren't kept innocent of all knowledge. I know something about the birds and the bees, but you'll have to fill in the gaps. You're the expert."

Not about this, he wasn't. He could scarcely breathe. "The birds and the bees don't have near as much fun, and anatomy is only interesting when two study it together."

She gasped and then, beneath his hands, relaxed, moved against him ever so subtly. His hands explored her slowly, the mounds of her perfect breasts, the swell of her abdomen, the curve of her buttocks, and back to her abdomen. All of it silk. His mouth moved to one of her breasts, his tongue lingering, swirling, while his hand cupped the other, felt her heart flutter like a captured bird. They arched together at the same time, the need, the want, all-consuming.

Somehow he'd have to abbreviate the lessons.

"There's much more to lovemaking than a bride needs to know the first time, but . . ." His hand caressed her thighs, his hand sliding up the inner thigh, gently parting them.

She gasped in pleasure, and then he parted her lips with a kiss, his tongue stealing into her mouth, mimicking the movement of his hands.

While his tongue readied her, his hands roamed over her, taunting, teasing, then moving back to her thighs again, reaching higher and higher, finally touching the intimate heart of her. And again. Till she moaned beneath his touch.

"Lizzie, the first time it may hurt."

"I don't care. . . . Zack, please."

His fingers were teasing her to distraction, in and out, and then he moved over her, poised above her, hesitant. . . .

"Zack . . ." As she arched up against him again, he slid into her, and as they became one, he kissed away her cry of pain, paused, then as she calmed, drove deeper until she arched again . . . and again, their bodies seeking each other, blending in nature's oldest dance, their movements instinctive, the climax shattering, inevitable. He poured life into her, the moment as awesome as when he'd pulled that baby into life. All pink and bawling new in the universe. And he was glad he'd bided his time, cherished the final coming together.

They lay entwined for a long time, neither speaking, both lost in their own rapture.

Because she'd never been with a man before, there was much she assumed. She didn't know desire, and so many of her assumptions were enchantingly wrong. To his benefit.

She assumed all men kissed a woman before coming together with her. She assumed they took their time exploring a woman's body. She assumed they whispered words of endearment.

She assumed all men and women came together like this. Oh, God, this was sweet. He'd have to tell her that love-making wasn't always like this, though. He'd have to place his soul in her hand, and damn the consequences. Only not tonight. Just for tonight, he'd leave her naïveté intact, pretend she loved him before she told him otherwise.

"You can sleep in my arms," he said finally, satiated, trembling at the feel of her. "Or you can have half the bed to yourself."

"The choice is mine?"

He shut his eyes, sated. What would she do when she knew what he felt? Feel obligated to pretend a mutual affection? Perhaps she never would tell. Perhaps he could douse the lamp and take her in his arms this way for the rest of their lives, and she'd never know what he felt.

Her reply was so soft he could barely hear. "I think on my wedding night the way we are is fine. Do you?" Hesitant.

He cradled her head to his shoulder, hoping she wouldn't notice the joyful jump of a muscle in his jaw. "Perfect, Lizzie," and lay awake long after she slept, planning their future, wondering how he could have been so lucky as to end up in Eden Creek.

Elizabeth lay with her eyes shut but was awake a long time, marveling. How could she ever have known such a feeling in her life? His way with the marriage bed was, typical of Zack, both fierce and tender. She'd thought for a minute their hearts had beat in time. What would it be like if he actually loved her? She couldn't begin to imagine.

*   *   *

The next day she awoke alone in bed and at once missed Zack. Hurrying, slightly panicked, she rose and reached for her gown, but before she could put it on, he came in from the kitchen. Warmth from the stove radiated in through the door with him. He wore his trousers and nothing else, and his hair was tousled from sleep, his face stubbled dark with a night's growth of beard.

"Zack, I thought you'd gone without me."

"Silly goose." He was staring at her strangely, his eyes dark, hooded.

It occurred to her she was standing there naked except for the gown, which she held against her to cover her from breasts to knees. She let it drop and stood still, watching his reaction, seeing how quickly she affected him, how his body responded to her instinctively. Unashamedly.

At once she ached for him in all the new ways he'd taught her, couldn't move for wanting him. And then he was there, scooping her up and onto the bed, kissing her, caressing her. Together, laughing, they shed his trousers, and they fell back again. He came to her at once, with no preliminaries to their desire, but a long lingering crescendo.

For a long time there was no talk of going anywhere. They lay wrapped in each other's arms, she wistful, half wishing they could stay, but afraid to say so.

He, too, was silent, thoughtful, and she wished she could read into his mind. Was he happy? Glad, on this morning after, that he had married her?

Later that day they helped each other dress. She wanted to learn to button a man's shirt, to knot a tie, he to master the hooks and eyes of a woman's dress, to lace her corset. Then they parted in a reluctant embrace, he returning a moment later to kiss her once, then once again. It was as if, once joined, they were reluctant to be parted.

"Where are you going?" he whispered.

"To get your wedding gift . . . and to say good-bye." Her voice caught. Actually she needed to talk to Orville

Gustavson about the orchard. "And you?" She supposed he'd say farewell to Ben and Maddie.

"To the depot first," he said.

"Don't leave without me," she teased.

"Not a chance, Mrs. Danvers." His gaze went from her head to her feet as if the layers of clothing were not even there. Suddenly he looked into her eyes, his own eyes dark blue and oh, so anguished.

"Zack . . ."

"No, we have to leave." Zack made himself say the words. If he kissed her, her skin would taste of violets and he'd never get out of the house. "You want to leave, don't you?"

Elizabeth's face fell a bit. Had she expected him to make love to her forever? He'd married her, given her a respectable name. Wasn't that enough? "I gave you my vow, but you won't be long? Clara's coming by."

His smile was wry. "Doesn't that child have any respect for honeymoons?"

"She's only eight, Zack."

"Then meet me in one hour, and don't tell Clara." He whispered the place in her ear.

Hesitant, she wanted to say no. Not there.

"Lizzie, it's important. We can't leave until you know something, and it has to be said there." He was tempted to stay, to linger over her, but he pulled back, forced himself to let go of her.

Ever since he'd seen her crying at their wedding he'd been racked with second thoughts about leaving Eden Creek. Now he'd decided what he was going to give her for *his* wedding gift, and what he planned would not take long. He mounted his horse and waved. She looked small and vulnerable. And she was his.

Elizabeth watched Zack ride off, his face sad. Not even marrying had made him happy. There had to be something in this world that would give him joy. . . . She could think of only one thing, but it was a start. And after wrapping herself in a cloak, she went off to visit Orville Gustavson.

Two hours later she was packing her trunk when Zack appeared in the doorway, face flushed, hair tousled.

"You weren't at the creek to meet me."

"Not quite. I have three trunks and a crate full of books and—"

He shut the lid on the trunk and took her hand. "Come with me for a walk. You'll be safe, I promise."

Minutes later she stood at the water's edge, staring down at one of the little rowboats, which Zack had hauled up from the hotel.

"You want me to get in?"

He had already stepped in and was waiting to hand her in. "There's an old saying about falling off a horse and getting back on again."

"I know that. Why do I ever need a rowboat again?"

"Get in, Lizzie, and I'll explain."

Swallowing her fears, she stepped over the side, bracing herself while the boat wobbled. Quickly she sat opposite him.

"Good girl." He handed her a train ticket. "Your wedding present."

Tears welled up in her eyes. She couldn't look at it. The finality of it was too much. A pair of ducks paddled by, then disappeared into the reeds at the shore. The little boat rocked gently back and forth.

Before she said another word, she simply handed him his gift, thrust it into his hands without a word of explanation.

After a moment during which he stared at her bowed head, he ripped the envelope open and pulled out bills. Money. Mouth open, eyes dark with suspicion, he looked at her.

She looked up. "It's to help you start your practice in Chicago." At his puzzled look, she said simply, "I sold my half of the orchard to Orville."

"You did what?"

"You're not angry, are you? That I sold the orchard without consulting you?"

A slow smile spread across his face, and to her amazement he picked up one of the oars and raised it over his head like some triumphant Viking warrior.

Her shock must have shown in her eyes.

"Darling Lizzie." He thrust the train ticket at her. "You've been so busy looking at the date you never looked at the final coupons. Turn them over."

She looked at them and frowned.

"But, Zack, there's a mistake. This is a round-trip ticket . . . to Chicago"—she looked up—"and back to Eden Creek."

"That's right. I telegraphed Harry's father and told him I was coming. He wired back his congratulations and wished me well. He wished me well, Lizzie. He wished me all the happiness that would have been Harry's, and he wants to meet you."

The world stood still, except for the gentle rocking of the rowboat. "What are you saying?"

"We're not going to move to Chicago, Lizzie. Would you mind terribly if we came back and I set up practice here? We'll buy more apple trees if you want." He took the ticket back from her, reached into his pocket, and handed her a narrow blue box.

Her heart was in her throat as she opened it. Nestled on a bed of black velvet was a necklace of garnets, sparkling dusky wine, a whole string of them dangling from a golden chain. This was not the gift of a man marrying out of duty, of a man who felt honor bound to rescue her reputation.

"What are these for?"

"To wear when you have nothing else to wear. To pass on to our daughters, to our granddaughters. They're very old, so Ben and Maddie say; they were my mother's . . . and we'll buy more. A garnet for every harvest, and then—"

"Zack, what's wrong with you?" She'd sold the orchard. Eyes shimmering, she looked up into his eyes and saw reflected back more than she'd dared to dream. "Why are you giving me all this? Garnets? A life in Eden Creek?"

It took all of Zack's courage to answer that question, to risk rejection.

"I love you, Lizzie."

The words hung there, fragile, connected to his heart, and oh, so breakable. "You gave me my life, Lizzie. If it was scary for you to get back in this boat, it took ten times more courage for me to tell you how I feel." He looped a finger over the string of garnets. "It seemed easier to have a gift in hand, in case you didn't want the fancy words. That's all I wanted you to know. I love you." He looked away, out over the water. "There's nothing you need to say."

She reached for his hand, covered it with her own.

"Yes, there is. I love you, Zack. With all my heart . . ."

Clara came along while they were still kissing. She was the first person Elizabeth told the news to, that they'd be coming back here to live for good.

Zack looked at Elizabeth. "If you meant this to be a secret, I think you erred in telling Clara."

"On the contrary," Elizabeth smiled shyly. "I told her on purpose. It'll take her a while to run off and tell the whole town, don't you think?"

And they leaned into another kiss. There was all the time in the world to walk back through the trees.

❀

Epilogue

Another harvest . . .

The hiding places were all changed, of course, but when Clara climbed atop the ridge overlooking Eden Creek, she saw that the orchard stood strong, the Idaho wind still ruffled the branches, the sky was still as wide and blue as ever, speckled with magpies. Those things never changed.

Nor did her fascination with the solitary apple tree up on the ridge. The years had seen it grow tall and yield a bounty of crimson apples, and most of all, the years had seen a legend grow up around it, as ever present as the manicured grass surrounding it, as homely as the rope swing that dangled from a limb. And never was the legend more alive for the children, both loved and lonely, than it was at harvesttime in Eden Creek.

Clara had made it her job to know all of the children, especially the lonely ones, and each year at harvesttime she climbed with them up to the ridge to pluck apples and not a few memories, and to tell again the story of how the tree had once bloomed at harvest. Only once.

Always the questions were the same, over and over, no matter how many times a child had heard the legend.

"How did the tree get up here all by itself?"

"My brother hauled it up. He and I planted it in the sage and rocks when it was no bigger than a broomstick. And we watered it and weeded around it."

"But where did you get it?"

"Elizabeth gave it to us. Elizabeth and Zack, too. In the summer, when that poor tree almost gave up hope and died of a broken heart."

"Where did Zack come from?"

"He arrived here one day, on the same train as Elizabeth, neither knowing the other."

"Were you here then?"

Clara smiled. So many secrets to share. "Oh, yes, I was here. I was right up there at the depot, watching. It was after a war, you see, and they both came, with no roots of their own, and the Eden Creek band was there right beside me as the train came in, and it began playing a song, the grandest song. . . ."